You're About to Become a

Privileged Woman.

INTRODUCING
PAGES & PRIVILEGES™.

It's our way of thanking you for buying
our books at your favorite retail store.

— *GET ALL THIS FREE* —
WITH JUST ONE PROOF OF PURCHASE:

◆ Hotel Discounts up to 60% at home and abroad

◆ Travel Service - Guaranteed lowest published
   airfares plus 5% cash back on tickets

◆ $25 Travel Voucher

◆ Sensuous Petite Parfumerie collection ($50 value)

◆ Insider Tips Letter with sneak previews of
   upcoming books

◆ Mystery Gift (if you enroll before 6/15/95)

You'll get a FREE personal card, too.
It's your passport to all these benefits– and to
even more great gifts & benefits to come!

There's no club to join. No purchase commitment. No obligati

As a Privileged Woman, you'll be entitled to all these Free Benefits. And Free Gifts, too.

To thank you for buying our books, we've designed an exclusive FREE program called *PAGES & PRIVILEGES*™. You can enroll with just one Proof of Purchase, and get the kind of luxuries that, until now, you could only read about.

Big HOTEL DISCOUNTS

A privileged woman stays in the finest hotels. And so can you—at up to 60% off! Imagine standing in a hotel check-in line and watching as the guest in front of you pays $150 for the same room that's only costing you $60. Your *Pages & Privileges* discounts are good at Sheraton, Marriott, Best Western, Hyatt and thousands of other fine hotels all over the U.S., Canada and Europe.

Free DISCOUNT TRAVEL SERVICE

A privileged woman is always jetting to romantic places. When <u>you</u> fly, just make one phone call for the lowest published airfare at time of booking—<u>or double the difference back</u>! PLUS—

you'll get a $25 voucher to use the first time you book a flight AND <u>5% cash back on every ticket you buy thereafter through the travel service</u>!

FREE GIFTS!

A privileged woman is always getting wonderful gifts.
Luxuriate in rich fragrances that will stir your senses (and his). This gift-boxed assortment of fine perfumes includes three popular scents, each in a beautiful designer bottle. <u>Truly Lace</u>...This luxurious fragrance unveils your sensuous side. <u>L'Effleur</u>...discover the romance of the Victorian era with this soft floral. <u>Muguet des bois</u>...a single note floral of singular beauty. This $50 value is yours—FREE when you enroll in *Pages & Privileges*! And it's just the beginning of the gifts and benefits that will be coming your way!

FREE INSIDER TIPS LETTER

A privileged woman is always informed. And you'll be, too, with our free letter full of fascinating information and sneak previews of upcoming books.

MORE GREAT GIFTS & BENEFITS TO COME

A privileged woman always has a lot to look forward to. And so will you. You get all these wonderful FREE gifts and benefits now with only one purchase...and there are no additional purchases required. However, each additional retail purchase of Harlequin and Silhouette books brings you a step closer to even more great FREE benefits like half-price movie tickets...and even more FREE gifts like these beautiful fragrance gift baskets:

L'Effleur ...This basketful of romance lets you discover L'Effleur from head to toe, heart to home.

Truly Lace ...A basket spun with the sensuous luxuries of Truly Lace, including Dusting Powder in a reusable satin and lace covered box.

ENROLL NOW!
Complete the Enrollment Form on the back of this card and become a Privileged Woman today!

Enroll Today in *PAGES & PRIVILEGES*™, the program that gives you Great Gifts and Benefits with just one purchase!

Enrollment Form

☐ *Yes!* I WANT TO BE A *Privileged Woman.*

Enclosed is one *PAGES & PRIVILEGES*™ Proof of Purchase from any Harlequin or Silhouette book currently for sale in stores (Proofs of Purchase are found on the back pages of books) and the store cash register receipt. Please enroll me in *PAGES & PRIVILEGES*™. Send my Welcome Kit and FREE Gifts -- and activate my FREE benefits -- immediately.

NAME (please print)

ADDRESS   APT. NO

CITY   STATE   ZIP/POSTAL CODE

▶ DETACH HERE AND MAIL TODAY! ▶

Please allow 6-8 weeks for delivery. Quantities are limited. We reserve the right to substitute items. Enroll before October 31, 1995 and receive one full year of benefits.

**NO CLUB!
NO COMMITMENT!**
Just one purchase brings you great Free Gifts and Benefits!
(See inside for details.)

Name of store where this book was purchased_____

Date of purchase_____

Type of store:

☐ Bookstore   ☐ Supermarket   ☐ Drugstore

☐ Dept. or discount store (e.g. K-Mart or Walmart)

☐ Other (specify)_____

Which Harlequin or Silhouette series do you usually read?

_____

Complete and mail with one Proof of Purchase and store receipt to:

U.S.: *PAGES & PRIVILEGES*™, P.O. Box 1960, Danbury, CT 06813-1960

Canada: *PAGES & PRIVILEGES*™, 49-6A The Donway West, P.O. 813, North York, ON M3C 2E8   PRINTED IN U.S.A

"Why did you do that?"

Christine was frowning.

"Why? What kind of a question is that?" Wood ran a hand through his hair. "Because I've wanted to for a long time."

"But that's what I mean," she said. "Why would you want to? I don't understand."

"What I don't understand," he shot back furiously, "is how a woman as beautiful as you are got to be—what, twenty-eight, twenty-nine years old?—without knowing how to handle a simple little kiss. What gives, damn it? *Tell* me."

She mumbled, "I think…we ought to just forget it."

"Not on your life, darlin'," Wood said softly, his voice deep and husky with meaning. "That was something I won't be forgetting anytime soon, I can promise you that."

Dear Reader,

We're back with another fabulous month's worth of books, starting with the second of our Intimate Moments Extra titles. *Night of the Jaguar* by Merline Lovelace is the first of a new miniseries, Code Name: Danger. It's also a fabulously sexy, romantic and suspenseful tale of two people who never should have met but are clearly made for each other. And keep your eyes on two of the secondary characters, Maggie and Adam, because you're going to be seeing a lot more of them as this series continues.

Award-winner Justine Davis presents one of her irresistible tormented-but-oh-so-sexy heroes in *Out of the Dark*, another of her page-turning titles. And two miniseries continue: Kathleen Creighton's Into the Heartland, with *One Good Man*, and Beverly Bird's Wounded Warriors, with *A Man Without a Haven*. Welcome bestseller Linda Randall Wisdom back to Silhouette with her Intimate Moments debut, *No More Secrets*. And try out new-to-contemporaries author Elane Osborn, who offers *Shelter in His Arms*.

As promised, it's a great month—don't miss a single book.

Enjoy!

Leslie Wainger
Senior Editor and Editorial Coordinator

Please address questions and book requests to:
Silhouette Reader Service
U.S.: 3010 Walden Ave., P.O. Box 1325, Buffalo, NY 14269
Canadian: P.O. Box 609, Fort Erie, Ont. L2A 5X3

ONE GOOD MAN

KATHLEEN CREIGHTON

Silhouette®
INTIMATE™ MOMENTS®

Published by Silhouette Books

America's Publisher of Contemporary Romance

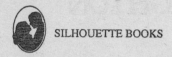

SILHOUETTE BOOKS

ISBN 0-373-07639-8

ONE GOOD MAN

Copyright © 1995 by Kathleen Modrovich

Printed in U.S.A.

Books by Kathleen Creighton

Silhouette Intimate Moments

Demon Lover #84
Double Dealings #157
Gypsy Dancer #196
In Defense of Love #216
Rogue's Valley #240
Tiger Dawn #289
Love and Other Surprises #322
Wolf and the Angel #417
A Wanted Man #547
Eyewitness #616
*One Good Man #639

Silhouette Desire

The Heart Mender #584
In from the Cold #654

Silhouette Books

Silhouette Christmas Stories 1990
"The Mysterious Gift"

* Into the Heartland

KATHLEEN CREIGHTON

has roots deep in the California soil, but has recently relocated to South Carolina. As a child, she enjoyed listening to old-timers' tales, and her fascination with the past only deepened as she grew older. Today, she says she is interested in everything—art, music, gardening, zoology, anthropology and history, but people are at the top of her list. She also has a lifelong passion for writing, and now combines her two loves in romance novels.

Here's to all survivors!
Sisters, this book is for us.

NOTES AND ACKNOWLEDGMENTS

My heartfelt thanks are due to many people who helped me with the background research for this book. First among them, Dawn Morse, R.P.T., of Anderson Physical Therapy in Anderson, South Carolina, for answering all my questions with humor and patience, for her generous sharing of time and materials, and for giving me a new and profound respect for these patient, compassionate and mostly unsung medical professionals. Any errors herein are mine, and no fault whatsoever of hers.

Thanks also to Marti Anderson of the Iowa Attorney General's Office and to her wonderfully helpful and friendly colleagues with the Crime Victim Assistance Division for information on Iowa's antistalking laws. And last, but certainly not least, to my cousin Nina Mueller of Sioux City, for braving an Iowa snowstorm to take pictures for me.

It must be noted and emphasized that, although Sioux City has two excellent medical centers, Riverside Hospital and the adjacent Physical Therapy Clinic and medical center are based on neither. Rather, they are a product of my imagination, composed of bits and pieces of all the medical institutions that are part of my own (blessedly limited) personal experience.

Chapter 1

The telephone was ringing, a polite, electronic trill that sounded as if it might have been apologizing for having disturbed her at such an unseemly hour.

In the charcoal darkness her mind struggled to separate safe, sterile reality from the sweaty tangle of nightmare. Clear images of exactly what she'd been dreaming had already slipped beyond her recall, but it didn't matter. She knew the dream well. It was always the same—the sense of lurking evil; abject and mindless terror; futile, slow-motion flight on legs of lead; breathing achieved in excruciating sobs that burned like acid. In another moment she would have been screaming—raw, throat-rending, silent screams. Ordinarily it was the screams that woke her.

The numerals on the clock-radio beside her bed gave the time: 3:07 a.m. Very slowly she drew her knees up, curling into her body's own warmth for solace. She lay with her cheek pillowed on one closed fist and stared into the darkness, while the telephone rang on, and on and on.

Thunder. Wood had never heard such thunder. He could feel it in his molars. And the air, thick as blackstrap molasses; the

*darkness, so impenetrable the lightning came like flashes of
cold steel, a physical assault on the retinas...*

No, not lightning. Of course not. He'd been in the Marine
Corps long enough and had seen enough action to know mortar fire when he heard it. The Serb guns were putting on a real
show from their positions in the hills around the city tonight,
lighting up the sky like one helluva good old Iowa thunderstorm. They were zeroing in on the highway now, on the relief
convoy, trying to find the correct range. Looked like they'd just
about got it right, too. Wood could feel the explosions in the
seat of his pants. He set his jaw and gripped the truck's steering wheel more tightly, straining to see through the blackness
beyond the mud-spattered windshield.

*The flash and the explosion came almost simultaneously, so
he knew the lightning had struck close by.*

*Someone swore—that had to be Dad. His mother screamed,
not loudly, just a sharp little cry of fear and surprise. He heard
her gasp, "Ed..."*

*The world tilted, bucked and spun like a world-class bronc.
Wood struggled to sit up, to hold on, but his body wasn't his to
command. His arms and legs were flailing and flopping around,
making him feel helpless as a rag doll in a washing machine.*

*The world rushed up and hit him in the face. There was a
sickening, grinding* crunch, *and finally, silence. Still, black silence. Blessed and absolute...*

A voice, calm but insistent. Just a voice, no words. He fought
to ignore it, fought to return to the silence, but the voice
wouldn't let him go. It went on and on, compelling him to respond.

Pain!

"That's it, stay with me now, there's a good fellow...."

The pain seemed to ride in on the words. It poured over him
like a dump-truck load of sand, weighing him down, suffocating him.

"No, you don't. Come on, now, stay with me. What's your
name? Hey—can you tell me your name?"

Of course he knew his name. Wood Brown, that was it. No,
officially it was Edward Earl Brown. After his father.

"Good...good, you're doing fine. Do you know where you
are, Woody?"

Did he know where he was? Of course he knew. Bloody
freakin' Bosnia, that's where, trying to keep kids from starv-

ing to death and a whole damn city from self-destructing. Or was that the other place—what was it—Somalia? It was hard to tell the difference. The eyes of hopeless children all looked the same.

One thing he did know for sure—he was stuck with driving a lousy truck again. No goddamn springs, but what did he expect from a military vehicle? No, wait—that wasn't right. He wasn't in the military anymore, although sometimes it was pretty damn hard to tell the difference about that, too.

"Come on, buddy, do you know where you are?"

The hell with that. Once a jarhead, always a jarhead. He was Wood Brown, and proud to be a United States Marine.

"Okay, Soldier," the voice soothed. "We'll have you out of there in a few more minutes. You hold on, now, you hear me? What year is this? Can you tell me that?"

"Sure." Wood didn't know which was worse, the pain or that voice. "Nineteen ninety..."

The pain won, hands down. Unconditional surrender. Somewhere other voices were shouting, but he didn't care. He was slipping wonderfully down a long black chute, straight into oblivion....

"Mom? Dad?" The car was upside down. He couldn't see through the windshield. It was silvery and opaque, except for a jagged hole where his mother's head rested against it. His hands were covered with something sticky and warm. He wanted to cry, to scream, but instead he began to swear, the same ugly, forbidden word over and over again, like a litany....

Someone was swearing, the same word over and over again. Someone else took Jesus' name in vain and added, "Willya look at that, geez, look at his legs... God in heaven, poor devil. Poor devil."

The calm, commanding voice said, "Easy...easy. You're going to be fine, Woody. Just fine."

"I'm gonna be sick."

"All right, gotcha." Careful hands held his head and spinal column steady. "Turn on the count of three. One, two..."

Just in the nick of time.

"Well, Mr. Brown. I've got some good news and some bad news."

That voice Wood recognized. It spoke English with a distinctly Southern accent, and was one of several that came to intrude relentlessly on the twilight world he preferred—a world in which he floated, suspended by tubes and wires, on undulating waves of pain, and in which time was measured only by the peaks and valleys of that pain, ticked off in disconcertingly erratic electronic beeps.

The face that went with the voice loomed into his line of vision, showing teeth. "Which would you rather hear first?"

Wood made a garbled sound he hoped would be understood for "bad."

The face backed out of range. Wood tried to follow it with his eyes, one of the few things he could still move, but it hurt so much he closed them instead. Offscreen, the voice continued.

"Son, fact is, the only femurs I've seen busted up worse than yours were in Vietnam, and we lost most of those."

What exactly do you mean by "lost," Doc?

"Given the conditions, most of the time we didn't have a whole lotta choice but to amputate. But now, the good news is—"

Cut off my leg and I swear I'll hunt you down, Doc, if I have to crawl on my belly to do it.

"Easy, Son, easy." Still off camera, the voice chuckled. "Like I said, the good news is we've got a few more options here we can try for you. Okay? The thing is, we need to do whatever we're goin' to do as soon as possible. You feel up to hearing the choices?"

"Shood," said Wood, and frowned. He'd meant to say, "shoot."

"What's the matter, Son? Having some pain?"

Pain? Some pain? Pain was always with him, but it wasn't a constant. It had different colors, he'd discovered. Pulsating purple; vicious stabs of red; hot, searing yellow; and the worst, explosions of blinding white, like supernovas. After those, what he usually did was throw up. Or pass out.

He tried to shake his head and frowned again as panic closed around his throat. "Can't...move. Am...I...''

Another chuckle. "You're not paralyzed. It's just a little something we're giving you to keep you still so you won't make things any worse than they already are. Okay? Don't worry....''

"...Don't worry, Son, it's just a little something to help you sleep."

"No—no drugs. I don't want to sleep. I have to—"

Lucy's face, frozen and pale. *"You don't have to do anything, Earl, you hear me? You just sleep now, sleep...."*

"They're dead, aren't they? They're dead. It's my fault. I really messed up, Lucy. I should have been driving. I should have..."

"You were driving, Son, don't you remember? And it sure as hell wasn't your fault. From what they tell me, the truck ahead of yours took a direct hit—pretty much blew up in your face. Nothin' in the world you coulda done. Fact is, you're just plain lucky to be alive...."

"...You're lucky to be alive, young man. And right now the only thing you have to do is get some rest. This is going to help—"

"No! No drugs, I don't want any drugs. Lucy—no—"

"Shh, it's okay, Earl, it's okay. Shh...it's going to be okay...."

Something cool and soothing touched his face. Two faces hovered above him now, like twin moons—the doctor, looking concerned, and a nurse, looking peeved. The tone and pitch of the electronic beeping had changed—some kind of alarm going off.

"No drugs," he said distinctly.

The nurse ignored him and leaned to fiddle with something above his head, so that her breasts occupied his entire field of vision. He heard her speak to the doctor in a scolding tone, and then the breasts disappeared, to be replaced by white acoustical ceiling tiles. Wood felt a momentary pang of quite normal masculine regret—they were very nice breasts—and then he was drifting once more, helpless as a newborn baby. And angry.

"I know you're probably feelin' pretty helpless, maybe mad as hell about it, and a little bit scared, too," said the doctor with the Southern accent. "Right, Son? That's natural. But listen, we're going to get you put back together. It's just gonna take a little bit of time. What we want to do is get you into surgery as soon as possible, you understand? I need to tell you some options, so you can decide which route you want us to go. You think you can do that?"

Wood didn't even try to nod. He stared up at the acoustical ceiling, feeling angry, helpless, scared, trying to make sense of what the doctor was telling him about the pros and cons of putting metal rods in his legs versus some pins and a couple months in something called "skeletal traction." Either one sounded about as much fun as a forced march in Georgia in July.

"No question about it, the rods would get you up and around quicker," the doctor was saying, his voice growing hollow and tinny. "But they do take gettin' used to and are probably going to limit your movement some..."

Limit my movement? Some? What the hell does that mean? How much? Permanently? I'm an athlete, for crissakes! I'm a soldier—a United States Marine. I'm not going to be a god-damn cripple! Am I? Oh, God... am I?

"...And then sooner or later they're most likely going to have to come out. On the other hand, you're looking at at least six weeks in traction, another six to eight in casts and wheel-chair and..."

Wood summoned every last ounce of his strength and managed to lift his head a centimeter or two from the pillows that supported it. "No rods," he growled, and tumbled headlong into the waiting silence.

"Hey there, Son, howya doin' this mornin'?"

"Hey," Wood responded. He'd figured out that in Southern American "hey" meant the same thing as "hi."

He held up his left hand, which someone had thoughtfully strapped to a board, presumably to keep him from disturbing the hose-size needle that was sticking out of the back of it through a thick swath of gauze. "What the hell's this?"

The doctor chuckled, which Wood was beginning to find kind of annoying, since he couldn't think of one single thing about his situation that might be considered amusing. "That's your own personal pipeline, Son. All kinds of things been goin' through there, helpin' keep you alive and more-or-less com-fortable."

Comfortable? People around here sure did have a strange idea of what that word meant, along with a few others, like *some pain.* He hurt from his hairline to his toenails. Both of his legs seemed to be suspended by a complicated system of weights and pulleys so sensitive to movement that every time somebody walked by within three feet of his bed his spine curled. Plus he had tubes in places he didn't even like to think about.

"...Blood, fluids, antibiotics, basic nutrients, painkillers—they showed you how to use your morphine pump, I suppose? I guess we'd abeen hearin' from you if they hadn't, huh?" Another chuckle.

Wood made a small, impatient motion with his head, unwisely risking awakening the buffalo herd that had been stampeding around inside it all night. "Not the needle. These." Lifting his left hand seemed to have exhausted his store of energy, so he just aimed his eyes down at the right one, which lay nestled in a matching mitten of white gauze on the sheet beside him. "Wha's wrong with my hands?"

"You mean the bandages? Aw, they're just a little bit cut up...burned. Nothing too serious, should heal up pretty fast. You'll be doin' chin-ups on that thing in no time." The doctor gestured toward the triangular metal bar suspended in the air above Wood's chest.

"Right..." Wood snorted, then winced. "Feels like there's a goddamn elephant sitting on my chest."

"You got a few caved-in ribs, and of course the lung underneath wasn't any too pleased about that for a while, but we got 'er pumped up again just fine. No permanent damage. You were lucky. If it'd been on the other side..."

"What else?" Wood demanded in a dark tone.

"You want the whole laundry list, huh?"

"Everything."

"Everything. As in, 'Give it to me straight, Doc.' Well...okay." The doctor heaved a sigh and sat down on a chair beside the bed, leaned forward and clasped his hands between his knees. That made his face just about level with Wood's, who noticed for the first time that the doctor had smooth, round cheeks and thin, reddish brown hair and looked as if he could be anywhere from sixteen years old to sixty. He studied Wood for a moment with compassionate eyes.

"I meant what I said, Son. You're pretty lucky to be here. You've got major compound fractures of both femurs—that's your thighbones, in case you're wonderin'. That's about the worst of it. Then you've got the broken ribs, like I said, a fair-to-middlin' concussion, a whole mess of cuts and bruises—"

"What's wrong with my face? I can see..." Wood tried to look at the white blob where his nose was suppose to be but couldn't quite manage the effort it took to cross his eyes. He let his head sink back onto the pillows. "Ah geez, I broke it, didn't I? I broke my damn nose." Four years of high-school football, an automobile accident and ten years in the Marine Corps, and it took a Serb mortar shell . . . Now *that* was amusing. Or maybe just ironic.

"Ow," he said in surprise. Obviously, laughing was out of the question.

The doctor wanted to know what was funny, but Wood was still fighting his way through a fog of pain and didn't quite have the energy to explain about the Rosewood Nose, the famous family feature that, of the current Brown siblings, only his sister Lucy had had the misfortune to inherit. Or the fact that there'd been times when he'd wished he could trade his own classic but unremarkable profile for Lucy's magnificent hawk's beak. Or how much it had always embarrassed him to be referred to as "handsome." At least it looked as if that wasn't going to be much of a problem for him from now on.

"Family joke" was all he said, closing his eyes once more.

"Tell me about your family, Son. You married?"

"Nah . . ." He hadn't stayed in one place long enough to get serious, let alone married. It wasn't something he'd thought about much.

"Where you from? You got folks back home?"

"Iowa . . . far western part. Sioux country. Yeah, I got a sister—Lucy—she's married to some famous newspaper columnist. Mike Lanagan, maybe you've heard of him . . . But she still runs the family farm. Has a little girl now, too. My brother Rhett lives in Des Moines—last I heard, he's some big-shot lawyer. He's married and has two kids, one of each . . . ."

It suddenly occurred to Wood that he'd never seen his nieces and nephew, except for the pictures that were sent from time to time, and which had caught up with him in various far-off places. Had it really been that long since he'd been home? *Home.* Even the word seemed alien to him, like a language he'd spoken as a child and since forgotten. *Iowa.*

A wave of totally unexpected homesickness overtook him, and in his weakened state there was nothing he could do to protect himself from its consequences. He felt the cool tickle of tears under his eyelashes, then in a line from the corners of his eyes down into his hair. He'd never felt so humiliated, so helpless.

"How long since you've been home, Son?" The doctor's voice was gentle with compassion, which didn't help matters.

Wood swallowed and muttered thickly, "Ten years."

"Your parents still living?"

"No." God, he didn't need this. He wished the damn doctor would just go, leave him alone. He didn't want anybody to see him like this. "They were killed in an automobile accident when I was eighteen. I was...with them. In the back seat. Didn't get a scratch. Guess I was just born lucky."

"Yeah, I guess you must have been." Wood heard rustlings as the doctor stood up. He felt the brief weight of a hand on his shoulder. "Either that, Son, or the Lord's still got somethin' important in mind for you to do. Hey, I'll be back. You get some rest now, you hear?"

Wood didn't answer. He waited until he heard the footsteps fade, then swallowed again and yet again, trying to make the tears stop. He hated this...*hated* it. He hadn't cried in years—not since the night his parents had died. It was thinking about home that had done it, he was sure, thinking about Lucy, the farm ... grain elevators etched on a huge, empty Iowa sky; the smell of new-turned earth in the spring; that damned prairie wind. It had caught him by surprise. Who'd have thought he—Wood Brown, toughest damn grunt in the Corps—would ever be shedding tears over something like that?

But he felt so helpless, so alone. Just like a little kid lost in the woods, scared to death and crying for his mommy. All he wanted in the whole wide world was to go home.

Sioux City, like the rest of the nation's midsection, was enjoying a false spring. With two weeks left of February, the temperature was expected to make it to the upper fifties, maybe even an unheard-of sixty degrees. The sun was shining, the sky was blue, the snow from the last blizzard had melted even from the protected, shady places. Birds could be seen in the bleak, bare branches of trees, singing and chasing one another as if there wasn't still March to be gotten through, as if the next storm was not even then zeroing in on the suburbs of Seattle, soon to hurtle the Rockies and come barreling across the plains on its mindless drive toward the eastern seaboard.

Christine Thurmond, like most Iowans, knew better. Which was why she reported for work at the Riverside Physical Therapy Clinic wearing her usual fake-fur-trimmed parka and mittens, her only concession to the springlike weather being the decision to forgo the top half of her long johns. In their place under her usual tunic-length sweater she was wearing only a sleeveless cotton-knit turtleneck, and she hoped she wasn't going to regret even that. It seemed as though she felt chilled most of the time these days, no matter what the temperature.

She breezed through the empty waiting room and pushed open the double glass doors marked Please Wait for Therapist Before Entering, giving Megan, one of the young assistant P.T.'s, a wave as she paused at the reception window to pick up her schedule.

"Whose birthday is it?" she asked Roxanne, the receptionist, pulling off her mittens as she nodded at the florist's arrangement of white roses on the counter.

"Aren't they gorgeous?" Roxie ambled over to the window and propped her elbows on the countertop, wistfully shaking her head as she sniffed one perfect ivory blossom. "Wish I knew who they're for. There wasn't any card—believe me, I checked."

"Strange," murmured Chris, because it was the expected thing to say. Inside her parka she shrugged away a small shudder. "Who delivered them?"

"I don't know. They were already here when I got in this morning. Meggie found 'em outside the front door and brought 'em in. Nobody seems to know anything about them. Sure looks like somebody's got a secret admirer, huh? Too bad we don't have any way of knowing who it is. Those roses must have set somebody back a pretty penny. Can you imagine? A dozen white roses this time of year?"

"Eleven," said Chris. "There's one missing."

Roxie counted for herself. "Hey, you know, you're right. This gets stranger and stranger, doesn't it? And *white* roses. I mean, don't you think that's kind of unusual? Aren't they supposed to mean something? You know, like yellow means friendship, red means love...."

Chris picked up her clipboard and schedule and said in a cool, absent tone as she studied it, "I'm sure there's a perfectly ordinary explanation. Somebody here probably ordered them to give to somebody else, which would explain why there's no card, right? I'm sure somebody will claim them before the day's out. Who knows—maybe John ordered them for his wife."

"Hey, John..." Roxie leaned around the bouquet of roses to grin at the owner of the clinic as he came through the double doors as if on cue. "You been a bad boy again? What did you do now?"

John Mason frowned and looked vaguely confused. Roxie winked at Chris; it was an accepted fact that, while their boss was as good-looking as a soap star, if he had a sense of humor, no scanner had yet been invented that could discern it. He nodded and mumbled a polite "Good morning" to Chris, then looked to Roxie for an explanation.

"The roses," Roxie said, obliging him. "They came without a card. We were wondering if maybe you might have ordered them for your wife."

"Nope, not mine," Mason said, disposing of the distraction with obvious relief. "Listen, can you get me Mrs. Olmstead's file? And my messages, please. Thanks."

Chris waited until he'd turned away from the counter and was making for his office, sheaf of messages in hand, then fell into step beside him. "John, can I talk to you a minute?"

Her boss glanced up briefly, then went back to shuffling memos. "Sure, Chris, what's up?"

"This new-patient evaluation you've got me scheduled for this morning—"

"Right, the ex-marine. Brown. Came in last night. What about it?" He gave her a distracted frown. "There a problem? We can make it later if you—"

"No, it's not—it's just that I've got kind of a full patient load right now. I don't know if I..."

Mason pulled out the file he'd tucked under his arm and waggled it at her. "Well, for starters, you're losing Mrs. Olmstead—seems her family's decided they want her to be closer to them, so they're moving her out to California. That should free up some time. And what's her name—the head trauma—Julia? She's going to be coming just twice a week starting Monday. Shouldn't be too difficult for you to work this in."

"Yes, but does it have to be me? Why..." She realized that the edgy intensity in her voice was earning her an appraising look, so she shrugged and deliberately lightened it. "I mean, isn't this more Brad's kind of thing? He usually gets the sports injuries. I just think—"

Mason parked one hand on his office doorknob and turned to face her, obviously girding himself for the task. Chris had no idea why she made him so uncomfortable—not that he was the only one with the problem. She'd noticed that a lot of men seemed ill at ease around her, which was one of the reasons she preferred to work with elderly stroke patients and children.

"Look, Chris," said Mason with a touch of impatience, "the fact is you're the senior therapist on my staff, and this is going to be a tough case. That's why I want you on it." He took a breath and softened his tone a little. "That, plus I think this guy will do better with you than he would with Brad. He's an ex-marine—hurt in some kind of accident in Bosnia—"

"Bosnia? I thought we weren't sending troops in there."

"I said *ex*-marine. He was working for some international relief agency, from what I understand. Anyway, they're picking up the tab, and it's going to be a whopper. He's looking at some long, hard months before he's even back on his feet, and that's the problem. I don't think he's going to be the type to adjust to limitations very well. You know this guy's going to be very highly motivated, and in this case I'm afraid that might work against him."

Chris sighed and nodded in agreement. "He'll try to push the envelope just as hard as he can, every chance he gets."

"Right. Plus, with a big, strong guy like Brad, he's going to feel a certain—"

"Competitiveness," supplied Chris wryly. "The macho thing."

Mason nodded. "With you, I'm hoping he might be willing to be a little bit more patient with himself. Let himself be—"

"Babied." This time she finished the sentence for him with a reluctant smile. It was a well-established fact that the biggest, strongest guys were apt to be the biggest crybabies.

"Yeah...right." Mason looked pointedly at his watch. "Well, you'd better get on over there. Come talk to me when you're through, okay? We can discuss where we're going to want to go with him once you've seen him, talked to him. If you still think there's going to be a problem—"

"No problem," said Chris firmly, hugging her clipboard to her chest. She took a deep breath and added to the director's closing door, "No problem at all."

* * *

A tunnel had been constructed to facilitate pedestrian traffic between the hospital block and the complex of doctors' offices and satellite medical facilities known as the Riverfront Health Center. There was talk of eventually building a skywalk like the ones downtown across the wide, busy thoroughfare, but so far nothing had come of it, and completion was at best a long way off. Meanwhile, the tunnel was clean, well lighted, protected from the weather and wheelchair accessible.

And unless she was with someone, Chris never used it.

It shamed her to admit it even to herself, but the tunnel frightened her. It echoed with ghost-footsteps and sinister whispers, raising the fine hairs on her neck and the specter of old childhood terrors of things unknown lurking in dark places. And so, on a morning when everyone else in the city was reveling in the feel of the sun on their faces and the wind in their hair, she kept her hood up and clutched tightly under her chin and hurried past the tunnel entrance with pounding heart, every nerve vibrating with a sense of foreboding, as the child she'd once been had scampered past the half-open closet door.

While she waited to cross the busy street, she carefully monitored vehicle and pedestrian traffic as she always did, then scurried across, feeling as exposed and vulnerable as a squirrel on a wire. Safe on the hospital side, she turned right as she always did and hurried around to the ER entrance, which was more closely monitored by security than the main entrance, and where casual visitors weren't allowed to go. These precautions had become second nature to her, as had the way she glanced around as the automatic door whooshed open in her path, her mind recording and cataloging every person in sight before she stepped through it into the familiar, antiseptic cocoon of the hospital.

She actually liked the hospital smell; she associated it with safety. When her senses were especially heightened, as they were today, she could distinguish the different smells underneath the prevailing odor of disinfectant. Each department had its own—Physical Therapy was sweat and oil of wintergreen; Pathology across the hall was formaldehyde, so strong sometimes it made her eyes water. When it was busy the ER smelled of blood and vomit and fear. This morning it was quiet, although down at the far end an orderly was mopping up after what had apparently been a hectic night shift.

At the moment, the only patient in the place seemed to be a boy of about nine or ten, who sat hunched on an exam table cradling one towel-swathed arm while his young, ponytailed mother stood nearby in earnest consultation with the resident on call. The police-band monitor over the nurse's station squawked briefly as Chris passed. The nurse on duty glanced up, smiled in recognition and went back to filling out forms.

Just past the chapel, which always smelled of candle wax and stale flowers, another automatic door whisked open to reveal an empty corridor of gleaming vinyl tile and sand-colored walls tastefully decorated with graphics in Native American style, and lighted signs that pointed the way to Radiology, Laboratory and Cardiac ICU. It was all as familiar as home to Chris. Familiar and safe. Here at last she could relax.

She took off her parka in the elevator, and when she checked in at the nurse's station, deposited it temporarily on the counter while she inquired briskly as to the whereabouts of her patient.

She was rewarded with a look of profound disapproval from Florence, the duty nurse, a dark, dour woman of around fifty. Florence wasn't one of Chris's favorite people, and since the feeling was obviously mutual, there wasn't much point in wasting time on pleasantries.

"You're late," Nurse Florence commented without looking up. "You've missed the doctor."

"I know...sorry." Chris was smiling, breathlessly ingratiating, which was her involuntary response to tacit disapproval. "He decent?"

Florence gave her a stony look over the tops of her glasses. "Doctor left you this." She thrust a sheet of paper over the counter at Chris. "Room 312—right over there."

She took the paper with a sigh, absently muttering, "Thanks," as she glanced over the list of notes and instructions before affixing it to her clipboard. She'd have liked to ask a few questions about the new patient's physical and emotional condition before meeting him for the first time, but she knew that, with Florence, it would be a waste of time. So she drew a fortifying breath, then turned and marched resolutely down the hall to Room 312.

The door was closed. She paused a moment before knocking to sneak a peek at her new patient through the small glass panel. Her heart gave a queer little lurch of dread. Oh God, she thought, I knew it was going to be something like this. I knew it.

It was even worse than she'd feared. The face on the pillows bore no resemblance to any spit-and-polish young marine she'd ever seen, or, for that matter, to any battle-scarred veteran she might have imagined. True, it was bearded and fierce, the features sharply honed, still shiny with newly healed scars, the eyes unreadable, sunk deep in shadowed sockets. But it was... an arresting face, Chris thought, fascinated in spite of herself. A beautiful face. Dark and beautiful as the face of Lucifer.

Chapter 2

"I can't do this," she whispered to herself, even as the contradiction and the reassurance were taking shape in her mind.

Yes, you can. He's injured...helpless. You're in control. You are the one in charge here.

She became aware, finally, of the cool press of the doorknob in her hand, of Florence's watchful eyes boring into her back. Affixing a smile on her lips like a badge of authority, she turned the knob and pushed the door open.

"Mr. Brown—hi, good morning."

The eyes came to life in their shadowed sockets, flaring like coals in a breath of wind. They fastened upon Chris with a stare of such intensity that she felt, as she approached the patient's bedside, almost as if she were advancing against the point of a sword.

"I'm Chris," she continued, doggedly smiling and cheery. "I'm going to be helping you get back on your feet, Mr. Brown..." She glanced at the clipboard and amended, "Ed. Or do you prefer Edward?"

The eyes continued their unwavering examination. "Ed was my dad's name. Call me Wood." The voice was as cracked and raspy as wood—old wood, rough and weathered.

Chris repeated the name and nodded, still smiling as she made a note of it on the list affixed to her clipboard.

She had to force herself to keep her body language open, accessible, when with every ounce of her being she wanted to hug the clipboard to her chest like a shield. But she was a trained professional, and she knew how important it was at this stage in establishing rapport with a new patient that she do everything she could to inspire confidence. It was important that the patient feel relaxed and comfortable with his therapist. Important that he begin to feel he could trust her.

And *she* felt as if she'd just stepped into a cage with a wild leopard.

"Florence tells me your doctor was just here. Did he pretty much answer all your questions, or is there anything you'd like to know before I start asking *you* questions?"

"Yeah, there's something you can tell me." His tone was blunt, though without being rude. He managed to hitch himself up slightly on his piled-up pillows without altering that intent, dark stare so much as a millimeter. "Where in the hell do I know you from?"

Now her clipboard did come up. She couldn't help it—it was pure reflex. Her arms folded across it, hugging it firmly in place against her breasts. The question was totally unlike any of the responses she usually got from men, and therefore totally unexpected.

She murmured, "I beg your pardon?" A little chill wafted through her, roughening her skin in all the most sensitive places.

The man in the hospital bed cleared his throat with edgy impatience. "I know I've seen you before. Just can't for the life of me figure out how I could have. I've been away for close to twelve years. It's driving me crazy."

"In that case, I don't see how you could have, either, because I've been right here." She kept her smile in place and her tone light, but coated it with a furring of frost that she hoped would be unmistakable. "I'm sure I just remind you of someone else."

The coolness was apparently wasted on Wood Brown.

"No... no," he muttered thoughtfully, "I don't think I'd forget a face like yours. Had to be a long time ago, though... Hey—wait—hey, *what are you doing?*"

What Chris was doing was making an elaborate show of inspecting the weights that hung suspended from the foot of the patient's bed. She was doing it quite deliberately because she knew it would distract him, if nothing else would. And it did.

Having jerked his gaze away from her at last, her patient was reaching toward the weights with a protective and imploring hand—a hand, she noticed, that still sported a patchwork of tape and gauze over half-healed wounds.

"Just don't... touch anything." He sounded very young suddenly, with that note of near-panic in his voice.

In spite of her own uneasiness, Chris began to feel twinges of sympathy and understanding and decided she could risk a smile, now that she had the patient's mind safely focused where it belonged, on his own injuries. She murmured soothingly, "It's okay, Wood. Don't worry, I know how sensitive those pins are. Just the slightest little bump—"

"Bump, hell," he said with a wry grimace. "Every time somebody walks by the foot of my bed, I cringe. I swear, I can feel the breeze."

Oops, Chris thought, time to nip that self-pity in the bud. She said flatly, "Look at it this way—you could be numb from the waist down." She nodded toward the other bed in the room, the occupant of which was absent at the moment, and added, "Like Grady there."

"Ah, yes..." Wood sank back onto his pillows with an audible exhalation. "My roomie—that's his name, huh? I haven't had much chance to get acquainted. They came and got him pretty early this morning."

Chris looked at her watch and nodded. "He's probably in the therapy pool right about now."

"So... what's wrong with him?" Wood shifted uneasily. "You say he's paralyzed?"

She didn't cushion it. "From the waist down. He was shot—an innocent bystander at a convenience-store robbery. The bullet severed his spine."

Wood swore and looked away, his expression once again fierce and angry.

Chris continued in a gentler tone. "Wood... your injuries are extremely serious, and the healing process is going to be slow and involve a great deal of pain. I'm not going to lie to you about that. The rehab is going to be a long, difficult haul for you. But in the end, you know you're going to walk again. The fact is, eventually, you should be able to do almost everything you did before you were hurt."

He was avoiding looking at her now as steadfastly as he'd been scrutinizing her a few moments ago, but Chris saw what he was trying so hard to hide from her. He mumbled, "Yeah, well, it's that word *almost* that I don't much care for."

He's afraid, she thought, and felt the tension inside her ease a little more. *He doesn't know what's going to happen to him, and he's scared to death.*

She found herself moving away from the safety zone she'd established for herself near the foot of the bed, drawn closer, almost against her will, to that disturbing and beautiful face. She even put a hand briefly on his shoulder, an instinctive urge to comfort that she knew she'd have to fight against. With every new patient there came a moment of truth, a moment when she had to decide which role she should adopt in order to get the best results—whether to be tough taskmaster or gentle persuader. She was almost certain she knew which would work best with this man. She'd seen his type before. He'd fight against sympathy and gentleness, and in the process, push himself too hard and too fast. She took a breath and hardened herself—her face and eyes, her voice and her words.

"Wood, I know you want someone to tell you you're going to come out of this exactly the same as you were before you were hurt. That just isn't going to happen. From what I can see, you've suffered some bone and muscle loss. You're not going to get that back. What you *do* get back, as far as strength, movement, coordination and so forth, is going to depend mostly on you. It's going to take a lot of hard work and pain, and a lot of determination and patience on your part. You're the one who has to make it happen. You understand?"

There were a few tense moments of silence, and then his eyes came slowly back to hers, gleaming with a different light—little sparks of amusement, like stars on a moonless night. He touched a temple with one bandaged finger and his teeth flashed white against the dark stubble of beard. "Yes, *sir*, Coach."

It was the first time she'd seen him smile, and something inside her stirred, responding to it as naturally, as inevitably as a furled flower bud to the spring sun. She wanted very much, suddenly, to smile back with the same genuine, infectious smile, one that would touch her eyes and flood her soul with light and warmth and joy. It had been so long since she'd smiled like that.

Instead she kept her mask intact, frowned and reached for his hand. Her fingers closed with expert care around his wrist, felt the pulse beat hammering beneath the tendons, felt the smooth, warm skin and the coarseness of hair. She cleared her throat.

"Mostly what we're going to be doing right now, while you're still in traction, is work on your upper-body strength. You're going to be needing it once you get into a wheelchair, and especially when you start learning to walk again. We're probably going to be using some electrical stimulation on those leg muscles, too, to keep them from atrophying as much as possible while they're immobilized."

"Ouch," said Wood. But his voice was low and friendly now, the rasp making it seem almost intimate. She could feel his eyes on her, and kept hers focused narrowly on his hand. She carefully spread his fingers, feeling the resistance. "Still kind of sore," he explained with a soft grunt of pain.

She nodded. "We're going to want to work on that stiffness. I'm going to work with you to soften up and stretch the scar tissue, and I want you to start some exercises right away, to get those joints loosened up and some strength back. Are you using them at all?"

He stirred irritably and muttered, "I can manage to feed myself. Shaving's a little difficult."

She could tell by his voice that he'd turned his face away from her again. She glanced up, compassion flooding her at the sight of his battered profile, so stark against the pristine, white pillows. She murmured, "So I see. If you like, I can get someone to shave—"

It was the wrong thing to say, she realized almost at once. As his eyes snapped back to hers she was reminded again of the leopard, and belatedly understood his rage at his confinement and most especially his own helplessness.

"Thanks," he growled, pulling his hand from hers, "but I've kind of gotten to like the beard."

Chris nodded, but the warmth she'd enjoyed just a few moments ago was gone. She felt chilled again, as if that spring sun had been covered by clouds. She took a quick breath and a step backward and said, "Well, okay then. I'll, um . . . I'll come see you tomorrow, get you started on those exercises. In the meantime..." In the meantime what? Have a nice day? "Take care, now, okay?" she chirped, and added dismally, "Hang in there."

"Oh, I'm hangin'," Wood said in a dry tone, nodding at his prison of pulleys and wires.

Chris hesitated, then turned to flee, only to find her retreat blocked by a barrel-chested black man in a wheelchair. She stood aside to let the wheelchair pass, once again hiding behind the barricade of her folded arms and clipboard as she murmured a greeting to Grady, whom she'd seen around quite a bit, even though he wasn't her patient. The orderly with him was Sal Ramos, one she'd worked with before, so she said hi to him, too, hoping he wouldn't notice and wonder about the breathlessness in her voice that she couldn't seem to control.

As soon as the doorway was clear she slipped through it and made good her escape, but not before she heard Wood Brown call after her, "Hey, Chris, what's your last name? I still say I know you from somewhere. Where'd you go to school?"

"You're wastin' your time, man," drawled the guy in the wheelchair as he maneuvered past the foot of Wood's bed.

Wood watched him until he was safely clear of the hanging weights, then unclenched his jaws and said, "Yeah? How's that?"

The black man tilted his head toward the orderly. "Tell him, Sal, my man." Then, while Sal was nodding in verification, he leaned forward and stretched out a long, muscular arm. "Hey, I'm Grady. And you are . . ."

"Wood." He held up his bandaged hand and grimaced in apology. "Sorry."

"Hey, no problem. Now, what you want to do, Wood, is save yourself a whole lot of trouble and heartache. You got to listen to the voice of experience here." He jerked a thumb at Sal and shook his head in sympathy.

Sal grinned. "Just a minor case of frostbite, is all. Hey, I learn fast. Look but don't touch. I can live with that." He shrugged and turned the wheelchair a neat one-eighty. "Okay, Grady, let's go . . . upsy-daisy."

Wood watched for a moment with a hard, cold knot of empathy in his stomach, then turned his face away while the painful transfer from chair to bed was completed. Partly to fend off the queasiness, he said, "Uh . . . we are talking about Chris, here, right? The physical therapist—the one that just left? Come on."

Sal and Grady looked at each other and made identical clicking noises of regret. "Uh oh, too late," said Sal.

Grady sighed. "I know what you're thinkin'. The face of an angel and the body of a *Playboy* centerfold—and I'm one of the few men alive around here who can testify to that last fact, because I've seen her down yonder in the therapy pool." He gave a low, meaningful whistle.

Sal straightened up from setting Grady's bed to rights and took hold of the wheelchair handles. "Look, don't feel bad," he said to Wood, "there's probably not a male in this place over the age of puberty who hasn't had the same thoughts you have about that woman."

"Maybe you don't know what my thoughts are," said Wood.

Grady snorted. "Hey, man, if you ain't gay, you've got the thoughts."

"Trust me," said Sal. "She's ice."

"She didn't seem all that frigid to me," Wood said thoughtfully, looking toward the door as if he could still see her standing there, smiling at him like a burst of spring sunshine. He thought about the way she'd touched him, held and manipulated his hand, then amended with a grin, "Oh, well, I guess her hands were a little cold, but you know what they say—cold hands, warm heart."

Grady snorted. Sal said, "Believe me, that lady is cold all the way through. Hard to tell if she's even got a heart. Now, don't get me wrong, she's nice enough—polite, I guess you'd say, and a good P.T. Just doesn't get involved. Ever. With patients or anybody else."

"It's been suggested," Grady drawled with a hint of a smile, "that she don't care for men much at all."

"I'll bet it has," Wood said dryly. Among the guys he knew, that was pretty much the standard excuse for striking out with a woman. In this case he didn't really believe it was true, but it was kind of an unsettling thought. He shrugged it away. "Maybe she just doesn't care much for getting hit on all the time, you ever think of that? A woman who looks like that, she's got to get it a lot."

"You'd think so," Sal said, thinking it over, "but from what I've seen and heard, not as much as you'd expect. You want to know the truth, I think she scares people off—I know she scares the hell outa me. Such a thing as being *too* good-looking, know what I mean? I mean, what would you do with a woman like that? Geez, you'd be afraid to touch her."

It wasn't a situation that would ever have occurred to Wood, but he didn't say so. He could sort of see how it might occur to somebody like Sal—not that he was a bad-looking guy or anything. But still...

"Ah, hell," he said, "she's probably just reserved. She's Scandinavian, right?" She had to be, with that coloring—silvery hair the color of moonlight; eyes the pale, translucent blue of a summertime sky; ivory skin, the kind that turns to warm honey in the sun. "I used to know a lot of Scandinavians—went to school with 'em. They were the first white settlers where I come from. They're sort of like that." He squirmed irritably; the conversation was beginning to bother him, for reasons he couldn't quite pin down. For one thing, something was prowling around the back door of his memory, and he wanted to be still for a minute and see if it would come on in.

Before it had a chance to, though, the phone on the stand beside his bed rang, startling him enough to jolt him and send some pretty high-voltage pain shooting through his legs and deep into his guts. While he was fighting it, the elusive memory bolted for good.

Swearing and dripping with cold sweat, he reached clumsily to pick up the phone and only succeeded in dropping the receiver on the floor. Sal picked it up and wedged it between his ear and shoulder for him, murmuring, "There you go, man."

Wood muttered his thanks, cleared his throat and croaked, "H'lo?" into the phone.

"Earl? Oh God, is that you? What happened? Are you okay? What's wrong with your voice?"

Wood was about to snarl, "Who the hell's this?" when it occurred to him that there was only a very small and select group of people alive on this earth who would ever call him Earl. And only one who could fire a barrage of questions that fast without stopping for a breath. Something cracked open inside him, pouring warmth through his chest. It felt just like a slug of neat whiskey, banishing all pain and leaving him slightly winded.

"Well...hi there, big sister," he said huskily, and sank back into his pillows, smiling from ear to ear. "How're you doing?"

"How am I doing? How am *I* doing? Edward Earl Brown, I swear, I may have to kill you myself!"

"Hey... Lucy." The idea of his tough-as-nails sister crying was awakening painful memories, memories he didn't want to have to deal with right now. Especially while he didn't have any privacy to speak of. He forced a chuckle through the constriction in his throat and said, "You wouldn't kill me before I've had a chance to see my cute little niece, would you? How is that Rosie, anyway?"

It did the trick. He heard a quick intake of breath, a gulp and then, "Oh, fine—growing like a weed."

"I'll bet. How's Gwen?" Wood nodded at Sal, who was pulling the curtain between his bed and Grady's. The orderly waved and went out of the room.

"She's fine—she's right here, waiting to talk to you. But Earl—"

"And that husband of yours—do I get to meet him sometime before I die?"

"Don't talk like that, Earl. Don't you dare."

"Hey... Luce—Lucy, it's okay. I'm okay. Honest. Hey, I'll be home to visit in no time. Soon as they let me out of this get-up they've got me in—"

There was a liquid-sounding chuckle. "You've got to be kidding. You don't think I'm going to wait that long, do you? I'm coming to see you, you idiot. That's why I'm calling. Is tomorrow okay?"

"Are you kidding?" His voice cracked. "Can't you get here any sooner?"

Another chuckle, less shaky now, more like the Lucy he remembered. "You can't have forgotten *that* much in twelve years. This is a farm, remember? I have to get somebody to do the chores, and find a sitter for Rosie—"

"For Pete's sake, bring her!"

"They won't let her in to see you, anyway, Earl. And you don't want her jumping around on you, trust me. Don't worry, I'll bring pictures. Okay, so Gwen and I'll be there—"

"Gwen, too? That's great. So what about the husband? When do I get to meet him?"

"Mike's in Chicago—he'll be home on the weekend. I'll bring him next time. Look, I wasn't going to wait any longer to see you, dammit. I've been worried to death about you, don't you know that? When they called and told me what happened—"

"Hey, I told you, I'm going to be fine." He tried another sidetrack. "You hear much from Rhett? How's he doing? Still keeping the streets of Des Moines safe for women and rugrats?"

"And kissing babies for all he's worth, I'm sure." Wood smiled as he heard his sister's voice plummet a few degrees in temperature. Ah, yes . . . just like old times. "His wife tells me he's tied up in court right now and can't get away. I told her to tell him even a big-time lawyer could manage to find the time to give his little brother a call. I take it he hasn't yet?"

"Not yet," said Wood easily. "But I'm sure he will. Ease up on him, Luce, I just got in last night. Poor old Rhett's not so bad."

"Yeah, well, you haven't seen him in a while, have you? He's changed, Earl. I think he's clean forgotten how to smile." She caught a quick breath and abruptly shifted gears, as only Lucy could. "We'll talk about all that when I see you. Tomorrow morning, okay? First thing."

"It's a date."

"Oh God . . . I can't wait to see you."

Wood chuckled uneasily. "Uh . . . I'd better warn you. You might not recognize me." Hell, there were times he didn't recognize himself.

"Why?" The word was a breathy gasp of alarm. "What have you done—"

"I've picked up a few battle scars is all. It's been a long time, Luce." *I'm not your "handsome" baby brother anymore, Sis.* He rubbed at his jaw, smiling darkly to himself at the rasping sound the beard made against his fingertips. No, he seriously doubted that particular word would ever be used to describe him again. Which was okay with him. He chuckled once more. "Hey, don't worry. I don't exactly give nightmares to small children."

He said goodbye and managed, after a couple of misses and some bad language, to return the receiver to its cradle. Then, exhausted by the effort, he lay back on his pillows and closed his eyes.

Not small children, maybe. I'm not so sure about women.

He was suddenly remembering the physical therapist, Chris, and the baffling flash of fear he'd seen, for just one moment, in her eyes. . . .

* * *

Where did you go to school?

With those magic words her mind had cleared, like a year-book falling open at just the right page.

Twelve years...no, more than that. Thirteen years ago. She'd been barely sixteen, a lowly sophomore and in just her second semester on the staff of the school newspaper. How thrilled she'd been—and how terrified—to have been chosen to interview the senior-class president and captain of the basketball team. The team had just won the championship of their division in a stunning upset victory over the top-ranked team in the state. And Earl Brown was just possibly the most popular boy in the entire school, certainly the best looking. She'd been so nervous...tongue-tied, painfully aware of her shabby skirt, made over from one her mother had worn in the sixties, and of her shapeless sweater and thick glasses. So certain she was about to make a complete fool of herself.

How well she remembered the way Earl Brown had exploded into the journalism lab that morning in an almost visible cloud of euphoria, riding his victory and fame like a magnificent white charger, absolutely on top of the world. Conceited, she'd told herself. Much too full of himself. An arrogant snob. But even she had known he was only using disdain as a means of combating paralyzing awe.

And then—somehow, she never knew quite how he'd managed it—he'd turned everything around. Grabbing up a layout roller, he'd begun to interview *her,* in the flamboyant style of an "eyewitness" television reporter, leaving her breathless, bemused and completely charmed.

"So tell me, Chris Thurmond, where do you go to school? Ah, ha—the best school in the whole state of Iowa, right? And what do you think of West High's chances of winning the state championship this year?"

So she'd discovered that not only was Earl Brown popular and good-looking and smart and a star athlete, he was also *nice.* If she hadn't known how ridiculous it would be, she probably would have fallen head over heels in love with him right then and there. But Chris Thurmond was a realist, and much too practical to even imagine such a thing....

Earl Brown. Could it possibly be? She hadn't recognized the gaunt, compelling face on those pillows, but he'd been through a lot, and so much time had passed. More than twelve years. Hadn't he said he'd been away that long? And he'd insisted he knew her. Oh God, she thought, please don't let him remember me.

She stared at the notes on her clipboard until they blurred. Edward Brown. No middle name given. *Ed was my dad's name... call me Wood.* Maybe. Maybe it was a recent nickname. It sounded like something a marine might come up with. And if he was a "Junior," they could easily have called him Earl while he was living at home, going to high school.

It could be true. So what? She didn't understand why her entire body suddenly felt hollow and jittery. The weakness in her knees appalled her. Why should it matter that she'd just encountered someone from her distant past? She wasn't even that person anymore. *She wasn't.*

"Aren't you forgetting something?"

Chris started violently and blinked, bringing Florence's steely glare into focus. "I'm sorry?"

"Your coat." The nurse nodded at Chris's parka with a look that made it plain its presence there was about as welcome as she imagined a cowpat would be on her front lawn.

Chris absently murmured her thanks, picked up the coat and threw it over her arm. It was much too warm to put it on; far from feeling perpetually chilled, as she seemed to lately, her body felt overheated, her face flushed, as if all her vital signs had been kicked into high gear. She hurried back to the health center in a haze of memories, too distracted for once to notice anything—or anyone—around her.

The Riverside Physical Therapy Clinic was humming, the morning's activities in full swing. Brad was goading Paul, a trucker injured in an interstate pileup, into taking a few more painful steps with the aid of the parallel bars, at the same time keeping an eye on a knee-injured high school football player who was sweating and grunting through his Nautilus routine. Megan was on the floor pad, coaxing Tonya, a brain-injured six-year-old, through the slow and tedious task of "reprogramming," while her mother looked on, learning the process. Over in the far corner frowning and self-absorbed, a figure skater recovering from an ankle injury was plodding away on the stair climber.

Chris paused in the waiting room to offer a few words of encouragement to her first patient of the day, a sixty-eight-year-old stroke victim named Gracie—a real sweetheart and a favorite of hers. Then she dropped her coat off at her desk before reporting to Mason's office for the promised briefing on the new patient.

She had a busy day ahead, which was the way she liked it, with a full schedule of patients, all with problems that made hers seem piddling by comparison. As always, she threw herself into the work and, by concentrating hard on her job and doing her best to avoid the reception counter and the gorgeous bouquet of white roses there, was almost able to forget the fear that was with her every waking moment.

Almost. Because wherever she went the fragrance of the roses seemed to follow her, clinging to her like an annoying party guest, demanding her attention. And in the back of her mind a phrase kept recurring, playing over and over again like a line from a particularly irritating song.

I know you... where did you go to school?

After work it was still too warm for the parka, so she tossed it over the passenger seat for the short drive home.

She lived on a quiet, shady street in an older part of town. In the summertime it was a friendly, busy neighborhood full of the sounds of plastic tricycle wheels, bouncing balls and children's laughter, full of the smells of home cooking and newly cut grass. She had an apartment she loved on the top floor of an old-fashioned frame house with blue-painted siding. The house had once been a genteel family residence—a doctor's house, someone had told her—but had been converted into five tiny apartments, two each on the first two floors, and hers by itself on the third, tucked in under the high, peaked roof, in what had probably once been the maid's quarters, or perhaps the nursery. The ceilings were low and the rooms small, and since she was not, there were times when she felt a little like Alice after nibbling on the wrong mushroom.

There were a few other disadvantages, too, in living where she did, but as far as Chris was concerned the advantages far outweighed them. First and foremost among them being a distinct lack of privacy. The street positively teemed with inquisitive children, protective mothers and elderly people with nothing much to do except keep an eye on their neighbors. Strangers could not come and go unnoticed and unremarked upon.

"You had a delivery," Mrs. Furman, one of her first-floor neighbors announced, coming out into the vestibule while Chris was checking her mailbox. "Florist, it looked like."

The muscles in the small of Chris's back went into spasm, as if someone had run an ice cube up her spine. She murmured, "Oh, really?"

Mrs. Furman nodded. "One of those pretty, long gold boxes. I had him leave it at your door. It's not your birthday, is it? Oh, I hope I didn't miss it. I'd have baked you a cake. I always like to do that, you know—a nice, homemade cake, from scratch. You have to tell me what kind you like—Mr. Furman always liked apple spice, you know, with walnuts. And extra cinnamon."

"That's okay," Chris assured her. "It's not my birthday."

Mrs. Furman beamed, her eyes bright with the hope of getting more information. "Oh, then you must have an admirer!"

"They're probably from a patient," Chris murmured as she sorted blindly through her usual assortment of junk mail, doing her best to make it seem as if that sort of thing happened all the time. "Thanks for telling me."

She waved and stretched her lips in a desperate smile, then turned and ran for the stairs.

The box lay on the carpet in front of Chris's door, just as Mrs. Furman had described it. Long, gold foil, tied with gold ribbon. She bent down to pick it up, juggling purse, parka, keys and mail, dropping first one thing, then another. Her skin was crawling, her fingers icy cold and clumsy. She finally managed to gather everything haphazardly into her arms, unlock the door and stumble inside.

She dropped her parka and mail on the floor and left them where they fell, threw her purse onto the couch and her keys onto the coffee table. The florist's box she carried to the kitchen, quaking inside, breathing in short, angry whimpers. With her eyes burning with tears that refused to fall, she laid the box on the countertop and took a knife out of a drawer. Her movements were jerky and fumbling as she cut the ribbon. Though she didn't want to, she lifted off the lid.

Inside the box was a single white rose. Its stem was long and carefully plucked free of thorns, its leaves glossy and still beaded with moisture. The perfect, urn-shaped bloom lay beside the stem, nestled in crispy green tissue paper. It had been cleanly severed at the neck.

Chapter 3

"Earl—my God, you look awful!" Lucy exclaimed the minute she laid eyes on him.

Wood just smiled; he was learning to quell the urge to laugh. "Thanks, Luce. Now I know for sure I'm home. H'lo, Gwen."

At least, he thought, there was one thing that hadn't changed. The old lady looked exactly as he remembered—tall, thin and straight as a rail. Still wearing jeans at—what must she be now? Eighty? Oh, no, it had to be more than that; she'd been close to eighty for as long as he could remember. Her hair was a little whiter, maybe, still worn in a knot at the nape of her neck, with that whimsical halo of curls around her face. And there was still that gleam in her eyes, that arch to her eyebrows, that look of laughter just about to bust loose.

"Lucy's right," she said in the lovely, melodious voice he remembered as she bent to kiss his cheek. "You do look terrible."

Wood shrugged it off with a grin and drawled, "Yeah, that's what happens when a truck falls on you." Inside he was beginning to quiver with unexpected—and unwelcome—emotions.

His sister wasn't making any effort to hide hers, which didn't help matters. She'd been hanging back with one hand clamped over her mouth, and now, with a long, quivery sniffle, threw up her hands and exclaimed, "Look at you—I don't even know where to hug you! I swear to God, Earl . . ." She shook a fist at him, as if she thought he'd hurt himself on purpose just to aggravate her and it was all she could do to keep from popping him a good one herself. She was laughing and crying at the same time, which was something he remembered she was inclined to do at moments like this.

"You can hug," he said in a gravelly voice. And Lucy being Lucy, he hastily added, "Just whatever you do, don't shake the damn bed."

Then he braced himself for the familiar feel of her hands on his face, the unfamiliar dampness of her cheek, the quivering in her body that reflected his own. It didn't help; he still felt the sting of those childish, treacherous tears that had plagued him so much lately. He was frowning like an embattled eagle in an effort to camouflage them when Lucy suddenly reared back to stare at him.

Then to his surprise, she burst out with a gurgle of laughter. "Oh, Earl—now you've got it, too. The Rosewood Nose."

He touched it ruefully. "Yeah, I know. I could have had 'em fix it for me, I guess, but I don't know...I kind of like it. What do you think?" He put on a wicked grin.

Lucy snorted. "You look like a pirate, that's what I think. What's with this stuff, anyway?" She tugged on his beard, none too gently.

"Ouch—hey." He evaded her, trying desperately not to laugh. "It's too much trouble to shave right now, that's all."

"That's not all that must be trouble." Lucy was looking with dawning realization, then horror, at the complex system of pulleys, weights and wires at the foot of his bed, at the sheets carefully tented across the lower part of his body. "How in the world do you—"

Wood coughed and shifted position and subject. "Hey," he said with all the heartiness he could muster, "*you* sure are looking good. I guess married life and motherhood must agree with you, huh? When am I gonna meet this guy you've shacked up with? You've been married how long now? Five years? And that little Rosie Ellen—you promised me pictures. I'll bet she's just as cute as the dickens."

He noticed that Gwen was laughing in that melodious way she had, like the sound of a cold brook running over mossy pebbles.

Lucy glared at him in that particular way *she* had, like a little bitty hawk about to take a chunk out of something. "It's your own fault you've never met Mike, or your own niece. Edward Earl, you could have come home for a visit." Her voice broke, but she went furiously on. "It's been *ten years*. You didn't even come for the wedding."

She looked so fierce he had to turn his face away. God, he knew her so well. He knew he'd hurt her, so of course the guilt made it hurt to look at her.

"Hey...I know, Luce, I'm sorry. I just..." He waved a hand, incapable of coming up with an excuse. He'd tried a few times, that first couple of years after he'd joined the Marine Corps. *Coming home*... The truth was, it had hurt too damn much, and he'd been too selfish to come again.

"That reminds me," Lucy said abruptly, shifting gears with a typical burst of energy that made him cringe and brace himself. "I brought you something. Gwen, where did I—oh, there it is."

She'd left it by the door. He didn't know how he'd missed seeing it, except that with Lucy around it was hard to notice much else. Now, as she whirled and swooped down upon the dark, pebbled leather case, he felt something inside him turn and twist, kind of like a knife in his guts. She turned back to him with it hugged in her arms, her face so radiant he had to fight to control his, hoping desperately he wouldn't spoil it for her. It occurred to him, somewhat irrelevantly, that his sister really was looking great. Almost beautiful.

"Your old guitar," she said breathlessly. "I thought you could use something . . . you know—to pass the time." She laid it with unwonted care—almost reverence—across his stomach.

He couldn't think of anything to say. Maybe he was incapable of speech, being simply too overwhelmed with the memories. He felt as if he was drowning in them.

"Sing me, Mama, sing me some more. I want the old-cotton-fields one. Sing me 'Cotton Fields,' Mama."

"All right, honey, but you have to help me. Ready? 'When I was—'"

"I want to do it, Mama. Let me do it."

"Just let me show you, honey . . . put your fingers—"

"No! I can do it by myself. See? Look, Mama, I'm just like Elvis. 'You ain't nothin' but a houn' dawg!'"

"Oh, Earl!"

"Mom, I hate 'Church In The Wildwood.' It's dumb—'Oh, come, come, come, come—' Rhett just likes it 'cause he gets to do the bass. Why do we always have to sing these old songs, anyway? Why can't we sing something... You know, cool?"

"Like what?"

"How about 'Sunday Mornin', Comin' Down'?"

"That's hardly appropriate for church, Earl."

"What do you mean? It's about Sunday, isn't it?"

"...I can't do it, Lucy. Please...I can't."

"'Peace in the Valley' was Mama's favorite, Earl. Please, do it for her. You know how much she would have wanted—"

"I said I can't, dammit! Don't ask me to. Don't ever ask me to sing again! And I don't ever want to see this stupid thing again, either—never, do you hear me? Never...."

He didn't remember moving, but he felt the rough, pebbly texture of the guitar case beneath his fingers and realized that he was stroking it. He had to say something. Lucy was waiting for him to say something, her eyes tear bright, her face shiny with hope and happiness. Behind her Gwen's face hovered, lined in perpetual laughter, but her eyes were filmy and sad, soft with understanding. He cleared his throat, opened his mouth to speak. But nothing came out.

He was a United States Marine, battle scarred, tough as nails. He'd looked death in the eye a dozen times or more, on the sandy wastes of Kuwait, in the treacherous streets of Mogadishu and Sarajevo. There wasn't any situation he didn't feel capable of handling himself in, any emergency he couldn't deal with.

But here in this damned hospital bed, strung up with pulleys and wires, with his mother's guitar sitting on his chest, he felt almost totally helpless. He felt crushed beneath the weight of his sister's love and expectations, bludgeoned by his own emotions. And as close as he'd ever been to complete panic.

Just at that terrible moment when the tension had reached the point of breaking, there was a sharp knock on the door. Wood jerked his eyes toward the source of the interruption like a doomed man hoping for salvation.

The door opened. A voice sweet as bird song called out, "Oh—hi, sorry to intrude. Would you like me to come back later?"

Chris had known about the visitors. Florence had told her with obvious satisfaction, as if she thought she'd be throwing a monkey wrench into Chris's plans with the news. However, after a pretty much sleepless night, Chris was in no mood to be bullied *or* thwarted.

"Great," she'd said with set jaw and forced smile. "I've been hoping for a chance to talk with his family about his therapy." And off she'd sailed, on a wave of annoyance mixed with determination, armed with her clipboard and false cheer.

But nothing could have prepared her for the look she saw in Wood Brown's eyes when she opened that door. She wasn't sure what it was, what it meant, that look of terror and desperate hope—like someone clinging to a precipice by his fingernails and looking to her to throw him a rope. But it hit her like a sneaky punch to the stomach. She paused momentarily while her heart lurched and the breath left her lungs, and her body grew hot with a purely instinctive urge to respond. Then she did what she always did in the face of a terrifying and unexpected attack on her emotions, the only thing she knew how to do: she threw up every defense, every wall she had. And barricaded herself behind them.

"I'm Chris," she said when no one spoke, keeping her voice cool and her manner calm as she aproached the older of the two women in the room with outstretched hand. "I'm going to be helping your son with his physical rehab. But I can come back, if you—"

"No, no, that's okay." Wood's voice was a croak. He struggled to raise himself beneath the weight of the guitar case. "Uh...this is my aunt Gwen, my sister, Lucy..."

Chris murmured the appropriate phrases as she took each woman's hand in turn—the old lady's, blue-veined and fragile as balsa wood, then the sister's smaller one, brown, callused and amazingly strong. She had to steel herself to meet the look of half-recognition and thoughtful speculation in the aunt's shrewd old eyes. The look in the sister's, a chilly reserve that was almost hostility, she was used to encountering in women near her own age, especially those in the company of their menfolk. She merely shrugged it off, having given up wondering about the reason for it.

"Actually, it's good that you're here," she said, briskly professional. "You might like to hear what we're going to be doing, kind of get an idea what to expect. Is that okay with you, Wood?"

"Sure," said Wood with a slight shrug. He seemed more relaxed now, Chris thought; seemed even to be enjoying himself in purely male fashion, as the only man in a roomful of women. Whatever the source of the tension when she'd walked into the room, it appeared to be gone now.

"Is this yours?" she asked casually, picking up the guitar.

There was nothing casual about the spasmodic movement he made toward the guitar. Or the way he coughed and muttered, "Uh . . . yeah. Used to be. My . . . Lucy brought it. She, uh, I guess she thought—"

He'd been hiding one hand, with its scars and bandages, under a fold in the sheets. Chris heard a soft, stricken sound from behind her.

She turned with the guitar to smile reassuringly at Wood's sister, who had clamped a fist over her mouth and was staring at her brother's hands with bright, shimmering eyes, apparently getting a good look at them for the first time.

"What a good idea. This should be great therapy for those hands. Speaking of which . . ." She set the guitar case on the floor under the bed and reached into the pocket of her tunic. "I brought you something." She held up a pair of small, hard rubber balls. "I want you to start squeezing these—gently at first, just whenever you can. While you're watching television or whatever. Okay? Work on building strength, working out the stiffness."

She took one of Wood's hands in hers, turning slightly to include the two women in what she was saying. "We want to work on the hands first, so he can start making use of the trap bar, get that upper-body strength built up." While she was talking she was gently working the hand, straightening each finger, pushing against the resistance in the joints. "He's going to be in traction probably for another three or so weeks, and once he gets his casts he's really going to need that strength in order to handle the chair."

"Chair?" said Lucy faintly, still looking stricken.

"Wheelchair," Chris confirmed cheerfully, placing the hand she'd been massaging on the sheets and picking up the other one. "That's when the real fun begins. He'll have about two weeks of training in the use of the chair, learning how to do things for himself, and then he'll be ready to get out of here."

"Hallelujah," Wood muttered with a little grunt of pain.

Unable to help herself, Chris glanced at him. She found his gaze resting on her with that black, unnerving intensity, only now it was much nearer than before, barely an arm's length away.

"You can do this yourself," she said as she returned his hand to its resting place on the rumpled sheets, silently thanking Providence for the presence of the sister and the aunt. "Work on stretching those joints, and start working with the balls. And as soon as you can, you might try gripping the trap here, okay?"

She touched the bar that was suspended above his chest, setting it to swinging gently, and turned to flash a professional smile at the two women. "Well, it was nice meeting you. Wood, I'll be back tomorrow. Is this a good time for you? Okay, then . . . see you in the morning. Hang in there."

"I'm hangin'," Wood drawled sardonically after she had gone. But he was smiling to himself.

"Oh, brother!" said Lucy.

"What?"

"I've seen that look, Ed Earl. What is it with you and Rhett? What is this . . . this *thing* you've both got for these cold, statuesque Nordic types, anyway?"

"I wouldn't exactly call Chris statuesque," he said placidly. Unless he was miscalculating badly, under that tunic he'd bet she had a waist he could get his hands around. "More like . . . willowy."

Lucy sniffed. "Give her a few years—and twenty pounds."

"Lucy!" Gwen chided, but on a note of forgiving laughter.

Wood *tsked* in gentle reproof. "Catty isn't like you, Luce. I can't believe you'd be jealous of somebody just—"

"I'm not jealous! Why on earth should I be jealous of blond hair, gorgeous eyes and—and legs up to *here* and boobs out to *there?*" She paused suddenly in her ranting and smiled with a faraway look, as if she was remembering something . . . nice. Then she shrugged and was somber again. "I just can't bear to think of you getting involved with another cold fish like Elaine, that's all. Poor Rhett—and those poor kids of his. I wonder sometimes . . ."

Wood allowed himself a cautious chuckle as he lay back on his pillows, trying without much success to ease the discomforts in his lower back and hips without setting off the fireworks in his thighs. "Look, I'm hardly 'involved' with her. She's my physical therapist—that's it. But I'll tell you this much—she's nothing at all like Rhett's wife. Nothing, not even close. Definitely not cold.''

"How do you know?" Lucy demanded. "You only met her yesterday."

"I just know." He frowned thoughtfully at the door, seeing again the vision that had been playing over and over in his memory for the past twenty-four hours. A tall, slender girl in a shapeless, too-big sweater, pale blond hair pulled sleekly back from a perfect oval face, a too-bright smile and a lost, scared look in her silvery-blue eyes. It was a vision that haunted him because it called up elusive memories from the distant past, and he couldn't for the life of him complete the connection. "There's something about her..."

"Yeah? Like what?"

"I don't know. She looks familiar to me. I just can't—"

"She looked familiar to me, too," said Gwen thoughtfully.

"She did? So who in the he—world—is she?"

But Gwen only shrugged and smiled in that maddeningly serene way of hers. "Oh, I don't know, I can't seem to place her. It'll come to me."

Wood let his breath out in exasperation. "I can't place her, either, and it's been bothering the hell—sorry, heck out of me. I don't know what it is, but I'd swear that woman's hiding something." He grinned suddenly. "It might be a kick, though, finding out what it is."

"Oh, *Earl*," Lucy said in mock disgust, swooping like a sparrow hawk to peck a kiss on his forehead. "I swear to God, you haven't changed a bit, have you?"

"Guess not," he murmured. But when he tried to smile, he discovered that it was hard to open his eyes. He suddenly realized that he felt lousy—weak, sweaty and clammy.

"I think Earl's tired." Gwen's voice seemed to come from a long way off. "Lucy, we need to go now...let him get some rest."

Wood heard himself protest, but in truth he wanted very much to be left alone.

"...Be back again soon...bring Mike next... Get better...love you."

His family's farewells left him dizzy with exhaustion. He listened with his eyes closed to the sound of the closing door, while the bed floated and the world slowly revolved around it.

"You haven't changed a bit."
Oh, but Lucy, I have . . . I have.

He'd changed; everything had changed. He didn't recognize his own face in the mirror. His body, which he'd spent a lifetime keeping fit and healthy and which had served him so well, was no longer his to command. His career as a soldier was over, that was for damn sure, and he didn't have a clue what he was going to do from now on. He didn't even know who he was anymore.

The new storm arrived that night, right on schedule and with a vengeance, restoring reality with wind chills in the subzero range. Chris woke to find three inches of snow on the ground and the air full of stinging flakes blowing almost horizontally in a wet, bitter wind. It was a gray, cruel and unforgiving morning, but no worse than was to be expected.

Chris didn't spare the weather a second thought, but dressed for work methodically in her maximum number of layers. She ate her usual vegetarian breakfast—coffee, two slices of fat-free toast with fruit-only spread and a sliced banana in skim milk with artificial sweetener sprinkled over it—while she watched the early local news on television. Breakfast over, she checked the clock and decided, as she usually did, to pass up a second cup of coffee. There'd be coffee at work, although she seldom found time for it there.

She gave her dishes a quick rinse and left them to drain, then made a last trip to the bathroom to brush her teeth and put in her contact lenses. Restoring clear vision gave her an unpleasant shock—purplish smudges under her eyes that she didn't remember being there before. Certainly not this bad. And those strain lines around her mouth... Oh God, she thought, I'm not even thirty. I don't know how much longer I can take this.

She snatched up her parka, purse and keys, gave everything a last once-over and went out, carefully locking up behind her.

Downstairs in the entryway of the old house she paused, as she always did, to put on her parka and to peek out at the street through the cut-flower pattern in the frosted-glass door panel. Satisfied, she reached into the pocket of her parka for her mittens.

The mittens were there, as always; she was very organized, a creature of regular habits. But this morning something else was there, as well. Something made of paper. She drew it out and stared at it, frowning. It was a piece of paper torn from a notepad, the kind people use to scrawl hurried notes to themselves, fold once and stick in their pockets, to be forgotten until washday, when they emerge as small, indecipherable wads of pulp. There was nothing unusual about it at all. Except that she couldn't remember having written herself such a note. Or putting one in her pocket.

She didn't want to unfold the note, but her fingers did so, anyway. It took her several tries, because they were cold and stiff, and very clumsy. The penciled words on the paper, neatly printed in black letters, swam almost reluctantly into focus:

Too bad about the kid in ER, isn't it? You know the one— the broken arm. But that's what happens to people who aren't careful. Let that be a lesson, Crissy. Never let your guard down. I'm always watching.

She didn't realize what she was doing until a single tear fell on the paper in her hands, soaking in instantly and making a round wet spot in the middle of the word *careful*. Then, as if someone had released the Mute button on a remote-control device, she heard herself saying, "Oh,no, oh, no, oh, no. . ." over and over in a high, keening voice, which shocked her immediately into silence.

She hastily brushed at her eyes as she glanced around her, thankful, at least, that there'd been no one around to see or hear, then shoved the note deep into the pocket of her parka. Half-blind and trembling, she fumbled for the doorknob, opened it and stumbled into the swirling snow.

Oh no, oh no, oh no . . .

She hardly felt the cold. Her heart was pounding, racing, her pulse like drums in her ears.

When? Oh God, when? How?

She couldn't think, couldn't make sense of anything. Because it didn't make sense. How could he have done it? And when? She couldn't remember . . . couldn't *think*.

She felt like a hunted rabbit, exposed and vulnerable. Helpless.

She barely remembered how she got to her car, but the key was in her hand and she was unlocking the door. *That's what happens to people who aren't careful.* In terror now, she darted quick looks all around her, certain someone was right there behind her, ready to grab her. She realized that she was breathing in whimpers, the way she did in her nightmares. And then she was inside and fumbling at the locks.

Safe. Except she knew now that she wasn't safe anywhere, not even in the hospital. Her own hospital.

How had he done it? How? She started the car and sat shivering in the cold while she waited for the engine to warm, thinking about it as hard as she could. She remembered the ER, the child and his mother, the doctor, the orderly mopping down the floors. Could it have possibly been—oh, no, please God. That would mean he had a security badge now. *Oh no, oh no, oh no . . .*

Had he been waiting there for her, hiding in the chapel, perhaps, being familiar with her routine? Or had he followed her in, followed her upstairs, where her parka lay unguarded on the counter at the nurse's station? He must have written the note with Florence not five feet away, trying to look oh, so busy so as not to appear unduly interested. He might have chatted with her, maybe flirted a little to distract her while he slipped the note into the pocket of the parka.

I'm always watching. . . .

She wasn't safe. Not anywhere. And she was never going to be safe again. Not as long as he was alive.

"You gonna play that thing or just hold it?"

Wood shook off his memories, looked over at the next bed with a lopsided smile and lifted his hands off the guitar, holding them up by way of an excuse.

Grady nodded in acknowledgment of the bandages, then shrugged. "Hey—it'll come. Don' worry about it." His voice was very deep; it rumbled out of his chest like tympany.

"Oh man . . . I don't know." Wood eased his head back on the pillows with a sigh. "It's been a long time since I played." He could feel the guitar strings under his fingers, could almost feel them vibrate. "A long time . . ."

"You played when you were a kid?"

"Yeah. Started when I was real young—maybe six or seven. My mom taught me."

Grady gave a low whistle. "That's young."

Wood shrugged. "I guess. I can't really remember a time when I didn't play—or sing—something. Music comes kind of naturally in my family." He paused to chuckle softly. "For my mom and my brother and me, anyway. My dad and my sister, Lucy, couldn't carry a tune in a bucket."

Grady chuckled, too. "That's me, man. You're lucky, you know that? To have the music."

"Yeah," said Wood, "I guess." His fingers stirred across the strings of their own accord; they answered with a warm, welcoming murmur. *"Look, Mama, look at me...."*

Grady was saying something. Wood jerked away from the memory and said, "What?"

"I said, why'd you quit? Playin' music, I mean. Man, if I had a gift like that..."

The polished wood felt warm under his hands, almost as if it were alive. The strings seemed to be waking to a rhythm of their own, like a heartbeat. "It was hard..." Wood cleared his throat. "After my mom died. Too many memories."

"Hey, man, I'm sorry." There was a pause, and then he asked softly, "How'd it happen?"

"Car accident. Week before I graduated from high school. My mom and dad were both killed." The guitar had gone stone cold and lifeless. Wood lifted it away from his chest and lowered it carefully to the floor beside the bed.

"Yeah, that's rough," said Grady. "That's rough." After a moment he shook his head and laughed almost silently, a dry, whispering sound. "I never knew my old man. Died before I was born. Got shot in a bar. They *said*—" he glanced at Wood with a wry, roguish look "—in an altercation involving a *wo*man.... So my mama raised me to stay outa bars. And look at me—I get mine in a Seven-Eleven."

"That's rough," said Wood, because he didn't know what else to say. But after a few minutes of silence, he cleared his throat and blurted out the question that had been on his mind for two days now. "How do you do it? I mean, how do you deal with it, man? I'm not handling *this* very well." He waved an angry hand at his pulleys and wires. "I don't know what I'd do if I—"

"If you knew you'd never walk again?" Grady's voice was soft and thick.

Wood just nodded; he couldn't look at him.

"Hey, it's *hard*. I'm not gonna lie to you." There was a long pause. "You wanna know what got me through?"

"Yeah." Now he did look, frowning and intent. "I want to know."

Grady laughed, a rich rumble from down deep in his belly. "You think I'm gonna say faith in the Lord, or something, don't you? No, truth is, it was my wife got me through—she's got faith enough for the both of us. No, man, I'm tellin' you. You know what she said to me, the first thing I can remember after I got shot? *'You're alive, honey. You're alive.'* That's what I remembered, what's carried me through. I'm alive. That's what matters. And I still got things to do, man. I got things to do."

"What are you going to do?" Wood asked. "I mean, have you thought about it? What'd you do before?"

"Drove heavy equipment for the state highway department—snowplows in the winter, graders and whatnot the rest of the year. That's pretty much out, but I figure there's got to be other ways to make a living, even for a man in a wheelchair, know what I mean? I'm thinkin' 'bout goin' back to school, maybe learn about computers. Hey—if my ten-year-old kid can figure 'em out, how hard can it be?"

"Yeah," said Wood absently. It still seemed hard for him to believe—a man in the prime of his life, a big, powerful man... He turned his head to look at him, frowning. "So you really are okay with this? With what's happened to you?"

"Hell no, I'm not okay with it!" Grady brought a ham-size fist down on his rolling tray, so hard that it scooted away toward the foot of the bed. "You think I don't pray every day that it's some kind of bad dream, and I'm gonna wake up and get outa bed and *walk,* man? But that ain't gonna happen, is it? And I gotta accept what *is,* not what I wish was. That's *life,* man."

He was quiet for a while, and Wood could see him looking inward, paging back through a lifetime's worth of memories. Memories of the man he used to be. Then he looked over at Wood with a half smile and said, "You want to know how I see this thing? Way I see it, my friend, is that I didn't have no say about what happened to me, so I ain't gonna let myself spend time and energy worrying about that. What I *do* have a say in is whether I'm gonna let it mess up my life or not. You dig?"

"Yeah," said Wood. "I dig."

"Tell you something, though," Grady went on, "it sure does help to have somebody who you know is on your side, somebody you can count on, who loves you enough to stick by you, no matter what. My wife and my kids, man, that's what I got goin' for me. Hey—so what about you? You married?"

"Nah," said Wood. "Never had time."

"That's bull, man. You just haven't found the right woman yet, is all. You find her, you gonna *make* time. Trust me."

"Yeah, maybe." Wood was wishing he could shift into a more comfortable positon, thinking there were times he could almost envy Grady being numb from the waist down—on a temporary basis, of course. "So, when do I get to meet this wonder woman of yours—what's her name, by the way?"

"Joanna." The big man's face suddenly changed, got dark and sad, as if a cloud had covered up his sun. "Wish you could, man, wish you could. She ain't here. She and the kids went back to Georgia to stay with her folks. Had to—only way she could work and have somebody to watch over the kids. Oh *man*, I sure do miss her." His sigh seemed to come from the soles of his feet. "Seein' her face every day...it was like watching the sun come up, you know what I mean? Now she's gone, it's like the sun don't come up no more."

Wood didn't say anything, because he'd just heard the doorknob click and start to turn. As he looked toward the door, he felt his heart lift in his chest and his pulse rate quicken in expectation. *Ah, yes...right on schedule.*

And he found himself thinking how lucky Grady was, and how barren his own life must be when the high point of his whole day was a visit from his physical therapist.

Chapter 4

The minute she walked in, he knew something was wrong. Chris was smiling as usual, but this morning the effect wasn't anything at all like the sun coming up in spring. It was more like a cold, rainy day in December, when the holiday cheer can give you the blues so bad you just want to crawl into a corner and cry.

Which, it occurred to him, was exactly what she looked like she'd been doing.

She pulled herself together, though, so quickly he might almost have believed he'd imagined that wild, distracted look she'd come in with, like someone coming into shelter from a fierce and frightening storm.

She gave him her usual bright, "Hi, how are you doing?" as she crossed the room, and the same for Grady while she was drawing the curtain between the two beds. Her movements were brisk and businesslike as always, but for some reason Wood thought they seemed sort of stiff, as if she didn't quite have her nerve impulses under control. As she came around the bed, he watched her narrowly, for once not cringing in dread of disturbances in his suspension system; watched her drop the parka she'd been carrying over one arm onto the chair and smooth back her hair with both hands. He couldn't help but notice that there were dark, purple smudges under her eyes.

"Well," she said as she moved the guitar gingerly to one side and took one of his hands in both of hers, "let's see how these are coming along, shall we?"

Her fingers were cold as ice. Wood couldn't stop the hiss of an indrawn breath between his teeth.

"I'm sorry," she said in a remote, expressionless voice. Her lashes dropped like curtains over her eyes. "I know my hands are cold. I was...running a little late this morning, so I came straight here. I guess I haven't had a chance to warm them up yet. I'm sorry. Here, I'll go—"

But before she could, Wood turned his hand and captured hers. Held on to it. Surprise made her catch her breath, but it was no greater than his was. Her eyes flew open, giving him a stunning glimpse of silvery blue, like the flash of water in the distance or the miraculous leap of a trout toward the sunlight. It took *his* breath away.

"You've been doing your exercise," was her only comment, her voice cool, even. Thick lashes again veiled her eyes. "That's good. And I see you've taken off some of your dressings."

"Pickin' away at it," Wood drawled, hiding the unexpected loss of composure in that slow, raspy way of talking. It was a habit he'd adopted long ago in the Corps, a way of protecting his tough-guy image when he wasn't feeling tough at all. "And I don't mind cold hands. You might just as well warm 'em up on me as someplace else."

She didn't say anything, but went methodically to work on his hand, massaging, bending and straightening the fingers against the resistance in the joints.

It felt good—even the pain was a good hurt—but Wood's mind wasn't on it. He was watching Chris, watching her aloof and lovely face, thinking that she had incredible skin, the kind of features artists dream of capturing on canvas, the kind of bones that love a camera. Briefly he wondered if that was all it was that kept giving him that elusive sense of recognition—just that she reminded him of some famous model or movie star. But...no, he knew that wasn't it. It was more than just her face, it was the whole thing—the look, the attitude, the way she moved, even something about her voice. If only he could remember...

He wanted to ask her about it again, but resisted the urge, partly because it sounded to him like an old and tired line, but mostly because he didn't want her going cold and distant on him the way she had the first time he'd mentioned it. It could wait; they were going to have lots of time together, by the looks of things, and one of these days it was going to come to him.

Instead, in his gentlest and most nonthreatening manner, he murmured, "If you don't mind my saying so, you look a little upset this morning. Something the matter?"

The pristine mask of her face altered only slightly with her smile. "It was one of those mornings," she said without looking up from her task. "There, that's coming along. Let's have the other one."

Wood obligingly changed hands, but not the subject. He said, "Yeah, I know about mornings like that," with a wry half smile of his own. "Want to talk about it? Sometimes it helps—you know, get it off your chest."

"No, I don't think so." Her head made a quick motion of denial. "It really isn't worth talking about—just a lot of little things. You know how it is sometimes."

"Yeah, I know." He watched her work his hand for a moment, then casually asked, "Family or car?"

Her glance flicked at him. "I beg your pardon?"

"That's what it usually is, isn't it—mornings like that? Either the people you live with driving you nuts, or something's wrong with your car."

"Really, it's nothing like that." Her smile was remote, dismissive. "Here—I want you to try reaching for the trap bar. Can you do that for me?" She helped him, slowly raising his arm until he winced and exhaled sharply in pain.

"Ribs," he explained airlessly. "Still a little sore."

"I can see that." Frowning with concern, she placed her hand on his side. "Right in there, huh? Is it just on the one side? Here, let's try the other arm." Still keeping her hand pressed gently over his newly knitted ribs, she supported his opposite arm while he carefully lifted it.

"Better," he muttered, breathing heavily through his nose. She smelled fresh and clean, an elusive scent that called up memories of just-washed sheets flapping in a cool spring breeze.

"Good. We'll start with that arm, then. You really should be more comfortable once you start using that bar, Wood. It helps quite a bit—you know, with things like bathing and making up your bed—'' She broke off with a soft gasp. Wood had just pressed his elbow against his side, capturing her hand in the warm cavity between his arm and body.

"Why don't you leave it there awhile?" he said easily, smiling at her with his eyes. "Let it warm up a little. Matter of fact, want to put the other one in, too?"

She wasn't even flustered. He'd have liked it better if she had been. She just smiled at him as if he were...oh, about ten years old and full of harmless mischief, and deftly slipped her hand out of its trap. Then she became very busy writing notes to herself on her clipboard.

Wood watched her for a few moments, then tried another tack. In a purely friendly way he asked, "Hey Chris, you have a family?" She didn't answer, either trying to make him believe she was too intent on what she was doing to hear him, or just plain ignoring him. He shifted restlessly. "Hey, you know, I'm not asking to be nosy, here. I'm just trying to make conversation."

Now at least she was looking at him, eyebrows arched in exaggerated courtesy. After a moment of that she said coolly, "Everyone's got some sort of family, I suppose. If you mean am I married, which is what you really want to know, the answer is no, I'm not."

She was beginning to frustrate the hell out of him. Wood cleared his throat. "Look. I'd like to get to know you better, that's all. You and I are going to be seeing quite a bit of each other for the next couple of months. What, am I out of line?"

Her gaze wavered, then dropped almost desperately to the clipboard as if, he thought, she'd suddenly forgotten her place in the script and hoped to find her next line written there. Then all at once he saw her shoulders relax, and she hugged the clipboard to her chest, crisscrossing it with her arms. Her eyes came back up to meet his, and in that soft, emotionless voice that aggravated him so much, she murmured, "No, of course not, Wood. I'm sorry. Obviously, *I* was."

All at once he wanted to reach her so badly, get through that shell of hers somehow, that he felt like grabbing her and physically shaking her.

"Hey," he said harshly, "what am I going to do, put a move on you? *Look* at me, for God's sake! I can't even move enough to pee. How can I possibly be a threat to you? What the hell are you afraid of?''

What are you afraid of? She would like to have told him, but for the first time in months, Chris realized that she didn't know the answer to that question herself. It had suddenly become very complicated. She wished she could have told herself it was the same thing she'd been afraid of when she'd discovered that note in her pocket this morning, or when she'd opened the lovely gold foil box and found the sick, cruel gift of a decapitated rose. She wanted so much to be able to believe that the heat in her cheeks and the tremors in her belly were only leftovers from her nightmarish drive to work this morning, imagining deadly pursuit every inch of the way. But she couldn't. Because the strange thing was, *that* particular fear had vanished the moment she'd set foot in this room.

Strange... She realized it only now, when her heart was pounding and her palms were wet with a new and wholly different kind of fear. But it was true. The instant she'd heard the door of Wood's hospital room click shut behind her, she'd felt...*safe*. Here with this man in a tiny space curtained around with only flimsy white vinyl, she'd felt cocooned, somehow... protected as if by castle and moat.

Until she'd touched him. His body. Felt the intensity of his life force, the resilience of muscle, the smooth, firm skin, the *heat*...

Oh yes, it had frightened her. She'd thought of the leopard again, had that feeling of being too close to something wild and dangerous. Something...unpredictable. But what made things so complicated was that fear was only one of the things that had crossed her mind in that brief flash of awareness before she'd managed to free her hand from the warm, sultry place in which he'd imprisoned it.

Of course, part of her was angry with Wood for doing such a presumptuous thing. Such an unexpected thing. And part of her was surprised that she could experience such an intense reaction to a man's body. She hadn't thought she would ever feel that way; nature must be more resilient than she'd believed possible.

Surely, she told herself, that was all it was—hormones. That time of the month. She'd have to check her calendar.

But another part of her, a shameful, deeply buried part, exulted. *Oh yes! I am alive! My body, my senses are alive. I'd forgotten how good it can feel....*

Of course. She'd just forgotten what it felt like to work with a young man's body, one that was strong and firmly muscled and vital. Usually she managed to steer the young male patients—the accidents and athletic injuries—to one of the other P.T.'s. The flesh she was accustomed to touching had either the soft, sweet tenderness of the *very* young, or the flabby fragility of blue-veined age. She simply hadn't prepared herself for someone like Wood, that was all. Now that she knew what to expect, she'd be able to guard against any reaction like the one she'd just experienced. It wouldn't happen again.

So, what *was* she afraid of? Wood was right—he was totally helpless. Not to mention in pain. She had absolutely nothing to fear from him, right? Under the circumstances, she could certainly afford to let her guard down a *little,* couldn't she?

She made the conscious effort to relax, letting the clipboard slide downward. Her breath emerged unevenly, broken by soft, embarrassed laughter. "I'm sorry. Really. I guess...I'm just not used to being asked personal questions. My patients are usually pretty wrapped up in their own problems. So what... would you like to know about me?"

"Oh, I don't know. Everything." The corners of his mouth quirked upward and his eyes had the dark luminosity of semiprecious stones. Like onyx, she thought. In spite of her resolve she felt a tight little inner shiver, which she was surprised to discover wasn't entirely an unpleasant sensation. "How about we start with your name. Chris—now, is that short for Christine?"

"That's right."

"Okay, so Christine...what?"

"B-Bendix." Her voice stumbled over the name, but only slightly; she didn't think he'd notice. But she couldn't possibly tell him the name he'd known her by, the name she'd taken back after her divorce. *Christine Thurmond.* Surely he'd remember *that.*

"Bendix..." He sort of growled the name, deep in his throat, while she, hearing it, felt the bitter burn of acid in hers. "Damn—I'd have sworn..."

"What?" It was a breathless, guilty puff of sound.

"Oh, nothing—just, I'd have sworn you had to be pure Scandinavian, with your bones and coloring. But with a name like—"

"It's my married name." She was already turning away, but broke in with the explanation before he could say the hated word again.

"I thought you said—"

"I'm divorced."

"Hey," Wood protested, "you're doing it again."

Again her breath caught nervously. "Doing what?"

"Come back here. Now tell me, what in the hell's wrong with being divorced?"

"Nothing's *wrong*." She felt childish, keeping her face averted from him, but those eyes of his demanded too much. "I just don't like talking about it."

"I can respect that." His voice was soft now. Disarming.

She took a careful breath, delicately cleared her throat. Oh, but this was hard—she had no practice at it. Almost whispering, she said, "Listen, I don't like talking about my past very much, that's all. It, um, it wasn't a great time for me."

"None of it?"

She shook her head helplessly. The incredulity and compassion in his question made it impossible still for her to look at him, although taking a deep breath did help her finally to reply. "Pretty much. That's why I'd just as soon forget about it, okay?"

"Yeah . . ." But he said it absently, obviously thinking hard, and when she started to turn from him again, he reached out a hand to stop her. "I mean, no! No—hey, you can't just...forget about your past. You can't just pretend it doesn't exist."

But suddenly she was gone. Wood stared for a long moment at the closing door, then silently finished it. *You have to face up to it, mistakes and all. And then . . . try to forgive yourself for them.*

Not a bad piece of advice, he thought. He should listen to himself more often.

"Hey, Grady," he called softly, "you still there?"

"Ain't goin' nowhere, my man."

"Guess you heard all that, huh?"

His roommate gave a gusty sigh. "Sure hope you know what you're doing with that woman. I mean, I know she's somethin' to look at, but... Shoot, beauty don't keep you warm, know what I mean?''

"I know...I know." Wood lay back on his pillows, but he couldn't relax. He felt keyed up, stimulated in ways he'd rather not be, under the circumstances. "It's not just her looks, though. Swear to God. I mean...well, sure, she's attractive...."

Actually, he couldn't even think of a word to describe her kind of beauty. *Rare, timeless, ethereal, elegant*—all true, but still inadequate. Right now she was every man's erotic fantasy in the flesh, but he had a feeling this woman was still going to be beautiful when the flesh was shriveled and shrunken, the flawless skin spotted and wrinkled with age.

"It's something else," he said restlessly. "I don't know what it is, but...there's something going on with her. For one thing, I *know* I've seen her before, and when I figure out where, I have an idea it's going to explain a whole lot. But besides that..." He paused. "Did you—you heard everything, right? What did you think?"

"Think?" Grady chuckled softly. "What I think is I've got icicles hangin' off my ears. That voice of hers gives a man frostbite."

"Yeah, but you didn't see her face. Know what I think? I think that woman has some serious problems."

"Man, you got that right."

"No, I mean, I think she's hurting about something. Bad. Deep down inside, know what I mean? It's like she's all walled in, like she's trying to protect herself from the pain. You look at her and you see all this ice, right? But then you look closer— I mean, *really* look—and you can see this...this person in there, looking back at you. And it's like she really wants to get out of the ice, you know? Only she can't."

"Lemme guess. And you think you're just the man to melt the ice, right? You're gonna thaw out the ice maiden."

"Damn right," said Wood, grinning at himself both over his ego and the cliché.

"Man," said Grady, "you have got it *bad.*"

"Hey—what else am I gonna do here? It'll keep me from getting bored, anyway."

"Yeah, well, watch out for that frostbite. And don't say I didn't warn you."

Wood just laughed.

About then Sal, the orderly, came and took Grady away for his morning swim in the therapy pool. Wood's nurse had already been in for her daily torture session, and his day yawned bleak and empty before him. In sheer desperation he picked up the TV remote and punched his way through the morning talk shows, but couldn't work up much of an interest in teenagers with eating disorders, wives who'd taken in the offspring of their cheating husbands or cross-dressers in the workplace. Old "Gilligan's Island" reruns didn't appeal to him, either. He thought about picking up the phone and calling Lucy, but a look out the window at the weather reminded him that she'd probably still be outside seeing to the livestock.

He listened to the sounds of the hospital for a while. And to the sounds of his own body. His pain had a sound, he'd discovered, sort of a low-voltage humming. If he really tuned in to it, after a while it got to be almost hypnotic. He imagined he could hear his bones stretching.

"This is ridiculous," he muttered between clenched teeth, and reached for the guitar.

It wasn't Chris's usual time to be in the hospital. Evening, she found, had a very different feel to it. In contrast to the late-winter darkness outside, the light seemed softer, almost cosy. And it was very quiet. The dinner trays had been dispensed, and evening visiting hours for the surgery floors were still half an hour off. The corridors were almost deserted; doors stood open here and there to emit the muffled murmurings of a television set, the sporadic tinkle of stainless-steel dinnerware.

Chris checked in at the nurse's station, explained her mission to the night duty nurse, a Korean woman named Jackie Sung whom she'd met before only briefly, then proceeded on to Room 312. Unlike most of the others she'd passed, it was closed. She was about to give her usual courtesy knock when something stopped her. Made her draw quickly back before she could be seen in the glass door panel.

It was a sound—music, but not from any TV set or cassette player. It was the soft strumming of a guitar, a single chord repeated over and over in slow and steady rhythm, like a chime tolling away seconds...one, two, three, four, five, six, seven.... Chris found herself counting with it before she was even aware of doing so.

And then a voice joined in, nearly whispering at first. It gained strength and volume little by little, but didn't lose the raspy, rusty quality that somehow made it sound as if it came straight from the depths of a battle-scarred heart. The voice sang of love, and taking chances, and being afraid, and having hope. Chris didn't know which touched her more, the words of the song or that scratchy, ravaged voice, but she found that her throat was aching and—even more strangely—that her skin had shivered with goose bumps.

She waited until the last notes died away, haunting echoes of the opening chord, broken now, like the petals of a flower torn apart and left floating on rippled water. Then she carefully cleared her throat and knocked.

"Yeah—come in." The voice still had the rasp in it, thickened now with something that might have been embarrassment.

She opened the door and stuck her head inside. "Hi—I'm not disturbing you, am I? Maybe I should have called...." The guitar was leaning against the wall beside the bed. Wood's hands lay on the sheet in front of him, innocently drumming and only succeeding in making him look guilty as sin. Chris found that she had to try hard to keep from smiling.

"No—no, hell no, you're not disturbing me. Come on in." He cleared his throat, obviously surprised and uncharacteristically thrown off-balance by her visit. "This is...kind of a strange time for you to be hanging around here, isn't it? Shouldn't you be home eating dinner about now?"

She shrugged evasively. "I had some paperwork to catch up on. Since I was late anyway, I thought I'd, uh...I wanted to stop by and..." She caught a quick breath, as if she was getting a good grip on a lifeline, then plunged in. "Wood, I wanted to apologize. For this morning. I'm sorry—"

"Hey," said Wood gruffly, "not necessary."

But she couldn't let it go that easily. "I'm just...not comfortable talking about myself. Especially my past."

"No problem. I was out of line. Your past is none of my business." He brushed the subject aside with a finality that left her feeling vaguely incomplete and disappointed, as if she'd psyched herself up for a contest, only to have it canceled at the opening bell. He nodded at the brown paper bag in her hand. "Hey—what's that you've got there?"

"Oh..." She gestured with it, peered into it as if she didn't know, either, what it contained, then set it down on the already-crowded nightstand beside his bed.

I shouldn't be here, she thought. I must be losing my mind. This was turning out to be much harder than she'd imagined it would be. It just wasn't something she usually did, getting this involved with a patient. Visiting one on her off-hours was unheard of.

She cleared her throat, fighting for her customary composure. "It's just... you know, some things I thought you could use to help you regain your manual dexterity." She tried a smile. "Plus, they might help you pass the time. There's a deck of cards, a couple of board games—things like that. I thought maybe you and Grady—where *is* Grady, by the way?"

Wood grunted and shifted as if in mild discomfort. "I don't know. He said something about watching a basketball game on TV. Sounded like he and the orderly had a bet going."

Chris glanced at the silent set mounted high on the opposite wall. "You don't like basketball?"

"To play, not to watch." There was a slight pause, as if he were listening to a replay of what he'd just said. And to Chris it seemed that his bright, inquisitive eyes darkened for that instant, as if a shadow had crossed them.

Sympathy flooded her. No—more than that, it was a sudden awareness, as shocking as hitting a light switch in a pitch-dark room, a full understanding of what it must be like to be a strong, physically active man—an athlete—facing the possibility of permanent impairment. She teetered on the brink of saying something that would show him she understood, while he squirmed restively, as if the whole subject was something he'd prefer to avoid.

In the end, it was Wood who had his way. In a voice edgy with false heartiness, he said, "Hey, you haven't eaten, have you? You must be hungry. Why don't you—"

She hurriedly broke in with, "You're right. It's late. I should go. I'm keeping you from your—"

"No, no, you're not. Actually, I've had all I want. What I was going to say was why don't you help yourself to some of mine? They give me so much to eat in this place you'd think they wanted to fatten me up for market or something. Go on—dig in."

"Oh no—no, really, I couldn't. I'm sure it's...the nurses would probably have a fit. I'm sure they like to keep track..."

Wood snorted expressively, and Chris instantly felt herself warming with embarrassment. And empathy. This—all of it, the loss of control, of privacy—must be so hard for him. He pushed awkwardly at his tray table, trying to swivel it out of his way without disturbing his apparatus, and as she moved forward to help, she found herself talking rapidly to distract him from what she knew might be taken as an additional affront to his pride.

"I really should go," she murmured, putting out her hand in a vague little gesture of uncertainty.

"Don't go." To her utter surprise, he caught her hand and held on to it.

Strange, she thought, how different it feels. It was, after all, a hand she'd touched more than once, a hand she'd taken in hers, examined, manipulated and massaged. But this was different. He'd taken *her* hand; the initiative and control were his. And all she could think about was how warm it felt, and how big it really was, and...oh yes, how gentle the rasp of his fingertips felt across the sensitive base of her palm. It was as disconcerting, in a way, as that day so long ago when he'd turned the tables on her in that high school interview.

He must have seen something in her face, because the intense black glitter of his eyes softened instantly to an ironic sheen, as if someone had turned down the flames that burned behind them.

As he released her hand, he gave a little shrug, perhaps of apology, and his smile turned crooked. "Why don't you stick around awhile? Unless...there's someplace else you need to be?"

"No." She had to unglue her tongue from the roof of her mouth in order to say it. "Not really."

"Then you might as well hang around here, right? Pull up a chair. Make yourself comfortable."

Although comfort wasn't something Chris could even begin to hope for, she did pull the visitor's chair closer to the bed and perch gingerly on the edge of it. Searching wildly for diversion, her eyes found the brown paper shopping bag she'd brought with her. "Would you like to, um—" her throat made a small sticking sound when she swallowed "—play cards or something?"

He made a clicking sound with his tongue. "Never did care much for cards, to tell you the truth."

"Checkers?" she offered hopefully.

He started to answer, then paused and smiled as if he was remembering something. "Oh man . . . checkers. My dad and my brother, Rhett, used to always play checkers. Long winter evenings, you know?" He shrugged it aside. "Nah . . . I guess I'm not much of a one for board games, either. Actually, you know, what I'd rather do is just talk."

"Oh," said Chris earnestly, "but you really should try to use them as much as possible anyway. It's very good exercise, especially the cards. Shuffling, holding them—things like that? It will force you to use those small muscles, help you get back your coordination and dexterity faster. Even if you don't . . ."

She saw that he was laughing, almost without sound or movement. When she hesitated, he put on an exaggeratedly solemn expression and murmured, "Sure, Coach. Okay, Coach. If you say so."

Chris sat for a moment looking at him. Then she said evenly, "Or you could always play your guitar instead."

The bright, amused gleam in Wood's eyes wavered and went out, like a candle in a gust of wind.

Chapter 5

She hadn't intended to mention the music, ever. But Wood's teasing, even so gently done and probably innocently meant, had made her feel vulnerable and small. Humiliated and helpless. For a moment, just a moment, he'd made her feel like a schoolchild again, with a body too tall and big-boned for grace, wearing glasses, long braids and clothes that didn't fit. Retaliation was the only defense she had, and she used the only weapon at her disposal.

Hiding her anger in a cool, carefully modulated voice, she said, "I heard you playing, you know. Right before I came in. It sounded very nice. What was the name of the song you were singing? I've heard it before, but for some reason I can't place it."

Wood coughed with great care before he answered. "It's called 'The Rose.'"

"Of course," she murmured. "Well, it's a lovely song."

"Thanks." He looked away, his expression dark with what might have been pain.

Normally Chris would have responded to the pain with compassion, but now it seemed to her a small victory. Emboldened by it, she pressed harder on the vulnerable spot she'd found, forgetting caution. "I was wondering why you seem so shy about playing. I don't know much about music, but to me you really did seem ... quite good. If you're worried about disturbing the other patients ... ''

He flicked her a smile, one without much amusement in it. "Thanks for reminding me. I didn't even think of that."

His self-deprecating attitude disarmed her for a moment, reminding her that she was on treacherous ground. She struggled to maintain her balance by smiling a superior little smile and saying in what she knew was a rather patronizing tone, "Oh, no—I'm sure you wouldn't be. As long as you didn't play in the middle of the night, or something like that. No, I just thought—"

"It isn't that," Wood said, interrupting her with an exhalation that sounded to Chris like surrender, and she leaned forward, eager to savor it. When he went on at last, the hesitancy with which he spoke betrayed his extreme discomfort, and she couldn't help but think, with a small sense of triumph, *Good— let him feel what it's like to have his best-guarded secrets relentlessly probed.*

"It's kind of a case of too many memories, you know? My, uh...my mom and my older brother and I used to play and sing together a lot. Mostly just for fun, but sometimes we'd sing for church, weddings, things like that. My mom's the one who taught me how to play. And after she died ..."

"Oh..." Chris touched her lips with her fingertips, as if with the gesture she could take back the words she'd spoken so recklessly. Too late she understood the danger to herself, recognizing the trap only as she was tumbling into it. And then she could only murmur, "I'm sorry."

"It was awhile ago," Wood said with a shrug that was meant to camouflage his pain. His half smile failed miserably in that attempt as well. "Both my parents were killed in a car accident the week before my high school graduation. It was a long time ago, but...I don't know, it seems like this accident of mine has brought it all back. Seems like it was just yesterday, you know?"

Chris nodded; she couldn't speak. Inside, her heart had begun to flutter like that of a wild bird as it hears the trapdoor clang shut behind it.

How could she have done such a thing? It was something she never did—getting involved with her patients' private lives and personal problems. Never. She didn't want to. Especially *this* patient. She didn't want to know, didn't want to *care*. It hurt too much, and she had too much pain of her own.

His voice was matter-of-fact but relentless. "My sister, Lucy, wanted me to sing for the funeral service. Rhett was willing, but I . . . I don't know, I just couldn't do it. Even thinking about it made my throat close up. Still can't sing the old hymns—anything that really reminds me of Mom. Just . . . closes the old pipes right up."

He smiled again, one of those agonizing, completely fraudulent smiles she knew so well because she employed them so often herself. "Anyway, when my sister asked me, I guess I was, um . . . pretty short with her. I seem to remember I almost threw the damn guitar at her. Well, *hell,* I was a kid. One minute I was sitting pretty up there on top of the world, and the next minute my whole world fell apart. And then I guess I was feeling pretty guilty, too."

"Guilty?" Chris said faintly. *"Why?"*

His eyes found hers and held on, with neither the burning intensity of the caged cat nor the soft sheen of irony, nor the hard luster of semiprecious stone. She wanted to look away, but they were deep and dark with anguish now, and it was all she could do to keep from drowning in them.

"Because," he said softly, "I was in the car when it happened. We were coming home from my awards banquet. There was a terrible storm—hail, funnel clouds, the whole bit. I should have been driving. Mom didn't like to drive at night because of her eyes, and Dad had a bad knee from where a bull kicked him once. But I'd been out partying the night before—celebrating, you know?—and I was tired. Maybe a little bit hung over. Crabby as the dickens, I guess, because I remember I was pretty nasty with my mom when she asked me to drive. I said I didn't feel like driving, and I crawled into the back seat and just conked out. So Dad was driving, bad knee and all, and I think that's why . . ."

He coughed, struggled with it for a moment, then took a deep breath and plowed on. "Maybe not. Who knows? But the fact is I blamed myself for a long time. And it didn't help any that I didn't even get hurt. Not a scratch. A few bumps and bruises, that's all. Dammit, it didn't make sense to me. In fact, it wasn't until *this* happened that it started to make any kind of sense at all."

Chris broke in, almost desperate now to distract him. "How did it happen—your accident?" She didn't want to know about that, either, but listening to him talk about his youth and family had dredged up things from the mucky bottom of her memory that she'd tried hard for a good many years not to disturb. She felt shaken, as if it had been she who'd survived disaster, not he. "I understand you were in Bosnia?"

He nodded, seemingly unaware of the effect his confidences were having on her. It was a fact for which she was both glad and sorry. If, she thought, he knew how uncomfortable he was making her by unburdening himself of painful memories and feelings, then perhaps he would stop. But then, of course, he would probably wonder *why*...

"Being in Somalia kind of got me thinking about what was happening over there. Bothered me, you know? I thought we should be there, doing something to help. So after I left the Marine Corps I went to one of the private relief agencies that were trying to get food and supplies into the area. I figured I had the time, a little money saved up and nothing in particular waiting for me back home, right?

"Anyway, I'd done a bit of truck driving in the Corps, so I offered my services. Things were getting desperate, I guess, because they didn't keep me standing around. The shelling had been pretty heavy and cold weather was setting in, and we hadn't been having much luck getting the convoys through. There'd be a supposed 'cease-fire,' and that'd last just about long enough for us to get the trucks rolling, and then the shells would start falling again and we'd have to turn back. We'd been getting reports of kids starving to death, doctors trying to smuggle injured kids out of the city because there wasn't enough medicine and supplies to save them. So a bunch of us decided we'd go for it—take the damn convoy in, come hell or high water. After the usual negotiations and all sorts of delays, we'd made it to the outskirts of the city. It was nighttime, and the shelling was heavy. I remember thinking it sounded just like a good old Iowa thunderstorm...."

His voice faded. Chris found that her heart was beating much too fast. "What happened?" she whispered.

Wood shook his head. Shrugged. "I don't know—don't remember much about it. They told me a shell hit the truck ahead of mine and exploded. I couldn't stop—plowed into the wreckage and rolled. I guess I was pinned in the mess for a while before they cut me loose. I'm told I'm lucky to be alive." His grin was ironic.

"Again. Like I said, it brought it all back, my mom and dad dying and me walking away without a scratch. And I'm starting to think maybe somebody's trying to tell me something, you know?" He frowned, looking thoroughly perplexed. "Ah hell, I don't know."

To her profound shock, Chris found that she was reaching toward him, a small, involuntary gesture of sympathy motivated by an instinctive desire to comfort. She wasn't sure what she would have said to him, or whether she would have found any words at all.

She was saved from having to find out, because at that moment the door opened and Grady rolled in, followed by an orderly she didn't know, the two of them arguing with good-natured vehemence about the game they'd been watching. There were the usual greetings and introductions and casual four-way conversation, and then it was easy for Chris to make her excuses, say her goodbyes and go.

But leaving that room and Wood Brown, even after his agonizing personal revelations, was not an escape. She knew that as she stood with the closing door at her back, facing the brightly lit hospital corridor, abustle now with flower-laden visitors with apprehensive eyes and determined, painted-on smiles. She felt as if she were leaving a haven in a raging storm, and for a moment she wanted nothing more than to turn back into the warmth and safety and stay there.

But... to think of a hospital room as *warm?* Ridiculous. Unheard of. Until she realized that the warmth didn't emanate from the room, at all, but from the person in it. It was *Wood's* warmth, as natural a part of him as his scratchy voice, black-jewel eyes and dusky skin, that drew her like a campfire on a cold, dark night.

I'm losing it, she thought bleakly. The constant war of nerves, being afraid every moment of every day and in terror of the nights, was getting to her. She had to do something. She *had* to. She didn't know how much more of this she could take.

"Man, you are full of surprises," said Grady with a chuckle. The orderly had settled him in his bed and gone away. Outside in the corridor the chimes were sounding the five-minute warning for the end of visiting hours.

Wood snorted softly. "Hey, I was as surprised as you are, let me tell you."

"Wish I coulda been a little fly on the wall. Just to see how you operate, man."

"Come on . . . I don't *operate.*" Wood shifted restlessly, trying without success to relieve both the numbness in his backside and the gnawing sense of guilt Grady's words inspired. The truth was, of course, that when it came to women, he'd spent most of his adult life doing exactly that. Might as well face it— as the baby of a household dominated by three strong feminine personalities, he'd learned early on how much could be accomplished with sweet sincerity and a killer smile.

"And if I did," he growled, "I wouldn't even know where to begin with that lady. . . ."

The trapeze bar dangled like a lure above his head. He eyed it, gauging the distance, psyching himself up. Reached for it, gritting his teeth. Felt the cool smoothness of the bar in his hand, the jagged edges of pain in every muscle, nerve and sinew.

Remembering the first day of football practice, the coach yelling in his face, he summoned more strength than he knew he possessed and lifted his torso a fraction of an inch off the bed, held it and collapsed back onto his pillows, awash in cold sweat and trembling like a newborn calf.

"I swear," he said, panting, "every time I think I'm getting somewhere with her, something happens. Just now, when I was talking to her, I know I saw something. Real feelings—warmth, compassion, the whole nine yards. Then she just...cranks down the old thermostat another notch or two and runs like a scared rabbit. And I do mean *scared.* Wish I could figure out what's going on with her."

"Hey, she came to see you, didn't she? After hours, on her own time? She mighta run, but the rabbit is definitely interested."

"I don't know about that." Wood was glaring at the bar as if it was a defensive lineman getting ready to pound him into the turf. He reached for it, grabbed it hard...grunted, pulled, held it while his muscles screamed and quivered . . . then released it and lay back, breathing as if he'd just run ninety-eight yards with the entire defensive backfield on his heels. "She . . . just came by... to bring some stuff... I'm supposed to use for therapy."

Grady laughed softly. "She *says*. What kind of stuff she bring you?"

"I don't know—playing cards, games. Things like that. Supposed to be good exercise for my hands." He looked at the bar, then closed his eyes. *In a minute, maybe.*

"Hey, that's cool—you play gin rummy?"

Wood gave a dry snort of laughter. "You know something? I *hate* cards—always have. Maybe because when I was a kid my older brother and sister were always playing games like that. Mostly in the wintertime when the weather was bad. Me, though, I just wanted to be outside—*doing* something. Games, cards and things always make me feel like I did back then... sort of cooped up, restless...." His voice trailed off.

After a moment Grady's voice came, quiet and deep, like a string bass played softly. "I understand you, man. But I'm going to tell you somethin'. Take it from somebody who *knows*. You got to have patience. *Patience,* you follow me? Patience with the lady, *and* with that." He pointed at the trapeze bar and chuckled suddenly. "You try to go too fast with either one, and you just gonna mess things up for yourself. Take you longer to get where you want to go. You hear me, man?"

"Yeah," sighed Wood, "I hear you."

In his head, though, he was hearing something else all of a sudden, like a note of bird song out of the blue. As a matter of fact it was a song, a song about love... and patience. A song called "The Rose."

"Yes, ma'am," the cop said, looking politely attentive. "But can you be a little bit more specific? How, exactly, has this person been harassing you? Has he threatened you? Has he, uh... made sexual advances toward you? What are we talking about here?"

Chris's mouth felt dry and her heart was racing. Strange, she thought. I feel as though *I'm* the criminal.

She cleared her throat carefully and told him about the phone calls in the middle of the night, the flowers... the decapitated rose.

The cop, who'd been jotting things in his notebook, looked up and said, "The flower was cut off the stem?"

"That's right."

"And ... you don't think it just accidently broke off."

"No," Chris said firmly, "I don't."

"I see. Anything else?"

"He left me a note. In the pocket of my parka. I have it ... right here." She took the crumpled paper from her purse with jerky, uncoordinated hands and tried to smooth it as she placed it on the desk. The officer picked it up, read it, frowned and put it back down.

"He calls you Crissy? You know this person?"

She swallowed, nodded. "Yes, sir. I'm certain it's my ex-husband. Alan Bendix."

"So you think this is meant as a threat? Seems to me you could take it either way. The part about 'watching over you—'"

"It's a threat," Chris said tightly. "I know him."

There was a long pause. The officer frowned as he fidgeted with an assortment of odds and ends scattered on his desk top. Finally he cleared his throat and said, "Mrs. Bendix—"

"It's Thurmond," Chris broke in. "*Ms.* Thurmond."

"Ms. Thurmond. How long have you and your husband been separated?"

"Divorced. We've been divorced almost six years. But I've been away—going to school. I only moved back here a year ago. The, uh ... calls and things started a couple of months after that. Lately they've been getting worse and worse. I don't know what to do. I can't—"

She broke off, because the officer was no longer there. He'd left his chair and was rummaging through a rack of pamphlets over by the wall. Willing her body to utter stillness, she watched him return and take his chair, all the while carefully avoiding her eyes. And she felt the familiar sense of helplessness ... *aloneness* ... encase her like a thick veneer of ice.

"Ma'am, I'm going to give you a couple of pamphlets here that'll help you understand just what our stalking laws are, and tell you what we can and can't do."

"You're telling me you can't help me," Chris said dully. "I've wasted my time coming here. I'm sorry." She started to rise.

The officer stopped her with a gesture. "No, that's not exactly true. Look, I can pursue this if you want me to. I can press charges against your ex-husband—assuming we find out he's the one responsible for the phone calls and the, uh, other things. But I gotta tell you, so far all he's guilty of is a misdemeanor. Now, I don't know what kind of man your ex-husband is, but chances are if we arrest him and slap him with a fine and maybe a few days jail time, all you're going to do is *really* piss him off. Then again, maybe he'll get the message you mean business and leave you alone."

The officer finally looked straight at Chris. His face was clear and boyishly young, his eyes old and tired and jaded. He shrugged. "Whatever you want to do, I'll do. It's your call, ma'am."

After giving the matter some thought, Wood decided to take Grady's advice to heart. *Patience.* Although he'd never been known to possess much of that particular commodity in the past, he decided it would be his watchword from now on.

So, he told himself, there would be no more trying to get Chris to talk about herself, her past or her problems. From now on he'd make sure the conversation stayed completely casual. The weather. "Seen any good movies lately?" Things like that. If the woman wanted to maintain a certain air of mystery, so be it. In fact, he had to admit it made her that much more intriguing—a nice little challenge to help pass the time.

And no more probing into the dusty corners of his memory in search of the elusive sense of recognition he still felt each and every time he saw her. Like Gwen, he would simply have to learn to wait serenely for it to come to him.

No overt flirting, no suggestions of a personal or intimate nature, and above all, no physical contact—except, obviously, whatever was initiated by Chris herself in the normal course of their professional relationship.

Which was going to be tough on him, because the fact was, Wood was a natural toucher and he did love to—well, flirt, in what he considered to be an entirely playful and harmless way, of course. He did it because he liked to watch a woman's eyes start to sparkle and her cheeks turn rosy and her body kind of swell and arch, then begin to move and sway in that unconscious response, as if somewhere in the back of her mind she was hearing the rhythms of a song as old as time. In his lifetime he'd observed the response in young women and old, fat and thin, homely and drop-dead gorgeous, and always it struck him as wondrous and as reassuring, in its way, as the budding of new leaves and flowers in spring.

But on the few occasions when he'd flirted with Chris, touched her hand or even just teased her a little, he couldn't help but notice that she'd recoiled from him like one of those sea creatures with the wavy fronds that shrink into inert-seeming mud pies at the slightest touch.

In spite of that he didn't really believe—and he was honest enough with himself to admit that this *might* have been his ego talking—that it was him personally she was reacting to so violently. It hadn't been aversion or distaste he'd seen in her eyes when he'd touched her. No, sir, he'd swear that what he'd witnessed had been more like . . . fear.

Fear—he'd seen it in her eyes before. But he was beginning to realize that again, it was not fear of him specifically. Why on earth *should* she be afraid of him? As he'd pointed out to her, he was pretty much incapable of causing harm to anyone. And besides, she didn't seem to show any uneasiness around him as long as it was strictly business and she was initiating the touching. No, as incomprehensible as that seemed to him, it had to be intimacy itself—or the slightest suggestion of it—that scared her.

Why, dammit? Had she been hurt, abused, betrayed? And by whom? He thought it almost had to be her husband. Damn, but he'd sure like to know what could have happened to cause such a warm and beautiful woman to seal herself off from the world inside a wall of ice the way she'd done.

But, no. Patience. He would have patience. He couldn't ask. He wouldn't push. And above all, he would not touch.

The telephone rang the next morning just as Chris was dashing through the last stages of her getting-ready-for-work routine. There were several reasons why she picked it up without even a twinge of premonition. It was an unusual time of day for the phone to ring, not *his* customary time at all. *He* always called in the dead of night or the cold, lonely hours before dawn, when her defenses were down and the psychological effect was the greatest. And it had been snowing most of the night. Sometimes when the weather was bad, morning patients would be rescheduled for afternoon, after the snowplows had had a chance to clear the streets. She thought it might be Roxanne calling to tell her not to come in until later.

And then, of course, she was simply rushed, distracted and not thinking clearly after a night tormented by strange, elusive dreams.

She grabbed for the receiver and tucked it between her ear and shoulder, gasping, "Hello?" as she struggled to button the front of her tunic. Meanwhile her feet were searching under the edge of the bed for her shoes. When she heard the whisper of an exhalation, she felt the cold stirring of the hair on the back of her neck, and her fingers froze on the buttons. An instant later she snatched the receiver away from its intimate contact with her skin, as if it were something slimy and unspeakable.

"Where were you last night, Chrissy?"

"Alan..." Her heart was thumping wildly, painfully, out of control. With every ounce of strength she possessed, she willed it to be quiet, but it was no use. She whispered, "Alan, why are you doing this?" all the while saying over and over to herself, *He can't hurt me, he can't hurt me.* Saying it with all the conviction of a terrified child whimpering, "There's no such things as ghosts."

"Answer me, Chrissy. I know what time you came home. Where were you?"

"I was—" She closed her eyes in utter futility "—I stayed late at the hospital. To see a patient. That's all."

"Don't lie to me, Chrissy."

As always, she was beginning to tremble. She couldn't seem to help it, no matter how hard she tried. "Alan, I'm not lying. Why would I lie to you?" She took a breath, drawing in courage along with the oxygen. "Whatever I do, it's none of your business. Can't you accept that and just . . . leave me alone?"

She heard a soft, angry hiss. "Of course it's my business, Chrissy. Have you forgotten? *Till death do us part.*"

She slammed the phone down then. Her hands curled into fists, her body shuddered and her teeth clenched as she tried in vain to hold back sobs of bitter rage and utter helplessness. But her eyes burned dry in aching sockets. She had used up all her tears long ago.

It was all well and good for Wood to take a solemn vow of patience. Patience was easy enough to practice. Words, actions and facial expressions could, with a certain amount of effort, be controlled. The one thing he couldn't do, though, was stop his thoughts. Most of those were more-or-less predictable and, he was pretty sure, were shared by every red-blooded male who'd ever set eyes on Christine Bendix. They'd be what Grady had been referring to when he'd said, "If you ain't gay, you've got the *thoughts*."

He lay awake at night, wondering things like whether her breasts were really as lush and full, her waist as tiny and her fanny as round and as firm as it seemed they might be, so tantalizingly suggested beneath the loose and shapeless layers she always wore.

Released from its unforgiving knot, would her hair be thick and long, and would it cascade down her back and tumble over her shoulders and bathe his face with its fragrance, like a cool spring shower?

Would her skin feel as soft to the touch as the velvet it seemed to imitate? Would her mouth taste like wine and be as intoxicating?

Were her legs really that long and slender, and what would they feel like, wrapped around him? What would it be like to cradle himself in her body and lose himself there?

And if the thoughts were predictable, his response to them and to their countless variations was even more so, which in his present circumstances caused him no end of difficulty and inconvenience. On the other hand, he couldn't help but be gratified by the fact that at least *one* part of his body still functioned the way it was supposed to, and without any help whatsoever from medical science.

Other thoughts came to him in the wee small hours of the sleepless hospital nights, though, that were less easily justified and explained. Thoughts that caused him as much discomfort, on another level entirely, and that were just as capable of robbing him of his rest.

More and more often, it seemed, he found himself segueing directly from fantasies involving Chris to thoughts about his own life. Not even thoughts, exactly—more like images, flashes of memory, bits and pieces of his life jumbled together like shards of colored glass in a kaleidoscope, constantly shifting and reassembling into patterns . . . now of his childhood, then some event from his more-recent past, again of a time long ago and half-forgotten.

But the strange thing was that, whether the moments revisited were happy or sad, traumatic or joyful, they afforded him no pleasure. He felt instead a vague sense of regret, of dissatisfaction, almost of... failure. What, after all, had he to show for his life? Twice he'd cheated death, and for what purpose? All the years he'd spent in the Marine Corps, taking such pride in the belief that he was serving his country, protecting his loved ones, liberating countries and feeding the hungry, doing something *important*...and now it occurred to him that maybe what he'd been doing was only running away, because he was too cowardly to face up to the things that were *truly* important. Things like making a life, a home, a future with someone. Finding that someone. Having a family. Kids. *His* kids. Lots of kids.

Funny, he thought. Funny and ironic, the fact that he should pick now, of all times, to start thinking about settling down, having kids. Now, when he didn't have a clue what in the hell he was going to find to do to support himself, much less a family. In the past, when he'd thought beyond his career in the Corps, it had been vague, at best. Something in trucking, maybe, or heavy-equipment operations. Just as long as it wasn't farming—that was Lucy's thing, not his. Definitely something physical, though; something with his hands. Something that would keep him active. He'd always depended on his body—his strength and athletic ability—to make his way in the world. It simply hadn't ever occurred to him that it could let him down.

Fear. Oh yeah, Chris wasn't the only one who knew what it was to be afraid. Wood knew that, for all the times he'd listened in the darkness for the whine of incoming SCUDs, mortar shells and sniper bullets, he'd never been more scared in his whole life than he was right now.

What he couldn't figure out was why all his disquieting yearnings, self-doubts and sleepless nights seemed to be connected somehow to his blatantly carnal and thoroughly entertaining fantasies about his physical therapist.

But he couldn't pursue it. Nosiree, he had to be *patient.* Wait for her to thaw enough to open up of her own accord, while he talked to her about the weather. Hospital food. Sports. Just like he had to lie here in this damn bed and wait for his body to heal all by itself. Which, he thought, was sort of like watching grass grow. Sometimes he wondered whether it was worth the pain and effort. Any of it. Had it really been worth all this just to keep from having a few metal rods in his legs? Was Chris—was *any* woman—worth this much aggravation?

That's what he'd ask himself. Then she'd walk through his door.

Chapter 6

"You're going over to the hospital again?" Roxie asked when Chris stopped by the reception counter on her way to lunch. "You've been spending an awful lot of time over there lately, haven't you?"

"My own time," Chris mildly pointed out, nodding at the clock on the opposite wall. "I'm taking my break. Tell John, will you? And if my one o'clock shows up before I get back, could you ask Brad to get her started with some heat?"

"Sure." Roxie ambled over and leaned her folded arms on the countertop. Chris knew she had to be dying to ask why anyone in her right mind would voluntarily eat lunch at a hospital. But after pondering the question—and chewing on the inside of her lower lip—for a moment or two, the receptionist apparently thought better of asking it and posed another one instead. "So, how do you like your new apartment?"

Chris, involved in the process of putting on her cold-weather layers, pulled the zipper of her parka up to her chin before she answered, with a shrug of her own, "It's okay. You know how it is—moving's never fun."

"So why did you? I mean, you had such a neat place, that adorable old house and everything."

Concentrating on her mittens helped her keep her voice neutral. "I know, but I wanted a place closer to work. I was getting tired of driving in this weather. And it really was too small."

"Well," said Roxie with a sigh, "I wish you'd told me. I've been thinking about getting my own apartment. I guess it's probably about time. My mother's starting to get on my nerves, you know?"

Chris didn't, really, but didn't say so. "It was kind of a spur-of-the-moment thing. The opportunity came up . . . you know how it is."

"Yeah." The receptionist shrugged and straightened. "I guess there're advantages in living in a big modern apartment complex like that, huh? Pool, hot tub, tennis courts and stuff like that. Lots of single guys?"

"I don't know, I haven't really asked." There'd been a different set of questions on Chris's priority list. Such as how good was the security, and whether there was controlled access to the lobby, parking garage and elevators.

"What," Roxie said with a huff of incredulity, "you mean you haven't checked it out yet? C'mon, Chris, get with the program, here."

In spite of everything, Chris had to laugh. Roxie was so young, and sometimes made her feel so old. She was still so innocent, in so many ways naive. Lucky kid. The fact that she still lived at home at twenty-three said a lot about what kind of family she came from.

"If you ever decide to get a roommate," Roxie said, sounding a shade wistful, "you know, keep me in mind?"

Chris smiled and waved a mittened hand as she went out.

A roommate—now there was a thought. She hadn't actually considered it before. But . . . would having a roommate really do much to protect her from Alan, or would she only be involving someone else in her nightmare? And while on the one hand she might feel safer, having someone else around, there was so much of herself, her past and private life, that she wouldn't want to share with anyone. Ever. She just wasn't sure she could manage to live with someone and still guard her secrets.

Secrets. Who would guess to look at me, she thought bleakly, that crossing a street makes my heart race and my skin crawl with dread? That I jump and turn cold every time the phone rings? That every time I look in the mirror I feel only guilt and shame? They say…people tell me I'm beautiful, but they don't know. *They don't know.…*

Thank God *he* doesn't know, she thought as she raced up the surgery wing's deserted fire stairs, her feet echoing on the concrete steps, the iron rail burning cold under her hand. These days she took a slightly different route every time she went to the hospital, and varied the times of her visits, as well. Just one of the suggestions the police officer had given her, but she found it unsettling and disorienting to have to give up the familiar routines and habits that kept her from having to think too much. Remember too much.

Thank God Wood hadn't remembered her. But what would he think of her if he knew her secrets…if he knew about her past? Edward Earl Brown, with his idyllic home and childhood like something out of an old black-and-white TV show—"Father Knows Best" or "Leave It to Beaver." Wood Brown, whose most painful recollections were of playing the guitar and singing hymns with his mother and brother in church—what did he know of the kind of ugliness that fouled *her* memories?

He'd get sick to his stomach with disgust if he knew, Chris thought. She just hoped to God he never, ever found out.

Exactly why she cared so much about what Wood thought of her was something she didn't want to examine too closely—as were most of her other thoughts and feelings about her patient in Room 312. When it came to Wood, she preferred to keep a curtain drawn between the analytical part of her mind and the part that roamed unfettered and unfenced, beyond her control.

For once she found the third-floor nurse's station deserted. She was beginning to dread Nurse Florence's raised eyebrows and fishy stare, which somehow made her feel she ought to stop and justify herself for being there. Evenings were better—Jackie Sung was nice—but evenings were dangerous, and walking to her car alone afterward was an ordeal she didn't even like to think about.

Today, though, she paused outside Wood's door, taking advantage of the rare, unobserved moment to prepare herself both physically and mentally before entering. She took off her mittens and parka with painstaking care, tugged down her tunic and smoothed her hair. Schooled her face to smile, her breathing to become calm and her heart to take on a slower, more dignified cadence.

Finally, as ready as she could be, she raised her hand to knock, at the same time stealing a peek through the glass panel.

She didn't mean to spy, only to make sure she wasn't about to intrude on Wood's privacy—privacy being a rare-enough commodity in a hospital, as she knew only too well. But in that brief glimpse she felt she'd done exactly that. She could see that he'd cranked up the head of his bed and was staring into the tilt-up mirror in his tray table. Obviously thinking himself unobserved, he was studying his face with a look that reminded Chris of the one he'd greeted her with that very first day. A look both searching and intent, as if, she thought, he was trying to identify someone he'd just met.

At her knock he pushed the tray table aside with guilty haste, though when he looked up his expression remained brooding and dark. When he recognized Chris, however, it seemed to her as if someone must have flipped a switch and turned on a whole bank of lights, suddenly flooding his face with warmth and . . . what might almost have been joy.

Oh God, that look. It caught her off guard, and her unprotected heart responded like a sea-weary lookout on a homebound ship glimpsing the lights of shore. . . .

Wood was cursing himself for his carelessness. Big mistake, he knew, to lose his grip on his feelings like that. But he hadn't expected her; she'd caught him unprepared. He'd felt momentarily dazzled, as if he'd suddenly turned a corner and found the sun was hitting him right in his eyes.

"Hey, Coach," he said gruffly as he mentally donned dark sunglasses.

She was smiling, but it was her too-bright, professional smile. "Hi—where's Grady?"

Wood was glad to have something to talk about while he pulled himself together. "Grady's gone—shipped out this morning. They've got him in some kind of halfway house— occupational therapy or something. They're supposed to be teaching him how to do things for himself, be independent, take care of himself, I guess—stuff like that." Chris was nodding, so he shrugged and added, "I guess you'd know."

"Yeah . . . too bad," Chris murmured absently. Then, as if something had momentarily distracted her, she pulled her attention back to him. "I'm really sorry. I wish I'd had a chance to say goodbye. Have they told you whether you're going to be getting a new roommate right away?"

"Don't know about that. They don't consult me." There was an awkward little pause, during which Wood noticed that Chris didn't seem to want to look at him. He thought then that he must have been mistaken about the way her eyes had flared and her face brightened up when she'd first walked in. A trick of the light, he told himself. That's all it had been. That, and wishful thinking on his part.

He shifted position a fraction of an inch and cranked up his smile again. "So, Coach. What brings you here at a time like this? It's not even your day."

"I know." Her smile seemed so strained it made his own jaws cramp just to look at her.

Wood knew he wasn't mistaken about one thing, and that was the amount of tension in the room. Chris fairly vibrated with it, for reasons he couldn't begin to imagine. And his own body felt so rigid he thought they could probably wheel the bed out from under him and he wouldn't even know it. Tension filled up all the space between the two of them like a solid but invisible object, but it was impossible to tell, just then, whether the object was a bridge . . . or a wall.

Chris hauled in a breath, finally, and stuck her hands in her pockets. "I just came by to see how you were doing. I heard you have a big day tomorrow."

"Oh," said Wood. "Yeah, I guess."

"Wow. Yeah, you *guess?* I thought you'd be thrilled to be finally getting your casts on."

"Oh, sure I am. I'm thrilled to be getting out of this . . ." He grabbed the trap bar and gave it a tug, then let it go. "I don't know," he said on an exhalation as he watched it swing, "I guess I don't know how I feel about . . . the rest of it." A chuckle bumped painfully through his chest. He really wished they'd picked another day to move Grady. He really could have used the man's special brand of wisdom and insight right about now. "I don't know if I'm ready for the idea of myself in a wheelchair, you know?"

"Oh, but it's a big step. You've made such wonderful progress," Chris said in a chirpy, rah-rah kind of voice. "Only three weeks in traction—"

"Six," he reminded her. "I had three weeks in Germany, you know, before they shipped me home."

"Even so, six weeks in traction—that's very good. And now we can start making some real—" She broke off, probably because he was shaking his head and silently laughing. In irony, not amusement.

"Right, Coach," he drawled. And then, before he knew he was going to, perhaps because he was wound up so tightly, he heard himself plunge headlong into forbidden territory. "Hey—you know what you can do for me?" He felt dark and reckless, resentful and rebellious. He struggled to turn his upper body, wincing as he pointed to his left shoulder. "Ow—I'm so damned tense it feels like my whole head is screwed on too tight. Think you could use those magic fingers of yours, maybe get some of the kinks out?"

He wasn't sure what he expected her to do—freeze up, withdraw, run screaming?—but he'd forgotten both her professionalism and her control. She was, after all, a physical therapist. Massaging people was what she *did*—part of it, anyway.

"Of course" was all she said, in a tone both soothing and polite, and stepped right up to his bedside. "I'll try. Is it your neck? Oh my... you *are* tight, aren't you? Okay, now, just try to relax...."

As he exhaled and closed his eyes, he felt her hands settle between his shoulders and the base of his neck... her cool, strong hands, her clever, probing fingers. They tightened, dug deep. His trapezius muscles screamed bloody murder, then slowly turned to jelly. His neck melted. Though he tried his best to forget whose hands they were, waves of tingly, peppery nerve impulses rippled outward from where they touched him, lapping into every nook and cranny in his body.

Heat engulfed him. He could actually feel the blood surging through him, every drop of it heading for the same location in one helluva hurry, as if each and every artery was having a race with every other artery to see which could get the most blood there first.

"Oh...God," he groaned, unable to help himself. He wondered if she had any idea at all what she was doing to him.

"Hmm... right there, huh?"

"Yeah. Right there." No, of course she hadn't a clue. He wondered what she'd do if she ever found out.

Her fingers were working their way up the back of his neck now. "That's it...try to relax." Her voice sounded breathy, as if she might be smiling.

Wood opened his eyes to see if she was, and saw that she had her eyes closed and her head slightly turned, as if she was listening to signals from some private kind of radar in her fingertips. Then she did smile, slightly, and murmured, "Your hair's getting long."

"I know," he said in an air-starved croak. "I guess I need a haircut."

"It doesn't look bad." Her fingers pushed upward, sliding under his hair to stroke muscles that for some reason had gone rigid as iron again.

"Can't get used to it," he said through clenched teeth. "I...look in the mirror and I...don't know who in the hell that guy is in there."

"Is that what you were doing—just now, when I came in?"

"You saw that, did you?" A gust of rueful laughter relieved his tension slightly—and dangerously. Right now tension was the only thing keeping him from reaching for her, pulling her down into the bed with him, regardless of the consequences. His fingers hummed with the need to touch her. He was like an overtightened guitar string, and he hated to think what would happen if he snapped.

"I'm sorry about that," she murmured, her lashes dropping. "I didn't mean to peep."

Peep? The word made him chuckle. "No, it's okay. Just a little embarrassing, is all. I don't want you to think I spend a whole lot of time staring at myself in the mirror. It's just hard to get used to, you know?" He paused for a moment, then laughed again, but not because anything was funny. "Do you have any idea what it's like to wake up one day and look in the mirror and not recognize your own face?"

She didn't say anything at all for a few moments. But because he was watching her so intently, he saw her eyes fly open; caught their silvery flash, then just as quickly darkening, as if a roiling mass of thunderclouds had blocked their light. Her face seemed to lose all color, all luster and life. But even if he hadn't seen, he'd have felt that something was wrong, because on his neck her fingers suddenly stumbled and came to a halt, utterly devoid of strength and tension, like a prizefighter whose knees had buckled.

"I can't imagine," she said in her cool, emotionless voice.

Wood knew then, beyond any doubt, that she lied. He'd have given just about anything to know why.

But she was avoiding his eyes again. As she took her hands from his neck and stepped away from him, every move was spare and carefully controlled. So was her voice when she said, "You should try and get some rest now. Big day tomorrow."

"You gonna be here?" Now it was his voice he didn't recognize. It was a self-conscious croak, the words pulled out by a need he didn't understand, despite the barrier of his pride.

There was a pause. Then, as if the words were pulled from her as well, she said, "Yes, I'll be here. I'm not sure when, but . . . I'll stop by." And she was gone.

It didn't hit Wood until after she'd left that, unless he was very much mistaken, something pretty incredible had just happened between them. Something about it—the whole episode—had been so . . . he searched his mental dictionary and came up with the word *intimate*.

Whatever it was, he found it unsettling . . . and sort of exhilarating, too, in a way. Even a little bit frightening, like jumping out of an airplane for the first time. The fact was, he'd made love with a lot of women in his life, in a lot of different and thoroughly uninhibited ways, but he'd never experienced anything quite like this before. This seemed to be a kind of touching that went beyond skin, and even flesh and bone. A joining that had nothing to do with bodies.

Although his body definitely *was* involved. Oh, yes, indeed. Painfully so. He felt like a volcano about ready to blow.

In agony, he eyed the plastic pitcher of drinking water that was sitting on his nightstand, sweating cool moisture droplets onto its matching tray, and thoughtfully considered its possibilities. The only thing that kept him from dumping the contents where they would do the most good was the prospect of having to explain to that gimlet-eyed dragon of a nurse how his bed had come to be soaking wet.

Chris almost decided not to go. She'd spent a miserable night, unable to sleep because of a single ghastly image that she couldn't shake no matter how hard she tried. Awake, it hung above her in the darkness like the face of the moon, seeming to follow her wherever she went; when she closed her eyes, there it was again, like a ghost image imprinted on the backs of her eyelids.

It was only a face…but a hideous, gargoyle face, swollen to a shapeless mass, mottled with purple and green and blue, with slits for eyes and a bloody mass where the mouth should be. And the most horrible part of it was, she knew the face was her own.

She'd given up, finally, and had stumbled into the bathroom to bathe her face and sticky eyes with cold, soothing water. But the face she saw staring back at her in the harsh glare of the vanity lights was no more familiar to her than the one that haunted her sleeplessness. Eyes sunken deep in shadows, skin stretched tight over bones that seemed too sharp, too vulnerable; mouth pulled downward, bracketed by lines of despair… With a small, stricken cry she threw out a hand and hit the light switch, plunging the bathroom into darkness.

Oh God—she remembered it all so well. Everything, every detail. The horror, the pain, the rage… Incredible, she thought, shaking with silent, bitter laughter—laughter that produced the tears her sobs could not. *Nothing's changed.* She thought she'd escaped it, but it seemed she hadn't, after all. It was all still here, right here in this room with her, right now and for always, wherever she went. Maybe it just wasn't possible to escape from the past. Maybe Wood was right.

Wood. Saying his name, even in her mind, was like hearing a tolling bell that ushered in a cold, gray dawn. *Earl Brown.*

Calmly now she patted her face dry and made her way through rooms still hazardous with boxes and packing materials, zigzagging her way to the kitchen. There she sat on a straight-backed chair with her knees pulled up and her arms wrapped around them for warmth and watched the blackness outside the window thin gradually to the pale and lovely lavender of a late-winter morning.

The coffeemaker clicked on, trickled interrogatively for a few minutes, then launched itself into the new day with bubbling, belching gusto. Elsewhere in the building she heard doors slam, the thud of footsteps, the quiet roar of plumbing. Down below in the street the rhythms of rush-hour traffic began. Stiff and exhausted, Chris finally unfolded herself and hobbled on icy feet to the counter to pour herself a cup of coffee.

What was I thinking of? she thought as, leaning against the counter, she drank it, the black, bitter liquid burning its way into her belly. Yesterday she'd promised Wood she'd be there to see him after he got his casts on. Why? He wouldn't be ready for her yet, not until at least tomorrow. Why had she promised such a thing?

The answer was simple. Because he'd asked her to. Just like he'd asked her to massage his neck, and without a word, without a thought, she'd done his bidding. She was losing control of things where that man was concerned, that was very clear. And she couldn't let that happen. She'd made one mistake; she knew she'd never survive another one. She'd have to—at least she knew she should, for her own sake—get out of it now, right now. She should quit, turn this case over to Brad. John wouldn't understand, he'd be furious with her, but what could he say? What could he do, fire her? There were worse things to lose than a job.

Her stomach twisted into a knot. She closed her eyes, swaying with a sudden wave of dizziness. *Oh God, what was I thinking of?* That business yesterday with Wood—what in the world had she been doing, massaging his neck like that? She hadn't felt like a physical therapist treating a patient. What she'd felt like was a woman. Just a woman, touching a man. And even now her whole body ached at the thought of it...the way it had felt, his skin...so warm and smooth under her hands.

Shaken and jangled, she thought, I can't do this. Not now, not ever. It's impossible.

And again: What was I thinking of?

This was Wood Brown—*Earl Brown*—one of the "good kids." From a good home, a good family, raised by good parents with all sorts of love and high moral standards, laughter and singing and church on Sundays. How could someone like that ever understand what *her* life had been like?

And why on earth would someone like that, a good, decent man, ever want to have anything to do with...someone like her? Oh God, she thought, if he knew...

Her stomach rolled once more; the coffee turned to acid in her throat. As she poured the last of it into the sink she felt calm at last, her eyes clear, her resolve strong. All right, she'd just be careful from now on. She wouldn't lose control again. She couldn't allow herself to get too close to the man, that was all there was to it. Getting close to someone—anyone—would risk giving away her secrets. Getting close to *this* someone would almost guarantee it. And never, *ever* did she want to see the inevitable result: a look of utter revulsion in Wood Brown's eyes.

There was one good thing about the incident with Wood, Chris thought wryly as she checked her rearview mirror on the short drive to work that morning. At least it had served to take her mind off her "other" problem, if only for a little while. She hadn't had a middle-of-the-night phone call since she'd moved to the new apartment and changed her telephone number again, but she knew better than to let that fact raise any false hopes that the respite would last. Sooner or later Alan would find her. He always did.

She wasn't sure whether she would actually have asked John to transfer Wood to another physical therapist; she never got the chance to find out. When she got to work, Roxie informed her that John was going to be in Des Moines at a seminar for the rest of the week. Shortly thereafter, both Brad and Megan called in sick. So in any case she was, blessedly, too busy to worry about Wood, or to give a thought to how little sleep she'd had the previous night. Only after the last patient had gone home and she was preparing to lock up—which, as senior P.T., was her responsibility in John's absence—did it occur to her that she had a decision to make.

Should she run across to the hospital for a few minutes to see how Wood was getting along with his new casts, or not? Would she do it for another patient, if asked? Probably. Then why not for *this* patient? Because she was afraid she wouldn't be able to keep her emotions under control? Ridiculous.

In the end, of course, there was no question at all. No question and no choice. She'd said she'd be there, and so she would. Simple.

But when she got to the third floor, slightly out of breath from having dashed the long way around through the parking lot and in by the cafeteria entrance, Jackie Sung informed her that Wood was asleep. Had been most of the day, in fact, sleeping off the effects of the anesthetic.

Chris wondered whether the flat, sinking sensation she was feeling inside was due to disappointment or relief. "Okay if I look in on him?" she asked Jackie, pleased that her voice betrayed only casual, certainly no more than professional interest.

Jackie smiled and said, "Sure." What a dear she was.

Chris smiled back and said, "Thanks," and went on down to Room 312 with a nice, professional firmness in her step.

She slipped into the room without knocking, then stood for a moment just inside the door, realizing that once again she hadn't prepared herself for this. What was it about this man, she wondered desperately, that her normal defenses always seemed so woefully inadequate?

He seems so...exposed, she thought. The bed, stripped of the hanging weights and pulleys, looked denuded and open—the leopard cage without its bars. Only now, of course, the leopard was safely asleep.

She moved closer to the bed, her heart pounding. She had no idea why. He was sleeping so soundly, he wouldn't wake up—she knew that. She *did*.

Was there anything more vulnerable, she wondered, than the face of a strong man sleeping? All the more so because of being so seldom caught in that unguarded condition...relaxed and at peace, relieved of the necessity of always appearing manly and tough and brave? No one should see him like this, she thought, except the one he shares his life with. It was just too intimate a trust.

And yet... It came as rather a shock to her to realize that, although she'd been married herself for nearly seven years, she'd never been moved to such reflections before. The truth was, the sight of her husband's sleeping countenance had brought her nothing but a sense of relief. A momentary surcease of anxiety. She couldn't recall that she'd ever, even in the earliest days of her marriage, looked at her husband asleep and felt like this—as though her heart had grown too big for her chest.

Her fingers itched to touch him, to smooth the dark, soft-crisp hair away from his forehead. But she didn't. "Wood Brown," she whispered, in awe and dismay. "Edward Earl..."

She knew she should leave, that there was no point in her staying. But all at once she felt exhausted, weighed down, somehow, by what she'd just discovered. All the implications, the total impossibility, seemed too much for her sleep-deprived mind to cope with. Sticking around was both pointless and dangerous, she knew that. But the task of leaving seemed...insurmountable.

I'll just stay a minute, she thought as she pulled the comfortable visitor's chair closer to Wood's bedside. Just a few minutes...then I'll go.

* * *

Wood was sure he'd dreamed her. He'd been drifting again, his return to reality a gradual, on-again, off-again process in which the drifting kept being interrupted by periods of stability, something like a leaf sifting down through a tree, now coming to rest on this branch or that, then tumbling on again at the whim of the next breeze. It was during one of those periods of stillness and lucidity that he opened his eyes and saw he wasn't alone. That someone was curled up in the chair beside his bed, sound asleep.

For one disorienting instant he was a child again, and it was his mother sitting there watching over him, just as she'd always kept vigil through his various childhood fevers. It didn't even surprise him much to see her; he'd already wandered quite a bit through his youth and childhood in the twilight sleep of anesthesia withdrawal. But then she exhaled softly and shifted position, and in the gray hospital half-light he caught a glimpse of her hair. A single lock of silver, slipped loose from its moorings to wash across her cheek like a pale ribbon of moonlight.

"Chris?" He'd croaked her name in wonder and disbelief— or had he only dreamed that as well?

Because the next time he opened his eyes, she was gone.

"Good morning, Mr. Brown! And how are *we* feeling this morning?"

Reveille, thought Wood from the depths of his laughing-gas hangover, was easier on the ears.

"Come on, up-up-up! No more lounging around, Mr. Brown. We're going to get you up this morning! How does that sound?"

Like fingernails on a blackboard, Wood silently groaned as he covered his eyes with a forearm against the blast of daylight the nurse had just admitted with one ruthless yank of the window blind's cord. Not Florence, thank God. Ida, this time. Nurse Ida, a remorselessly cheerful woman with frizzy, gray-blond hair and a severe overbite. She was okay. Ordinarily he'd even flirt with her a bit, but this morning he wasn't up to it.

"Up?" he croaked. "You gotta be kidding." As near as he could tell, the bottom half of his body seemed to be encased in cement.

Nurse Ida was energetically bustling about, making unseen adjustments to his bed and its coverings. Then she beamed at him and hit the control button that raised and lowered the upper half of his bed.

"Hey!" said Wood as it hummed and whined and started heaving beneath him. Up it went...and up. His head swam. He felt like he ought to hold on to something.

"Don't worry, Mr. Brown. I know it feels a bit strange, but you won't fall off, I promise." Ida seemed to think that was extremely amusing. Wood didn't, not in the least. To him it seemed like an imminent possibility.

"Now then," said the nurse, as if she was announcing that he'd just won a new car on a TV game show, "What we're going to have you do this morning is dangle!"

Dangle? Wood didn't dare even ask what that meant; he was too busy making sure the bed wasn't going to tip over.

"That's right—no more lying around like a lazy dog all day for you. Later on you even get to bathe yourself—how about that! But first we'd just like to have you get used to sitting up for a few minutes, all right, Mr. Brown? Would you like a bottle? No? Okay, then, now you just stay right there—don't go away. I'm going to go and get an orderly, just in case you decide to take a nosedive." Again, for some reason, that seemed to strike Ida as hilarious.

Wood watched her go, mentally grinding his teeth. With her departure the world stabilized and his brain started functioning again.

Bottle...bathe myself...orderlies...what the hell do they think I am, a damned baby? Sitting up, for God's sake—he'd been doing it all by himself since he was six months old. How hard could it be?

Already he felt better. He was getting used to this—being upright again. What was it he was supposed to do, just dangle his feet over the side of the bed? Piece of cake—he was a marine, after all. Hell, he'd jumped out of airplanes, climbed mountains in desert heat, run obstacle courses in full battle gear. He for damn sure didn't need some orderly watching him make a fool of himself.

He threw back his blanket, made sure he was decently covered, then sat for a moment just looking at the brand-new fiberglass shells that now encased his legs from his hips to mid-calf with what seemed to be hinges at the knees. He swallowed hard a couple of times; the idea of moving them seemed terrifying.

But this was a kind of fear he could understand and deal with. To him it was simply one more challenge, a spur to his will, something to be overcome, an enemy to be vanquished. Clenching his jaws and summoning his courage, he placed his hands on one of the casts, closed his eyes and lifted.

Chapter 7

Chris couldn't remember a stranger night. Being shaken awake in Wood's hospital room by Jackie Sung at the close of evening visiting hours had left her disoriented and demoralized, with that cold, queasy feeling as though it were very late, somewhere in the wee hours of the morning. Except that it hadn't been. It was only eight-thirty in the evening. Consequently, the drive home had seemed almost surreal, a montage of noisy traffic and a downtown ablaze with multitoned lights that splashed color and an illusion of warmth across the frozen mounds of piled-up snow.

She barely remembered how she got to her apartment, but once safely locked inside, perversely, she'd felt restless and keyed up, in an aimless, utterly useless kind of way. She'd seemed unable to settle down and concentrate on anything—unpacking or tidying up, going though the mail, reading a book, even watching television. In the end she'd bolted down a can of tomato soup and a cup of coffee and had tumbled, exhausted but wide-awake, into bed. There she'd tossed and turned and dreamed weirdly troubled dreams, finally dragging herself out of bed to see if a hot shower would help her relax, only to discover that it was already morning and she'd overslept.

That wouldn't have been so terrible, but then she remembered that in John's absence it was her responsibility to open up. She had no choice but to throw on her clothes and dash out the door, no time even to take a shower or do her hair. Her parka would cover it, she told herself, until she got to her desk and had a chance to brush it out and put it back in its usual sleek and practical knot.

But rush hour was at its peak; when she pulled into the rehab center parking lot she could see Roxie and Megan already waiting at the front door, hugging themselves and shifting from one foot to the other, huffing clouds of vapor into the crackling cold air.

"Oh gee, you guys, I'm sorry," Chris panted as she ran up to them, keys at the ready. "Been waiting long?"

Megan's only reply was a pitiful-sounding cough. Roxie, however, was breathless but cheerful. "Just got here. What happened to you? Are you okay?"

"I'm fine. Overslept." That got her a couple of shocked looks; it was simply not something that had ever happened before.

Chris unlocked the door, then glanced at her watch and handed the keys to Roxie. "Finish up for me, will you? I'm supposed to be at the hospital right this minute. Got a patient coming out of traction. Thanks, Rox—I owe you!" The last bit she threw over her shoulder as she was running for the green light at the corner.

She took off her parka in the elevator, as usual, and that was when she remembered her hair. God, what a mess. She didn't need a mirror to know that the knot was half-undone and falling down her back, a halo of loose wisps floating around her face and standing straight up on the top, thanks to the static electricity generated by the fake-fur lining of her parka hood.

Frantically, she jammed her parka between her knees, ripped off the fastenings that held her hair secure in its practical bun and stuck them in her mouth while she finger combed the whole waist-length mass into some semblance of order. Swiftly she gathered it in both hands, twisted it into a thick rope and looped it into a loose knot, just as the elevator came to its bumpless halt. Not as neat and tidy as she liked, but it would have to do.

The corridors were bustling at that hour, the third-floor nurse's station deserted. Chris considered leaving her parka there, thought better of it and rushed on by.

The door to Room 312 was open for once, she saw as she approached. She slowed, hesitated in the doorway, then gasped, "Oh my God!" and dropped the parka. Hurling herself forward, she managed to get her arms around Wood just in time to prevent him from sliding bonelessly, rather like a load of wet laundry, onto the vinyl tile floor.

He was a big man. She'd known that, of course, but it took having a sizable portion of his weight collapsed unconscious against her to make her realize just *how* big. Even though he was very thin, with not an ounce of fat on his body—he'd undoubtedly lost weight since the accident—his frame was large and well covered with muscle that six weeks of inactivity didn't appear to have softened one bit. She could feel the breadth, depth and solidity of his chest through the thin cotton hospital gown he wore, feel his body's heat soaking through it and into her own. Feel the reassuring thump of his heartbeat.

God, he was heavy. It was all she could do to keep him from falling, which would certainly result in catastrophic consequences to his injuries. Whatever else happened, she knew she must *not* let him fall. So she just braced herself and held on.

She couldn't think. Her mind seemed numbed, which was probably to be expected. It had just received two very severe shocks, the first being the sheer masculinity of the man she now supported almost totally in her arms.

If she had for even one moment believed this man to be harmless simply because he was injured, she'd been deluding herself. Dear God, he exuded maleness and sexuality from every pore, telegraphed it with every pulse beat, like some kind of low-frequency signal. The rasp of his beard whispered it against her cheek, like promises in the dark; his musky scent wrapped her in it, enveloped her like fog.

Considering her personal history and the significance of such things in her life, she knew she should have found so much rampant masculinity repugnant. That she did not was the *second* shock.

It occurred to her suddenly that Wood's face, leaning against hers, felt damp and clammy. She really did need to get his head lowered somehow. Bracing herself and taking most of the strain of his weight in her legs, she managed to lift his upper body, then ease him gently backward onto the bed. There, that was better—except that now her arms were pinned under him and she couldn't straighten up.

She tried to free them—the last thing she wanted was for her patient to wake up and find her collapsed across his chest like a sack of oats. And he was probably going to return to consciousness pretty quickly now that he was lying down; already she could feel the warmth flooding back into his skin.

But for some reason she couldn't seem to find any strength in her arms. She felt weak and panicky, whimpery and ineffectual. And then, to make matters worse, the loose, heavy knot of her hair slithered forward over her shoulder right into Wood's face, and she couldn't do anything about it.

One of his hands came up, clumsily at first, groping.... When it found the knot of hair, it halted, then with one deft tug, untied it so that the whole mass tumbled free.

"Your hair's loose," he said in a muffled, slightly drunken tone.

"Coulda fooled me," Chris muttered furiously. God, this was awful. So embarrassing. She was beginning to sweat.

"That's weird, it really does feel like rain...."

"What?"

The body under hers jerked and came to full awareness. *"Chris?"*

"Yes," she managed to gasp in a constricted croak. "Listen, you fainted. I can't get . . . my arms . . ."

She had *his* arms pinned just above the elbows, but the lower parts, which included his hands, were managing to do a considerable amount of exploring. One was weaving through the pile of her hair, lifting and crushing it in wondering fistfuls. The other she could feel moving slowly up and down her back.

She hadn't thought matters could get any worse, but just then they did. There was a soft but horrified shriek, and then a voice cried, "Oh, my goodness! Mr. Brown—*Christine*—what are you doing? Oh, my *word!*"

"Help me," Chris gasped. Oh boy, this was all she needed. At least, thank God, it wasn't Florence. "He fainted. I can't . . . lift him."

"Oh, my *word* . . ." That seemed to be the only thing Nurse Ida was capable of saying at the moment. But strong hands were already coming to Chris's aid. She felt the weight on her arms ease.

"Careful—watch his legs," she gasped as she slipped her arms from under Wood's body and stepped back out of the way, allowing the nurse and Sal, the orderly, to take her place.

She was seething—that was the only word for it. Flushed, disheveled and breathing as if she'd just run a hundred-yard dash. Angry and embarrassed, more upset than she'd thought she possibly could be. Trembling. And oh, so thankful to have a few moments to pull herself together while Sal and Nurse Ida screened her from Wood's view.

Ida was clucking and scolding over her patient like an old mother hen with one chick. "*Shame* on you, Mr. Brown. I *told* you to wait until we had Sal to help. Honestly! You could have been seriously hurt, couldn't you? *Please* don't try to do anything like that again, now, do you hear me? Oh, my—you nearly gave us a heart attack, Mr. Brown. What am I going to do..."

Sal, on the other hand, looked as if he found the whole thing absolutely hilarious.

"Sorry," Wood mumbled, looking beyond Ida's shoulder and addressing the apology to Chris. Normal color was coming back into his face, though it still had a waxy, moist appearance. In spite of that his eyes were glowing at her from under his black brows like something wild and playful, caught out in his mischief but at heart unrepentant.

"Guess I shouldn't have tried to rush it." His voice was thick, the words still a little slurred. "I've never done that before in my life. Never occurred to me you could faint sitting down." At least now he had the grace to look chagrined.

"Not sitting down—sitting *up*. You've been lying down for six weeks, remember?" Chris said acidly, then paused to let the edge in her voice subside. She injected as much ice into it as she could muster under the circumstances, and continued from the safety of her position, clear across the room near the door. "Actually, this is quite common, especially with male patients. That's why we take precautions. What you did was incredibly stupid. To risk six weeks' progress just to prove some—some macho point or something—"

"Come on," said Wood softly.

"—Really makes me angry. And I can't—"

"Angry?" The light in his eyes wasn't playful any longer. His voice, however, if anything became even softer. "Really? You coulda fooled me."

Chris grew still. Her heart began to hammer hard against her ribs, a completely different cadence from the physical stress of a few minutes ago. She said calmly, "What would you like me to do, shout and throw things?"

"That'd do for a start, yeah."

"Ok-kay..." trilled Nurse Ida, hastily stepping between them, "are we ready to try again, Mr. Brown? Feeling stronger now, are we? Come, Sal, give us a hand. Let's see if we can dangle this morning, after all. Ready, Mr. Brown? Upsy-daisy..."

Sal, who had been grinning unabashedly and watching the exchange between Chris and Wood like a spectator at a tennis match, recovered himself and jumped forward to take an arm. Together he and Nurse Ida eased Wood upright, then slid his legs around, casts and all, and lowered his feet carefully over the side of the bed. Chris kept her distance and watched.

"Now then," said Nurse Ida with an air of immense satisfaction, "we're doing just *fine.* If you begin to feel a little woozy, now, you just let us know, okay?"

Wood didn't reply. He was leaning slightly forward, staring down at his feet. His brow was creased with what looked almost like puzzlement.

"How are we doing, Mr. Brown? Feeling okay?"

"Fine," said Wood. But his voice had a stifled sound to it, as if he might have forgotten to breathe.

Chris continued to watch in silence, trying to distance herself emotionally as well as physically, holding herself across her middle and concentrating hard on controlling her facial expression. She knew very well how Wood was feeling, and "fine" didn't begin to accurately describe it. Right now the blood would be rushing into his feet, pooling there, making them feel like balloons blown up until they were ready to burst. They'd be throbbing. They'd be hurting like hell.

He didn't say a word, just sat gripping the edge of the bed and rocking himself slightly. His eyes were closed, and his forehead bore a fine beading of sweat. Chris could hear him breathing through his nose, slowly and evenly, fighting his silent battle against the pain. It grew too hard to watch him.

She shifted her gaze to his feet. It struck her that they looked oddly defenseless, toes stretched and angled upward, like someone walking on hot sand. She noticed that below the casts his legs were bony and pale and covered with coarse black hair;

that the calves were bunched and rigid, as if knotted with cramps. With any other patient, she'd have been on her knees on the floor right now, massaging those charley horses, helping ease the pressure on those poor feet....

"Hey," said Wood in his stifled, airless croak, "where are you going?"

Already on her way out of the room, Chris paused, but kept her back to him. She wanted desperately to ease her inner turmoil with a deep breath, but was afraid even that might betray emotions she didn't want to have, much less reveal. Instead she said lightly, "You're in good hands. I have patients who need me." She turned then and tossed the last in his direction without meeting his eyes: "I'll be back tomorrow. Bye, now. Have fun."

When she got to the rehab center, the first thing she saw was the huge bouquet of white roses sitting on the reception counter. Even before she counted them, she knew there would be eleven.

The twelfth she found when she was getting ready to go home that evening. The long, thornless stem was tucked beneath her car's windshield wiper. The severed blossom lay nearby, like a single, pristine dollop of snow on the dark blue, winter-grimed hood.

Wood was teaching himself to pop wheelies in a section of the hospital corridor just around the corner and out of sight of the nurse's station when he happened to see Grady rolling toward him from the direction of the elevators. He wheeled himself out to meet him, grinning from ear to ear, and when he got close enough, sang out, "Hey!" The Southern-style greeting had apparently rubbed off on him and stuck.

"Man, what you tryin' to do with yourself?" Grady teased as they rolled up alongside each other and clasped hands in the bent-elbow, raised-forearm style. "You tryin' that fancy stuff already? Didn't I teach you nothin'? And you barely outa training wheels!"

Wood had forgotten how good it felt to cut loose and laugh from the belly up without having to worry about hurting himself. In the weeks since he'd gotten out of traction, he hadn't felt much like laughing. "Hey, what are you talkin' about? I'm getting ready to blow this joint."

"No kiddin'?"

"That's what they tell me. Soon as I find a place."

"That's great ... that's great."

"So, what the hell are you doing back here? I thought you were long gone."

"Came to say goodbye." Grady's smile was gentle and slow, but Wood noticed that there was a gleam in his eyes and that he seemed like he was about to burst. "I'm goin' to Georgia. Gonna be with my wife and kids."

"No! Hey, that's great."

The gleam in Grady's eyes became a softer sheen. "Yeah... Joanna's found us a place, one that'll handle my chair. It's gonna be good to see 'em. Awful good. Damn, I've missed 'em."

"I'm happy for you, man."

"Got me a job, too."

"No kidding? Doing what?"

"Dispatcher for a sand-and-gravel company. Don't pay much, Joanna'll still have to work, but I'm gonna be takin' some classes—computers, electronics, that kind of stuff. Just a matter of time till I find something better."

Wood nodded and made appropriate noises, but he didn't really know what to say. The truth was, he was finding it un-expectedly hard to say goodbye to Grady. He'd seen a lot of buddies and bunkmates come and go during the course of twelve years in the Marine Corps, but he didn't think he'd ever felt closer to anyone than he did to the man he'd shared his hospital room with. Nothing like a combination of vulnerabil-ity and boredom to foster confidences, he thought. But, of course, with Grady it was more than that. Wood wasn't sure what it was—maybe something about him that reminded him of his dad. No doubt about one thing, though. He was going to miss the man.

"So," said Grady, finally breaking one of those awkward little silences that tend to fall at times like that, "how 'bout you, my man? You're lookin' good, anyway."

"Gettin' there," said Wood. "Gettin' there."

"And ... how's it goin' with the ice maiden?"

"Ah, hell, I don't know!" Wood laughed out loud, and again it felt good, like scratching an itchy place.

Grady propped his elbows on the arms of his wheelchair, laced his fingers together across his middle and leaned forward slightly. "Tell me about it."

Wood shrugged. "I mean it—I don't know what's going on with the woman. I was taking your advice—about being patient, you know? And things seemed to be going...okay. I mean, we'd talk a lot, not about anything special, just casual stuff. She won't talk about anything very personal, nothing about her past, or when she was a kid, or anything. It's kind of weird, in a way. It's like talking to somebody who just hatched, you know? No history. But I was making some progress, I thought. Little things—like, did you know she's a vegetarian, of all things?"

Grady gave a low whistle. "All *that* from *veggies?*"

"No lie. And she's into all these causes—saving whales and boycotting tuna and all that stuff. We really got into it one day over the spotted owl, can you believe that? It was great."

"So?" said Grady. "What's your problem? Sounds like you just gotta keep doin' what you're doin', man. She'll come around."

Wood dejectedly shook his head. "Yeah, that's what I used to think. Now I'm not so sure."

"What happened?"

"Wish I knew." He sighed, then laughed uneasily and confessed, "Ah hell, I do too know. At least I know *when*. I'm just ashamed to tell you about it, is all. See, what happened is, the day after I got my casts on, I was, uh...trying to sit up on the edge of my bed, and uh...well, shoot. I fainted."

Grady laughed his tympany roll. "You're kiddin'."

"Swear to God. Never happened to me before, man. One minute I'm sitting there thinking I don't feel so hot, and the next thing I know I'm lying flat on my back, and Chris is lying on top of me with her arms wrapped clear around me, and her hair is all over my face."

He stopped and scrubbed a hand over his face, more shaken by the recollection than he'd expected to be. Then he shook his head. "And ever since then, it's like she's...shut herself off. I mean, she's there, but she isn't, you know? Anyway, I can't reach her, no matter how hard I try. I'm beginning to think you and Sal were right. The whole thing's just not worth it."

Needing activity on which to vent his frustration, Wood gave his wheels an angry slap and moved off a little way down the empty corridor. After a moment Grady came rolling silently up beside him. "Sounds to me like you startin' to care about this woman."

Wood snorted and snapped him a look as they rolled on slowly in tandem. "Of course I care about her."

"Uh-uh." Grady's voice was soft and low, like a string base. "I mean *care*. Like, you having *feelings* for her, my man. Like she's not just some kinda challenge to you anymore, is she? Just a little—" he fluttered his fingers in the air and grinned "—diversion to help pass the time. Ain't that right?"

Wood let his chair glide to a halt. "I don't know," he muttered, shaking his head, "maybe I am starting to have feelings for her. If I am, that's what scares me. I mean, think about it— what if I fall in love with a woman who won't love me back? What kind of a fool does that make me? It's pathetic!"

Grady chuckled. "Nah, it ain't. It's happened to better men than you, my friend, believe me. But that's not what's got you scared. Is it? 'Cause you don't believe for a minute you ain't gonna bring that woman around, sooner or later."

Wood couldn't help but laugh, because Grady was right. He'd never failed to win over any woman he happened to be interested in, and he usually didn't have to spend much effort to do it. In fact, come to think of it, he'd never in his life had to put this much effort into a woman. If a woman gave him grief, he just said, "So long," and moved on to somebody else. Plenty of other fish in the sea, right?

He waggled his shoulders uneasily, frowning again. "Okay, so let's say she does come around. What the hell am I going to do with a woman like that? I mean, she's got problems, man. Problems I don't think I can fix."

"It's tough," Grady agreed with a sigh. "Don't know what to tell you, man."

This time the laughter didn't feel good to Wood. It felt forced and painful. "What? Come on."

Grady's smile was wry and gentle. "Sounds like you got some heavy thinkin' to do, my friend." He swiveled his chair with practiced ease. "Hey—take care now, you hear? Let me know how it comes out."

"Where you off to?" Wood asked as the big man waved and began to move away.

"Got a few other people I want to say goodbye to before I go. You?"

"I don't know—think I'm gonna see if I can find some air that doesn't smell like disinfectant and sick people."

Grady laughed. "I hear you."

"Hey, stay in touch," said Wood gruffly.

"I will. I'll send you my address, soon as Joanna and I get ourselves settled. Where'bouts you want me to send it?"

Wood thought about that while he was catching up with Grady's chair. "Why don't you send it care of the P.T. clinic? Way it looks, I think I'm going to be around awhile yet."

"Yeah, good idea. Well…" Grady smiled wryly and held up his right hand.

Wood grasped it and held on for a moment. "Take care, now."

"I will. You hang in there, my friend."

"Hey—I'm hangin'…" He sat slumped in his chair and watched Grady roll away down the corridor, casting a long shadow across the polished floor. Then he turned and wheeled himself slowly back to the elevators.

Nice thing about hospitals, he thought as he punched the buttons. Everything was all set up for people like him and Grady. "Handicapped Accessible," wasn't that what they called it? Funny, but it hadn't ever occurred to him that that phrase was going to apply to him someday. At least in his case, though, it wasn't permanent. Not like Grady.

He really was glad Grady had stopped by, but saying goodbye had made him feel more depressed than ever. It was this place, he decided. Hospitals were hard to be optimistic in. He needed to get out of here, that was all. Even for a few minutes.

The elevator arrived with a muted *ding*. Wood had to maneuver himself awkwardly out of the way to let some people off, then grab for the door to keep it from shutting before he could get on. One of the people who'd just gotten off—a young woman volunteer, by the looks of her pink pinafore—was kind enough to hold it open for him until he'd gotten himself sorted out. When he thanked her, she said, "No problem," and smiled at him with what was probably meant to be sympathy and compassion. But it made his belly burn.

On the ground floor he turned right, but skirted the main lobby. He had an idea that going out that way in his wheelchair and pajamas would probably raise a few eyebrows, if not alarms. He envisioned Klaxons, sirens and searchlights going off as he passed through the automatic doors, and loudspeakers blaring, "Red alert—escaping patient! Red alert!"

Instead he followed the signs for the cafeteria. He knew there was an atrium somewhere nearby, because he'd spotted it yesterday from a window in the third-floor lounge. It had looked pleasant and sunny, protected from the prairie winds, with tables where people could sit outside and eat when the weather was nice.

But he found the atrium closed and deserted. He'd forgotten what March was like out here on the northern plains. Growing up he'd always thought March the cruelest of months, teasing and whispering promises of spring, only to break them in the very next moment with taunting blasts of more—and more—and *more* winter. Through glass walls he could see the tables, clothed now in white and fringed all around with icicles, sleet riming the wet, black branches of leafless trees, stubby swords of daffodils poking up through lacy crusts of snow that had partially melted and then refrozen. It looked bleak and lonely and cold, which come to think of it pretty much described his own mood.

Not quite ready yet to call off his sortie and go back and face the solitude of his room, Wood rolled himself to the elevators and pressed Down instead of Up. He knew the hospital's little-used physical therapy department had to be down in the basement somewhere. He also knew there wasn't much he could hope to do there at this point except look around, but hey—anything was better than another afternoon of soap operas and talk shows.

The air in the basement was muggy and reeked of chemicals—he identified chlorine from the therapy pool and formaldehyde, probably from the pathology lab or the morgue.

It was also very quiet after the constant bustle and babble of the hospital above, and seemed deserted. Chris had told Wood that these days most patients were sent across the street to the new Riverside Clinic, which was larger and better equipped. She'd proudly informed him that in case he didn't know it, Iowa was one of the most progressive states in the country in the field of physical therapy. As a matter of fact, Wood had learned quite a bit about physical therapy in the last three weeks or so; it was one of the few subjects he could discuss with Chris without her freezing up and shutting down.

It isn't worth it, he told himself. *She* isn't worth it. No woman in the world was worth this much grief. Maybe it was about time to give it up. Find something—or someone—else to occupy his mind and his time.

Following signs and the odor of chlorine, Wood found his way through the maze of corridors to the pool, which at first seemed as empty as the rest of the place. He was about to move on in search of the other P.T. facilities when he heard the rise and fall of voices, which seemed to be coming from an open doorway to his right. One of the voices was unmistakably Chris's soft alto; the other sounded young and angry, a shrill and tremulous tenor.

Before Wood could maneuver himself around the corner and go to investigate, he heard a loud noise, as if something heavy had fallen over or been dropped. He heard the whir of stainless-steel wheels, and then a chair shot from the doorway like a ball from a cannon. Wood had only a brief impression of a thin body bowed with physical exertion, a pale, narrow face with furious eyes set deep in shadowed sockets, a shock of red-blond hair, straight as a sheaf of wheat. And then the wheelchair barreled past him, narrowly avoiding a head-on collision.

"What the hell?" muttered Wood aloud, but softly. Intrigued, he began rolling himself toward the doorway from which the other wheelchair had come. On the way he had to pass by the observation window of what appeared to be an office. As he did, he caught sight of something that brought him to an abrupt and silent halt.

Chris was sitting slumped on the corner of a desk, her face turned slightly away from him, one arm hugged tightly across her middle and clasping her waist, the other hand pressed to her mouth. As he watched, though, she slowly raised both hands, clenched now into fists in a classic gesture of helplessness and frustration.

And her face...watching her face, Wood thought, was like watching something of exquisite beauty—a porcelain egg, perhaps—suddenly crack and break into tiny pieces. And underneath that fragile shell...oh God, it was all there, the passion, the grief, the pain, the rage, all the emotions he'd convinced himself she was capable of in spite of any evidence to the fact. Now he could see it for himself, naked and unrestrained. So much emotion, so raw and intense it was hard to watch her. He hadn't realized how much empathy there'd be. Hadn't known that her pain would become his.

Almost...*almost* he decided to back away and leave her undisturbed. But something else compelled him forward instead. He rolled silently on past the window, rapped on the wall beside the open door and called out, "Hey—anybody here?"

Chris was just bending over to retrieve a straight-backed, wooden chair that had evidently been knocked over by the young wheelchair hot-rodder in the course of his hasty exit. She straightened with the chair in her hands and smiled at Wood, her eyes too bright and her color high.

"Oh, hi. My goodness, what are you doing way down here?" Her voice was cool and light as always, the only remnants of her private outburst just a hint of breathlessness and an unfamiliar edge of strain.

"Exploring, looking for some air," said Wood casually as he slipped through the doorway. He jerked his head back toward the pool. "Who was that? Sure in a hurry."

"Oh—that was Kevin." She tossed it off with an airy wave of her hand. "A...patient of mine." She set the chair on the floor, frowning as if its correct placement was a matter requiring a great deal of thought and careful consideration.

"He seemed a little upset."

"Oh...yeah, he was." She lifted one shoulder in an offhand shrug, still apparently absorbed by the problem of the chair. "He's having a little difficulty with adjustment." She glanced at Wood as if that needed explaining. "He's finding it hard to accept his handicap. It's not uncommon at this stage. He still has a lot of anger to work through."

"Must be hard."

"He's suffered a great loss." Evidently satisfied with the chair at last, Chris shrugged and returned to the seat she'd occupied before, on one corner of the desk. She picked up a clipboard from the desk top and folded it against her breasts, the way she held it reminding Wood not so much of a shield or barrier, but more of a hurt child hugging a teddy bear or a favorite doll for comfort. "With any loss, there's a grieving process, certain stages that must be worked through if there's to be healing. Anger is just one of those stages. It's perfectly normal."

"I didn't mean the kid. I was talking about you. It must be hard for you, especially somebody so young."

She smiled at him gently, as if he'd said something ingenuous—sweet, but rather foolish. "I don't let myself get emotionally involved where my patients are concerned, Wood. If I did I wouldn't be much help to them, would I? It's the same as for a doctor or nurse. We can't afford to lose objectivity, for our own good as well as the patient's."

"So . . . you've never let a patient get to you?"

Her gaze was steady, clear and unflinching, the soft, smoky blue of midsummer skies. "That's right."

"Never? Not even once in a while?"

She let out a breath, but her smile didn't waver. "No. I simply don't allow it."

"Christine, you're a liar," said Wood softly. "A liar and a fraud."

Chapter 8

She didn't say anything at all for a moment. Then she stiffened and turned pale, and her eyes became slivers of blue ice. Wood could almost see puffs of frosty vapor come out of her mouth when she said, "I beg your pardon?"

"Come off it, Chris," he said harshly, and closed part of the distance between them. She didn't seem to react at all, just sat there like some kind of lovely frozen sculpture, which infuriated him more than he'd thought possible. "I know damn well you let patients get under your skin sometimes. Don't try to deny it, because I've seen you myself. Dammit, I've *seen* you."

At that her mask finally slipped. Not a lot, just enough so that he caught a glimpse of the inexplicable fear that appeared now and then in her eyes. "What...do you mean, you've seen me?"

"Just now, right after that kid—what'd you say his name was, Kevin?—left. I was coming by the window and I saw you, sitting right *there*. Right where you are now. And don't try to tell me you weren't upset, lady, because you damn sure were."

She jerked her eyes away from him and he could see her body slump. She hugged the clipboard closer, while just above it her throat moved convulsively once, twice... and again.

"Come on, it's no big deal," he said, more gently now, even trying to joke about it a little. "I sure as hell didn't mean to spy on you. Hey, you've caught me in a private moment a time or two. I guess you could say we're even, right? Anyway, I'm not planning on giving away your secret, so why don't you just come clean with me? Might help—you never know."

He wasn't sure what he expected from her; if she hadn't responded at all he'd have been disappointed, of course, but not surprised. As it was, when she finally drew a long, uneven breath and set the clipboard aside he felt a sense of pure elation, as if he'd won a major victory.

"It's just Kevin," she said on the exhalation. A smile flickered and went out as she added in wry understatement, "He's been . . . a tough one."

Wood planted his elbows on the arms of his chair, laced his fingers across his middle and leaned forward, the way Grady had done with him a little while before. "Tell me about him."

Another breath, another exhalation. "Oh, it was such a stupid, unnecessary tragedy. One of those things that just makes you sick and furious inside, you know? One night a bunch of kids—Kevin's older brother Matthew and a couple of his friends—decided to go joyriding in Kevin's dad's pickup truck. They'd been drinking—Kevin's parents were out of town—and decided it would be great fun to go cut hogs on the front lawn of the junior high school. They were going to make Kevin stay home—he's only twelve—but he threw a fit about being left behind, so they finally agreed to let him and the family dog ride in the back of the truck."

Wood said, "Oh sh—" and leaned back in his chair. He could see what was coming.

Chris nodded in mute confirmation. "Matthew was driving. He lost control of the pickup and flipped it. Kevin and the dog were thrown out. The dog's fine. Kevin's spine was fractured."

"The other boys?"

"They weren't badly hurt, but the family's been just about destroyed by what happened. And Kevin . . . I think the hardest part of it for him is that he can't find anyone else to blame for what happened to him. He'd like to blame his brother, but he knows he's the one who begged to go along. He can't handle the fact that in a way he did this to himself." Chris shook her head and smiled wryly, still not looking directly at Wood.

"I think kids have a lot harder time than older people when it comes to accepting the fact that they're not perfect. They haven't made enough mistakes yet."

Wood was scowling; he knew now what she'd meant by "sick and furious inside." "So," he said gruffly, "the kid's paralyzed?"

Chris shrugged. "For now he is. From the waist down."

"For now? Then it's not permanent?"

"There's just no way of knowing. There's always a chance— the spine wasn't severed. The damage was pretty extensive, but . . . miracles have happened." She took in another breath, as if she was trying to ease a heavy load. "I just wish . . ."

"What?"

"Oh . . ." She said it with a small gesture of frustration, a flash of the anger he'd seen before. "I wish I could get Kevin to stop feeling sorry for himself and start *fighting*, that's all. In this business, if miracles do happen it's not because somebody was lying around wishing for one. They happen because someone puts all his will and determination and hard work and effort into *making* it happen. Kevin's not doing that. I think he's given up. And I can't . . . reach him. I've tried everything. I can't . . ." She caught a quick breath that sounded very much like a sob.

Wood remembered that one brief impression he'd had, of a whip-thin body bowed with tension, and eyes flashing fire. The kid had the strength, all right—all he had to do was find the will.

"Hey," he said softly. He reached for Chris's hand, impulsively raised and kissed it, then let it go before she had time to react. "You'll find a way. Don't give up. My money's on you."

She gave a strange little hiccup of laughter, one he'd never heard from her before, and gulped, "Thanks."

"Any time."

Her eyes found his as her voice dropped both in register and volume, almost to a whisper. "No, I mean . . . thank you. Really."

"I mean it, too," said Wood. "Any time."

There was a long silence during which the air in the little office seemed to become warmer and even more humid. Chris's face no longer appeared the least bit frozen; her cheeks were a soft petal pink, and seemed almost to glow, as if lit from inside. Wisps of silvery hair floated free around the perfect oval of her face and clung damply to her neck. Her skin looked as if it would be moist and velvety to the touch. In fact, Wood found himself thinking how very much he'd like to touch it. Thinking, too, with a mild sense of shock, that he'd certainly have done just that if he'd been able to reach her.

Small gusts of anger and frustration drifted through him, briefly ruffling his emotions like a breeze across a quiet pond. Following that was an equally gentle impulse to chide himself with laughter; he was used to looking down at beautiful women, not up. Evidently he was going to have to get used to operating for a while from a height approximately two feet shorter than his normal six feet plus.

She looked away from him suddenly, breaking what had become a curiously tense mood. Almost, he thought, of a kind of…expectation. She opened her mouth as if she was about to say something, but he beat her to it.

With a soft cough, he said, "Well, I guess I'd better get back upstairs before the warden puts out an APB."

"Warden?" She said it straight-faced, smiling with her eyes. "You wouldn't be referring to Nurse Florence, by any chance?"

"Good ol' Nurse Florence…" Wood drawled, then paused in the process of turning his chair toward the door to inquire of no one in particular, "Why in the world do you suppose somebody like that decided to become a nurse? Don't think maybe she got carried away by the name, do you? Thought she was—"

"Florence Nightingale?" Chris chimed in, her laughter blending with his chuckle. "Oh my, I never made that connection. Do you suppose that's it?" She followed him through the door, then strolled along beside him in a companionable sort of way, her clipboard tucked under one arm. When they reached the elevators, she leaned forward to push the Up button, getting to it just ahead of him, then glanced at him and said casually, "I spoke to your doctor this morning."

"Yeah?" said Wood, just as casual as she was. "What'd he have to say?"

"He says he's about ready to release you from the hospital, provided you have someone to stay with you. Did he tell you?"

"Yeah, he told me."

"Well, I know how glad you must be to finally be getting out of here." There was a pause, and then she asked even more offhandedly, "Have you made your arrangements?"

The elevator arrived, taking its sweet time about it, the way hospital elevators do. Wood waited for the doors to open and wheeled himself aboard before he shrugged and answered, "I'm working on it. Problem is, I don't exactly know where to begin. I have to find a place first. That's a little hard to do from in here."

"I thought you might be going to your sister's."

Wood glanced at her, wondering about the odd note that had crept into her voice, something just a little jarring, like one slightly out-of-tune guitar string.

"Lucy's? Nah—it's too far out of town, for one thing. I'd have to make other arrangements for my physical therapy." He grinned at her, wondering how far the new ease in their relationship extended, and whether he'd be a fool to test it so soon. He decided to risk it. "And if you want to know the truth, I'd really hate like hell to do that. I don't want to lose you, Coach."

Then he coughed and hurried on so she wouldn't be left searching for a reply to that. "Plus it's an old farmhouse—not exactly what they call 'handicapped accessible,' if you know what I mean. I figured I'd just get some little place here, close by. Finding somebody to stay with me—now that's another problem."

"Not really." The elevator had arrived at the third floor. Chris held the Open Door button while he exited, then went on holding it, staying where she was and speaking to his back. He could hear an odd breathlessness in her voice. "Your insurance will most likely pay for home care in a situation like this. I...might be able to look into it for you, if you'd like."

He didn't turn around, afraid of what she might read in his smile. "Yeah, sure, that'd be great. Thanks." He gave his wheels a push, then stopped, turned his chair halfway around and looked back at her. "You're not getting off here?"

She shrugged, smiling ruefully and, he'd have sworn, with a hint of regret. "I want to go see if Kevin's okay." She let go of the Open Door button and pointed toward the ceiling. "Fifth floor. Pediatrics."

"Oh—sure. Right. Well..." The doors began to close. "Guess I'll see you tomorrow, then."

"Yes. See you..." She waved and stepped back. Just before the crack closed completely, Wood saw her raise both hands and carefully smooth those whimsical, curiously endearing wisps of hair.

"Tomorrow," murmured Wood, smiling now without restraint. He didn't feel at all depressed, not anymore. He wanted to dance, kick up his heels, leap for joy. Until he remembered that tomorrow was Saturday.

When Chris got home that evening she found the hallway outside her apartment half-filled with packing boxes, and the door across from hers standing wide open. Instead of unlocking her own door right away, she went over to the open doorway, a brace of plastic grocery bags dangling from one hand and her keys in the other, and called tentatively through it, "Hello? Anybody here?"

A thin, pretty young woman with red hair cut spiky-short like a boy's emerged from one of the back rooms, smearing black newsprint smudges from her hands onto her face and the front of her already-dirty T-shirt. "Yes? Can I—oh, hi."

"I'm Chris—your neighbor from across the hall? We've met a couple of times...."

"Yeah, I know. I'm Debbie. Seems like you just got here, and now we're moving. Sorry I didn't have a chance to get to know you better."

"I'm sorry, too," said Chris. "Where are you moving to?"

"Indianapolis. Jerry got transferred. He's happy about it—he's originally from Fort Wayne. Far as I'm concerned, moving is the *pits*, no matter how you slice it."

"Yeah, I know what you mean," said Chris. She did, too; she'd done more than her share of it the last couple of years. "Well, I won't keep you. I know you have a million things to do. Listen, if you need anything, just holler, okay? And...good luck in Indianapolis."

"Yeah, thanks...."

Chris left Debbie sitting on a box dejectedly surveying the wreckage of her apartment, returned to her own and hurriedly unlocked it. Bypassing the blinking message machine and her mail, she made a beeline for the kitchen and dumped the grocery bags onto the counter. The few things that couldn't wait she shoved into the fridge's small freezing compartment. Then she snatched up her purse and keys and headed back out again, carefully locking the door behind her.

The manager's apartment and office were in another building in the complex, on the opposite side of a landscaped parking area. As Chris was coming out of her building, she saw a man just getting into a silver gray van parked in front of the manager's office. It was dark, and she caught only a quick glimpse of him, but it was enough to jolt her heart right out of her chest and make her shrink back into the shadows behind some evergreen shrubbery until the van had backed around, bumped out of the parking lot and sped away down the street.

She waited until the taillights had winked out around the corner, then crossed to the office on unsteady legs and rapped sharply on the door.

"Hi, I'm sorry to bother you so late," she said to the man who answered, trying to keep her teeth from chattering.

"No bother—come on in." The manager of the complex was a tall, very thin man with thick salt-and-pepper hair and a bushy mustache, who almost always wore argyle sweater vests over plaid shirts. A nice man, though. So was his wife, who was as round as her husband was lean and who Chris happened to know worked at the hospital in the food-service department. Their name was Spickler, but in her mind Chris always called them The Sprats.

"I'm Chris," she said. "In B-432? I just got home, and I see that the apartment across from mine is coming available. You d-didn't happen to rent it to that man who just left, did you?"

"No...no, he took an application, but like I told him, it won't be ready to let for another week or two yet. I was planning on getting the painters in there first. The Briskies are paid up to the fifth."

"Oh..." Chris gulped, relief making her light-headed. "Oh, thank goodness. Because I have a big, big favor to ask...."

Wood's Saturday was looming ahead of him even more empty and depressing than usual. After breakfast he struggled through the tedious process of bathing. He briefly considered shaving off his beard, more to have something to do than anything else, but decided against it. Come summer, he promised himself. When it gets hot. *Then* I'll shave it all off. He did trim it up a bit, though, shaping it around his mouth so he didn't look quite so much like a hard rock miner come to town looking for a good time.

After that he worked out with the barbells Chris had given him until he actually worked up a good sweat. That felt good, but then of course he needed to bathe again, which always left him feeling unpleasantly damp and not really clean. He decided showers were one of the things he missed most. That and fresh air, being outdoors. Oh yeah—and cold beer. And silence. Hospitals, he'd discovered, were very noisy places.

By midmorning he was so restless he thought he'd go nuts if he didn't get out of his room for a while. Damn, he missed Grady. Even a new roommate would have been a welcome diversion and worth the loss of privacy, but the bed next to him remained unoccupied. Sal, the orderly, had the day off. There was nothing on television but cartoons.

It was the cartoons that made him think of Kevin. Kids, cartoons—they just seemed to go together. The next thing he knew he was in the elevator punching the button for the fifth floor and hoping he wasn't butting in and about to make a bad situation worse.

He found Kevin in what seemed to be some sort of playroom, watching the hapless coyote blow himself to kingdom come in futile pursuit of the roadrunner. The boy wasn't alone; he was sharing the room and the TV set with several other kids, mostly younger. The little ones were giggling over the cartoon; Kevin was looking surly and bored. He glanced up when Wood rolled into the room, his eyes flickering a little with uncertainty, but immediately went back to watching the mayhem on the television screen with studied disdain, as if determined not to display anything that might be taken for interest or curiosity.

Wood parked his chair next to Kevin's and gave him his Southern greeting. "Hey. How ya doin'?"

The boy flicked his eyes in Wood's direction and mumbled, "I'm okay," as if he didn't really care whether he was or not and considered it a waste of his time to answer such dumb questions.

Wood stuck out his hand, which surprised the kid so much he took it. "My name's Wood Brown. Saw you yesterday down at the pool. You probably don't remember—you were in a pretty big hurry."

This time Kevin didn't even bother to reply. He shrugged and went back to the TV. Wood watched with him for a few minutes, then said, "Hey, I guess we've got the same physical therapist."

The kid kept his eyes glued to the screen while he muttered what sounded like it might have been, "Big deal." Or something slightly more colorful.

"Yeah," said Wood, "I guess she can be pretty rough."

Kevin lifted a shoulder. "She's okay."

Wood gave up and watched the cartoon in silence until it ended and a commercial for a multicolored breakfast cereal came on. Then he abruptly backed his chair around, jerked his head toward the door and said, "Hey—whadaya say we blow this place? Come on, I'll buy you a drink."

Again, that seemed to surprise the kid enough to get a response out of him. After a moment's hesitation, he actually followed Wood out into the corridor, although slowly, with the wheelchair equivalent of dragging his feet. But as they were dawdling along toward the nurse's station, curiosity finally got the better of him. He pulled his chair up even with Wood's and inquired grudgingly, "Okay, so where we going?"

Wood glanced over at him and shrugged. "We could go to the cafeteria. Or we could go down to my floor, I guess. There's a waiting room there for the ORs—it's got some pretty good vending machines."

Kevin snorted. "Big deal. Granola bars and fruit juice."

Wood chuckled. "Probably. So what about it—you on?"

Kevin hesitated, then finally shrugged and said in a careless tone, "Sure, why not?"

"Great," said Wood. "Why don't you wait here for a minute while I go talk to the warden about getting you sprung."

When he returned, equipped with the head nurse's permission and blessing—evidently Chris wasn't the only one who found Kevin a pain both in the heart and in the rear—he found the kid maneuvering his chair in tight figure-eights with the total absorption of the hopelessly bored.

Wood rolled up to him and said, "Not bad. You learn to do wheelies yet?"

Kevin gave him a scornful look, muttered, "'S easy, man," and proceeded to demonstrate his skill.

Wood watched in admiration, then shook his head and held up a hand. "Don't look at me. I'm still working on three-point turns."

"So," Kevin said as they were proceeding side by side down a long corridor on the way to the elevators, "what happened to you, anyway?" He had a deep voice for such a skinny kid. Kind of low and scratchy, as if he didn't use it much.

"Broke my legs," said Wood. "You?"

"Back." And then, after a moment's hesitation, he added, "Chris prob'ly told you I'm paralyzed."

"Yeah, she did. That's rough." Kevin shrugged. They pushed along in silence for a while, then Wood said, "I knew a guy once, had almost the same kind of injury you've got. Marine Corps buddy of mine."

"You were in the marines?"

Wood could feel the kid's interest perking up. He still kept it casual, though, just rolling along. "Yeah. Anyway, this guy got hurt during Desert Storm."

"You were in Desert Storm?"

Oh yes, he had him now. "Yeah. My friend—Dan's his name—my friend was in the Marine Corps Reserves. Before he got called up and sent to the Gulf, he was a baseball player— minor leagues. Pitcher. Played Triple A ball out in California. Had a real chance at the big leagues, too. Then he got hurt and everybody said he'd never walk again."

"Bummer," said Kevin.

"Yeah, well . . . ol' Dan just refused to believe 'em. He was bound and determined he was going to prove all those doctors and experts wrong. Swore up and down that someday he was going to walk back out onto a baseball diamond under his own power."

They'd reached the elevators. Wood pushed the Down button and placidly watched the indicator lights plot the slow progress of all three cars from floor to floor.

"So?" Kevin finally blurted, his voice cracking. "Did he?"

"Did he what?"

"Did he—your friend—ever walk again? Did he get to play baseball?"

Wood looked over at him in surprise. "You mean you never heard about it? Season opener last year at Dodger Stadium. In front of fifty thousand people. Ol' Dan walked from the dugout to the mound under his own steam and threw out the first pitch. Got a standing ovation."

"Yeah, but did he *play?*"

"Not that day," Wood admitted, "but hey, I wouldn't put anything past that guy." He shook his head as he wheeled himself onto the elevator. "Dan's got guts. And he never gives up. If anybody can do it, he will."

Kevin didn't say a word on the slow trip down to the third floor. Neither did Wood; he was looking up toward the ceiling, silently praying for forgiveness. He'd made it all up—actually, he'd borrowed the whole thing from the plot of a movie he'd seen on television last week. He just thanked God Kevin hadn't been watching the same channel.

After a stop at the nurse's station to say hello to Nurse Ida, who of course had to fuss over Kevin like an old mother hen, Wood took the kid on down to the OR waiting room to see what the vending machines had to offer.

They found the room occupied by a middle-aged couple, which, since it was a Saturday morning, seemed to indicate some sort of dire emergency. Wood didn't want to intrude, so he bought two bottles of apple juice and a bag of cheese-flavored popcorn for Kevin, who looked like he could use some fattening up, and a cup of coffee for himself. They left the couple to worry and grieve together in private.

"Which one's yours?" Kevin asked as they meandered along, sipping coffee, glugging down juice and companionably sharing popcorn.

"Right here," said Wood. "Want to come in for a minute?"

"Sure, why not?"

Wood held the door while Kevin rolled in ahead of him, then followed.

"You got your own room?"

"For the last couple weeks, yeah, so it seems. Used to have a roommate—great guy, name of Grady. Wish you could have met him. He's paralyzed, too. Not like you and Dan, though. He got shot—bullet severed his spine. No way *he's* ever going to walk again."

Kevin didn't reply to that. He was already wheeling himself over to Wood's bedside, surveying everything with a child's unabashed curiosity. He stopped suddenly and turned halfway around, and for the first time looked straight at Wood, his pale eyes deep in shadowed sockets a fleeting but jolting reminder of another pair that very same silvery blue. He made a motion with his head and in his cracked, rusty-hinge voice said, "That your guitar?"

* * *

For the second time Chris heard music as she approached the door to Room 312...the soft strumming of a guitar. Not "The Rose" this time, nor any other song, so far as she could tell. Just chords, halting and tentative. The door stood open, and through it she could hear voices as well, first a low, querying mumble, then Wood's clear reply:

"That's it—no, you gotta lift your wrist, stretch all the way over to the G string. *Now* you're getting it. Okay, now here's where your pick comes in. This is what you call an acoustical guitar—that means the only amplification comes from the box, this part right here. Your pick gets you a little more volume, plus it saves wear and tear on your fingers. Here, let me show you what I mean."

Chris stood as if she'd taken root in the doorway, utterly transfixed. *How is it, Wood Brown, that you just keep surprising me?* Such gentle surprises, like a doe crossing her path on a walk through the woods, or having a butterfly alight on her hand. Surprises that made her gasp softly and then smile. Surprises that lingered, making her feel blessed and warm. Is this, she wondered, what it feels like to be happy?

She had no idea how long she stood in that doorway or how long she might have remained there, watching the two heads bent together in total absorption, one glossy black, with hair that was long and slightly curling, the other red-gold, unruly as a bird's nest. Watching the two chairs parked at a slight angle, so that knees rather than wheels touched; two pairs of shoulders, one so bony and thin, the other broad and strong...two pairs of arms taking turns cradling the glossy, almost feminine body of the guitar.... Watching big hands—sure and confident hands wearing pink ribbons of healing scar tissue—guiding small hands still clumsy with a child's uncertainty.

I'll remember this, she thought. *Always.*

Chapter 9

"Chris—hey!"

The tableau came to life, the three participants in it moving almost simultaneously and with varying degrees of surprise and guilt. The two wheelchairs backed and pivoted as if part of a choreographed dance. Chris started and walked toward them, feeling a little self-conscious about how long she might have been observed standing dumbstruck in the doorway and how much her unguarded face had revealed.

"Hi, guys." She made the best of it, putting on her brightest and most-confident smile, smoothing all traces of emotional tumult from her voice. "Kevin, what a nice surprise. I didn't know you two had met one another."

Wood cleared his throat loudly and jumped in to rescue Kevin, who was scowling furiously and blushing to the roots of his hair. "Oh, yeah, well . . . we just sort of ran into each other awhile ago. Didn't have much else to do, so we thought we'd hang out for a bit. I was just showing Kev a few licks on the ol' guitar. He's pretty good, too. What about it, Kev, you want to try it again tomorrow?"

Kevin mumbled, "Yeah, I guess so, sure." He was already edging toward the door with his head down and his chin tucked into his chest, the back of his neck and ears glowing hot and pink. "Well, gotta go...see you around."

Chris touched his shoulder as he wheeled past her. "See you on Monday, right, Kevin? Downstairs, eleven o'clock?"

He paused and looked back over his shoulder, but his eyes slid past Chris, seeking someone else. She saw him hesitate, and then subtle but unmistakable changes come over his face. The almost imperceptible lifting of the chin. The slightest reshaping of the mouth into firmer lines. And something else...like some sort of light kindling behind those sullen blue eyes. Then his shoulders shifted and straightened, and when he spoke, even his voice seemed different. Older, somehow. More adult.

"Sure," he said. "Monday. I'll be there."

"What are you, a miracle worker?" Chris said lightly a few moments later. That was all she could allow herself, having managed to hold it back until she was sure the boy was out of earshot. Inside she was laughing out loud, running around in circles, jumping up and down and shouting, "Yippee!"

"Who, me?" asked Wood with a perfectly straight face. But his eyes were gleaming; she could tell he was pleased with himself.

"What did you do?" she demanded. "No one, either here or at home, has been able to get that boy to take an interest in anything since the accident. What did you say to him?"

Wood shrugged. "Actually, I didn't do anything. He saw the guitar and asked me about it, so I...one thing sort of led to another. No big deal."

"Well, it is a big deal." Chris had to fight to keep her voice even; she was riding perilously close to the edge. Looking for a way to distract herself, she casually picked up the guitar, which Wood had just placed on the bed, and pretended to examine it. It was the wrong thing to do. The polished box still held the heat from his body; even the strings seemed to vibrate with his life force. She set the guitar aside, glanced back at Wood and said quietly, "You may just have turned that child's life around, you know. I can't tell you how delighted I am."

"Yeah, you can. Try." Wood's voice was very soft, but his eyes had that black intensity she found so unnerving...like a physical touch.

In automatic response to it she folded her arms protectively across her body. "I...don't know what you mean."

He was leaning slightly toward her across his laced fingers, giving her his full attention. The faint smile on his lips did nothing to soften the jewellike brightness of his eyes. "Come on, Chris. Tell me how happy you are. Better yet, *show* me."

Tremors began to course through her body, undercurrents of a strange excitement. She fought to keep them out of her voice. "Look, Wood. I know it seems to bother you that I don't like showing emotion. I'm sorry, but that's just me. It's the way I am. Some people—"

"Hey—" He said it sharply, cutting off her words as ruthlessly as if he'd wielded an axe. "Don't give me that. I've seen the way you show emotion, remember?"

"That was..." She cried out before she could stop herself, then looked away and finished it silently: *Unfair... unfair!*

Instantly his voice gentled again. "It's okay, you know. I don't plan on telling a soul. Your secret's safe with me."

She swallowed twice but didn't say anything. After a moment she heard the almost soundless whisper of his chair, and felt the softest brush of fingertips across the back of her hand.

"Look, so the kid gets to you. Nothing wrong with a patient getting to you now and then. I bet even doctors and nurses have patients get under their skin sometimes, have things happen they can't let go of when they leave this place."

There was a pause. She felt his fingers curl around hers, turn her hand and gently enclose it. His voice deepened, until it, too, became almost a caress. "Most of them, though, have somebody waiting for them when they get home, somebody they can share the burden with. Tell me, Chris—who's there for you? When somebody's problem hitches a ride home with you, who do *you* have to help you unload?"

She looked up at the ceiling as if in profound exasperation, then drew a shuddering breath and closed her eyes. She felt his fingers working against the resistance in hers until they yielded and allowed themselves to be swallowed up in his hand.

"Hey," he urged softly, "come on...."

His words, his will, his compassion and gentleness pulled at her like magnets. Unable to resist him any longer, she finally turned her head toward him, but gave her eyes a surreptitious brush first, just to be safe.

"Yeah," he murmured, "that's better."

When she saw that he was smiling, she couldn't help herself—a little whimper of laughter bubbled up from the cauldron of emotions inside her and burst free. To her astonishment, it brought tears with it. She jerked her hand out of Wood's grasp and swiped at them, then stared at her fingers in dismay.

"That's good...crying's good," said Wood matter-of-factly. He leaned over to pluck a tissue from the box on his bedside table, handed it to her and said in a voice suddenly gone gruff, "Have one—on me."

"But I'm not crying," Chris hastened to explain as she dabbed at her eyes. "See? I only do this when I laugh."

And then he was laughing; they were both laughing—quiet, gentle laughter that had an oddly soothing, healing quality to it, like a spring bubbling up and spilling over onto parched soil. Chris could feel something inside her that had been barren and lifeless slowly uncurl and stretch tremulously toward the light.

She wiped her eyes once more, blew her nose and dropped the tissue into the wastebasket beside the bed, and suddenly she didn't seem to know what to do with her eyes. She was aware, too aware, of Wood's eyes on her, and had to resist a compulsion to fiddle self-consciously with her hair.

Once again she picked up the guitar, held it against her breasts while she stroked her thumb across the strings. The soft, melodious thrumming seemed to wash over her like balm, and suddenly she was hearing again the haunting words she'd heard Wood singing that day, the words to the song he'd called "The Rose." *Love...* Was it possible? Did she even dare believe that it could still happen, even for her?

Oh God, she thought, I'm *frightened.* What an unexpectedly painful thing it was, this reawakening of hope.

In the awkward silence, Wood cleared his throat and said, "So, what brings you here on a Saturday, anyway?"

Chris drew a shaky breath and once more set the guitar aside. "Actually," she said, straightening up with a smile and using both hands to smooth back her hair, "I came to see if you feel up to a field trip."

At that his head came up like a wolf catching a scent on the wind. "Come again? You mean a trip—as in *out?* Outa *here?* What'd you have in mind?"

"It's...a surprise."

"Hell, who cares? I'll go anywhere as long as it's away from this place." He was already putting the guitar away in its case, but paused and looked up long enough to fire a volley of questions at her. "When do we leave? Is this officially sanctioned by the warden, or are we planning a jailbreak? Do I need clothes, or are they going to let me go in my jammies?"

"We leave right now, I've already cleared it with your doctor," Chris told him, laughing, "and you don't need clothes...." Her voice faltered and she suddenly had to look away. His thin, ravaged face had lit up, softened, become younger, transforming into the face of the golden boy she'd been so in awe of all those years ago in high school.

She cleared her throat and went on, talking in breathless bursts as she bustled about getting him ready to go. "Just tuck your blanket in good around your legs ... like that. Your slippers are fine. I have some warm things over at the clinic you can wear—we'll take the tunnel over there, it's heated pretty well. Okay, ready to go?"

"You bet. Lead on, move 'em out!" he shouted, making a sweeping gesture with his arm. His grin would have illuminated a stadium.

And at that moment Chris knew she'd gladly spend the rest of her life doing whatever it took to make him so happy.

"You've trimmed your beard," she murmured distractedly, saying the first thing that came into her mind. The revelation had unsettled her.

"Yeah ... about time, don't you think?" His grin turned piratical; his voice became a throaty growl that unnerved her even more. Something about it—the grin, the voice, the gleam in his eyes—made Chris aware, all at once, of the way her body moved as she walked ahead of him to the elevators.

Funny, always before when a man looked at her that way she'd felt stripped and violated...awkward, self-conscious and ashamed. She'd wanted nothing so much as to cringe into a dark corner and hide. Now, although she was still painfully conscious of the way she looked, it was in a very different way. For the first time in a very long time she didn't want to avoid a man's admiring glances. She actually wanted one—*this* one— to think she looked nice. For him she wanted to look...pretty.

Oh, but her clothes were so baggy and her hairstyle so dowdy, and she wasn't wearing any makeup at all! And he was ... Wood Brown, the most popular boy in school, who could have had any woman he chose. What must he think of her?

Did he find her attractive? she wondered. Sometimes he seemed to, but she kept remembering the day he'd interviewed her back in high school and the way he'd dazzled her with his all-inclusive smile. Maybe it was just part of his natural charm.

Oh, thought Chris, what a terrible thing it is, this adolescent mixture of excitement and anxiety! One minute euphoria, the next, self-doubt. What in the world is the matter with me?

What the hell's the matter with me? thought Wood. He felt as excited as a little kid at the thought of going outside again. Actually, euphoric described his mood pretty well. So did giddy.

Worse, he kept having this urge to pull Chris down across his lap, lay her back on his arm and kiss the living daylights out of her. He might have given in to the impulse, too, except he didn't know if his chair would stand up to such treatment—or his casts, either, for that matter. They seemed pretty strong, but since it wasn't exactly something he could ask Chris about, there was probably no way to tell for certain except to put them to the test. He vowed that someday soon he was going to do just that, but not now. Now yet. Too soon. *Patience.*

All the way down in the elevator they played a flirtatious game of avoiding eye contact. He would feel her eyes on him, but when he looked at her she'd be studiously gazing off somewhere else. So he'd stare at her, timing it so that he looked away just a split second before she finally had to risk stealing another glance at him. Suppressed laughter, hidden smiles, excitement and tension vibrating through both their bodies and filling the very air around them...God, it was fun. Sexual awareness, pure and simple.

Chris seemed to lose her smile while they were going through the tunnel, though, and while tension remained with them, he thought that for her it seemed a different kind now—sort of watchful and uneasy. She kept looking nervously around her in a way that made Wood wonder whether she was looking for something or was maybe just a touch claustrophobic.

And then the elevator carrying them back up to street level bumped to a halt and the doors opened, and the brilliance of sunshine and the biting cold of an Iowa wind hit him full in the face. The uneasy moments in the tunnel were forgotten.

"Yee-ow!" he shouted, and laughed out loud for the sheer joy of it. And then he pushed off with a mighty shove of his wheels, calling, "Hey, Coach—race you!"

She managed to arrive at the door of the rehab center two steps ahead of him. Both of them were breathless with cold and laughter. Chris's cheeks were pink and her eyes sparkling like sunlit water, and all Wood could think about once again was how much he wanted to tumble her into his lap and kiss her. Her nose was red tipped; it would feel cold as snowflakes against his cheek. Her lips would be cold, too, before he warmed them with his own. Oh, to feel them melt... soften... open under his; to taste her, feel her tongue quivering, tangling with his...

His stomach churned audibly.

"Wow," said Chris as she held the door open for him, "what was that? Sounds like I'd better feed you before we do anything else. What would you like to have?"

Oh boy. Since he couldn't very well tell her, he said the next best thing he could think of, almost choking on his swallowed laughter. "Cheeseburger, large order of fries and a tall, cold beer."

She groaned, then laughed. How it pleased him to see her laugh like that, as if she truly felt it, with warmth that seemed to bubble up from deep inside her. Right now, in fact, she seemed to glow with an inner warmth and all the colors of spring—the pale gold of sunshine, the pink and white of dogwood and apple blossoms, the clear, sapphire blue of the sky.

"Didn't know you were open on Saturday," he commented as he rolled through the empty waiting room. Beyond it, through double glass doors, he could see people working out on weight machines, doing stretching exercises on padded tables. God, how he envied them.

"Oh sure—some of our patients aren't free any other time," Chris explained. "Come on, I'll introduce you to some of the other therapists while we're here."

So Wood met Brad and Megan and Chris's boss, John, and a few others whose names slipped out of his head as soon as she said them. His mind wasn't concentrating on polite small talk; all he could think about was getting out of there, being with Chris. Making her laugh, touching her... holding her. He wanted to stand up on his own two legs, take her in his arms and kiss her until *she* couldn't stand up any longer, then lay her down and make slow, sweet love to her all the long afternoon. That was what he wanted. The fact that he wasn't going to be able to do anything about making it happen for a long, long time was threatening to drive him crazy.

Patience, he told himself, mentally grinding his teeth. He was a United States Marine, by God. He could handle this. After all, self-discipline was a way of life in the Corps.

Sure. It took all the discipline he'd learned in the last twelve years and more to resist the urge he kept having to reach for her as she helped him into a parka in the privacy of her office. He kept having to remind himself that just because she'd had a breakthrough of some sort on the emotional front, in no way, shape or form did it mean she was ready for anything physical.

When she had him bundled up to her satisfaction, Chris led him sedately back through the main exercise room and lobby and out the front door to where she had her car parked and ready in a handicapped zone. Getting from his chair into the passenger's seat was a process Wood hadn't learned yet, and it turned out to be a bit more painful than he'd expected. At least it had a quieting effect on his rampaging libido. As he'd already discovered, it's hard to keep sex on your mind when you're fighting the urge to throw up.

"Are you all right?" Chris asked when they were out of the parking lot and heading toward downtown.

"Better now," he said, breathing through his nose. He smiled crookedly. "That was just a little more acrobatics than I'm used to."

"It gets easier with practice," she assured him.

"When are you going to let me in on where it is we're going?" She'd just turned off the main street, heading away from the river. This was a newer part of the city, built since the last time he'd been here.

Chris smiled. "No secret. First, I promised you lunch, right? How's this?" She made a quick right, following arrows into the drive-through lane of a familiar fast-food place.

"Great," said Wood, breathing deeply, drinking in the mouth-watering odor of charbroiling meat. He'd forgotten how good the smell of cooking could be.

"Let's see. . . ." Chris was studying the menu board. "That was a cheeseburger and fries, right? Sorry, they don't have beer here. Should I order you a Coke instead?"

"Better make it milk." He'd already learned to stay away from coffee and soft drinks as much as possible while he was trapped in the wheelchair. "And make that a double cheese-burger while you're at it—since you're paying."

He could see that she was smiling as she cranked down the window a crack and hollered their order through it. From his angle he could also see the hint of a dimple he hadn't noticed before. And a long ribbon of hair the color of vanilla ice cream that had worked its way out of its knot and was just slipping coyly down inside her coat collar.

Yielding to temptation, he reached out, got a finger under the strand and lifted it free. And instantly her hand was there to reclaim it, poking and tucking, patting and smoothing, setting it to rights again while a rosy pink wash crept slowly up her neck and into her ears. Something about that combination, perhaps—the pure, elegant lines of her neck and that exposed and vulnerable ear—made Wood's throat ache unexpectedly.

"So that's it—that's the field trip?" he said when they'd picked up their order at the window and were heading back the way they'd come. But he was teasing her; he could tell by the sparkle in her eyes that the day was just getting started. "Well," he said with a sigh, "it may have been short, but I gotta tell you, Coach, it was well worth it just for these." He stole one french fry from the bag on his lap and ate it with his eyes closed, savoring the greasy, salty taste of it. Pure heaven.

"Go ahead, eat if you're hungry," Chris invited, her voice soft and smiling.

"What about you?" He'd noticed that she'd ordered a salad for herself, one with lots of vegetables, a few cheese crumbles, some hard-boiled egg slices and not much else. He added with sly innocence, "Want me to feed you while you drive?"

Again he caught a glimpse of the dimple, and was reminded fleetingly and unexpectedly of his sister, Lucy.

"Oh, that's okay, I'll eat when I get..." She caught her lip between her teeth, then finished "...when we get there. It's not far. We're almost there."

She was right. A few blocks past the medical-center complex she made a right turn, went four or five blocks, then left, and right again into the newly landscaped grounds of a modern apartment complex. When she bypassed the parking lot and used a plastic card with a magnetic strip to gain access to a garage underneath one of the buildings, the light dawned.

"You live here." It wasn't a question.

"Yes." Her expression had suddenly become enigmatic.

So, thought Wood. One mystery solved and another one hatching. Chris had brought him to her place, which was an amazing development in itself. But why?

There wasn't much time to wonder. He had to swallow his questions along with the last bite of his cheeseburger and concentrate instead on getting from the car to his chair without passing out.

A small, rather jerky elevator carried them up to the third floor. Wood followed Chris down a carpeted hallway—which took a little more effort than he was used to—and waited while she used her key to unlock a door. She pushed it open, then stood back to allow him to go in first.

"Well," she said after a long moment of silence, "what do you think?" Her voice was breathy with suppressed emotions, the nature of which Wood couldn't begin to guess.

Without turning, he cleared his throat and ventured cautiously, "To tell you the truth, I expected more . . . furniture."

She surprised him with a ripple of delighted laughter, reminding him of nothing so much as a child holding a secret surprise behind her back.

She shook her head and pulled in a quick breath, talking rapidly as she went to join him. "My apartment is across the hall. This one's yours. If you want it. The people just moved out yesterday. I gave the manager a deposit and asked him to hold it until I could arrange for you to come and look at it. But there's no obligation. If you don't like it, or you think you'd rather not . . . I knew how much you wanted to get out of the hospital, so when I found out this was available, I just thought... I know there's a problem with furniture, but I think the manager would be willing to rent it partly furnished—you know, just with the bare essentials. And, um, I can always find some extra towels and dishes and things like that that you could use. It is wheelchair accessible. Plus it would take care of the problem of getting you to the rehab center for your therapy—"

"Whoa!" said Wood, laughing and holding up both hands in self-defense. He hadn't thought anybody besides his sister could talk that fast. "Hold on a minute. What about the doctor? Didn't he say I'd have to have some kind of live-in help?"

He'd begun rolling himself around the apartment, peering into doorways. "This place seems kind of small for two people."

Chris followed him, holding her arms tightly across her waist in a futile effort to quiet the turmoil inside. What had possessed her to do this?

She caught another quick breath and said, "I've already spoken to your doctor. I explained that I'd be close by in case you needed help or anything. Also that I'd, um, be willing to provide you with transportation to and from the med center for therapy and checkups."

"And...?" He'd stopped in the middle of the only bedroom and had swiveled his chair so he was facing her. His eyes had that black intensity that always disturbed her so.

She shrugged, evading his gaze. "He seemed to think it would work out okay. He said it was pretty much up to you— whether you felt ready to take the step." How professional she sounded, how calm and objective. Inside she was vibrating with tension.

"Ready..." He rolled a few turns toward the window, then back again, pulled in a breath and expelled it in uneasy laughter. "Yeah, I guess it is a big step. I didn't expect it to be so...I don't know. Scary, in a way." He looked awkward saying the words, as if they embarrassed him.

Chris cleared her throat. "It's natural. Really. Everybody goes through it. When you're that sick and helpless, when you're in the hospital, everything—I mean *everything*—is done for you. It's like being an infant again, in a way." She smiled reassuringly, then let the smile become a teasing grin. "Just wait until you try to stand up for the first time."

He tried to smile, too, but it was lopsided. "Yeah, well, it's going to be good to feel like an adult again, I can sure tell you that." Then the smile faded completely and his eyes took on that black-onyx shine. "Look, this was nice of you. I can't tell you how much I appreciate it. This place—it's great, it's... perfect. You said you put down a deposit? How much do I owe you?"

He looked away distractedly. Chris could almost see wheels beginning to turn behind those brilliant eyes, wheels that had been idle for months and were probably rusty.

"Geez . . . I guess I'll need to transfer some money, won't I? Open up a checking account. I'm going to need some clothes. I have a bunch of stuff at my sister's place . . . I'll have to see if she can bring me some things. You said the manager's willing to rent me some furniture? And there're the utilities, phone...." He stopped and ran a hand over his hair, looking a little overwhelmed, then spun toward her. "Hey, when can I move in? Did the manager say—"

"Whoa," said Chris, imitating the defensive gesture and laughing tone he'd used with her. "Never mind all that right now. It's a big step, remember? So, one step at a time. First thing I'll do is go tell Mr. Spickler you want it—or *you* can, I guess. As for moving in, I imagine as soon as I finish painting—"

"What? Hang on a minute." Now it was his turn to hold up his hand. His head was tilted to a quizzical angle. "*You* finish painting? Why you? Paint this apartment, you mean? How come?"

"Oh, well..." Damn. She hadn't meant for him to know about her deal with the manager. "I knew how eager you were to get out of that hospital, so I . . . told Mr. Spickler I'd do it— just to speed things up. It shouldn't take long," she said desperately, trying her best to shrug it off, make it seem like a casual thing. "Maybe a week—"

"Less, if I help," said Wood firmly, and shook his head to forestall the protest he could see she was about to make. "Look, there's nothing wrong with my arms. You give me a roller and I'll paint the bottom half while you paint the top. Otherwise the deal's off. Got it?"

"Got it," Chris gasped, catching her lip between her teeth to hold back what would almost certainly have been a nervous giggle. What was the matter with her? Her heart was going like a trip-hammer. She felt as excited and happy as a child looking forward to a day at the circus. All because of the prospect of spending a day painting an apartment with Wood Brown. Oh, my goodness, she thought, and drew in a calming breath. "Then it's settled. I guess we just need to go talk to the manager."

Wood suddenly cocked his head, listening. "Isn't that your phone?"

Oh, God. Her heart lurched, knocking painfully against her ribs. Was it only yesterday that the calls had begun again? The respite had been so brief... She leveled her voice and smoothed out her breathing and said, "It sounds like it."

"You need to answer it? I can wait."

She shook her head. "The answering machine will pick it up." She had a machine to monitor all her calls now—another of the police officer's suggestions. She'd begun to keep a log, too. But whether the call was innocent or not, it had effectively ruined her mood and taken all the enjoyment out of the day.

She went to pick up her coat, purse and the bag containing her salad, which she'd left near the door, keeping her face turned away from Wood's searching eyes. In a calm, remote voice, she said, "I'd like to get things settled with the manager about the apartment, and then I really do need to get you back to the hospital before Nurse Ida sends out a search party."

"Yeah," said Wood dryly, "I keep forgetting I'm just out on furlough." He nodded at her salad bag. "Aren't you going to eat that? Or at least put it away in the fridge?"

She looked at the bag, opened her mouth and closed it again, then looked back at Wood, utterly stymied by the dilemma. Eat it or put it away? But if she did either of those things, it would seem strange for her not to invite Wood into her apartment for a few minutes...wouldn't it? What if he heard the message being left on her machine? Even if she stalled until this call had been completed, what if another came while he was there?

"What are you going to do?" said Wood. "Carry it with you?"

She turned away quickly, breathless with guilt. "No, I'll just...I'll go put it away. I'll just be a minute...." She unlocked her door with unsteady hands, listening tensely for the sound of a voice. Relief flooded her; the message machine was silent. She pushed the door open and gave Wood a smile over her shoulder, a smile she knew must look as false and ghastly as it felt. "I'm sorry—the place is such a mess. Boxes and...things. I just moved in myself not too long ago. I hope you don't mind if I don't ask you in. I don't know if the chair..."

"It's okay," said Wood softly, "I'll wait out here. Go on—put your salad away."

Chris flashed him a grateful smile and went, but she could feel his eyes following her, thoughtful eyes full of questions.

This is what it's going to be like, she thought, shivering inside with a strange combination of excitement and dread. It would be good having Wood...having a friend so near. But in some ways it was going to make things harder, too. Harder for her to keep her secrets.

Chapter 10

It was official. As of five o'clock on Friday Wood was a free man. He'd been disappointed at not being able to move into the apartment across from Chris's right away, but the manager had explained that the previous tenants' occupancy didn't officially expire until Thursday, and that in any case he'd need a little time to have the place cleaned and move in some furniture. Wood had no choice but to accept the delay, and spent the time as productively as he could, getting his financial matters in order and otherwise making preparations for reentering his life.

And when he wasn't writing letters or making phone calls, he was pumping iron like crazy. Chris had been right about one thing—without the use of his legs he found that he needed his upper-body strength as never before. He hadn't realized how much.

Something else he hadn't realized was how hard it would be to leave the hospital. Well, not the hospital so much as the people he'd come to know there—the doctors, nurses, volunteers and orderlies, people like Sal, Jackie Sung and Nurse Ida. Saying goodbye was hard, even wrenching in a couple of instances.

Kevin, for one. Wood spent as much time as he could manage with the kid that last week, working with him, helping him with his guitar. His parents had bought him one of his own, and he was picking it up fast. He really did seem to have a knack for it and a real ear for music. Wood promised to come back as often as he could to continue the lessons, but he could see by the set of the kid's chin that he didn't believe him.

Nurse Ida also took his departure hard. On Friday she brought him a big chicken-and-dumpling casserole as a going-away gift and even shed a few tears over it. Jackie Sung gave him a potted plant for his apartment and a paper bird that was supposed to be good luck. Even good old Florence Nightingale loosened up long enough to pat him on the shoulder and tell him in a rusty-sounding voice that she was going to miss having him around aggravating her to death. She reminded Wood a lot of his master sergeant in the Marine Corps.

In fact, there was much about leaving the hospital that reminded him of the way he'd felt driving away from a military base for the last time. Leaving his buddies behind, knowing that while at the time he'd meant every word he'd said about keeping in touch, he probably wouldn't. Leaving behind a familiar world, a life of structure and discipline and routine, knowing his life was about to change irrevocably for good or ill.

But by five o'clock on Friday, all that was behind him. The paperwork had been done—and as far as he was concerned, hospitals had the military beat all to hell when it came to red tape. He'd managed to get himself dressed in the sweats Chris had brought for him. At five forty-five he was sitting in the OR waiting room with his jacket across his lap and his guitar and overnight bag and Nurse Ida's casserole on the floor beside his chair, practicing patience while he waited for Chris to come for him.

When he heard her out in the hallway talking to one of the nurses, his heart gave a kind of leap. Joy, expectation, plain old sexual response—whatever it was, he was no longer surprised by it. He'd pretty much come to expect it and to accept it as the natural order of things for him now, like the little lift he always felt inside when he watched the sun come up, or the way his throat tightened when he heard an old, familiar hymn.

He *was* surprised, though, when she walked into the waiting room, because he could tell right away that something about her was very different. It wasn't just the red scarf she'd tied around her head, folded three-cornered like a kerchief and tied under her hair at the back of her neck, although that was the first thing he noticed. It was hard to miss when he was used to seeing her only in neutrals and misty pastels. Nor was it the fact that she was wearing jeans and a windbreaker instead of her usual tunics, loose-fitting slacks and that all-enveloping parka. It was more than that—something about her attitude, the way she carried herself . . .

"Hi," she said, smiling as usual, but with a kind of suppressed excitement and twitchy self-consciousness that were completely new to her. "All ready to go? Is this all you have?"

"Yeah," said Wood, "isn't it enough? Oh—and that plant over there . . ."

That was when it hit him, when she turned to see what plant he was talking about. "My God," he whispered. She looked back at him, her lips still smiling, but poised now on the brink of a question. "Come here a minute," he croaked, gesturing.

"What? Why, is something . . ."

"Nothing, just . . . come over here for a minute."

She came hesitantly, her smile faltering a little now. He beckoned her closer. When she was within range, he reached up and whisked the red scarf away.

"My God," he said again. "You cut it, didn't you? You've cut off your hair."

Her heart had been going like a trip-hammer, her stomach aquiver with butterflies. She'd been dreading this moment, but now that it had arrived, she felt a profound sense of relief.

"Well, not *all* of it," she said, trying valiantly for humor and failing miserably, for once unable to smooth the nervousness out of her voice. Unbidden, her hands had crept to her neck, to her ears and temples, her fingers burrowing through the unfamiliar waves, plucking at the feathery wisps around her face for reassurance.

"Why'd you do it?" Wood's eyes had that onyx sheen, that intensity that made it so difficult for her to imagine what he might be thinking.

Why? Why had she? How could she ever explain that she'd thought of a little girl with long flaxen braids, begging to be allowed to have her hair cut and permed like all the other girls. That she'd remembered her father's voice, the look in his eyes as he talked about her "crowning glory." His hands, reaching out, touching . . . And another voice, the voice she played back nightly now on her telephone answering machine, the voice of a man who had once praised and worshiped her long hair and steadfastly refused to allow her to cut it, as if it belonged to him and not to her at all.

She shrugged. "It was . . . something I've wanted to do for a long time." She waited, catching back a little hiccup of nervous laughter, and finally prompted, "So . . . ? Say something. What do you think?"

"What do I think?" He coughed and shifted in that way he had, without altering the black and steady focus of his gaze, then said slowly, "If I'm going to be completely honest, I have to tell you I'm a little bit disappointed, I guess. Hey—I can't help it, I'm a guy, and guys have this thing about long hair—don't ask me why. I used to wonder, you know? About what it would look like down . . ."

Chris swallowed and whispered, "You did?"

"Oh yeah . . ." It was a husky groan that stirred nerve endings she hadn't even known she possessed. Then he laughed and shook his head, raked a hand through his own hair in a gesture that both acknowledged and mocked such masculine folly. "But as far as what I think—hey, I think you look fantastic. Of course, I happen to think you'd look fantastic bald, but . . ." He grinned at her gasp of surprise and pretended to duck. Then the grin faded and his voice got raspy, the way it did sometimes. "But what I think isn't really important. What matters is how *you* feel."

"I feel a lot lighter," said Chris wryly, giving her head a shake, secretly delighting in the way the hair slithered back and forth across her neck, the way it tumbled over her ears and stirred and tickled her scalp. But that wasn't what he was asking, and she knew it. *How do you feel?*

I feel free. I feel strong . . . renewed . . . reborn.

Oh, but he was a man, and how could a man ever understand what it was to be a woman, what it was like to have men exercise power and control over you, to be made to feel that you had no rights or sovereignty even over your own body? How could she ever make him understand what a frightening, exhilarating thing it had been to take those scissors and feel them bite into her hair with a sound like ripping cloth? That it had been in a way her own declaration of independence, her bill of rights, her affirmation of personhood and of freedom?

"So how about it?" Wood asked her softly. "Are you glad you did it?"

"Yes," she said. "I am glad. It feels . . . good."

"Then that's all that matters." He held out her scarf, almost, she thought, as if he were bestowing a blessing.

And as she took it from him, she allowed her eyes to meet his for once, to lock for just a moment with that steady, black gaze. Time stopped. Her world seemed to darken; she felt as if she were being swallowed up in those terrible eyes. . . .

How do you feel? Why can't I tell him? she thought. Maybe he *could* understand.

Suddenly, more than anything in the world, she wanted to be able to tell someone. Just . . . tell someone what she really felt inside. Funny, such a simple thing, and for her, so hard. For a moment anger and sadness nearly overwhelmed her—sadness because she wondered whether she would ever feel comfortable enough, trust someone enough to be able to talk about her feelings; anger at the people and events that had destroyed her trust so long ago.

"And by the way," Wood murmured, "you look . . . beautiful."

Beautiful? How strange . . . it was a word she'd heard so often it had ceased to have any value or meaning for her at all, and yet when Wood said it she felt as if she were hearing it for the very first time. How strange that a compliment she'd come to dread and even resent at times should surprise and touch her so profoundly that it made her throat close and tears spring to her eyes.

All but undone, she managed to mumble, "Thank you," and bent to pick up Wood's things, salvaging what she could of her poise with the physical activity. But she kept hearing the word, spoken in his cracked and rusty voice. *Beautiful.* And those words he hadn't actually said out loud: *How do you feel?*

I feel . . . scared, she thought. And happy and sad and excited and hopeful. And sometimes I remember too much, and then I feel angry and guilty and ashamed. And I think I may love you.

But of course she couldn't tell him.

* * *

Wood propped his paint roller in its almost-empty pan and propelled himself backward half a turn, flexing his fingers as he surveyed his handiwork with a critical eye.

Not bad, not bad at all. He was proud of it, in fact, especially since the painting had turned out to be a lot harder work than he'd anticipated. He was glad he'd spent as much time as he had building up his arm and shoulder strength—although the job seemed to have discovered muscles he hadn't even known about before. He felt it in his wrists the most, probably because of having to work with the roller at such an odd angle, the same reason a blister was even now forming at the base of his thumb. He felt it in his neck, too, and in his lower back.

He rotated his head, trying to stretch and relax his neck muscles while he watched Chris just for the sheer pleasure of doing so. At the moment she was up on a step stool painting the narrow strip near the ceiling with a small brush. She had a supply of paint in the shallow lid of a paint can, held in her left hand like a palette. He couldn't help but wonder at the change in her, or keep himself from speculating about what might have caused it.

Because whatever the reasons, the ice was gone. There was no doubt about it; he could see her blooming right before his eyes. Gently curling locks of hair escaping from the red bandana clung to cheeks and temples rosy and moist from her exertions; sweat-dampened tendrils brushed back and forth across the topmost bump of her spine with every move she made. She was wearing a T-shirt advocating the preservation of some endangered species of wildlife—whales, he thought, although he hadn't got a good look at the front of it yet. She had the shirt tucked into the belted waistband of snug-fitting jeans, which made it obvious to Wood that he'd been right about her body proportions all along. And all the easier to speculate about what it might look like with even less camouflage—nothing at all would have been his own preference. The word *lush* came instantly to mind.

He must have made some involuntary sound or movement, because she turned to look at him, eyebrows raised as if in question.

"Nothing," he said with gravel in his voice. "Just . . . taking a little break."

"Is your neck bothering you?"

He hadn't realized he was rubbing it. She stepped down from the stool, laid her brush and the paint lid carefully on the drop cloth and came toward him, wiping her hands on her jeans. There was a kind of coltish grace about the way she moved that he found intensely sexy, all the more attractive because attracting was probably the farthest thing from its intent.

"Here, let me." She moved around behind his chair.

He closed his eyes and almost groaned aloud when she touched him.

"Goodness," she murmured, "you are tight in here. Just try to relax...."

Relax? His jaws were clenched so tightly they felt cramped. So were his hands, from fighting the urge to reach up and pull her gently down, curve around the slender column of her neck, fill with the silky masses of her hair and guide her mouth to his. His desire to hold her body next to his had become a need so powerful he felt it in all his muscles... pain and stiffness, as if they were being deprived of some vital element, like oxygen.

"This isn't helping," Chris said, sounding perplexed. "Your muscles are all knotted up. I think maybe we should take a break for a while. Would you like something to drink?"

"Sure," he said as she moved away from him, trying to let his breath out slowly and silently so she wouldn't hear. He could have told her it wasn't her professional expertise he needed. And what he did need, what he wanted from her so badly, for the first time in his life he didn't know how to get.

Simply put, he supposed he was just frustrated. But what he felt wasn't simple. His frustration went way beyond the usual aggravation caused by delayed gratification, and he was a long way from being some sweaty adolescent groping hopefully in the back seat of his father's car.

The truth was, Wood had always enjoyed the pursuit every bit as much as the conquest. He'd considered it fun, a game, one he rarely if ever lost, and if he did—well, *c'est la vie.* There'd always be a new game tomorrow. The stakes just hadn't ever been high enough to spend time worrying over. The irony of his present situation was that, for the first time in his life, he was playing for higher stakes, and he was finding that he didn't know how to play the game.

He could hear Chris in the kitchen, opening cupboards, the refrigerator, running water in the sink. He thought how easy it would have been in the past. He knew exactly what he'd have done; could see it in his mind—see himself following her into the kitchen, moving in close behind her, touching her shoulder, leaning over and whispering something casual in her ear. Then, if her response told him to, he'd lower his face alongside hers, bring his arms around her and pull her close against him....

It's the chair—this damned *chair*, he thought, slapping the wheels in silent and futile fury. It felt like a cage to him. He couldn't figure out how to—Grady's word *operate* came readily to mind—from its confines, that was his trouble. Funny, there seemed to be all kinds of people ready to teach him how to get in and out of bed, drive a car, fix a meal, bathe himself and answer nature's call from a blasted wheelchair, but nobody— *nobody*—who could tell him how to go about wooing a woman from one. And there was no one he could even think of to ask.

God, he wished he had someone to talk to! Not only about sexual mechanics, but about Chris and the way he was afraid he was beginning to feel about her. Because it was all new to him—like everything else in his life seemed to be these days. He'd have given just about anything to be able to talk to Grady right now. Or his dad. Or even Lucy. In her own gruff way his sister had always been there for him when he was a kid, making up in common sense what she lacked in subtlety. He missed her, suddenly. He missed them all. Dammit, he missed...home.

Chris was coming back from the kitchen. He swiveled to meet her, hoping the smile on his face didn't look too forced and artificial—and then he saw what she had in her hands and he didn't have to fake the smile anymore.

"Surprise," she said, smiling a little herself as she handed him a bottle of beer. "I got you a housewarming present. Hope you like this brand. I wasn't sure..."

"Oh, man," said Wood, laughing as he took the bottle from her. It was chilled, already sweating. "No, this is great. Perfect. Thanks." He tipped his head back and drank; the beer was cold in his mouth and warm in his belly, just the way he liked it. "Fantastic." Then he watched hungrily while she took a sip from her own bottle, watched her throat ripple when she swallowed and felt the warmth in his belly move lower...much lower. He shook his head wonderingly and said, "I didn't know you liked beer."

"I don't really." She took another sip and he could see it jolt her a bit, the way alcohol does when you aren't used to it. "Just now and then. You know, if it's hot and I'm really thirsty." She tilted her head, considering. "Or if the occasion seems to call for it."

"And this one does?"

She smiled and lifted her bottle to him. "Sure, it's a celebration. Cheers—you've just been sprung, haven't you? Let's drink to your freedom."

Wood laughed. "Amen to that! Here's to freedom." He glanced ruefully down at his chair and amended, "Of a sort."

There was the slightest hesitation before Chris clinked her bottle against his. "Here's to freedom," she echoed, but he saw her lips tighten almost imperceptibly. And before her eyes slid away from his, he thought they seemed to flare for an instant with a strange, almost-desperate light.

He shook his head, puzzled by the sudden mood swing and more than ever frustrated because he knew she was never going to tell him what ghosts had chased away her smile. He took another long drink and then sat up straight and said with forced enthusiasm, "You know what? I think this occasion calls for some real celebrating. Where's that music? Let's get some volume, here."

There was a portable radio on the floor beside the windows, one Chris had brought over from her place and which they'd been listening to all evening, tuned low to a country-music station. He rolled himself over to it, leaned down and twisted the volume knob with a flourish. The room suddenly filled with a lilting one-two-three rhythm and the rich and sentimental voices of violins.

"The good old 'Tennessee Waltz,'" he drawled, smiling darkly. After that he wasn't sure what came over him. A combination of things, he supposed—frustration and freedom and fear, not to mention his first beer in months.

He gulped another swallow of it and placed the bottle on the windowsill, then pivoted back to Chris and held out his hand. He didn't even pretend to smile. He was feeling entirely too emotional, and reckless because of it. Instead, in a voice filled with gravel, he said, "How 'bout it, Coach—excuse me—Ms. Bendix? Care to dance?"

"Wha-at?" Her smile was tentative, her laughter uneasy. "Dance? How—"

"Come on." He jerked his head, commanding her. "Give me your hand." When she did, he placed it firmly on his left shoulder. His left hand went around her waist, which felt as slender and supple as he'd always known it would. Then, using his right hand to maneuver the wheelchair, he began to roll slowly back and forth to the rhythm of the waltz...forward, two-three, back, two-three.

But after only a moment or two of that, he growled, "This isn't working. To hell with it..." And tightening his arm around her waist, he tumbled her neatly into his lap.

"Oh, God—Wood!" she gasped. "You can't—you shouldn't—you'll hurt yourself...."

"Sit still, darlin', and it'll be fine. I am feelin' no pain. Now...put your arm around my neck and hold on. Tha-at's right...."

He tipped his head back and smiled up into her pale, frightened eyes. "This song is made for slow dancin'," he murmured, his voice a rusty vibration in his chest. "That means holding your girl close in your arms. Can't be danced any other way. Sorry." He began to rock them to the slow, sweet rhythm, and his heartbeat kept time right along with the bass. "It's made to be sung along with, too. Come on...sing it with me, Miss Chris."

"I can't...." He could barely hear her. "I don't know the words."

"Then hum." He began to sing softly while he held on to her eyes, locked them to his with every ounce of his will and strength.

The world narrowed and shrank until it came down to just that—the music and her eyes and the thunder of his own pulse. And when the music stopped, there was only her eyes and the booming inside his head like the sound of surf pounding against the shore. It was was then he knew that mechanics didn't matter, that if something was meant to happen it would find its own way.

He was never sure exactly how he closed the gap between them, whether it was his hand on the back of her neck that drew her down to him or whether she came of her own accord. He remembered the soft sigh she made, the warm wash of her breath across his lips, and then the sweet tingle of that very first touch...tentative, testing...wondering and unsure.

He remembered that he pulled the red scarf from her hair for the second time that night, burrowed his fingers into the silken masses and fitted his hand to the elegant curve of her skull, and that when he did so her mouth seemed to meld with his, and it felt to him as if he'd found a missing part of himself he'd been searching for all his life.

His heart surged inside his chest, gave a wild leap of joy and exultation. Sensation flooded his body. He groaned aloud and sought to deepen the joining of his mouth with hers, as if by doing that he could somehow find relief from the exquisite agony he was in. But of course that only made it worse. The more he tasted of her, the more he wanted, and her mouth wasn't nearly enough. He found himself plucking at the fabric of her shirt, rubbing his hand up and down her thigh, chafing at the unforgiving roughness of her jeans.

Finally it was the sheer impenetrability of those barriers that forced his return to reason. Unable to go any further, he simply had no choice but to stop and come up for air.

To lessen the shock for both of them, he tried to surface slowly, withdrawing from her mouth in stages, ending at last with gentle nibbles and nips, the soft brushing of parted lips, exchanged breaths and merging sighs. And even then it was hard. Hard to return to a state of separation he had a notion would never feel right to him again. His hand still cradled her head . . . their cheeks touched . . . they rested their foreheads against one another's, quieting themselves and their breathing while their hands touched, groped and clung, like survivors of disaster looking for comfort.

"Chris . . ." he began, then stopped because he realized he didn't know what to say. While he was trying to think of something, she beat him to it.

She straightened up first, being careful not to put more pressure on his legs. Then she made a small, throat-clearing sound and said, "Why . . . did you do that?" She was frowning, but her tone was more curious than accusing.

Wood could only stare at her. *Why? My God . . .* It was a question he'd never been asked before, or asked of himself, either, for that matter. It threw him, because to him it seemed so obvious, and yet every answer he could think of to give her sounded too pat, too selfish, too glib . . . too wrong. For God's sake, why did any man kiss a woman? Because he wanted to, certainly. But more than likely because he wanted something more, too. He suddenly felt vaguely guilty about that, and resentful at being made to feel guilty about something that should have been so simple, so natural, so . . . right.

"Why? Geez, Chris." He ran a hand through his hair and tried to laugh it off. "What kind of a question is that? Because I wanted to, I guess. I've wanted to for a long time—probably since the first moment I saw you."

She levered herself carefully off his lap and moved away from him, at the same time crossing her body with her arms and rubbing mechanically at her upper arms in that protective way she had. He could see that something had upset her profoundly, but whether it was the kiss or its aftermath, he hadn't a clue.

"But that's what I mean," she said in a low voice, her back still turned to him. "Why would you want to kiss me? Just for fun? I don't understand."

"What I don't understand," he shot back furiously, giving in for just a moment to his frustration, "is how a woman as beautiful as you are got to be—what, twenty-eight, twenty-nine years old?—without knowing how to handle a simple little kiss. Geez, Chris, you act like it never happened to you before. What gives, dammit? *Tell* me."

She whirled on him then, her eyes smoky, searing as dry ice. He could see emotions piled up behind those eyes like a logjam in a flood, but when she opened her mouth, no words came out. Finally she shook her head and turned away again, saying in that cool, expressionless voice he hated, "So... that was it, then? You kissed me because I'm pretty and you felt like it—nothing of any great importance, right?"

"No!" He flinched back in his chair as if she'd struck at him with a fist instead of words. Because if he was honest about it, a month ago it probably would have been the way she'd just described it. But tonight, to the best of his recollection—which was admittedly a little hazy—he hadn't been thinking about what she looked like at all when he'd kissed her. And whether she was beautiful or not had been the farthest thing from his mind.

"Dammit, Chris, it wasn't like that, and you know it! You were there, too, remember? Why did you kiss *me?* No, wait—don't answer that. I'll tell you why—because you wanted to, pure and simple."

He stopped suddenly, because she was looking at him again, glaring at him with eyes full of anger and confusion, like a hurt child's. That look brought him back to his senses, finally, made him remember who he was dealing with—a woman whose secrets and enigmas had fascinated him from the very first, and with whom he'd vowed to take things slowly, to have patience. How could he have forgotten? He'd let his hormones override both common sense and sensibility, that's what he'd done. As his buddies in the corps would have put it—although a bit more crudely—for a while there it seemed he'd been sitting on his brains.

"Look," he said gently, "I didn't plan it and neither did you. What happened just...happened, because both of us wanted it to happen. And as for what it meant, or whether it was important or not...well, that's something I haven't figured out yet. I don't know about you, but it kind of...took me by surprise, you know?" He laughed softly and unevenly, shaking his head.

When he looked at Chris again, he found that she'd turned her face away from him and was looking fixedly at the dark windows. Her profile was cold and pristine, her expression closed. "Maybe," he ventured, his voice grating in his own ears, "it's something we ought to talk about."

He saw her take a deep breath. She mumbled something he couldn't catch. He asked her to repeat it, and she pulled in another breath, jerked her head toward him, cleared her throat and said, "I think...we ought to just forget it."

"Not on your life, darlin'," Wood said softly, his voice thick and husky with meaning. "That was something I won't be forgetting anytime soon, I can promise you that."

He could see her throat move with her swallow...again, and yet again. *And neither will you.* Silently he finished it for her, because although he knew beyond doubt that it was true, he knew with the same absolute certainty that she wasn't ever going to say it.

The radio blared suddenly into his consciousness, playing something wild and raucous, a foot-stompin' line dance jarringly inappropriate for the tense and unhappy silence that had fallen between them. Wood pushed himself over to it and punched the Off button, creating an emptiness in the room that was instantly filled with another, more distant sound.

Wood swore and said, "I think that's your phone," but he could see that Chris had heard it already. She'd gone stiff and still, like a wild animal sensing danger. Which seemed like a pretty normal reaction to him, since it had to be past midnight and in his experience telephone calls at that hour were seldom good news.

"Don't you think you should answer it?" he asked when she went on standing where she was, just listening to the rings.

She came to life as if he'd pressed a button that animated a frozen screen image. "No, that's all right." Her voice was soft and level, and oh, so delicately balanced. "The answering machine will pick it up."

What the hell? thought Wood.

"It's getting pretty late anyway," he said gently. "We aren't going to finish this tonight. Why don't you go on home, get some sleep? We can pick it up where we left off tomorrow."

Chris nodded, frowning distractedly. "I'll clean up . . . the rollers and things."

"No, leave it—I'll take care of it. Go on—you look exhausted."

She finally went like a reluctant but obedient child, but paused in the doorway to ask one more time, "Are you sure? I really don't mind. . . ."

"Positive. Go."

He saw the ghost of a smile, fleeting and uncertain, light her face. "Your first night home . . ."

He managed a smile of sorts in return. "Don't worry, I'll manage. Good night, Chris. See you tomorrow."

"See you . . . bye." The door closed behind her. But Wood went on sitting where he was for a while, staring out into the darkness and thinking.

Once, in a bazaar in Turkey, he'd happened upon a stall selling Russian nesting dolls. He'd liked their bright colors and whimsical designs, and the intriguing little puzzle each one presented—of boxes within boxes within boxes, until the last tiny treasure at the heart, the one that couldn't be opened any further. He'd bought a couple, he remembered, for Aunt Gwen and Lucy.

That's what Chris is like, he thought. Like those dolls. Once he'd thought solving her mystery would be a simple matter of breaking through the shell of ice that encapsulated and protected her emotions. Thawing out the ice maiden, as Grady had put it. But he'd done that, hadn't he? And found only another layer of mystery underneath the ice. Puzzles within puzzles . . .

How many layers, Chris Bendix? he wondered. How many do I have to open up before I get to your heart?

* * *

The message light was blinking furiously when Chris let herself into her apartment. It seemed angry and imperious, demanding to be heard. She crossed to it wearily, thinking that there was something almost comical about that malevolent red eye, in spite of its pervasive aura of power and menace. Like a thwarted Rumpelstiltskin throwing his tantrum.

She picked up the steno pad and pen that were lying on the table next to the telephone. Better to do it now, she thought, than in the morning. Get it over with. She'd sleep better. Maybe. *He can't hurt me . . . he can't hurt me.* She closed her eyes, took a deep breath and pressed the Playback button.

Heavy breathing...some muttered swearing. *Hang up, hang up hang up.* And then that voice . . .

"Oh, Christina . . . you shouldn't have done that. Did you think I wouldn't know? Did you think you could keep it from me? How could you do that, Chrissy? You know how I feel about your hair. Your beautiful, beautiful hair. You've gone and cut it all off...disobeyed me—like the Jezebel you are. Big mistake, Christina. Big, big mistake. You're going to have to be punished for this, you know that, don't you? Why do you do things that make me have to punish you? You make me do this...."

Trembling, she hit the Stop button, any impulse she might have had to laugh vanishing like a puff of smoke in the wind. Oh God, she thought, I can't do this . . . I can't.

But somehow she made herself rewind and replay the message until she had every awful word of it written down. Then, after a moment or two of breathing deeply and evenly to give the shaking in her body a chance to subside, she closed her eyes, said a small, silent prayer and allowed the tape to continue on to the next message.

It was shorter than the first. Short and very, very clear.

"I saw you tonight. I saw you with that cripple. You've betrayed me, Christina. I won't forgive that. I promise you, you'll pay for what you've done . . . and so will he. I'm going to have to kill you. The both of you. Soon . . . very soon."

Chapter 11

"Chris—got a minute? I'd like to speak to you."

"Sure, John, what's up?" Chris detoured across the busy exercise room to Mason's office.

"Come on in." He held the door for her, then closed it and gestured for her to take one of the chairs facing his desk. "Have a seat."

She did so hesitantly, but with more curiosity than trepidation. There'd been no problems with any of her patients that she could think of.

When he'd taken his own chair and had his desk safely between them, Mason cleared his throat and adjusted the dark-rimmed glasses he affected so as to look less handsome and boyish and more like he thought the head of a large medical facility should. Chris waited patiently.

Mason shuffled some papers, repositioned a pen, then looked at her over the top of his glasses. "Ah...I understand you've taken on Edward Brown's occupational therapy."

"Yes, I have," said Chris, startled first of all by the fact that the news had gotten out so soon, and secondly by the guilty leap of her heart at the mention of Wood's name.

"And that you've had yourself assigned to his home care as well."

"That's right." Damn. She could feel the color flooding into her cheeks and fought desperately to control it. "Is there a problem with that? It shouldn't interfere with my work schedule in any way. It seems to be convenient for me to drive Wood—Mr. Brown—here in the morning for his therapy and workout, and for any checkups he has at the hospital, and then to take him home on my lunch hour. He has no family in town, and the doctor felt—"

Mason had held up a hand to stop her. "I'm sure you've worked all that out between you. That's not what concerns me. Chris... ah, darn, this is hard."

He took off his glasses and frowned at them for a moment, then leaned back in his chair. "Listen, I know I don't have to tell you about the inadvisability of patient-therapist relationships. They happen. It's natural, I suppose, when you consider the elements—the physical proximity, the extreme vulnerability, dependence, etcetera. But the fact is, these things almost never work out. Once therapy is completed and the patient gets back into his life, the real world... ah, well, you've seen it yourself. That technician we had—what was her name?—Cindy. You know how that came out. And believe me, that's what happens nine times out of ten. Now I know—"

"John." Chris could hardly force the word out of her mouth, her jaws felt so cramped and stiff. At least she didn't have to worry about blushing anymore; she felt chilled and queasy, as if all the blood had suddenly drained from her face. "Why are you telling me this? I am not having a relationship with Wood Brown. I'm not even living in for the O.T. The apartment across from mine happened to come available, and I was able to put him in touch with the manager, and... so anyway, he's staying there. He hasn't moved in with me."

Mason sighed. "I know that."

"Then why," she almost whispered, "would you think that I—that we... Why would you even say such a thing?"

"Look... Chris," said the director, just as unhappily, "if I was wrong, I apologize. Lately I've been noticing the two of you together, and I thought... Listen, just forget it, okay?"

He rose abruptly and Chris did, too, though she still felt slightly light-headed and shaky in the knees.

Mason said with obvious relief, "Well, I should have known you'd have better sense than to get involved with a patient. You're a very levelheaded person. I've always thought you had a good head on your shoulders. I really do trust your judgment." He didn't quite put his hand on her elbow as he was guiding her toward the door. Just before he opened it he paused. "Like I said, Chris, if I was out of line I do apologize."

"That's okay," she mumbled. "I understand." She couldn't bring herself to look at him, though she could feel his eyes on her, studying her face.

"You seem a little tired," he said, his tone concerned and thoughtful. "Is everything else okay?"

"Fine."

"Good...good." For a moment longer he seemed to hesitate, then gave a slight shrug. "Well—thanks for coming in. Have a good weekend." He pulled the door open and held it for her.

She murmured something vague in response and slipped out, but had taken only a step or two when he called to her.

"By the way," he said when she turned, his face a study in perplexity, as if he didn't know whether he should smile or not. "I like what you've done with your hair. Looks very...nice."

Chris managed to croak a thank-you and continued on to the lobby with her steps firm and her head high. But inside she felt shaken, desperately exposed, humiliated and oh, so vulnerable.

Oh God...was it true? John had seen her with Wood and concluded that she was becoming "involved" with him? Was everyone else thinking the same thing? How could she have let this happen? She'd always been so good at hiding her feelings.

I saw you with that cripple. I saw you...I saw you....

John trusted her judgment, did he? What a laugh. Judgment would have to involve some kind of rational thought, weighing consequences, making decisions. Lately she hadn't been doing much thinking, rational or otherwise. All she seemed to be able to do was *feel*. And her feelings were a cauldron, a maelstrom, a swamp filled with quicksand. No matter which way she turned, the consequences were dreadful, disastrous, terrifying and unthinkable. How could she make decisions when she couldn't see ahead, couldn't see which way to go or even what the next step should be? All she could seem to do was *react*. The way she'd reacted last night when Wood had kissed her.

Oh, that kiss . . . What a foolish, dangerous, reckless thing it had been. She should never have let it happen. And yet not only had she let it happen, she'd kissed him back, she knew she had. And just the thought of it made her insides feel like jelly and the air she was breathing seem inadequate.

What should she do? Her head was telling her one thing, but her feelings . . . oh, her feelings! Every bit of common sense she possessed—and Mason was right, normally that was considerable—told her no good could possibly come of kissing Wood Brown. She'd known it would threaten the secrets she'd fought so hard and so long to keep inviolate. Now it seemed it could threaten her very life . . . and his.

But in spite of that she'd *wanted* him to kiss her. She had! And with every ounce of her strength, every cell in her body, with the very warp and woof of her being she wanted him to kiss her again. She wanted to feel again the way he'd made her feel when he touched her, held her. And not just once, either. She wanted to feel that happy, that valued, that cherished always . . . every moment for the rest of her life.

The idea that she might never know such happiness, might never feel so wonderful again, was simply intolerable.

Hopelessly lost in her emotional swamp and the tangled thicket of her own thoughts, Chris crossed the rehab center parking lot on autopilot, traversing well-known paths to the hospital across the street, although at that moment she'd forgotten why she was going there. Somewhere, some part of her thinking mind must have remembered that she'd promised Wood she'd look in on Kevin for him, just to let him know he hadn't been abandoned.

At the corner purely out of habit, she stopped for the light, and when it turned green, stepped into the street without a thought, without even a modicum of her usual care.

She was nearly to the other side, just a few steps from the safety of the curb, when she heard a shout, and almost simultaneously the roar of an engine, a rush of wind. She had an instant's impression of something huge in her peripheral vision, something coming straight at her, and then instinct and reflexes took over. She hurled herself forward, hit the curb and fell hard on her hands and knees as a vehicle brushed past her, barely inches away, rounded the corner with squealing tires and sped away down the street.

Hands reached for her. Voices exclaimed in anger, dismay and concern.

"Hey—hey, are you okay? Geez, did you *see* that guy? Never even touched the brakes!"

"Idiot! Anybody get his license number?"

"Ought to be in jail, that guy. How is she? She okay?"

"Yeah, I think so...just shaken up. Don't think he hit her."

Someone was kneeling beside her. She shook her head like a dazed fighter to bring the face into focus and was relieved when she recognized Sal, one of the orderlies from the hospital.

His hand was on her shoulder. "Hey, Chris, are you all right? Are you hurt?"

She wanted to answer him, but shock and pain seemed to have robbed her of breath.

"That's okay," Sal said soothingly, "take it easy. Can you stand up?"

She shook her head. Her knees and the heels of her hands were on fire. She wanted very much to throw up; only pride and an ingrained horror of making a spectacle of herself kept her from doing so. With Sal's help she did manage to roll over and sit on the curb. She sat there holding herself, rocking slowly, trying to cope with the pain and with the realization of what had just happened to her.

"I'm okay," she said in a low, tight voice, still short of air. "Can we go inside? All these people..."

"Sure," said Sal, "come on, I'll help you up. You probably ought to go to the ER anyway, let them check you out. Those hands look pretty bad."

"My knees are worse," Chris murmured with a shaky laugh. But she let Sal help her to her feet, and didn't object to the support of his arm around her waist as she hobbled through the sympathetic crowd of onlookers toward the emergency-room entrance.

Halfway there she paused to look back, just once, at the spot where someone had tried to kill her.

"It was something big, that's all I know," said Chris. "It happened so fast."

She was sitting on the end of a paper-covered examination table in the ER with her slacks rolled up above her knees. One of the nurses on duty was busy dabbing at the skinned patches on them with something that stung. A young uniformed police officer was standing just beyond the nurse, jotting things in a notebook with a stubby pencil. He'd come in with a teenager with a gunshot wound who, after the officer had put in an all-night vigil, had died without regaining consciousness. Unable to get a statement from the shooting victim, the officer was now taking Chris's.

"It was a van," Sal confirmed from the doorway, where he leaned with one hand braced on the doorframe, as if it was his job to keep it upright and in place. "Gray. I think maybe it had maroon pinstripes."

The officer made a note of that. "You happen to get a license number?"

Sal shook his head. "Like she said, it happened so fast. And anyway, I was looking at Chris. I thought at first the guy hit her."

"Guy? So you got a look at the driver?"

Sal opened his mouth, hesitated, then shook his head again. "Not really, I guess. I just had the impression it was a man, you know?"

"O...kay." The officer scribbled rapidly, then looked up at Chris. "Anybody you know have a gray van with maroon pinstripes?"

She glanced at the nurse, a stranger, then at Sal, who'd been kind. Her lashes dropped across her eyes as she said firmly, "No, not that I know of."

"Anybody who might want to harm you? Somebody carrying a grudge? An old boyfriend, maybe?"

"No, of course not," Chris murmured, holding her breath and trying not to hiss at the sting in her skinned knees.

"Well, okay then..." The officer tucked away the notebook and pencil and turned for the door, though he didn't look happy about it; it must have been a frustrating night for him.

Sal shook his head and went out ahead of him, but in the doorway the officer turned back for a moment, hovering. "Look, if you should remember something else about the, ah, incident, or if you think of anything else you'd like to tell us, be sure to give us a call, okay? Or just come on down to the station."

"Sure," said Chris. "I'll do that."

Still the man hesitated. Chris concentrated hard on keeping her face impassive as the nurse slapped a couple of no-stick dressings over the raw patches on her knees.

The officer shook his head, as Sal had done before him, and silently went away.

It was past two in the afternoon by the time Chris got home. Wood had been listening for her return, had left his door open, in fact, so as to be sure not to miss her. When he finally heard the click of a key in the door across the hall, he rolled himself out to intercept her, his wheels silent on the carpeted floor.

"Hi," he said, "that took a while. Everything okay?"

Before the first word was even out of his mouth, she'd started like a doe, almost as if she'd sensed someone there behind her and had reason to be afraid. Then just as quickly, as his words washed over her, identifying and reassuring, he saw her shoulders relax. The face she turned to him after the slightest delay was composed and even smiling a little. And as bleached and transparent as parchment.

"Oh—hi." Even her voice seemed brittle and thin to him. "No, everything's fine. Sorry it took so long. I had ... some things to take care of."

Her phone rang, and once again she gave a violent start, though he could plainly see that it vexed her to have her body's reflexes betray her that way. It rang only once; Wood was about to comment on the fact that it seemed to do that a lot, when, through the door she'd already opened a crack, he heard the answering machine click into action. He heard a woman's voice, young and excited, say, "Chris, are you all right? I heard about what hap—" And then Chris closed the door sharply, obliterating the rest.

She turned to him, her face no longer blanched, but flushed and rosy with guilt. At almost the same moment he saw that the knees of her slacks were torn and dirty and stained with blood.

"My God, Chris." He said it quietly, but his pulse had quickened with emotions and concerns he couldn't stop to ponder. Not then. "What happened?"

"Nothing."

But he didn't miss the small, reflexive movement of her hand, like an animal shrinking into its hiding place. He drew it forth despite her resistance and lifted it to the light, quelling a powerful urge to bring it all the way up to his lips, to kiss, oh, so tenderly, the fresh abrasions on the heel of her palm. Instead he held it, saying nothing, and waited for her to fill the silence.

She did so first with the smallest of sounds, the careful clearing of her throat. "It's nothing, really. I just ... fell. But I'm fine—they fixed me up in the ER."

"The *ER?*"

She gave a short, ironic laugh, the first thing she'd said or done that rang true. "It happened practically in their driveway. You can imagine how embarrassed I was."

"Yeah, I can," said Wood. And then, since her door was now closed and locked again, he jerked his head toward his. "Listen, you want to come in for a minute?"

She threw one quick glance back at her own door, then said, "Sure," and followed him across the hall to his apartment.

"Did you have a chance to see Kevin?" he asked as he rolled in after her. "Or did this—"

"I saw him." She was wandering and turning like a tourist in a museum. "Briefly. He was still a little sulky and hurt, but I think he'll be okay once he realizes you haven't abandoned him.... My goodness, you have been busy, haven't you?"

Wood gave a soft snort of laughter. He'd spent the morning painting everything in the apartment he could reach and had the blisters to prove it. "Yeah," he said dryly, "but that's all I can manage. You're going to have to finish it. Either that or get me a taller chair."

She turned to him, smiling, but whatever it was she'd planned to say she apparently forgot in the moment. The smile faded slowly. Silence came as an unexpected guest and quickly became as burdensome. Her eyes flitted across his face like silvery moths searching for a place to light, then as quickly slid away.

"I need to talk to you," Wood said finally, hearing his voice grate with the harshness of uncertainty. "About last night."

She said nothing, but sank onto the sheet-draped arm of a sofa. Her eyes were obliquely lowered, avoiding contact with his. He saw her throat move as she nervously cleared her throat. Still he hesitated, not knowing what to say to her.

He knew what he *wanted* to say, just as last night he'd known exactly how, if not for his confinement to the wheelchair, he would have pursued her and wooed her into his arms and, ultimately, into his bed. But he was operating now from a whole new perspective, not only in the physical sense, it seemed, but in other ways as well. He was finding that caring genuinely for someone else's feelings put him at almost as great a disadvantage in some ways as not being able to stand up on his own two legs and walk.

Not that he hadn't always tried his best to be a considerate lover, sensitive to his partner's moods and needs. His goal was to give a woman pleasure; after all, a happy, self-confident and fulfilled woman was a source of tremendous satisfaction for him, not to mention some incredibly intense and delightfully imaginative lovemaking.

Which was exactly the point. Even then he'd known that the motive for all his thoughtfulness and care was ultimately selfish, that its purpose was to achieve for himself in any liaison the greatest possible level of enjoyment. Sort of a splash-back effect: pleasuring a woman insured pleasure for *him*. Simple.

This was different. How it was different he wasn't exactly sure, but it definitely was not simple.

Originally he'd schooled himself to patience and had vowed to take things slowly with this particular woman as a means to achieving a particular—and altogether familiar—goal. But somewhere along the line, he wasn't sure when or how, the goal seemed to have changed, and he wasn't entirely certain anymore whether the achieving of it was even in his hands.

"About last night," he said again, groping his way. "I never meant to upset you." She shifted and said something so softly he had to ask her to repeat it, but when he did she only shook her head. So he frowned and went on, "For that I'm sorry. But I have to tell you . . . for myself, I'm not sorry I kissed you."

She'd been sitting hunched and tense, but looking away from him, as if, he thought, she was listening intently, but not necessarily to what *he* was saying. But when he said that she made a small, reflexive movement, straightening her spine. She stared for a moment at her hand, at the scratched and skinned place on its heel, and then her head came up and she said with what sounded oddly like defiance, "I'm not, either."

"You're not?" He said it with a gusty exhalation of relief or surprise. Perhaps both.

She slowly shook her head, then repeated, "No, I'm not."

"Oh. Well, that's—that's good." He could feel a smile beginning, but didn't know quite what to do with it. Nonplussed, he ran a hand through his hair.

Chris wasn't smiling at all. Her eyes burned blue-hot, like jets of flame. He felt seared by them. They seemed to heat the whole room, until he saw her through a wavering, shimmering haze.

How, he thought dazedly, could anyone ever have thought this woman *cold?* In all his life, in all the acts of sex and loving he'd ever experienced, beginning with his very first—which had taken place one memorable night the summer he'd turned seventeen on a blanket on the banks of the creek that ran through his father's soybean fields, and which had resulted in mosquito bites in places he still cringed to think about—in all his life he'd never known such passion. It enveloped him like a hot summer night, washed over him in humid waves. He could feel his body responding to it, swelling and tingling, and his pulse pounding thunder inside his head.

Then she did smile, finally, and it was as if she'd turned down those flame jets to a slow simmer. He could see them still flickering impishly in her eyes. He let his smile come then, too, feeling sweaty, winded, thoroughly and foolishly adolescent. They smiled at each other for breathless, uncounted moments, and he knew that their smiles, goofy as they must have been, were both an acknowledgment and a promise.

"I'm going to have a beer," Wood announced, swiveling his chair around and crunching off to the kitchen through drifts of plastic drop cloths and newspaper. "Want one?"

"Oh, no thanks." She slipped gingerly off the arm of the sofa and followed him rather stiffly to the door. She was evading his eyes again, perhaps inevitably self-conscious now. "Listen, I'm going to go and change my clothes, then come back and finish this. It shouldn't take too long ... you've already done so much."

"Okay. Why don't you bring over some utensils while you're at it? I'll cook us some dinner." He watched the smile leap into her eyes.

She gave a ripple of surprised laughter. "Are you sure you can manage? Already?"

Wood shrugged modestly. "To the extent that I ever could cook, sure. What's the big deal? Counters are a little higher than I'm used to, but hey—if I can reach the oven controls, we're in business. I've still got Nurse Ida's chicken casserole." And then, snapping his fingers, he added, "Oh, darn, I forgot."

"That's okay." Her smile became wry, slipped just a touch askew. "I'll bring some pasta and the makings for salad."

"Better bring a bowl to put it in, too," Wood reminded her as he "walked" her to his door.

Chris nodded, paused and then turned back. "That reminds me. Have you talked to your sister? Is she going to be able to bring your things?"

"I talked to her." He shook his head, rubbing ruefully at his neck.

"What did she say? Is something—"

"No, I'd just forgotten a couple of things, that's all. Like what spring is like on a farm. And how...blunt Lucy can be when she's feeling stressed. Marriage and motherhood have mellowed her some, I guess, but basically what she said was, 'Are you *crazy?* I can't get away now, you idiot, it's planting time!' Planting time means when the ground is right and the weather allows," he explained. "Which means that if the ground is right today and a storm is expected tomorrow, you plant all night long."

"I know. I understand," said Chris, and her mouth tightened in a way that made him wonder if she did, in fact, understand.

Which intrigued him greatly, because for her to have any knowledge of farms and farm life was the last thing he'd have expected. For some reason he'd always thought of her as city born and bred—just another of the many ways they seemed to be total opposites. Now, suddenly, he was remembering all the other things he didn't know about her, all the things that had intrigued and mystified him at first, things he'd lost sight of in the blinding light of recent discoveries. Things that made him pause, now, as he had back then, and wonder...

Chris unlocked her apartment with Wood watching from his doorway just across the hall, and because of that, did so for the first time in recent memory without trembling fingers and heart-pounding, stomach-squeezing dread. How good it felt, how unbelievably good to have him there, enveloping her in that same subtle web of safety, that same indefinable warmth she'd felt whenever she'd visited him in his hospital room.

And at the same time, how dangerous it was. Because she was so close to breaking...so close. That wonderful warmth and safety could be her undoing. It made her want to give in, bury her face in someone's nice broad chest, feel him wrap his strong, comforting arms around her and just . . . let go.

But I can't break down now, she thought. I must be strong. I must keep my head.

Yes, she would have to keep that level head that John Mason had mentioned if she was going to beat Alan. And she would beat him. She would.

I'm going to kill you . . . the both of you.

Funny, the way last night's threat seemed to have affected her. Far from frightening her, it had made her angry. More than that, it had given her anger focus, a sense of purpose. *Both of you.* He'd threatened to kill Wood, and she could not let that happen. Wood Brown was a good, kind and decent man, and he didn't deserve to have gotten caught up in her ugly little nightmare. She simply had to find a way to stop Alan before he harmed Wood.

At least, she reminded herself, she now had a "creditable threat" to take to the police. Of course, even if Alan was convicted, it would still be only a first offense, a simple misdemeanor with a penalty of no more than thirty days in jail, according to the pamphlet the policeman had given her. And although there was also the little matter of today's hit-and-run attempt, she'd probably never be able to prove it had been Alan who'd tried to run her down.

But then again, maybe the police would know how to find a way. In any case, she was planning to take everything she had documented so far to the police station tomorrow and file a formal complaint. Yes, tomorrow she would finally do what she should have done long ago. She was going to have Alan Bendix arrested.

But for now, just for today, she didn't want to think about it. So she ignored the blinking light on her answering machine. She didn't play back her messages or write them down in her notebook. And after she'd gathered up a package of pasta and a cooking pot, a jar of marinara sauce and the makings for a salad, the last thing she did before she left her apartment was unplug her phone.

Why not? she thought, her heart quickening and swelling with defiance. Is it too much to ask? It had been such a dreadful morning, she just wanted to spend the rest of the day with Wood, painting his apartment, fixing a meal with him, eating, laughing . . . talking about nothing. She wanted that more than anything in the world. Just to be with Wood. Surely, she thought, I deserve that much happiness.

Looking back on it later, she thought it might have been one of the best times of her life.

She went to work painting while Wood banged around in the kitchen, making enough noise for a whole army of caterers and loudly singing naughty little ditties he could only have learned in the marines.

When Nurse Ida's casserole was warming in the oven, a green salad crisping in the refrigerator and a pot of linguine simmering on the stove, he disappeared into the bedroom for a while, Chris assumed for matters requiring a degree of privacy. But when he came out again, she saw that he had the guitar case balanced across his knees.

She didn't say anything, barely moved, in fact barely breathed as, from the corner of her eye, she watched him place the case on the shrouded sofa, snap open the latch and lift the shining instrument from its velvet bed, then nestle it into his arms like a long-awaited lover. With his head bending low in total absorption, he caressed the strings, coaxed each one gently into perfect tune.

The first chords made her catch her breath; she had to fight hard to keep back rising bubbles of laughter, of purest joy. And when he began to sing, not loudly now, but softly and with that rasp of emotion she'd heard before, she felt again that strange and wonderful sensation in her skin, the shivering, tightening, tingling feeling of goose bumps, as if at a lover's touch.

He played country music songs at first, not the ones she heard now and then on the radio, but old ones like "Red River Valley" and "Will the Circle Be Unbroken." He sang folk songs she hadn't heard since long-ago childhood, like, "Where Have All the Flowers Gone" and "Michael Row the Boat Ashore."

Once he started a song about some old cotton fields back home, but after the first few lines his voice cracked and died, and he muttered, "Nope, sorry...can't do that one," and for a few moments was silent. Then he began to play again, one chord repeated slowly over and over like the tolling of a bell, and Chris recognized the opening notes of "The Rose."

Softly the words came, his voice a little hoarse, a little raw, and Chris felt a lump rise in her throat and a peppery stinging in her nose and the backs of her eyes. Oh God, she thought, I wish I could believe it. How I wish...

She wanted so much to hope that love might someday bloom for her. But hand in hand with the hope came fear. Love held such terrible risks—for everyone, she supposed, but for her the risks seemed almost insurmountable. She would have to give up so much. So many secrets. She doubted whether she would ever find the courage.

She finished the painting and washed out the brushes and rollers in Wood's bathtub. They ate salad and linguine, and Wood ate most of Nurse Ida's chicken casserole, and then they did the dishes together—Chris washed and Wood dried. And Chris thought she'd never had so much fun, and how strange it was that ordinary things could become wonderful and magical when the person you were doing them with was the right person.

I wonder, she thought, aching with longing, if this is what it would be like...*could* be like...to be in love. And to *be* loved.

But the risks . . . oh God, the risks.

The painting was finished, the dishes were done. There was no longer any excuse for her to stay. She wanted to stay forever; leaving seemed a cruel banishment to her. She even allowed herself to imagine, for just a few moments, what it would be like to stay, even to spend the night. To lie beside Wood in the hard double bed Mr. Spickler had provided . . .

To feel his hands, those long-fingered hands she'd massaged and manipulated and coaxed back to full strength and suppleness . . . What would they feel like on her skin, caressing her body, touching her most intimate places?

What would it be like to know the weight of his body, to be enveloped in its heat and musky, masculine scent, to open to him, take him inside her without tension, pain or fear? To share with him every part of herself, and afterward snuggle into the curve of his arm, feel the soft, cushiony press of his beard against her hair, and finally fall asleep with the steady and reassuring bump of his heartbeat in her ear...

Dreams . . . just dreams, that's all they were. Dreams that made her tremble with fear and ache with longing.

It was time to go back to her own apartment. She lingered over the goodbyes as long as she dared without betraying her reluctance to leave, standing in the hallway with her cooking pot hugged to her chest in lieu of a clipboard. But finally...

"I was wondering," Wood said, just as she turned to go. She looked back, eyebrows raised in question. He cleared his throat. "Ah...I was wondering if you'd maybe consider another field trip."

"Field trip?"

"Yeah. I was thinking, since my sister can't bring my stuff up here for me, maybe you wouldn't mind taking a drive down there. It's not that far, no more than an hour, I'd guess. Thought maybe we could go tomorrow, if the weather's nice. It's Sunday. We could leave in the morning, get there easily before lunch, spend the afternoon and be back in plenty of time so you can rest up before you have to go to work the next day. What do you say?"

She opened her mouth, but couldn't form words. His smile was pure, undiluted charm. "You met my sister and my aunt Gwen, right? So... here's your chance to see where I grew up, find out all my embarrassing secrets, which I'm sure they'll both be more than happy to let you in on. So come on, how about it? You'd be doing me a big favor. A little R'n'R wouldn't be bad, either."

When she still didn't answer, his smile slipped comically awry, and his voice became high and fruity, an imitation of an old-time schoolmarm lecturing her class. "Yes, a visit to the farm, boys and girls—wouldn't that be fun? See all the little cows and horsies and pigs and chickens."

Chris tried to smile with him, but the ache inside her made it impossible. Because of course she'd already seen, even through the tumult of her own emotions, what he was trying so hard to hide with the joking and clowning around. The homesickness. The longing, the yearning even he didn't understand. Oh yes, she could see how badly Wood wanted, perhaps needed, to go home.

Her heart felt heavy, the air too thick to breathe, the way it feels when tornadoes threaten and thunder grumbles in the distance. She swallowed, and it made a dry, sticking sound. "Tomorrow?" she said faintly, while everything in her, every instinct cried out in dread, *No, no, please...I can't, I can't.*

Go back *there?* She couldn't; it would hurt too much. The memories were too terrible. And the risks... Oh God, the risks.

But of course she would. Because Wood wanted to go, and because he needed her. And because, in some part of her, she acknowledged and accepted that there might be some sort of Providence at work, and therefore a certain inevitability about what was to come.

Chapter 12

Spring was definitely in the air. It seemed as if every yard in town was suddenly abloom with forsythia, bridal wreath, redbud and the joyous trumpets of daffodils. Out in the country it didn't show yet unless you looked closely; the grass on the roadsides still showed winter brown, and off in the river bottoms and creekbeds the trees were bare and gray, without even the faintest haze of new green. But on all the rolling hillsides tractors were busy plowing contoured furrows into the rich black soil. The air smelled of damp humus and newly turned earth, and Wood knew that if a person took the time to stop and walk in the bright, cool sunshine, he'd find all sorts of new shoots pushing up through the mat of last year's leaves, and tiny blades of green, fine as down, woven in among the stubble of the old, dead grass.

How good it smelled. How familiar and how strange it felt to be back. Wood experienced a curious combination of emotions—a quickening of excitement, an eagerness that made him feel like a child on the edge of his seat and, just beneath his sternum, a hard little knot of pain. He hadn't realized until now how much he'd missed being home.

So much was the same, and so much had changed. Wood kept exclaiming over examples of both, calling them to Chris's attention—blackbirds following a tractor, diving for tidbits turned up by the plow; a new fast-food restaurant or multiplex movie theater on the outskirts of a small town; a five-and-dime he remembered that was now a video rental store; the high school; his best friend's house.

She responded with polite murmurs and nods, but if there was tension in the set of her jaw and in the way she gripped the steering wheel, if her cheeks seemed more than usually pale, he was too preoccupied with his own emotions to notice.

"That crossroads up ahead," he said, "see there? That's our church. That's where my brother and my mom and I used to sing for services sometimes." He leaned forward, frowning at the cars that overflowed the parking lot, lined up along the driveway and even along the side of the road. "Wow—big turnout. I wonder what's..." And then he noticed the palm branches over the front door and twined around the handrails on the steps leading to it.

"Palm Sunday," he exclaimed softly, half to himself, realizing with a small sense of shock that the next Sunday would be Easter. And it hit him all at once, for the first time, just how many weeks and months—and in a way, he supposed, how many years—he'd lost.

"Do you want to stop?" Chris's voice seemed faint and hesitant; he could barely hear her for the whispery rush of memories, like a sudden gust of wind rustling through the branches of a great old tree. "Would your family be here?"

He shook his head. "Gwen would have been to the early service, and Lucy, if she's breaking ground, I doubt she'd go at all."

He fell silent. Through the car's open window now he could hear the congregation singing one of the traditional hymns, an old one, one of his mother's favorites.

"Are you sure?" Chris asked him, idling the car at the crossroads stop sign. "I don't mind, if you..."

He looked at her then, his lips stretched in an attempt at a smile, and saw that her eyes were fastened on him with a somber and steady regard. Instead of their usual throat-catching silver blue, they were the luminous and misty gray of rain-washed skies.

He felt something inside him give way... a breaking of barriers, a relaxing of tensions, as if someone had just whispered, *"At ease."* He didn't know how or why he knew, but all at once he did know, beyond any doubt, that he, his heart and its closest-held secrets were safe with this woman. With her he would never have to pretend.

He let his smile fade. "Nah," he said softly, "I don't think I could handle it. Too many memories. I get choked up when I hear the old hymns, you know?" He looked away from her, out the window again. The bells were ringing now, signaling the close of the service. "The fact is I don't know if I'll ever go back."

"I'm sorry," Chris murmured with a catch in her voice.

Wood shrugged, and this time when he turned to her he did manage a smile. "It's okay. Lucy's expecting us anyway. We go to the left here. Only a few more miles."

Chris felt as if she were driving in a dream, or in one of those nightmarish movie sequences where the camera takes the driver's seat and the viewer goes along for the ride. She had no real sense of being in control, but rather felt as if she was just holding on to the steering wheel while the car took her down the straight country roads, past modern brick bungalows and familiar, old, white clapboard farmhouses, barns of all sizes and shapes, silos and feed lots, fields of freshly turned earth and others awaiting the plow, still scraggly with last autumn's weathered stubble. Past a creekbed choked with winter-bare skeletons of cottonwoods and willows, then onto a gravel lane beside a huge, weathered barn, up a short rise to where a white-painted, oak-shaded farmhouse waited like a gracious dowager to receive them.

"Hey, the swing tree's gone," Wood said in a musing tone, more to himself than to her. "I remember now, Lucy said it blew down in a storm. Place sure looks different without it."

Chris said nothing, but stole a secret, calming breath as she forced herself to relax. This was difficult enough for him; he didn't need her tensions and fears complicating things. Besides, she told herself, it was going to be all right. She had no memories of this place, nothing and no one here to fear. This was Wood's odyssey, not hers.

"Brace yourself," he cautioned dryly. "Here they come."

At Wood's direction Chris stopped the car near the back-porch steps and turned off the motor, and together they sat in silence that was like a held breath and watched Wood's family converge upon them from all points of the compass.

First the two she'd already met—the old lady, straight and tall as a signpost, coming through the screen porch door to stand at the top of the steps, wiping her hands on the flowered apron she wore over a man's work shirt and jeans and looking as though any second she might burst into peals of surprised and delighted laughter; then Lucy, smaller than Chris remembered, all but swallowed up in a pair of overalls several sizes too big for her, striding rapidly from the direction of the tractor sheds and breaking into a run halfway there.

The other two, the two she didn't know, were approaching from another direction entirely, trailing them up the graveled lane from the barn—a tall man who, in spite of the overalls and plaid flannel shirt he wore, did not look like a farmer, and a very small child dressed in blue corduroy pants and a red windbreaker with a peaked hood, who was towing him along by one finger like a tugboat guiding the *Queen Mary* into port, the child in turn piloted by a medium-size black-tan-and-white dog.

They made rather an interesting picture, Chris thought. There was something about the man that seemed not entirely domesticated, possibly something to do with the brown fedora set squarely on his head and tilted slightly forward, in the manner of Indiana Jones or Dick Tracy. Or perhaps an international spy. Or a hit man.

"Must be my brother-in-law," said Wood in an undertone, watching in his side-view mirror. Chris remembered then that he was meeting the pair for the first time, too. "And my littlest niece, Rose Ellen." He glanced over at Chris and explained, "The Ellen is after my mother." Then he opened his door and was instantly engulfed in his sister's noisy and affectionate welcome.

After that, pandemonium set in. In the midst of it Chris got out of the car and went to get Wood's wheelchair out of the trunk. She was trying to extricate it when the man in the fedora took it gently from her, unfolded it and set it on the ground. He wiped his hands on his overalls, offered her one and said, "Hi—Mike Lanagan. Lucy's husband."

"Hi, I'm Chris," she murmured. "Wood's physical therapist."

"I know," he said, "Lucy told me."

Gwen called down to him from the top of the steps. "Mike, anything happening down there?"

"Not yet."

The child was peering solemnly from behind her father's legs. Her eyes, Chris saw, were dark like Wood's, bright as new buttons. "My horse is having a baby," she announced, husky and hushed with awe.

"Probably not imminently," Mike clarified with a wry grin as he lifted the wheelchair around to Wood's side of the car. "There you go, Wood. Hi, I'm Mike. You need any help with this, or can you manage it yourself?"

"Her name is Belle," the child told Chris in a confiding whisper, then went dancing over to her father so she could see better what was going on.

"I can handle it," Wood grunted. But still everyone hovered—Lucy with blanched anxiety; her husband more casually, but there at the ready just in case; the little girl with round-eyed fascination; and even the dog with ears perked up, alert and curious. Only Gwen had gone back inside, something in the kitchen evidently holding a higher priority for her than watching a man maneuver himself from a car into a wheelchair.

How hard this must be for him, Chris thought, inwardly squirming. How he must hate being fussed over, treated like an invalid.

She'd been mentally evaluating the house and yard from the perspective of someone wheelchair bound, noting the steps and narrow doorways, the thick grass, graveled drive and long, uneven slopes, and she understood now what Wood had meant when he'd said his sister's place wasn't exactly "handicapped accessible." How in the world were they ever going to get him into the house?

"Don't worry about the steps," said Mike, startling her with the ease with which he seemed to read her mind. "I built a ramp of sorts. Portable. It's going to be a little bit steep, but with us helping, I think it'll work." He turned to Wood, who was struggling to turn the chair in the coarse gravel. "You guys want to come in now, or. . .I don't know, take a walk around the place first? I guess it's been awhile since you were here, hasn't it?"

"Yeah," grunted Wood, "it's been awhile."

"You go on, show Chris around before we eat," Lucy said. "You'd just be underfoot inside anyway, while we're trying to get dinner on the table."

"They might want to freshen up a bit after the drive," her husband suggested mildly. He looked at Chris, who shook her head.

"Nah, I'm okay," said Wood.

"Good," said Lucy, taking her daughter firmly by the hand. "Come on, Rosie, let's you and me go help Gwen set the table." She started for the steps, the little girl dancing along beside her like a toy elf on the end of an elastic string, rotating now and then to wave at them with an engaging mixture of shyness and mischief.

Wood and Mike exchanged a look of masculine understanding that Lucy nearly intercepted when she turned to call, "Hey, Cage, you coming?"

"You bet," her husband said, making no effort at all to hide his grin from her as he touched the brim of his hat with a two-fingered salute. "I'm just going to get the ramp set up first—be in in a minute." He winked at Wood and Chris and went off toward the row of utility sheds at an unhurried pace, with the dog trotting amiably at his heels.

Lucy paused again at the top of the steps to call, "Dinner'll be ready in half an hour, you guys—don't go too far."

"Yessir, Boss," muttered Wood as the screen door banged shut behind his sister, but Chris could see that he was smiling. He shook his head as he returned once more to the problem of turning his chair around in the rough gravel. "Wow, I don't believe it—my sister's actually developing subtlety."

"Subtlety?" Chris moved quietly behind the chair and took the handle grips.

"Yeah, didn't you get it? Lucy's evidently decided I need to be alone for this. In case I want to get emotional, I suppose."

"Oh," Chris said with a little gasp, and took a step back. "I'm sorry. I didn't think. Would you rather I—"

Wood's hand shot out and fastened around her wrist. "Don't you dare," he grated in that raspy drawl she was beginning to know so well, placing her hand firmly on his shoulder and covering it with his to make sure it stayed right there. "Besides," he added with a smile in his voice, "if Lucy'd wanted me to be *alone* alone, trust me, you'd be in there helping set that table right now."

Chris laughed, though it bumped in her chest like pebbles, and said shakily, "Is she always so..."

"Bossy?" supplied Wood. "Yeah, Lucy does like to run things. Except, like I say, I think she's softened up quite a bit since she got married. Never used to have so much tact. Oh, hey, look—this must be the new bunkhouse Mike built. Sure doesn't look like the old one."

It looked like a doll's cottage, Chris thought, only larger, big enough for a person to sleep in. It was made of wood, white clapboard with a red shingle roof, blue-painted gingerbread trim and a tiny front porch with a climbing rose growing over it, just now showing the russet furring of new leaves.

"It's cute," she murmured.

Wood snorted. "Used to be a plain old bunkhouse. It was where the hired hand slept, on the rare occasions when we needed one. Also where my brother, Rhett, caught me trying to smoke a cigarette when I was about six. One of the hired men must have left 'em behind. First and last time I ever smoked.

"Anyway, there used to be a huge old oak tree right over there—had a swing hanging from one of the branches. Several years ago, Lucy wrote me, they had a bad storm. Lightning hit the tree and split it down the middle, and half of it came down on the bunkhouse. Didn't take out Gwen's chicken house, though, I see. That's right next door, on the other side of that evergreen windbreak, see? Then down there, at the bottom of the hill, that's the hog yard, farrowing sheds . . . all that stuff."

They crunched across the driveway, Chris pushing as unobtrusively as she could, Wood talking in fits and starts in a musing tone, more to himself, she thought, than to her. He pointed out familiar things, told her little stories about them and exclaimed over the changes that had been made—the old John Deere tractor, the first thing he'd ever been allowed to drive; the big, new, red International with the enclosed and air-conditioned cab; rusty old plows, including one, probably a valuable antique now, that his great-great-who-knows-how-many-greats-grandfather had used to break through the dense prairie sod. So many memories.

From time to time Chris made murmured comments and asked encouraging questions, but mostly she watched Wood, watched him anxiously, because she could see the memories building up inside him like a logjam in a flood. She wondered what he would do—what *she* would do—when it finally broke loose.

They'd come to a garage of sorts—a shed made of corrugated tin with big double doors on one side. A splintery board held the doors closed. Wood worked it loose and threw it aside, then pulled the doors open, one at a time. He rolled slowly into the shed, disturbing dust that rose swirling in the wedge of sunlight from the doorway.

Chris didn't help him, but followed closely, wrinkling her nose at the smells—old oil and diesel fuel and radiator rust and all the other things she didn't know the names of but that together made up the unique and unmistakable odor of every garage she'd ever been in.

"Ahh, there it is." Wood's voice was a crusty growl.

He gave his wheels a push and coasted over to a bulky shape covered with an old, faded quilt and a thick layer of dust. He pulled on the quilt, sending fresh billows of dust into the light, then dropped it in a heap and sat back in his chair, gazing at what he'd unveiled.

"Still here. I don't believe it." He moved his head toward her, but his eyes couldn't seem to let go of the gleaming chrome-and-black motorcycle. "My bike," he murmured. "My Harley. Oh, man... my best friend Kenny and I—we must have spent half our lives out here, putting this thing together, cleaning it up. You should have seen it when I bought it—it was a wreck. I thought my dad was going to blow a gasket...."

"Because you bought a motorcycle?" Chris asked when he didn't go on. "Or because it was a wreck?"

It was a moment before he answered; he was busy inspecting the motorcycle, maneuvering his chair with one hand while the other jiggled switches, thumbed levers and probed into unknown pockets. Finally his reply drifted back to her, muffled and distracted.

"Both, probably. There wasn't much he could do about it, though, because I'd bought it with my own money. See... we all—all us kids—got paid for the work we did on the farm. It was understood, of course, that we were supposed to save that money for something important, like college, or a down payment on a house someday. I guess wheels would probably have been a legitimate expenditure, but..."

Once again his voice trailed off. He sat for a moment brushing his hand lightly, almost caressingly across the top of the shiny black gas tank, wiping away the dust that was already trying to settle there. Then he shook his head, and Chris saw one corner of his mouth lift in a lopsided attempt at a smile.

"He never told me I couldn't spend the money, but he sure did let me know what he thought of my choice . . . how disappointed he was. Poor Dad." The smile became a wry little twist. "I'm afraid I was always pretty much of a . . . disappointment to him."

"A *disappointment?*" Chris asked in surprise. "Why? I don't understand." To her he'd seemed so perfect—good student, good athlete, popular, never in any kind of trouble. It was a mystery to her how any parent could be disappointed in a son like that.

"Why?" He pushed himself away from the motorcycle and into the wedge of sunlight, squinting at the unaccustomed brilliance. "This place, for one. I was supposed to take over for him someday."

"Not your older brother—what's his name—Rhett?"

Wood shook his head, laughing softly. "You'd have to know Rhett. No . . ." He spoke softly, half smiling, his face lifted to the sun's warmth and light. "Rhett always knew exactly what he wanted to do. He wanted to do something important— Lucy'd say he meant to *be* important, but my sister and Rhett never did see eye to eye on much of anything. Anyway, Rhett wanted to change the world, right wrongs, all that stuff, and he figured the best way to do that was to go into law, and then into politics. I really believe he may be governor someday, at the very least. Dad was pretty proud of ol' Rhett. He always had a direction, a purpose, and Dad approved of that. Me, I never did know what I wanted to do." He gave an ironic bark of laughter. "I guess I still don't."

The constriction in Chris's throat had become a lump, a swelling tightness, an ache that encompassed her jaws, her face, her neck. *Wood,* she wanted to cry out, *don't do this. Please, don't.* Instead, she laced her fingers together and pressed them to her lips to hold it all inside, and only started a little when he pivoted suddenly and violently and pushed himself out of the sunlight.

His voice came, cracked and husky, from the shadows. "I was the youngest, you know—the baby. And then I was always real close to my mom, and Lucy, too. I think Dad might have been extra hard on me because he was afraid I'd be spoiled—you know, turn out to be a 'Mama's boy'? I resented the hell out of him at the time, of course—fought him every inch of the way. But at the same time, deep down inside, I had this...something I wanted to prove to him. Maybe that was why I bought the Harley, I don't know. I know for sure it's why I joined the marines. Even after he died, I wanted to prove to him he'd been wrong about me. I wanted to do something to make him proud...."

Chris didn't remember moving, but all at once she was on her knees in the oily dirt beside Wood's chair and her hands were reaching up to touch his face, the springy softness of his beard was tickling her palms, and there was something warm and wet on her fingertips.

"Don't," she whispered brokenly, "oh, please...don't."

His fingers fastened on her wrist like a bracelet of iron. Her breath caught; she stared at him, her mouth open in mute appeal, but his face was only a darkness that blurred and swam through the rainbow glaze of her tears.

Then he said her name, a single harsh cry like a shout in a storm, and she felt his hands touch her face, take it between them and lightly touch, as if in wonder, the moisture there.

But briefly—for only a moment. And then they moved on, gripped her shoulders, and in what seemed almost like a spasm of pain, half lifted her and pulled her close. His arms came around her, and instinctively she arched into him and lifted her own arms to his neck. He held her with such tension and urgency she thought she felt his muscles quiver; she couldn't be sure, because she was holding him just as tightly.

Her fingers caressed his hair, combed and burrowed through it first, simply pleasuring themselves with the raw-silk texture, the newness of it. But her fingers were trained to ease pain and give solace, and almost of their own volition they slipped beneath his hair to find and stroke the taut muscles in the back of his neck. Downward they pushed, probing under the collar of his shirt, automatically seeking the rigid trapezius and the strategic places along his spine.

She felt tremor after tremor ripple through his body, then a gradual easing. She felt his chest expand with an indrawn breath, felt the trip-hammer beat of his heart while he held it, then the rush of an exhalation. His hold on her relaxed. His arms shifted, his hands came back to her face and took it oh, so gently between them and held it away from him, just far enough so he could look at her. His fingers pushed into her hair while his thumbs took tears from her eyes and smeared them across her hot cheeks.

She blinked, and suddenly she could see his face clearly. And there was that look she knew so well—so black and brilliant, so intense, almost questioning, as if he was trying to place her...or memorize her.

"My God—Chris." His voice was hoarse, his tone incredulous, stunned.

And then his mouth came down on hers and took it like a starving man given bread, without plan or thought, but with all care and awe and thankfulness...just tasting...savoring it first, until his hunger became too much for him.

Chris didn't breathe, didn't move, so intense was her fear of shattering the exquisite and fragile thing that was unfolding inside her. Could something so wondrous be happening to *her*? She couldn't believe it and so held herself still...so still, afraid a breath or the slightest tremor might burst the precious bubble.

Until his hunger became too much for both of them. She wasn't sure how it happened, or when, exactly. When she stopped thinking. When his mouth became a conflagration that all but consumed her. But suddenly she was on fire; his tongue invaded her mouth and she welcomed it! Now it was *she* who was hungry, insatiable, greedy for his touch, for the taste, the feel, the smell, the very essence of him.

Dimly she realized that he was unzipping her jacket, and she was glad. It had become cumbersome, binding and hot. It was in her way—in *his* way. Eagerly she shrugged it off, helping him as he pushed it over her shoulders, then yanked her arms from the sleeves with an urgency that bordered on desperation. And all the time the kiss went on . . . and deepened . . . and became unstoppable.

Wood arched above her, bearing her head back...and back, searching, it seemed, for the very center of her being. And she thrust her mouth upward beneath the force of his, meeting, yielding...inviting him in. She felt his hands tugging at her shirt and once again her own were there, helping him pull it from the waistband of her slacks. She groaned when he plunged his hands under the soft and giving fabric.

His hands...oh, his hands. They were everywhere on her body, spanning her back, stroking the sensitive places along her ribs and the taut, quivering muscles of her belly, breaking the clasp on her bra with an impatience that belied the gentleness, the reverence with which he then cherished what he'd uncovered. How gently he nested her breasts in his palms, cradling their weight, praising their firmness...then lightly, with feathery strokes, chafing the nipples to erect and tender buds.

She heard herself whimpering now, deep in her throat. The feelings were becoming too intense, the pleasure almost pain. Her legs began to tremble.

Almost at once, as if he'd sensed her distress, Wood's arms came around her. One hand hooked around her hips, and with the tremendous strength in his shoulders and torso, he lifted and settled her across his lap.

Then and only then did he finally tear his mouth from hers and nestle her hot, damp face in the hollow of his neck. He enfolded her in his arms, curving himself around her as if to protect her from harm, and, stroking her hair, whispered brokenly, "It's okay, Chris, it's okay...I'm sorry...I'm sorry."

It was a moment or two before she understood. When she did, she simply reached up and laid her hand along his jaw, turned his face toward her and raised herself to meet him, lips already parted, glazed and swollen.

He made a sound, a growl of pure hunger, and sank into her mouth as if he'd found something precious that had been lost. Her head fell back as she drank him in. Her eyes closed.

Once again the heat exploded inside her. There was a throbbing ache low in the center of her body; her breasts felt hot, her nipples tight; every nerve cried out to be touched.

And again it seemed as if he knew exactly what she needed. Because his hands weren't gentle now. Roughly, one shoved her shirt up, brushed aside her loosened bra and closed over a swollen breast, and it felt so good to her she made a pleased, chuckling sound low in her throat. She moaned aloud as his fingers found her nipple, tugged and teased it, sending new fire into every part of her until the sensation became too much to bear and she finally had to tear her mouth free and gasp for breath, almost sobbing with the exquisite agony of it.

His lips wouldn't abandon her even then. They brushed her throat, nibbled greedily along the side of her neck. And when he found the soft spot in the hollow near her collarbone, he pressed his mouth there and sucked with a hot, drawing pressure that made her gasp.

She tried not to squirm, aware even through the fog of desire of the precariousness of her position, and his. But it was hard, especially when his hand left her breast and skimmed downward over her ribs and stomach, hesitated at the belted waistband of her slacks, then pushed on across the zippered placket and slipped between her legs. She could only whimper and try to turn herself toward him a little in unspoken invitation.

He thanked her with wordless sounds of approval, deep-throated chuckles and low growls that vibrated through his chest like a tiger's purr. He stroked the insides of her thighs through slippery gabardine and finally cupped the hard, hot mound at their juncture, rubbing and probing with knowing fingers, seeking out her body's sensitive places even through layers of cloth.

To be touched so was both a relief and a torment—a relief because it felt so good . . . so good; a torment because it only increased her hunger for something she couldn't have.

Still, it was a torment Chris felt no compulsion or desire to put an end to. And neither, it seemed, did Wood, although he must have been as frustratingly aware as she that there was no way, just then, to bring what was happening between them to any kind of a satisfactory conclusion. Even so, her fevered mind was actually exploring possibilities, most of which, in saner moments, would have made her blush, when Wood's body suddenly went rigid and still.

"What is it?" she asked, her voice thin and air starved, her heart pounding. "What's wrong?"

"Lucy," he mumbled thickly. "Dinner must be ready." With obvious reluctance, he withdrew his hand from between her legs and pulled her shirt down more or less where it belonged. But he didn't release her—not yet. Instead he enfolded her as he had before, tucked her face into the hollow of his neck and pressed his jaw against her temple.

"This isn't over," he said in a fierce and ragged whisper as he stroked her hair back from her ear. "You know that, don't you?"

She could only nod. She didn't want to move, couldn't bear the thought of separating herself from him. She could feel the moist heat of his body soaking through his shirt and into hers, feel his frantic heartbeat, like a drummer's tattoo against her own breast.

"We have to go. Before they send somebody to find us..." He patted her bottom gently, then straightened, shifting her to a more upright position. "You gonna be okay?"

Again she nodded, because she was incapable of uttering such an obvious lie. Okay? She didn't know how she was going to stand on her own feet. Her body wasn't even muscle and bone, but only a mass of quivering jelly, rampaging hormones and roused nerves.

She felt his hands tighten on her waist, helping her, lifting her up, and again she marveled at the wiry strength in his arms and back and shoulders. Her feet found the floor; she stood, swayed and felt his hands steadying her. She could sense his gaze, knew he was concerned, but couldn't bring herself to meet it. Not yet... not just yet.

"My jacket," she mumbled, plunging her fingers into her hair and raking it back from her flushed and sweat-damp forehead. "Where did I..." Her tongue felt thick, her lips swollen, hot. She touched them with the back of her hand and looked around distractedly, overcome, all at once, by a bewildering urge to cry.

Oh, dear God, she thought, how will I ever hide this? Anyone looking at me will know...

It was such a familiar thought that it stunned her. Her body cooled and her head cleared, and in the sudden and terrible stillness within her she heard a voice whisper, *Of course you can hide it, Christine, as you always have. You're good at keeping secrets....*

A shudder rippled through her. She drew in a deep, calming breath, finger combed her hair into its new and blessedly carefree style, then picked up her jacket from the oily ground where it had fallen and shook it out.

"I'm fine," she said, and was pleased to hear that her voice sounded perfectly normal. "Ready to go."

She turned to Wood, and at the same moment gave a small gasp of concern, fingertips pressed to her lips and eyes wide with an unvoiced question.

But he was smiling, his eyes dark and ironic. "It's okay, darlin'," he said in his cracked and edgy drawl. "Just help me take my jacket off and put it in my lap. Then I'll be ready to go, too."

"Oh, God," said Chris in a small voice, and to her own amazement she burst out laughing.

Chapter 13

"Have some more chicken, Earl." Gwen was hovering at Wood's elbow with platter and serving fork at the ready, so he knew it wasn't a question.

He accepted another drumstick even though he'd already eaten more than he normally did in a whole day, then said, "Now for Pete's sake, come and *sit down.*" And those words played back in his mind like an echo from the past. How often had he heard someone say that, sitting at this same table in this same kitchen?

And of course, Gwen didn't sit down. She never did. She was already around on the other side of the table ladling creamed potatoes and onions onto Chris's plate. And because Wood knew how little Chris usually ate, he didn't miss the tiny spasm of dismay that flickered for one instant between her perfect eyebrows. But no one else would ever have noticed.

How does she do it? he wondered, in awe as never before of her flawless poise, perfect features and radiant smile. Because now he knew beyond any doubt what a cauldron of emotions boiled just beneath that protective shell . . . shell of ice, lovely as porcelain, fragile as crystal and false as a Halloween mask.

Well, he'd always known that it was false, hadn't he? He'd never for a moment believed that she really was cold, and in the last few weeks he'd been discovering more and more evidence of her vulnerability and natural warmth. Hadn't he, with his own eyes, seen her passionately angry, laughing and carefree, hurt and bewildered as a child? And just now, down there in that shed, he'd finally caught a glimpse of her fire.

Fire? My God, it had almost consumed him. He'd never known anyone so responsive. He couldn't get the visions of her out of his mind—her mouth, bruised and glazed from his kisses...her eyes, violet and slumbrous with desire. Or the feel of her breast in his hand, the sounds she made when he touched her...

But at the same time it troubled him to realize just how good she was at keeping secrets, when she wanted to. He wondered how he could ever be sure she wasn't keeping any from him. He thought again of the Russian nesting dolls, and wondered if he would ever really know whether or not there was yet another Chris inside her apparently seamless facade.

"I hope everybody saved room for dessert," Gwen sang, coming from the kitchen with a pie plate in one hand and a gleaming server poised and ready in the other.

Everyone groaned, because of course no one had. In Wood's memory, no one ever did on occasions like this—Thanksgiving, Christmas, all the special family times. But they always managed to eat plenty of whatever was offered, anyway, and then lay around moaning about how full they were for the rest of the afternoon. That much, at least, hadn't changed. Except that it should have been Dad sitting there in his Sunday-best overalls, and Mom bustling around waiting on everyone and ignoring everyone's pleas of "Sit *down*, Mama, *please*."

"Mmm-mmm, is that some of your cheesecake?" Mike was leaning back in his chair and rubbing his stomach in anticipation.

Lucy reached over and gave his front an affectionate pat and murmured, "Better watch it, Cage."

Gwen laughed her musical laugh and cut the first piece of cheesecake and handed it to Wood. Then she cut another and offered it to Mike.

"Too big for me," he said, piously declining. "That one's about right for Lucy. Cut me one a little smaller. 'Bout half. Tha-at's right."

Gwen gave him an amused look, then turned to his daughter. "What about you, Rosie? Want the other half of your daddy's?"

With a child's total frankness, Rose Ellen wrinkled her nose and squirmed back in her chair. "Don't like cheesecake," she announced with disdain, then dimpled winsomely. "Can I have a cookie instead?"

"*May* I," said Mike absently, having given his full attention to his morsel of cheesecake.

Gwen sighed. "You know where they are. Go help yourself."

"*One,*" Lucy specified as Rose Ellen hopped down from her chair and went skipping off to the pantry-laundry room across the hall.

"Chris, what about you?" Gwen asked, holding out a plate. "Won't you have some cheesecake?"

"No, thank you," she murmured. There was something about the way she said it, the way she sat with eyes lowered, hands folded in her lap, that reminded Wood of a well-mannered child.

For a moment Gwen seemed to hesitate, her hand still outstretched. Then she said, "Oh, of *course.*" And smiling, she lowered the plate to the table. "I wondered where I knew you from. For heaven's sake, you're the little Thurmond girl, aren't you?"

Wood's laden fork continued its journey to his mouth without a wobble. It was possible that the words simply hadn't sunk in yet. And when they did sink in, he didn't believe them. He sat there with the lemony sweetness of the cheesecake melting on his tongue, savoring the hint of almond flavoring Gwen always used, and waited for Chris to smile her brilliant smile and say, "I'm sorry, but you've mistaken me for someone else."

But she didn't. And her stillness was so profound it seemed to encompass the table, the room, the whole universe. She seemed not even to be breathing.

"The last time I saw you," Gwen went on in a pensive tone, apparently oblivious to the tension, "it must have been when your mother died. I took a cheesecake over to you and your father. That's what reminded me. And of course, Ellen—Earl and Lucy's mother—and I used to always take you the Sunday-school papers. Don't you remember, dear? We tried to get your parents to let you come to Sunday school, but . . . Oh my, you were always so *shy* . . . and now look at you. You've grown into a lovely young woman."

The old lady frowned, suddenly, and touched a curled forefinger to her lips for a moment. "You know, it seems as if we lost touch with you after your mother died. Your father . . ." Her voice trailed off, which for Gwen was unusual. She placed a gnarled, blue-veined hand on Chris's shoulder and squeezed it gently. "I'm so sorry about your father, dear. We all were."

Chris's only reply was a small, choked sound, possibly a futile effort to clear her throat. Her eyes darted into a far corner of the kitchen, as if seeking refuge there.

Say something. Please . . . Wood wondered how a living, breathing person could be so pale. She seemed to be made of ice—or glass. He felt that if anyone touched her, she would surely shatter.

In that stretched and frozen silence, Mike's courtesy cough was a startling interruption; Wood, for one, had all but forgotten anyone else was in the room. Chris jerked as if someone had poked her, but before either she or Mike could say a word, Rose Ellen came skipping back into the kitchen wearing an angelic smile and a telltale goatee of cookie crumbs. Neither of her parents thought to challenge her.

"Can—*may* I please be excused now?" she said in a singsong voice, looking as innocent as it's possible to look with a mouth stuffed full of cookies.

"Uh . . ." said Mike, and cast Lucy a look of appeal.

"I think you should go check on Belle again," said Lucy firmly. "Don't you?"

"Okay." Rose hopped around the table, obediently making for the door, but taking her time about it, the way kids do when they sense the grown-ups might be trying to get them out of the way. She paused to swing on the arm of Wood's chair, flirting coyly. "Can you come with me? We have baby kitties. Wanna see?"

"Uh . . . don't think so, Rosie," said Wood, a little surprised to hear his own voice. "I don't think I'd make it down there in this chair."

"'Cause you can't walk, huh." Rose Ellen nodded gravely. "'Cause your legs are all broken. But . . . they'll get better. My mommy said so." Buoyancy restored, she went bouncing off, to stop at Chris's chair. "*You* could come if you want to. Wanna see the baby kitties? We got this many." She held up four fingers. "That's how much I am, did you know that? I'm four."

Chris threw a look of mute appeal across the table, but not quite far enough to connect with Wood's eyes. She rose as if in a daze, and looked momentarily disconcerted when Rose Ellen reached for her hand.

"You know what?" Wood heard the little girl confide as she and Chris went out the door together. "My horse has a baby in her tummy. And you know what else? My mommy has a baby in—" The door closed, cutting off the rest.

In the silence, Wood leaned his elbows on the table, pressed his clasped hands over his mouth and exhaled sharply through them.

"You didn't know?" Gwen asked. Her usually amused eyes looked filmy and sad. No one thought for a moment that she might be referring to the news Rose Ellen had just revealed.

Wood closed his eyes and shook his head. He couldn't explain why he felt so disappointed when he'd all but expected something like this.

"Will somebody," said Lucy testily, "*please* tell me what is going on?"

"I knew I'd seen her before," Wood said with a sigh, rubbing at his eyelids with a thumb and forefinger. "I asked her about it, but she denied it."

Gwen shrugged and eased herself down onto a chair. "Could be she just didn't remember you."

He shook his head. "You saw her just now." God . . . she looked sick, he thought. Like someone whose worst nightmare was coming true right before her eyes. "No," he muttered, "she lied, I'm sure of that." He made a fist and gave the tabletop a restrained thump with it. "Dammit, I just wish I knew why."

"Well," said Gwen doubtfully, "they were a very strange family. . . ."

"Strange?" Mike pushed his plate out of the way and leaned forward on his arms. He looked deceptively relaxed, but Wood saw the sharp interest in his eyes and remembered suddenly that before he'd become famous as a syndicated columnist, his brother-in-law had been—and probably still was, in his heart— a newspaper reporter. "*How* strange?"

"Oh, you know…kept to themselves most of the time. Chris was an only child—there'd been several miscarriages, from what I understand, and a little boy who died in infancy. Mrs. Thurmond was a very quiet woman—I always thought she seemed rather sad, or maybe just tired and worn-out. Mr. Thurmond, now—he was a handsome man, big and blond. I believe Chris takes after him. But…there were rumors…."

"What sort of rumors?"

The old lady lifted a shoulder, as if it pained her to repeat such things. "Oh…you know. Abuse. There were all the miscarriages, and other injuries, too. Once in a while I'd see Mrs. Thurmond at the store, and she'd have a broken arm or a black eye. Other bruises. Then she started to put on weight—a *lot* of weight. So much that she couldn't get around much at all. If the rumors were true, I suppose it might have been a kind of self-defense, maybe—a way of fighting back."

Mike nodded. "It happens. But you said she died?"

"Yes, one day she just took to her bed and stayed there. Wouldn't go to the hospital, or have anyone in to care for her. It was months later that she died, apparently of pneumonia, from what I understand. Strange…very strange."

Again Mike nodded. Wood thought there was a grim set to his mouth. "How old was Chris when her mother died?"

"Let's see…she must have been about thirteen, I believe. Fourteen at the most. But her mother had been an invalid for at least two or three years by that time. I imagine the child was used to taking care of herself, and probably her father and the household chores to boot. She couldn't have had an easy life. I'm sure that was why she married so young—before she'd even finished high school. She couldn't have been more than seventeen. I'm sure she just wanted to get out of a bad home situation."

Mike sat back with a gusty exhalation. "Probably worse than you know. If her father was abusing her mother, chances are he abused her, too." He swore softly and reached for Lucy's hand.

"It's funny, though," said Gwen, looking thoughtful. "You never saw any sign of that, none whatsoever. I remember the little girl—Christine—always being so neat and tidy. Scrubbed looking, I always thought. Her clothes were shabby and out of fashion, perhaps, but scrupulously clean. And of course, she was so painfully shy...."

It occurred to Wood that he was feeling a touch nauseated, as if the room had become too stuffy. "Need some air," he muttered, shoving himself back from the table. "I'll be outside."

As he headed for the porch, he heard a chair scrape back, and over that Mike's voice saying, "You said something about the father. What did happen to him?"

And Gwen replied. "Now, that was the strangest thing of all. As I said, Chris got married very young—ran off with a salesman from the John Deere tractor place over in Millerton. I believe the man must have been ten years or more older than she was. Anyway, they found Mr. Thurmond the next day. They said he'd shot himself."

"*God.*" Wood groaned under his breath and covered his eyes with his hand.

A moment later he felt a light touch on his shoulder, heard a familiar voice ask, "Are you all right, Earl?"

He craned his neck to give his sister a twisted smile. "Not really."

Lucy's arms slipped around him from behind as she leaned down to lay her cheek against his. For a while she just held him like that, not saying anything. Then she sighed and said, "You care about her a lot, don't you?"

"Yeah..." He drawled the word, his voice gravelly and thick. "I do."

"I don't know, Earl." His sister straightened, but left her hands resting on his shoulders. "You sure you want to get involved with somebody with so much...I don't know, *baggage* to deal with?"

Wood gave a short, painful laugh. "That's the thing, Luce. I don't think I have a choice, do I? You don't exactly get to pick who you fall in love with, you know what I mean? It just sort of *happens.* And there's nothing you can do to make it go away, either, not that I've heard of, anyway. If somebody comes up with something—an antidote, maybe—I sure do wish they'd let me know." He gave his wheels an angry push and rolled out from under Lucy's hands.

She gave a low whistle and followed him over to the screen door, but didn't say anything. After a moment Wood shook his head and said quietly, "I didn't mean that. It just scares the hell out of me that I seem to be in love with somebody I don't even know. I *don't know her,* Luce. She . . . keeps everything inside."

She surprised him with a sharp little cackle of laughter. "I don't believe this. It's really funny—maybe it runs in the family. Do you know . . . when I fell in love with Mike I was in almost the same boat? He was on the run from the mob, hiding out, so he couldn't tell me anything about himself, not even his real name." She paused, smiling at something only she could see. "He called himself Mike Cage, back then."

"Ah," said Wood. "I wondered about it—why you keep calling him that."

She shrugged, and he saw her dimple, the one that was so like Chris's. "Yeah, well, I fell in love with him in spite of that, and it scared me to death, too. Believe me, I know how you feel."

Wood was silent for a moment, studying her. "You look happy now," he said finally. There was an incomprehensible lump in his throat.

She nodded, her face calm, serene . . . beautiful. "I am."

"I'm glad you found someone, Luce."

"Me, too. I thank my lucky stars every night of my life."

"Well," said Wood gruffly, "I happen to think Mike's the lucky one."

Lucy uttered her rusty little chortle, then suddenly stopped to give him a hard, thoughtful look, the one that always made him think of a little sparrow hawk getting ready to pounce. But when she spoke, it was in a soft, musing tone, and not at all what he expected.

"You know, Gwen believes it was Providence that brought Mike Lanagan to take refuge in my barn on the very same night that my hired hand quit. . . ."

"Providence?" said Wood, laughing. "You mean Fate? Like maybe I was *meant* to have that accident and wind up Chris's patient? You really believe in that stuff?"

"I don't know whether I do or not," said Lucy with a shrug. "But I do know things have a way of working out the way they're supposed to, if you trust your instincts. Something to think about, anyway." She pushed open the screen door. "Come on, let's get you down that ramp. You look like you could use some fresh air and sunshine. You've been cooped up way too long."

"Don't you think you should get Mike to help?" Wood asked uneasily as Lucy maneuvered him backward through the doorway.

"Hah—you're forgetting who's the farmer around here, little brother. Mike punches computer keys for a living. Just relax, now . . . here we go!"

At the bottom of the ramp she turned him toward the front of the house, then, flushed and laughing, lifted her hands to comb the wings of her hair back behind her ears. "Now go—find yourself a sunny spot. I think I'll get Mike to go down to the barn and rescue Chris from Rosie's clutches. You two need to talk!"

On the way down to the barn, Rose Ellen told Chris everything she knew about babies and where they come from, which, since she lived on a farm, was quite a lot. In fact, it seemed to be her favorite topic of conversation, which Chris supposed was only to be expected, considering the season. Especially if the news the little girl had spilled as they were going out the door was true. Looking forward to the arrival of a new brother or sister must be an exciting time for a child. At least, it should be.

Hastily swallowing the rising sickness in her throat, Chris helped the child pull open the weathered doors and followed her through them into the quiet refuge of the old barn. And was instantly enveloped in the warm barn smells—hay and manure, sweaty animals and old leather. Dust motes danced in a shaft of sunlight from a window high in the hayloft; a horse whickered a soft welcome from the shadows; a small calico cat came from an empty stall to wind around her ankles. How familiar it all was . . . and how different. She wanted to cry.

Rose Ellen picked up the cat and slung its front legs over her shoulder to balance the load, explaining as she did so that it was okay to pick up the mama kitty now that she no longer had babies in her tummy.

"Girls can have babies in their tummies," she solemnly explained. "Boys can't. You could have a baby in your tummy, because you're a girl. So could I, when I'm bigger."

She stretched to reach the top of a stall gate and opened the latch. The mother cat leapt from her arms and dropped to the floor with a soft thud, slipped through the half-open gate and made a beeline to the far corner, churring anxiously. As she curled around her nest of sleeping kittens, they came to life one by one, mewing frantically, tiny heads bobbing, blindly searching. Rose Ellen squatted in the straw and scooped a kitten up in her hands with the casual assurance and skill of one both experienced and well taught.

"Here, hold it like this," she instructed, thrusting the tiny creature at Chris. "So it won't get scared, see? Then if you put it under your chin, like this, he can nuzzle your neck and it...*tickles*." A peal of childish laughter rose into the humid air. "Now *you* take him. Try it—yeah, put it right there, like that. It really feels funny, doesn't it?"

Chris didn't dare laugh or even speak. She was too close to tears, and how would she explain that to a child?

Oh, you lucky child... sweet, funny, precious little girl—do you even know how lucky you are? She sat with the tiny kitten crawling up her collarbone, pricking her skin with its tiny claws and bumping her neck with its little, cold nose, and ached inside for the childhood she'd never had, for all the things this little girl had and would surely take for granted. *Do you know...*

"Hey, Rosie, Chris—you in here?"

Rose Ellen bounced to her feet. "Daddy! We're in here, lookin' at the kitties. I only picked up one, ver-ry carefully, so Chris could hold it. That's all."

"Good girl," said Mike, as his daughter danced through the stall gate to meet him. "You check on Belle yet?"

"Nope." She went skipping off to do so, while Chris returned the kitten to its nest and rose, stiff with embarrassment. She was brushing straw from the seat of her pants when Rose Ellen returned to report, "She's just standin' there, not doin' anything."

"Okay. Well in that case, your mother's looking for you." Mike scooped her up in one arm for a quick kiss, then set her back on her feet and gave her bottom a pat. "Better go see what she wants—go on, scoot."

Rose Ellen scooted, giggling. In the profound quiet following her departure, Mike pulled the stall gate open wider and waited for Chris to go through, then walked beside her toward the barn door. When they got there he turned, touched her arm and said quietly, "You okay?"

She gave a light laugh, not looking at him, and murmured, "I've been better."

"Gwen filled us in a little—about your family history."

Chris just nodded. Mike waited a moment, then said, "Wood's a little upset."

She tried the same light laugh, but it emerged as a small whimper of distress.

Mike said, "He's wondering why you didn't tell him."

She couldn't speak, just shook her head and looked away.

"I think I understand why you didn't."

Slowly she turned her head to look at him. She thought, *He's got such compassionate eyes....* And possibly because of that, or maybe because he was more of a stranger, and people sometimes tell things to strangers they would never dream of telling someone close to them, she drew an uneven breath and said, "I was just . . . ashamed."

"I know," said Mike softly, looking into her eyes in a way that told her he *might* really know. "But I think you're selling Wood short. I really think you should tell him."

Chris said with a break in her voice, "I don't know if I can."

"Just . . . talk to him," Mike urged gently. "Give him a chance. I think, when the time is right, you will be able to tell him. And I think you'll be glad you did."

They emerged together into the cool spring sunshine. Chris drew a long breath and laughed, another of the small, helpless laughs that was more like a whimper. She gave her eyes a quick brush and said unevenly, "Okay, where is he?"

"Front yard," said Mike. "Waiting for you, I believe."

She found him sitting in his chair on the frost-burned lawn, near a spot where a huge tree stump had been sawed off level with the ground. At his feet Chris could see clusters of green leaves, wild violets growing lush in the valleys between the roots of the old tree.

"Sure is a shame about this tree," he said, not turning or looking at her, but speaking as if he'd known she'd be there. "It was a great tree. Not just because of the swing, either. There was a robin's nest I could see from my folks' bedroom window. And it was a good climbing tree, too. I even tried to build a tree house in it once—I think I was about seven. Lucy helped me, but it was too much for us. We really needed Rhett, but I guess he was too busy being Big Man on Campus at the time."

Chris gulped air and said brightly, "He's . . . quite a bit older, isn't he?" Then she stopped where she was, still several yards distant from him. She knew she couldn't pull it off, not this time. Butterflies were dancing in her stomach, making her voice bumpy. She didn't want him to see that she was shaking.

Wood nodded. "Eight years. But he was okay, as big brothers go. I wish sometimes I'd had a chance to get to know him better."

He fell silent. Watching him, Chris thought how isolated he seemed, like an island there in his chair. Suddenly she wanted so badly to reach out to him, somehow make him understand. But she didn't know what to do.

She was making a try at it, had swallowed at the dryness in her throat and opened her mouth, meaning to say, "I'm sorry," when he finally spoke again in a slow and thoughtful voice.

"I've been sitting here thinking... about the kind of childhood I had. Actually, I've been doing that quite a bit the last couple months, mostly feeling kind of sad about it. I couldn't figure out why, but now I think it's because so far I can't see I've done much to live up to the start I got in life. I guess I didn't realize how much I've taken for granted. I mean, I've seen things—overseas in Somalia and Bosnia—and I've thought about what a lucky guy I am to have been born in a place where things like that can't happen. I guess it's hard to think about something... so close to home."

He lifted his head and looked at her, finally, with an expression in his eyes she'd never seen before. She crisscrossed her waist with her arms to try and stop the trembling, but it seemed impossible. She couldn't read him at all, couldn't see where this was heading. So all she could do was wait.

"You told me once," he said slowly, as if he, too, was feeling his way, "that your past wasn't a happy time for you."

She nodded, and the words came tumbling out of her shaky insides. "I'm sorry. Wood, I'm so sorry I lied to you about knowing you before. I didn't mean—"

His eyes flared, suddenly bright with his pain and anger. "Geez, Chris, I don't care about the lie. You didn't know me back then, what kind of a guy I was or anything. Hell, I'd have probably lied about it myself, in your shoes. But that was a long time ago, dammit. I thought things had changed. Was I wrong, or has something been happening between us? You tell me, Chris. What just happened awhile ago, down there in that shed? Was that just some kind of newfangled *therapy?*"

She shook her head helplessly. Her face felt swollen; her throat ached so.

Wood's voice dropped to a gravelly rumble. "*Why*, Chris? When you knew we were coming down here, why didn't you tell me then? All the time I was pointing out landmarks— Geez, I even showed you the high school! When were you going to let me in on the fact that you went there, too, and at the same time I did? Were you *ever* going to tell me, Chris?"

"I'm sorry," she said again in a low voice, desperately gulping back incipient tears. "I was ashamed. Of who I was then. I didn't want you to know."

He let out his breath in a rush, as if he'd been holding it. "I think I can understand that. Believe it or not, I can, even though I don't agree with your reasons. But it doesn't change the fact that... God, this scares me to death." He paused, pulled in another breath. "Dammit, Chris, I have all these feelings for you—hell, I'm in love with you, and I don't have a clue what's going on inside you. I don't know how you *feel*— about me, about anything. Tell me *something*, dammit. I know you have feelings. Can't you just... trust me enough to tell me what they are?"

Tell him, Mike had advised her. Give him a chance. And she wanted to, she wanted to so badly. But the risks...oh God, the risks.

"I do have feelings for you," she cried at last. Sobs were so close now...so close. "I do. But..."

"But what?"

But I still have things I have to tell you. And you won't want me when you know.

She shook her head helplessly.

"You have feelings for me?" Wood prompted, his voice gentler now. "What kind of feelings? Good feelings, bad feelings, funny feelings..."

Love... Oh, what a terrible word that was. What a terrifying word to utter. She was shaking so hard she could hardly stand. And she certainly couldn't look at him. Impossible. "I feel...I love you," came her whispered confession. "I have for a long time."

There was a strange little silence. So awful was the suspense that she had no choice but to look at him, and once she did, it seemed as though she'd never be able to tear her eyes away from his again. She'd never seen them so deep, so dark, so intense.

They seemed to drink her in, to draw from the wells of her very soul.

"Were you never going to let me know that, either?" he asked softly, his lips curved in a little smile.

She shook her head and looked away.

"Why not?"

A short, painful laugh burst from her. "Because... I didn't have the courage." How strange this is, she thought. To be standing here like this, so far apart, not touching except for our eyes... and talking about love. "I didn't think I had a chance with... someone like you."

"What the hell do you mean, 'someone like me'?" But he was definitely smiling now, his eyes shining like polished stones. "I'm nobody special—just plain old Earl Brown from Iowa."

"But... that's just it—you're *Earl Brown*. In high school—"

"High school! Forget high school. This is the real world. Besides..." he pushed himself toward her, eyes twinkling like stars in a midnight sky "...I thought you were cute back then, too."

"You *didn't*. You didn't even know I was alive."

And suddenly they were walking along together, strolling and rolling slowly, the two of them all alone in the world. And Chris realized that she wasn't shaking anymore, except for a warm, tremulousness all through her body, as if she were newborn and just learning how everything worked.

"I did too," said Wood. "You interviewed me once for the school paper—bet you didn't think I remembered, did you?"

"I remember that you ended up interviewing me instead. I always wondered... why did you do that?"

"Because you were so damned cute. Hey—you wore glasses back then, didn't you? What happened?"

"Contacts."

"Ah. Anyway, you looked so shy and scared. I wanted to make you smile." He reached for her hand, lifted it to his lips. "I still do."

But Wood noticed that although her lips curved upward, her eyes didn't smile. And it occurred to him that she still hadn't told him anything about herself, her past, her family. Not a word.

They left for the city soon after that, with the back seat and trunk of Chris's car crammed full of Wood's clothes and a few personal belongings he'd left behind years before, as well as some bedding, towels and kitchen supplies Lucy and Gwen had scrounged up for him.

He realized that he felt a whole lot different leaving than he had when he'd arrived. He felt a sense of peace and ease and lightness, as if he'd completed something important, left a burden behind.

Even saying goodbye to Gwen and Lucy, Mike and little Rosie was surprisingly easy, a casual thing, like bidding good-night to a close neighbor. Because he knew he'd be back, and often. Because he'd discovered that his childhood home, his family, his past weren't lost to him at all, they were right there waiting for him, and had been all along.

And when they passed the church at the crossroads, he rolled down his window, imagining he could still hear the sounds of the congregation singing hymns on a Palm Sunday morning. Only this time it made him smile, and when, presently, he began to sing himself, pulling a song from the dusty shelves of his memory, his throat didn't close. He sang hesitantly at first, but quickly warmed to it as to a dear friend from childhood met after long, long years apart.

"What is that?" Chris asked him when he paused at the end of the verse. "I think I've heard it before."

"Just an old hymn Mom and I used to sing," he said. "It's called 'Church In The Wildwood.' Here—it's an easy one. I'll teach it to you."

Of course, she protested that she couldn't sing, but she was wrong. Wood was delighted to discover that her voice, though it lacked confidence, was sweet and true, and by the time they were halfway home he had her holding the melody in her childlike soprano while he sang the harmony. She giggled when he slipped into a belly-deep bass for the "Come...come... come" part, and that made him feel good. He was finding that he was never happier than when he could make her laugh.

Deep down inside, he knew that all their talk of love and mutual confessions of feelings hadn't made her happy. That it had resolved nothing, and that for him it had raised more questions than it had supplied answers. He thought again of the nesting dolls. He knew there were still more layers of Chris Thurmond hidden inside the one he'd come to love.

But at least the singing made the trip home easier, made it almost possible to forget the tensions between them, the mutual awareness of so much yet unfinished, so many things unresolved. And of passions banked, but far from quenched.

It was dusk when they drove into the security parking garage under their apartment building. Wood was tired. His legs were aching pretty badly, so he took his time about getting from the car to his chair, while Chris took armloads of clothes and bedding out of the trunk. They rode up in the balky little elevator, all but filling it, the two of them loaded down with as much of Wood's stuff as they could carry. On the way Chris began to sing "Church In The Wildwood" again, very softly under her breath, humming when she couldn't remember the words.

A pool of warmth spread through Wood's chest as he brought in the bass harmony on cue. And when they'd finished the last "little brown church in the vale," just as the door was opening, he chuckled and drawled huskily, "You learn fast."

"You're a good teacher," she responded. Then, as if she'd just heard something in her own words, she tilted her head to one side and repeated thoughtfully, "You're a very good teacher. And you have such a way with children."

"Come on."

"No, you do. I don't, but you really do. The way you were with Kevin ... Did you ever think about ..." they were at Wood's door, so she paused and waited while he unlocked it, then held it for him to go through "...about being a teacher?"

He gave a surprised little huff of laughter. "I hadn't, no." And it wasn't something he wanted to think about, not just then. He shifted his lapful of clothing onto the sofa and waited for Chris to dump her armload, then said with gravel in his voice, "If you want to know the truth, the only thing I can think about right now, now that we're finally alone, is how much I wish I could make love to you."

She turned toward him, moving stiffly, a deep pink blush creeping into her face and neck.

He smiled, amused and tender. "Hey, don't be embarrassed, darlin'. After what happened between us today, I don't think it's any secret how I feel. And by the way, it's no secret how you feel, either. Right?"

She licked her lips, swallowed and slowly nodded.

"Chris," he drawled, and felt his perceptions narrowing down, laserlike, into one tight beam of high-voltage sexual awareness. "Like I said down there in that old shed, what happened between us wasn't finished. I sure would like us to do a lot more of that, only I'd like it to be under circumstances that aren't quite so frustrating."

"I'd like that, too," she finally admitted in a slurred voice. And he felt as if he'd just watched a child take its first step.

He closed the distance between then. "But at the same time, I don't think we can just put everything on hold until I get out of this damned chair, do you? I want to kiss you so badly I can taste it. I want to undress you, a little bit at a time . . ."

He reached for her, put his hands on her hips, slid them around to cup her bottom . . . and felt her tremble. "Ah . . . damn," he groaned as she swayed toward him. "Chris, you know the only thing keeping me from asking you to stay with me tonight is this damned chair."

Her hands were on his shoulders, her buttocks firm and tight in his hands. "You don't . . . sleep in the chair," she pointed out, her voice thick and husky.

"Oh, man . . ." He laughed raggedly. "Oh, darlin', how you do tempt me." Tempt wasn't the word; his body was heated and primed, and so tightly restrained it felt cramped, like one giant charley horse. Because even though his thoughts might have been muddled somewhat by his hormones just then, he had a vague sense of something incomplete, something not quite right.

So he sighed brokenly and held her away from him, which might have been the hardest thing he'd ever done, and said, "Listen . . . we're going to make love together, you and I. And when we do, I don't want anything getting in the way." He rapped on his casts with his knuckles, even though he knew very well he hadn't been referring to just the physical barriers to intimacy. "Understand?"

She nodded and pushed away from him, and he stifled a groan of regret.

"I'd better go," she mumbled, looking around in a lost, vague sort of way. "Check my messages and...things. I'll come back later, if you want me to—to help you put things away."

He grabbed a steadying breath and nodded. "Sounds good. Meanwhile, I'll fix us a bite to eat." He followed her to the door. She went out, leaving it open, and he watched her cross the hall, reach to put her key in the lock. "See you soon," he murmured, and pushed himself backward.

He was closing his door when he heard her scream.

Chapter 14

It wasn't much of a scream—more like a cry, hastily stifled. Even so, Wood was out his door and across the hall before it had died, every nerve, muscle and sinew in his body singing with adrenaline.

He could see Chris through her open doorway, standing with her back to him, shoulders hunched, both hands pressed tightly over her mouth. He called her name with an urgency that tore at his throat, and she whipped around, made a small, choked sound much like a sob...except that above her hands he could see that her eyes were dry.

"My God, Chris..." Wood pushed into the room, shaken to the core.

Through all his wars, he'd never seen such cruel and sense-less devastation. It seemed to him that everything that could be broken had been—sofa cushions sliced open and the stuffing pulled out, pictures torn from the walls and stomped on, ta-bles overturned, lamp shades crushed like so much wastepa-per. And all around on the walls, smeared across the windows, a sticky red substance he knew at once was not paint.

"My God:...who did this?"

It would have been a stupid thing to ask the victim of a break-in, except that even in his shocked state, he'd sensed something odd about her. Something that didn't fit. She didn't seem to be frightened, the way she should have been—the way anyone would have been—walking into her home and finding that it had been burglarized and vandalized in her absence.

What she was, he realized, was *angry*. Behind the bleached and frozen mask of her face, he could see it, see it in her eyes, hot and burning as dry ice.

"My God, Chris," he said again, his voice an appalled croak, "you *know*, don't you? You know who did this."

Slowly she nodded, her arms stiff at her sides, hands balling into fists. She licked her lips, and when she spoke her voice was scratchy and halting, as if it was something mechanical that hadn't been used in a long, long time.

"It was Alan." She cleared her throat, and that seemed to help a little. "Alan Bendix. My ex-husband." She began to wander aimlessly through the debris, picking up things and tossing them aside. "He's been calling me . . . sending things . . . making threats, for a long time."

Wood swore randomly under his breath; he could hardly form coherent sentences. Finally he managed to ask, "Have you gone to the police?"

She nodded. There was a bitter twist to her mouth. "They told me I didn't really have enough reason to have him arrested. They gave me a pamphlet and some suggestions. I've been keeping a journal. . . ." She'd been searching as she spoke. Now, having found the telephone, she was hauling it out from under piles of books and papers by its cord. "It must be here someplace, if he didn't take it with him."

Suddenly she dove down and came up with a small brown book. Its pages were crumpled and smudged, some of them torn. She glanced at it almost negligently, then handed it, open, to Wood.

He read what she'd written in her neat, pretty hand and felt the rage well up in his throat like sickness. He couldn't even speak, except to mutter once again, "My God, Chris."

She was looking around distractedly, frowning as if she'd misplaced something, or wasn't quite sure where she was. "He, um . . . he tried to run me down with his van yesterday," she said in a conversational, slightly bemused tone. "That's how I fell . . . hurt my knees." She looked down at the heel of her hand, then gave a short, dull laugh. "Funny thing is, I was going to go to the police today and file charges. I was finally going to have him arrested."

"But instead you went with me," said Wood slowly, so shocked, so appalled he could barely take it in. To think that all the time he'd known her... "For God's sake, Chris, why didn't you tell me? We could have gone to the police before we left town. *Why didn't you tell me?*" Then he just shook his head; it was becoming such an old song.

"Hand me that phone," he said grimly, because he couldn't even begin to maneuver his chair through the wreckage. She did, without a word. "Does it still work?" He lifted the receiver and found it stone dead.

"Oh, I forgot—I unplugged it last night." Chris dropped to her knees, found the end of the cord and plugged it into the jack.

Wood got a dial tone and punched in 911.

Giving the necessary information in a clear and rational manner helped calm him, so that by the time he'd hung up the receiver and handed the phone back to Chris, his anger was banked and under control.

"The police'll want to know if anything's been taken," he said, keeping his voice low and even. "You probably ought to check, but I don't like the idea of you going into the other rooms until they get here. No telling what kind of surprises he might have left you."

He drew a breath and leaned toward her across his clasped hands. "While we wait, I suggest you try telling me what's been going on for a change. I'd like to hear about this ex-husband of yours. Hell, I'd like to hear about a lot of stuff. You said he's been doing this for a long time? How long? No...wait." God, there was so much he wanted—needed—to know, that he didn't know where to begin. He didn't even know what to ask.

He snatched a quick breath. "Okay—first of all, how long have you been divorced?"

Chris sank onto the arm of her ravaged sofa, the phone still cradled in her lap, and said in an exhausted-sounding voice, "Six years."

"*Six years?* My God, you mean—"

"Oh no, this—all this didn't start until about ten months ago." She sighed and looked away. "I guess . . . I'd better start at the beginning."

"I guess you'd better," said Wood shortly.

But she didn't start at the beginning—nowhere near it. And he knew it.

"Alan always said he'd kill me if I left him," she said after a long pause, looking away from him toward the window, which the growing darkness outside had turned into a mirror, compounding the chaos inside. She shrugged. Her voice was so matter-of-fact it seemed eerie to listen to her, Wood thought; hard to realize what she was telling him. "But since I was pretty sure he was going to kill me anyway if I stayed, I figured I had nothing to lose and maybe a better chance if I left. So one day I did, with nothing but the clothes on my back and a little bit of money I'd managed to save.

"It was enough to get me to a women's shelter in Des Moines. I stayed there until I was able to take the high school equivalency test and get my diploma. The people at the shelter helped me find a job and a place to live that didn't cost much, and the next semester I enrolled in classes at a community college, and . . . that's pretty much how things went for the next five years. After I got my P.T.'s license, I applied around the state to various places. This one seemed like the best, and I thought . . . so much time had passed, I guess I thought I was safe."

She looked down at her hands, resting on the telephone in her lap, and slowly shook her head. "I still don't know how he found me. I suppose someone he knew, a customer, maybe, or a friend—he owns a farm equipment dealership, so he has lots of business acquaintances—must have seen me and told him. Anyway, about two months after I came back to Sioux City, he called me." She gave a high, sharp laugh. "He wanted me to 'come home.' Can you believe it? He can't seem to accept the fact that we're divorced. He keeps saying things like, 'Until death do us part . . .'"

A siren sounded in the distance. She tensed and jerked her head toward the windows, listening as it came closer.

"All this time," Wood said softly, half choking on his anger. "This has been going on the whole time I've known you, and I never had a clue. Not a clue. My God, Chris, why didn't you tell me?"

Her head snapped back to him, and his heart gave a lurch when he saw that there was color in her cheeks, and that her eyes were gray and glistening, like stormy seas. "It... never...came...up," she said furiously, biting off each word. "What did you expect me to say? 'Hi, I'm Chris. I'll be your physical therapist today. Oh, and by the way, my ex-husband is *stalking* me'?"

"Come on, Chris. That's not what I'm talking about, and you know it. What about yesterday? That bastard tried to kill you! And when I asked you what happened, you told me you *fell!* All those phone calls—that was him, wasn't it? And the reason you didn't want me in your apartment—you were afraid I'd hear him on your answering machine. That's it, isn't it? Why didn't you tell me when I moved in here, at least? I could have..." A thought seized him. "My God," he said, his voice hushed. "Is *that* why you did it? I wondered what—is that why you got me this place? *Is it?*"

She sat hunched and silent while the sirens screamed below the windows and then abruptly died. He saw a tear make a silvery track down one cheek; its twin followed a second later. "I was...so scared," she said at last, her voice high and tight. "I felt...so alone. I thought...if I just had someone—a friend—nearby..."

The significance of that took a moment to sink in. "You mean to tell me," he said slowly, "that nobody knows about this? You haven't told *anyone?*"

She brushed at the tears on her cheeks and whispered, "No."

Once again Wood could only shake his head and swear. Footsteps were coming down the hall, heavy footsteps, unmistakably official. As he made a three-point turn and went to meet them, he felt something akin to despair.

It's not going to work. The thought made him go cold and hollow inside, but he couldn't make it go away.

There were two policemen, both male, both young. They tried to act as if they'd seen it all and nothing could rattle them, but Wood could tell they were as shocked by the condition of the apartment as he'd been. Once they'd been given a capsule version of what had happened, one of them went off to interview the manager and the other tenants of the building in the hope of finding someone who might have seen a stranger near Chris's apartment, while the other stayed behind, taking notes.

Wood, having identified himself as "a friend," gave his statement and thereafter kept out of everybody's way, watching from the fringes of the activity while his mind scurried in distracted circles, always coming back to the same question: *How am I ever going to make a serious relationship work with this woman if she won't open up to me?*

Then it occurred to him it was the first time he'd ever thought of Chris—or anyone else, for that matter—in terms of "serious," and that realization shocked him almost as much as the devastation spread out in front of him. Because for him, "serious" had some pretty frightening implications.

It meant permanence—settling down, making a home, having children, putting up with in-laws, growing old together. It also meant giving and taking, sticking it out through thick and thin, enjoying the good times and helping each other through the bad. It meant intimacy and honesty and trust. It meant . . . sharing.

All this he was thinking, and with a woman he apparently knew nothing about, and who evidently didn't trust him enough to reveal the most basic facts about herself. He had to be crazy.

A second team of officers arrived, one of them a woman. She took Chris off to a relatively clear and quiet spot to talk to her alone. Wood could see the policewoman asking questions, but also doing a lot of the talking herself, which he hoped meant she was telling Chris some things she needed to know about how to protect herself from lunatic ex-husbands.

The officer who'd left to look for witnesses returned just as Wood heard Chris say, in a voice that sounded as if she might be reaching the end of her tether, "I don't know, I'm sorry. I can't imagine *how* he got in."

"I'll tell you how," said the officer, strolling over to join the two women. "The manager let him in. The guy told him he was from the phone company. Said you'd reported your phone out of order."

"On a *Sunday?*" Wood burst out, unable to keep silent. "You've got to be kidding."

The policeman looked at him and shrugged. "The guy told the manager that, because she was in the medical profession, it made it a Class-One emergency. The manager bought it—he's a trusting guy. He didn't have any idea she'd been having problems." He turned to Chris. "You know, you shouldn't keep something like this a secret. You want to tell your neighbors, your friends what's going on, so they can help keep an eye out for the guy. Okay? That manager—what's his name?— Spickler. He never would have let the guy in if he'd known about the trouble you've been having. Chances are he'd have called us, and we'd have the man in custody right now."

Chris only nodded. She looked like a chastised child.

The other two officers joined them, comparing notes, preparing to close up shop. The one who'd just reported in read from his notebook the description of the "telephone repairman" he'd gotten from Mr. Spickler.

"Six feet tall, heavyset, dark hair, blue eyes, receding hairline." He glanced at Chris. "That sound like anyone you know?"

She nodded, but had to clear her throat before she could answer, "Yes, that's Alan."

The officer with the notebook, who seemed to have taken charge, said reassuringly, "Well, ma'am, we're going to go see if we can locate Mr. Bendix, talk to him about what happened here, okay? Meanwhile, you need to give serious thought to getting a protective order from the court against your husband. That gives us a lot more to work with, understand?"

Chris nodded. The female officer touched her arm, gave it a comforting squeeze.

"You're probably not going to want to stay here tonight," said the take-charge officer. "You got anywhere you can go? A friend, family member..."

"She'll stay with me," said Wood. His voice seemed harsh and unnaturally loud in his own ears.

The policeman nodded and tucked away his notebook for the last time. All four officers converged on the door, taking with them their cameras and evidence kits, their aura of authority and an intangible umbrella of safety.

For a while after they'd gone Wood sat very still, listening to the heavy thud of footsteps fade away down the carpeted hallway. He couldn't seem to look at Chris, although he was intensely aware of her standing there so straight and tall in the midst of the wreckage. He kept waiting for her to say something, do something, although he had no clear idea what that might be. But of course she didn't, and it came to him suddenly that what he was waiting for was for her to react like any of the other women he'd ever known.

But Chris wasn't like any other woman he'd ever known; he'd realized that from the very first, hadn't he? And he suddenly knew that she was right, that he was expecting too much from her.

He'd forgotten to have patience, a lapse that might, he thought, have had something to do with this extraordinary discovery that he loved her. He'd had an idea that his loving her should magically solve all her problems. That just because he loved her she should automatically trust and confide in him. Why not? Love to him meant sharing. He considered her a part of him, and all her problems his problems, too. It was so simple to him. But obviously, to her it wasn't.

He let his breath out soundlessly and spoke as gently as he could, with so much of himself reined in and held under iron control. "Well, let's don't stay here. Is there anything you need to get? Toothbrush, clothes..."

Chris nodded and went off to the bedroom, moving like a sleepwalker. A few minutes later she returned, holding her toothbrush and nothing else. "My clothes are all pretty much ruined," she said in a soft, careful voice. "Except for what was in the laundry hamper. I'll have to wash something..."

"Do it tomorrow," Wood said tersely. "I'll find something you can sleep in." He wanted to get her out of there. Even with her awesome control, he figured she must be close to breaking. "Just get your purse. Lock up and let's go."

Although why bother? he thought as he took one last look around on his way out the door. There was nothing left to steal.

Back in his apartment, Wood closed the door and locked it, put the chain on and felt the silence of intense awareness settle in around them. He made straight for the pile of clothes on the sofa, rummaged through it and came up with a St. Louis Cardinals baseball shirt, an old favorite of his, soft and faded from many washings, many sunny hours spent flapping in the Iowa wind.

"Here," he said, tossing it to Chris, "that ought to do it. Sorry I can't do much about underwear. Don't think mine would fit you." He tried for a smile. "If you need bottoms, I can probably find some sweats in here somewhere...."

"No—no, this is fine. Thank you." Still moving in her bubble of artificial calm, she set the shirt and her purse and toothbrush carefully on the coffee table and went to gather up an armload of the clothes from the sofa.

"Leave those," Wood told her. "I'll put everything away tomorrow."

She glanced up, frowning. "But I thought—I'll be needing—"

"Forget that. We're short of blankets, remember? You can have half the bed."

She just looked at him, her eyes luminous and, for once, completely transparent.

"Come on, you're safe with me," he said. "You know that, don't you?" But his voice was so harsh and gravelly it seemed to contradict the words. And so he was taken by surprise when she smiled...a smile he'd never seen before, from her, anyway—gentle, a little slumberous and completely feminine.

Yes," she murmured, "I know."

Something about the way she said it made his mind go momentarily blank, and he had to struggle to remember what he'd been about to say.

"Ah...oh, yeah—you'd better take the first crack at the bathroom." Again he struggled to produce half a smile. "It takes me quite a bit longer. Or, if you don't feel like turning in yet—are you hungry? I can fix you some eggs or something."

She shook her head and murmured vaguely, "I'm not hungry. But I am tired. It's been...kind of a long day."

It had been that, he thought, noticing with a sharp pang of sympathy the dark smudges under her eyes. Especially for her. And as for him, he'd stopped counting all the places he ached. He'd been sitting far too long.

"Okay, good," he said, making it short and businesslike. "In that case, the bathroom's all yours. Holler when you're through."

He waited until he heard the shower running, then rolled past the bathroom and into the bedroom, where he found a pair of sweats for himself and checked to make sure he'd tidied up the place that morning before he'd left for the farm. And boy, did *that* seem like a year ago to him now.

After that he went back to the kitchen and puttered around until he heard Chris's call. Then he stalled a minute or two more, to give her a chance to get settled in bed while she had some privacy. To his surprise, though, when he went to take his turn in the bathroom, he found her standing in his bedroom doorway, as if she'd been waiting for him.

The sight made him feel as if he'd been hit in the chest with a medicine ball. The light from the room behind her glanced through her milky hair like streaks of sunshine through clouds and gilded the fine down on her long, bare legs. He thought she looked like a cross between a pagan goddess and a teenager at a slumber party.

As it turned out, that baseball shirt he'd loaned her gave him a good deal to think about. She was a tall woman, but he was a good bit taller, so it hit her about midthigh and covered her decently enough. However, being conventionally and unrepentantly male, he couldn't help but speculate about what she had on underneath the damned thing.

He just couldn't decide. Knowing how modest Chris was, he'd have bet she was wearing panties, at least. On the other hand, he knew how fastidious she was, and since she didn't have a change of underwear to put on... well, it would make an interesting little dilemma for him to ponder while he was struggling through the tedious process of getting himself washed and clothed for bed.

"I was wondering if you needed any help," she said, and he watched color wash into her cheeks, as if she'd suddenly become aware of the direction of his thoughts.

"Nah," he said gruffly, "I can manage. One or two things I'm not very good at, but I'm learning." He gave her his soon-to-be-patented half smile. "To tell you the truth, taking off my pants is the hardest part. Once I get past that, the rest is a piece a' cake."

He saw her gaze drift downward, saw her eyes darken and her throat move as she thought it over.

"Go on to bed," he said gently, disgusted with himself for teasing her, as tired as she was. "I may be awhile. Just leave the light on for me."

He figured she'd surely be asleep by the time he'd finished. And that was just as well. Just as well that they were both so tired, he told himself. It made things a whole lot easier.

But she wasn't asleep. She was wide-awake and again apparently waiting for him, lying straight as a lance on the far side of his bed with the covers flat and neat across her breasts and her arms folded over them. And he knew that, in his heart of hearts, he was glad. The sight of her tousled, vanilla-ice-cream hair on the pillow next to his seemed so natural to him, so *right*.

It also made every vestige of tiredness, every awareness of cramped and aching muscles go flying right out the window.

"Thought you'd be asleep," he mumbled just before he hit the light switch.

Her voice came out of the sudden darkness, soft as a caress, asking again if he needed any help.

He told her he didn't, but he was grateful she couldn't see him struggle.

When he finally had himself straightened out and flat on his back, he lay very still for a while, waiting for his vital signs to quiet down. But although his breathing did slow after a minute or two, for some reason his heartbeat refused to settle into normal rhythms.

All his senses and perceptions seemed to be focused and refined into a kind of radar. His body knew the shape of hers, even though several inches of space separated them. He could gauge her body heat, fragrant and humid from the shower, count her shallow, slightly uneven respirations. He knew that her pulse, like his, was much too fast for rest; that it would be throbbing at the base of her throat... That her eyes, like his, were wide open and staring into the darkness, her ears straining to catch the slightest movement, the slightest sound....

"Wood?" Again her voice stirred his auditory nerves like a lover's touch, raising goose bumps. "Are you all right?"

"Yeah, I'm fine."

"I just wanted... I need to tell you something."

"Shoot."

"I wish... you could understand."

"Try me," he growled softly. "You'd be surprised what I can understand."

He heard a quick intake of breath. "I never meant to keep things from you. It's a habit, I guess. It's just that...I've been on my own for so long. And when this started I thought I could handle it. I didn't want to burden anyone with my problem. I really thought...I could deal with it alone."

It was a moment before he could answer. "Well," he finally said, in a voice so thick and husky he hardly knew it for his own, "you're not alone now. You have me."

He heard the tiniest of sniffs, and realized suddenly that she was trembling. "But...that's just it. I want to tell you—I do. I've wanted to for a long time. But it's just so hard to break the habit, you know? I don't know...if I can let someone inside me. I've never done it before."

There were so many things he wanted to say to her, but all at once he felt overwhelmed by the enormity and the consequences of what he was getting himself into. And he for whom words had always come so easily suddenly found himself at a loss for even one.

Follow your instincts—that's what Lucy had told him to do. And so he did.

"Come 'ere," he growled, and reached for her. Felt the silky tickle of her hair on the inner bend of his elbow, got his arm under her head and around her shoulders. "Relax..."

It wasn't that she resisted, exactly. It was rather as if she wasn't quite sure what she was supposed to do. He felt as if he was teaching a beginner how to play an instrument, guiding her stiff body into alignment with his, nestling her head into the hollow of his shoulder. "Yeah...just like that. Now—are you comfortable?"

She gave a strange little chuckle, half laughter, half sob, and he felt her head move, bumping his chin. She turned herself toward him and her hand came shyly, tentatively to rest on his chest. He covered it with his own and felt a tremor cascade through her. And then another...and another.

"Easy," he murmured, as if he were crooning a lullaby. "I just want to hold you. You don't have to tell me anything right now. And you don't have to be afraid anymore, understand?

Because I'm right here, and I'm going to take care of you. I'm going to protect you. You just relax, now...go to sleep, okay?"

Again her head nudged against his chin. He felt her take a breath and let it out, and knew that she was trying her best to do what he'd asked.

And not doing any better a job of it than he was. After a moment she gave another of those minute sniffles and whispered, "Wood? I have to tell you something."

"No, you don't."

"Yes, I do. I'm trying to relax, but if I can't, I just want you to know it's not your fault. It's just that . . . nobody's ever held me like this before."

His breath caught painfully in his chest. "You're kidding me. *Nobody?*" It seemed impossible to him. Such a fundamental thing, affection. As necessary to life as food. "Not even when you were little?"

Her body seemed to shrink almost imperceptibly, and yet he felt it. "Not that I remember," she said, her voice gone curiously flat.

"Well, get used to it, darlin'." He covered the side of her face with his hand, stroking her hair, her ear, her temple. "Because I'm a toucher and a cuddler by nature."

He lay then, staring up into the thin gray darkness, his body tense and tingling with familiar urges, hot and aching in the usual places, thinking about all the women he'd held like this, but differently . . . almost always in the aftermath of sex, when bodies were sated and relaxed and sleep came easily. He thought about all the ways he'd made love to those women, all the physical intimacy he'd known, and realized that he'd never felt as close to a woman in his life as he did to this one, whom he hadn't made love to at all. Her body was still a mystery to him; he had yet to touch her in real intimacy, had yet to enter her body and bind her to him in physical union, and still, in a way more real and compelling than anything he'd ever felt before, he felt that she was his.

Then it occurred to him to wonder if maybe what he felt for Chris had happened *because* of his physical limitations. He was honest enough to admit that, in all his other relationships, the physical union had been his primary goal, and possibly because it was so easily achieved, he'd simply never bothered to pursue any other. But with Chris, he wondered if it was because he'd been denied access to her body that he'd come to know, and to love, the person inside.

The idea intrigued him, but did nothing at all to quench the fire in his loins.

You're not alone... no need to be afraid... relax... go to sleep.... That's easy for you to say, Chris thought, quelling a painful little ripple of irony. She couldn't possibly relax, for reasons she'd told Wood only half of.

It was true that she'd never been held, just held, in a man's arms before. But it was also true that she wanted much more than just to be held. The truth, impossible to deny, was that she wanted him. She more than wanted him; she desired him with an intensity that stunned her, because she hadn't thought she was even capable of such feelings. And the irony—oh, the irony!—was that the first time it happened to her, it had to be with someone who couldn't—or wouldn't—make love to her.

Go to sleep? How could she possibly, when her nipples ached so, when pulses throbbed in her most intimate places, when her whole body tingled with a sensation that was almost like an electrical charge? She had to fight against the need to touch, to rub, to squirm; had to fight with every ounce of strength she possessed to keep from turning her face into his chest and pressing her mouth against his smooth, warm skin, tasting him, inhaling his musky, masculine scent.

Oh God, she thought, what am I going to do?

This was torture, pure and simple. She couldn't move away from him; she couldn't possibly stay so close. She lay tense, rigid as a post—and suddenly realized that he was as tense as she was. The pectoral muscle that pillowed her cheek felt like iron.

"Wood," she said softly, "is something wrong?"

"No, darlin'. Nothing's wrong." His hand made a convulsive little movement, tightening over hers. "Everything's gonna be fine." His voice sounded slurred, but she knew he wasn't sleepy.

"You're tense," she said. "I can feel it. Are you in pain?"

His chuckle was curiously strained. "Yeah, a little. Muscles, mostly. I sat too long in that damn chair today, is all. I'll be okay."

She wriggled away from him and sat up. "Okay, turn over," she commanded. She could feel him staring at her, probably as if she'd lost her mind. She laughed, and it felt like things were bumping loosely around inside her. "It's okay, I'll help you. It's all right, I promise."

There was a pause, and then he muttered indistinctly, "Okay, Coach, you're the boss."

Wood raised himself on his elbows, then turned his upper body away from her. She felt keyed up, jittery, full of butterflies. She knelt beside him, put her hands on his hips, felt his buttocks clench as she rolled him onto his side. Carefully she adjusted his casts, rearranged his legs, then eased him over. He settled onto his stomach with a muffled groan.

He jerked when she first touched him, not at the shoulders, the trapezius muscles, as she normally would, but at his waist, just above the gathered band of his sweats.

"Are my hands cold?" she asked innocently, spanning his back with her fingers, digging into the ridges of muscle that lay along his spine. He shook his head and murmured something she couldn't quite hear. She smiled as she moved her hands upward, finding the different muscle groups, the sensitive places, sculpting his back with her hands, "seeing" it with her fingers.

When she reached his shoulders, though, she found that they were too broad, that the reach was too great, too strained for her comfort. It seemed a natural thing for her to straddle his hips.

"Chris...what are you doing?" Wood's voice sounded faint and airless.

"Giving you a massage," she told him gently. "Why, am I hurting you?" But she smiled as she leaned forward to grasp his taut trapezius muscles, adjusting her legs so that the sides of his waist brushed her inner thighs. She felt exhilarated, even a little drunk. It was heady, this feeling of feminine power.

"No...you're not hurting me. God, no..." His breath seemed to catch in his throat.

Chris, who was working her way down his spine, had just seated herself on his buttocks and was dipping under his sweats so that she could reach the small of his back. There was a furring of hair there, she found to her fascination. And twin indentations, one on either side, just above the gluteus maximis.... She leaned forward again, bending low in order to catch his strangled comment. "What did you say?"

"I *said*..." His voice was a sandy growl of pure frustration. "You're not hurting me, you're killing me. Dammit, Chris. Do you know what you're doing?"

"I think so," she murmured absently. She was rubbing his lower back in slow, sensuous circles...spanning the small of his waist again. She raised herself a little so she could slide her hands around and under him, pushing her fingertips into the damp, curling hair on his belly. Her thighs tensed and began to quiver.

She was completely unprepared when his body suddenly bucked and bunched beneath her. Using nothing but the tremendous strength in his arms and torso, he turned himself within the imprisoning V of her legs, and she uttered a sharp little gasp of surprise as she found herself sitting, not on the firm, rounded pillows of his buttocks, but on something much harder and much more specifically shaped.

Large hands—strong, warm hands—slid up her taut thighs and around to grasp her buttocks, and she knew at once that the power wasn't hers any longer.

"That's what I thought," he growled. "No panties."

Chapter 15

"Chris, darlin'...what am I gonna do with you?" Wood's voice was deep and low, a panther's purr.

Hers was high and breathless, not frightened, but...oh, she didn't know what—she'd never felt like this before. "They were dirty," she gasped. "I washed them."

She felt his body bump beneath her in silent laughter, although when he spoke it was with a groan, as if he were in pain. "That's not...what I mean...and you know it." His thumbs brushed the crevices at the tops of her thighs with a painter's strokes, light and delicate. She shivered and realized that her legs seemed to be opening wider still, all of their own accord.

Can this be me? she wondered. She felt no shyness, no fear, no shame. Only a deep yearning, a bottomless hunger, urges her body seemed to know and understand even though she'd never felt such things before. Touch me, her body demanded. Yes, there... And with every nerve crying out for attention, she couldn't hear the timid whispers of self-consciousness...nor, perhaps, of common sense.

Touch me.... She thought he may have said something, but words weren't what she wanted now. She closed her mind to them, listening instead to the clamoring within her. *Yes...like that.*

His hands rode slowly upward under the soft cotton shirt she wore, following the curve of her hips, thumbs trailing over the sensitive places along her pelvic bones, then sliding inward to all but encircle her waist. She gasped, sucked in her stomach and arched her back when his hands skimmed her ribs, pushing up and up to find and cradle her breasts...when his thumbs roughly circled, then delicately flicked each nipple to hardness, playing them like a master, coaxing thrumming chords of response from the deepest part of her.

She leaned forward into his hands, reaching for him, suddenly needing to touch as much as she craved being touched. Her hands flattened on his chest, her fingers fanned wide, acquainting themselves with the soft-rough textures of his hair. She leaned farther, hungry for him, searching for him, wanting the taste of him, the feel of him on her tongue.

"Chris...you know we can't do this." His whisper blew warm across her lips.

"Why not?" She breathed it back to him, brushing his lips with hers and shivering at the sensations that exquisite contact aroused.

His reply was inarticulate, just a primal sound relinquishing, for the moment at least, all good sense and control. His hands slid around her, flattened against her back; his torso tightened and curved like a drawn bow, his head and shoulders lifted, bringing his mouth to hers, and he plunged his tongue deep inside her, claiming her mouth once and for all time as his.

And she was consumed. Desire exploded through her like gasoline thrown on smoldering flames, blinding her, enveloping her in heat and obliterating all thought. She wasn't prepared; she'd never felt anything like this. It was holocaust, overload—she couldn't survive it.

Nor could she bring herself to stop.

But suddenly Wood's arms were hard and tight around her shuddering body and she was sobbing into the hollow of his neck, struggling for breath and for a measure of sanity. The most sensitive part of her body, resting on the hard, hot ridge of his, throbbed with a slow, steady pulse that seemed out of sync with her frantically racing heart. His chest rose and fell beneath her; she rode it like an ocean wave, and it seemed to help a little, quieting her panic without diminishing the fires that raged on inside her.

"Chris, this is crazy." Wood's voice was agonized, the sound of tearing cloth. "I don't...have anything to protect you with...understand? We can't...ah, hell."

He took her face between his hands, stroking away the moisture of sweat and tears and passion, staring into it as if he could see it in the darkness, trying to see all the way to the secret core of her soul, the part so vulnerable she kept it hidden away from the world. Love flooded him, so fierce and protective his body rocked with it, cataclysms of the heart so profound he knew he'd be changed by them forever. He lifted his head and kissed her from the depths of those cataclysms, rocking her with him, rousing and soothing her at the same time...because implicit in the kiss was a promise.

Chris must have heard the promise and understood; her whimpers of frustration became deep-throated chuckles, her tremors languid undulations that stroked his body from his sternum to his loins. Very slowly he eased her mouth from his and raised her, supporting her as she arched forward, bringing her breasts to him. He cupped one in his hand, stroked and tugged the nipple with his fingers while his mouth treated the other the same. He pulled it deep, sucking hard as he slid his hands downward over her writhing body to grasp and stroke her buttocks, coaxing her legs wider, urging her gently but firmly forward, telling her without words what he wanted of her.

She knew what he wanted. And oh, she wanted it, too, her need like pain, every nerve so sensitized she thought she would scream with it. She was grateful for his hands, guiding her trembling legs, half supporting her even as they stroked her inner thighs and the throbbing, aching places between.

She cried out when he touched the swollen lips that guarded her body's most intimate secrets, almost fell when he eased them apart with his thumbs. But he held her firmly, a captive even when in desperate panic she tried to shudder away from that exquisite torture, afraid she couldn't possibly survive it, let alone what had to follow.

"Easy..." he crooned, gently stroking her. And then he kissed her there. With tenderness and care his mouth closed over her most vulnerable place, bathed the sensitive bud in honeyed heat. Her bones melted . . . her muscles gave way. She swayed, light-headed, while star bursts exploded inside her, sending a rain of fiery pinpricks into her legs.

Then . . . oh, then . . . his hands held her fast while his mouth, his lips, his tongue tormented and cherished her, lightly sucking, deeply probing, laving with teasing, feathery strokes. Her cries became thin and high—primitive, animal sounds. She was beyond caring.

Her body bucked and crumpled. She might have screamed, and then she was falling, falling, wracked with spasms she thought would surely tear her apart.

Except that Wood's arms were around her, holding her close, holding her together while she shivered and cried helplessly, lying naked and utterly devastated upon his chest. "It's okay . . . shh, darlin' . . . it's okay," he kept whispering as he stroked the hair back from her wet cheeks, his lips pressing hard against the top of her head.

It took her body a long time to quiet down. Aftershocks kept rippling through her, tiny residual pulsings she felt deep, deep inside. Relaxation finally crept up on her unawares; she even dozed, although she didn't realize it until she gave a violent jerk and heard Wood's chuckle in her ear. Half-awake but all-aware now, she lay still and waited for the waves of shame to wash over her. She waited, but they never came.

At last she stirred, drew a sighing breath and murmured, "I may never forgive you."

"What?" His voice was soft with laughter. "Why?"

"I died, didn't I?" she whispered wonderingly. "I must have."

"Hmm . . . that's funny." His hand skimmed slowly, lightly up and down her back. She wondered when she'd taken off the shirt; she couldn't remember doing so. "The French do call it the 'little death,' you know."

"Yeah? I didn't know. . . ." She wriggled as his hand stroked deliciously over the curve of her bottom. When she did, she couldn't help but notice that he winced. She gave a small, contrite gasp and lifted her head from his chest. "Oh, God— Wood, I'm sorry. I didn't even think. How could I—"

"Forget it. I'll be okay." His hands tightened when she tried to shift her weight, holding her where she was. He laughed painfully. "Don't worry, I'll live to 'die' another day...."

"Oh-ho-ho...*no* you don't," she cried, wriggling out of his grasp. "If you think you're getting off that easily—especially when I have you at my mercy like this..."

Oh, she had her revenge. And she took her sweet time about it, too, paying him back in spades for every stroke, every touch, every caress he'd given her, more than making up in curiosity and sheer enjoyment of his body what she may have lacked in experience and know-how.

She pleasured him with her hands—her strong, sensitive healer's hands. She explored him, every inch of him, with her mouth... her lips, her teeth and her tongue. She all but drove him crazy, seeming to sense when he was about to explode and pulling back each time just enough to prolong the agony.

The only thing she couldn't do was keep him from doing what he liked with his own hands in the meantime...and what he liked was to touch her, every part of her he could reach, in every intimate and erotic way he could think of. So that by the time he did climax—so explosively he finally understood fully what she'd meant about dying—he had her moist and squirming all over again, as completely aroused as she'd been at the start.

So aroused she lay quiescent, almost in a daze, not uttering a murmur of protest when he raised himself and drew her legs apart, pushed his fingers through her damp curls. She moaned softly when he slipped a finger inside her and pressed deeply, and she lifted herself against his hand, asking for more.

He gladly obliged her, probed deeper still...and slowly withdrew, rubbing his hand against her swollen lips as he pushed into her again...and again. She began to move with him, panting, writhing in wanton, heedless rhythms. He found the tiny, sensitive bead at the center of her body and began to rub it with his thumb, and felt a surge of primitive, masculine triumph when she arched, gasped and cried out, and he felt her body jerk and clench, and then the rippling shock waves of *her* climax.

"Unfair," she whimpered. "Unfair..."

But he just laughed and held her until the trembling stopped, and after a while began it all over again.

They finally slept a little before dawn, awakening groggy and disoriented to a gray and rainy spring morning.

"Wha'time izzit?" Chris mumbled, raising herself on her elbows and looking around with eyes so unfocused Wood remembered suddenly that she normally wore contacts.

He squinted at his naked wrist. "I dunno...my watch is in the bathroom."

She nodded, frowning as if she was trying to remember something important. He saw it come to her—the realization and the embarrassment. She sat up jerkily, stiffly, holding the sheet to her breasts with one hand while the other raked through the dandelion thicket of her hair. He saw her lick her lips as she looked around her at the tumbled bed, and knew she was searching in silent desperation for the shirt she'd abandoned so wantonly in the night.

He'd been waiting for something like this. Expecting it.

He touched her arm and said her name with the rasp of morning in his throat, then tugged gently on the sheet she held, though leaving it safely in her grasp. "Look at me."

She turned her head toward him but avoided his eyes. A soft, pink wash stained her cheeks.

"Daylight doesn't change anything," he said, smiling even though he doubted she could see it, hoping she'd hear it in his voice. "It's still you and it's still me. Darlin', last night I explored every single inch of your gorgeous body. Don't hide it from me now." He pulled again on the sheet, and this time, after the slightest hesitation, she let it fall.

He let out his breath in a hiss of wonder and brushed the side of her breast with his fingertips, lightly traced its sweet undercurve with his knuckle, just for the sheer pleasure of watching the nipple grow rosy and erect before his eyes.

She gazed at him somberly, almost warily, he thought, her lovely, nearsighted eyes still glazed and unfocused. After a moment she leaned down and kissed him, a thoughtful, gentle caress that for some reason made his throat ache. Then, without a word, she slipped out of bed and walked naked to the bathroom, and every stiff, self-conscious movement was a reminder to him of how far they had yet to come.

While Chris was in the shower, Wood wasted no time getting himself up and into his chair; nature had been calling him urgently for some time now. She was back sooner than he'd expected, wearing her freshly washed underwear and forgetting to be shy about it. She had his watch in her hand and a stricken look on her face.

"Wood, look what time it is. I'm already late for work." She shoved a hand through her wet, tousled hair and glanced around distractedly. "What am I going to wear? I'll have to get something out of the laundry. Oh God...what am I going to do?"

"I'll tell you what you're going to do." He gave his wheels a shove and rolled up to her, reached for her hands and grasped them hard. "Geez, lady, who do you think you are, Superwoman? Besides, we have things to do this morning, remember? Like go down to the police station, go to the courthouse and pick up a restraining order, clean up your apartment. Probably should call your insurance company—you do have insurance, I hope? Maybe we'll even buy you some clothes. What you're *not* going to do is try to go to work and pretend like nothing's happened, you got it? So...first thing you do is, you go use your phone and call in sick."

She looked genuinely horrified. "Oh, Wood, I couldn't do that. I'm *not* sick."

"Well," he said with a wry shrug, "you could always try telling the truth."

He let go of her hands and pushed on into the bathroom, still talking to her over his shoulder. "Look here—why don't you go through that pile of stuff on the sofa? There's probably something there that'll fit you. Find me a shirt, too, while you're at it. Soon as I'm through in here we'll go over and make that call. Okay?" He closed the door on her look of consternation.

Wait! she wanted to cry. Stop—you're going too fast for me!

It was all happening too fast; everything was changing. The orderly and insulated world she'd created for herself was collapsing around her like a house of cards, leaving her standing naked and alone in the debris, with all her secrets exposed.

You're not alone now...you have me.

Last night Wood's words had been a comfort to her; this morning they were terrifying. He expects so much of me, she thought bleakly. Love and affection, intimacy, sharing and trust... it was so easy for him. He'd grown up with those things; even, as he'd admitted, taken them for granted. He didn't know—he *couldn't* know—how alien it all was to her. He couldn't know unless she told him. And she knew she had to tell him. She just didn't know how.

Give him a chance. Tell him ... you'll be glad you did.

Oh, how she wished she could believe that. But when she played it over in her mind, telling Wood her terrible secret, she always saw his face fill with horror and revulsion. How could it not? And then, inevitably, she saw him leaving, unable to bear even to look at her.

Maybe Mike was right and she was selling Wood short. But how could she be sure? The risk was too great, too great. Too much was at stake now. And with every moment that passed, the stakes grew higher. Why hadn't she known that falling in love was like plunging down the side of a mountain in a runaway wagon? It was going too fast ... *too fast.*

You didn't seem to mind the runaway wagon last night.

Oh... last night. She sucked in air, her nipples hardening, her body's center already throbbing at the memory. *But that was different.*

It wasn't true, what Wood had said about daylight not changing anything. Daylight changed *everything.* How she wished it was possible to separate night from day, to somehow draw a curtain between those two parts of her life.... She found herself smiling suddenly—and unexpectedly. The Secret Sex Life of Christine. It sounded like an X-rated movie title. *But who would have thought I had it in me?*

She felt herself grow hot. She was all alone in the room and blushing to the roots of her hair, every nerve in her body alive with total sensory recall. Oh God, I have to stop thinking about it, she thought. Otherwise how will I ever get through this day?

Wood must have hurried through his bathroom chores, because he seemed to be out in record time. At least she was dressed when he found her in the living room, in a pair of his jeans that were too snug in the hips for her, and a rugby shirt that, thankfully, was long enough to cover the fact.

"How's this?" she asked uncertainly, pausing in the process of rolling the sleeves of the rugby shirt to her elbows. "Do I look all right?"

Wood's face was a subtle and confusing mix of signals. His eyes were smoky hot mirrors of her own erotic memories. But his smile was gentle and wry, and his voice tender when he said, "You don't get it, do you? Darlin', don't you know you'd look great to me in brown paper?"

Oh God, she thought, and didn't know whether to laugh or whimper.

Especially when he gave his wheels a nudge, reached for her and growled, "Come 'ere, you ... I haven't kissed you properly yet this morning."

The bottom dropped out of her stomach. His hands pushed under the rugby shirt to find her waist, then slid down over her hips and on around to grasp her behind, girdled in skintight denim. She swayed forward, clutching at his shoulders for support. He uttered an inarticulate murmur of pleasure against her belly; his beard was a tease, an erotic tickle ... his mouth a brand. Her knees buckled.

He laughed softly and turned her around, settling her bottom against the arm of his chair and cupping the apex of her thighs in his hand while he trailed hot, open-mouthed kisses up her spine. She moaned and began to squirm, already swollen and aching where his hand was. She pressed her thighs together, but he pushed between them and rubbed hard along the ridge of denim. And she was lost ... lost. Earth and sky changed places, and day became warm, sultry night.

She lay against his chest; her head fell back on his shoulder. His hard-muscled arm was a chafing band across one breast while his hand shaped and molded the other; she uttered a sharp little cry when he caught the nipple between thumb and palm and gently pinched it, sending shock waves of sensation into every part of her. She arched and pushed in unconscious rhythms against his hand.

His hand moved to the button fly of her jeans ... and then stopped. His arm folded instead across her waist, and she felt a gusty sigh blow warmly past her temple. "Damn," he murmured, "what am I thinking?"

He ducked his head to nuzzle the hair away from her ear, kissed it tantalizingly and whispered, "Just proves I'm right, though, about daylight not changing anything. After all that...last night...I still want you so badly I can taste it. I can taste *you*. But...if I start this now we may never get out of this place. And I'm afraid we have to. We have things to tend to, remember?"

She nodded, and he eased her back to a sitting position. Oh, but inside she was seething, trembling, every nerve jangling. *Me remember? You started this!* she wanted to cry, furious with him for igniting her fires and then leaving her to burn in agony.

His hands steadied her until she'd found her feet, then lingered while he asked in husky-voiced concern if she was okay.

And she actually nodded—she wondered if it was an automatic response for her, maybe even reflexive, because, of course, nothing could have been further from the truth. She paused then and looked down at him, frowning. "You want the truth, right? About how I feel?"

"That's right," said Wood. "Always."

"Well, okay." *Here goes,* she thought, and grabbed a breath. "No, dammit, I'm not all right. I feel lousy. And I'm angry with you for doing that to me and then . . . and then—"

His expression was quizzical, his eyes warm and glowing. "I know," he said softly. "I was thoughtless. I'm sorry."

Chris glared at him uncertainly, surprised that it had turned out to be so easy, but not quite ready to forgive just yet.

He smiled wryly and reached for the sweatshirt she'd laid out for him on the arm of the sofa. "If it makes you feel any better," he muttered indistinctly from its folds as he was pulling it over his head, "I'm in at least as bad a shape as you are."

She glanced at his lap and said, "Huh—I doubt that." But it did make her feel better—a little. "I feel like I've been run over by a truck," she muttered, still a bit shakily, as they were making for the door.

"No, you don't," Wood said with a dark, ironic chuckle. "Believe me—I know."

Chris thought she was braced for the horror of her apartment, but it hit her again like a fist in the stomach just the same. In some ways she thought it was worse than it had been last night. She'd been in shock then. This morning the full extent of her loss was beginning to sink in.

"Take it easy," said Wood grimly. "Take a deep breath. Don't look at anything. Just get the phone and bring it over here. We'll tackle the mess later."

She nodded, grateful for the comforting strength of his hand. She hadn't even been aware that she'd reached for it, but somehow it was there, big and warm and comforting, enfolding hers.

She nodded, made her way to the telephone, punched a pre-programmed button and heard Roxie's familiar voice chirping, "Good morning, Riverside Clinic."

"Hi, Roxie, this is Chris."

"Chris! Hi! We were wondering—"

"Yeah...listen, I'm sorry. I should have called sooner, but...I'm not going to be able to come in today."

"Okay...gee, Chris, what's wrong? Are you sick? You don't sound like yourself. Would you like to talk to John?"

"No—no, that's okay. Listen..." Her eyes met Wood's across the jumbled wreckage and held on while she drew a deep, bolstering breath. "I'm not sick. I've had some trouble...." She closed her eyes. "My apartment was broken into yesterday. So I have some things I have to take care of today, okay? You know, the police...things like that. I should be back tomorrow, but I need you to reschedule for me."

"Oh my God, Chris, that's awful. What—do you—do the police know who did it? Did they—"

"Listen, I don't want to get into it right now, okay? It's kind of...a long story. I'll fill everyone in on it when I see you. Just reschedule my patients for me, and...I'm sorry about not calling sooner."

"Oh, hey—that's okay. You just take care, all right? Don't worry about a thing here. I'll tell John."

"Thanks, Rox." Chris hung up the receiver, feeling as if she'd just run a mile. She huffed out air and looked over at Wood, who smiled and gave her a thumbs-up sign. She shook her head and muttered wryly, "Hoo boy, that's hard."

"Don't worry," he said, his voice as soft as his eyes, "it gets easier with practice."

The phone rang, startling them both. Chris picked it up, expecting it to be John or someone else from the clinic, since Roxie had had just about enough time to deliver the news. Instead it was the police.

She listened, feeling oddly disconnected from what was being said and its implications. She heard someone asking questions, but didn't feel as if the voice she heard answering was her own. Presently she cradled the receiver, then stood motionless for a few moments looking down at it. The hand that rested upon it seemed distant and tiny, like something viewed from the wrong end of a telescope.

"Who was that? Don't tell me—"

She gave a start, looked over at Wood and shook her head. "It was the police. One of the same ones who was here last night, I think."

"Well? What's going on? Have they arrested him?"

She cleared her throat carefully. How odd she felt—cold and numb, except for a tiny, white-hot core of rage. "They can't find him," she heard herself say with frightening calm. "Apparently Alan didn't go home last night. And he didn't go to work this morning. It seems he's gone."

"Okay, I think we're gonna need a couple of ground rules," said Wood as he and Chris sat in her car in a handicapped-parking place outside the courthouse. The motor was running, and the windshield wipers beat a steady counterrhythm to the drumming of the rain. "Number one, it's okay to admit you're scared."

She didn't reply, but he saw her eyes flick to her rearview mirror, and her lips curve into a faint, ironic smile.

"And number two," he said grimly, "until this guy's caught, you don't go anywhere—and I mean *anywhere*—alone, you got that? Now, I can't be with you all the time you're at work, so you need to tell everyone there and at the hospital what's going on, and make sure you always have somebody with you. Hey, maybe I should get you one of those portable phones. That way if you see anything suspicious, you can call the cops. What do you think?"

Chris smiled and shook her head. "I think you're getting a little bit carried away."

"After what the cops told us? This guy is *nuts*. Most of the damage in your apartment was done with a helluva big knife, and they seem to think that was meant as a message to you."

He turned his head to look at her, his head rotating stiffly, his jaws clenched tight. "Look, you still don't get it, do you? You mean too damn much to me. I'm not going to take any chances on you getting hurt, you understand? I'll do whatever it takes to keep that from happening—and I mean *whatever* it takes. Nobody's ever going to hurt you again, not as long as I'm around. Nobody."

She gave him a quick, startled look. Well, hell, he'd surprised himself a little, too. He had to swallow hard a couple of times and stare out the side window until he had himself under full control again.

Chris reached for the ignition key and turned off the motor. For a few moments the silence was broken only by the ticking of a cooling engine.

"Wood," she said softly, "I'm very glad you're here with me. Having you care for me..." her voice broke, and she had to clear her throat to get it going again "...is probably the most wonderful thing that's ever happened to me...."

He smiled wryly. "I hear a very big 'but' in there."

She reached across the space between them and placed her hand over his. "Please try to understand. Wood, I'm not a child. I've had to struggle to get myself out from under the absolute dominance and control of the men in my life. I can't...let you take over my life for me."

He stared at her, shocked. "I'm not trying to take over your life! All I want to do is help you."

"I know." She smiled gently and gave his hand a squeeze. "But sometimes...you know, the best way to help someone is to stand back and let them go it alone."

He made an involuntary movement and a choked sound of protest, but she held up her hand, pleading with him. What could he do? He swallowed his frustration and listened.

"It's like...when I've worked and worked with somebody to get them back on their feet again, and that time comes when they have to stand up and take those first painful steps. I just want to reach out and—and support them, you know? It's so hard not to. Sometimes I think it's the hardest thing I have to do as a therapist—just...keep my hands to myself. And that's what I'm asking you to do for me, Wood. Please...be there for me, but let me do it myself...okay?''

Wood could hardly speak. What she'd said to him, and how hard it must have been for her to say it, touched him profoundly. He turned his hand, captured hers and clasped it tightly, then coughed and jerked his head toward the courthouse entrance.

''There you go, darlin','' he finally drawled, though still with gravel in his voice. ''It's all yours. I'll be right here waiting for you when you're done.''

Her eyes shimmered like sunlit waters. ''Thank you,'' she said simply, and leaned over and kissed his cheek.

He listened for the slamming of her door, then watched her walk away from him, breaking into a run to escape the rain. He watched with his eyes burning and his heart in his throat until she'd disappeared inside the courthouse.

She was right. It was one of the hardest things he'd ever done.

Chapter 16

Chris insisted on going back to work the next day, which didn't make Wood happy. He'd argued with her until he was blue in the face, as his dad used to say, giving her all the reasons why he thought she ought to wait at least another day or two. For one thing, they'd barely made a dent in the mess in her apartment. And as he'd pointed out to her, thinking that would be the clincher—and for any other woman he'd ever known, it would have been—she still didn't have anything to wear.

He kept forgetting she wasn't like any other woman he'd ever known.

The main reason Wood didn't like the idea of Chris going back to work, though, was because he was just plain worried about the toll the stress was taking on her. She wasn't eating, although it hadn't affected her gorgeous body much that he'd noticed—and he thought he would have noticed, since they'd spent the night once more exploring all the erotic possibilities each other's body had to offer. At least within his limitations. And that, of course, was another frustration entirely.

He wasn't sure why he was holding off consummating his relationship with Chris. He ached to be inside her; not a moment of the day went by that he didn't think about it. And it wasn't even that it was physically impossible. He knew Chris would have been more than willing to accommodate his temporary handicap, and the "astride" position happened to be one of his favorites, anyway. He'd even bought condoms during their stop at the grocery store. And the funny thing was, he knew he probably wouldn't have hesitated for a second, if that was all he'd wanted from her. But it wasn't. Although it surprised the heck out of him to be so old-fashioned about it, he just wanted it to be *right*. And while he was honest enough to admit to a certain amount of masculine pride, wanting to make love to her for the first time with his full strength and control of all his body parts, the main reason was that it just didn't *feel* right to him, not when Chris was still in so much emotional turmoil.

Because although she tried to be cheerful and behave as though she was perfectly fine, he knew better. It was her eyes that betrayed her. They had dark smudges under them that stood out on her pale skin like bruises. He thought they seemed, for want of a better word, *haunted*.

And the strange thing was, the closer he grew to Chris, the more Wood wondered if it really was her ex-husband she was so afraid of.

In any case, Chris had her way; he was discovering she could be damned stubborn when she wanted to. They went in early to the clinic that morning so they could stop by the hospital first to see Kevin. Wood felt bad about the way he'd been neglecting the kid lately, so he rounded up Sal Ramos and got him to escort Chris across the street to the clinic while he stayed on awhile to give Kevin a guitar lesson.

When Wood got back to the clinic, he could see that Chris was busy with a patient, so he rolled on into her office and used the phone on her desk to call his family and fill them in on what was happening. Lucy was out in the barn with a calving heifer, so it was Mike he talked to. In a way he was glad. There were some things he wanted to know, and he had an idea his brother-in-law might be able to tell him.

He told Mike first of all about the break-in and the vandalism, and about the trouble Chris had been having, being stalked and threatened by her ex-husband. Then he said, "You know, Mike, you were right about the abuse. Except it wasn't her father who was abusing her, it was her husband. If she did get married to escape from a bad home situation, it looks like she went out of the frying pan into the fire, so to speak.''

"I'm sorry to hear that," Mike said after a moment's silence. "Sounds like she's had a pretty rough life."

"Yeah. Listen, I don't know very much about this domestic-violence stuff. You, uh...you seem pretty knowledgeable on the subject, and I was wondering..."

"I've taken an interest it it, yeah. Written a few columns about it."

"I don't mean to pry, but any particular reason?"

"You mean, personal? Nah—I just don't like bullies. Never did. What was it you wanted to know?"

"Okay—you've met Chris, right? You can see for yourself what kind of a person she is—I mean, she's bright, she's intelligent, beautiful...*boy*, is she beautiful. And yet she stayed married to that abusive sonuvabitch for six years. *Six years*, Mike. What in God's name makes a woman do that?"

"Low self-esteem," Mike said, and for some reason his voice suddenly sounded cautious. "That's usually the reason. Somehow they've been made to feel they deserve it."

"But—my God, *Chris*? You've seen her—she's fantastic. Why in hell would somebody like that have low self-esteem? I can't understand it, man. And I can't help but feel like it's important, too, you know?" He paused, dragged a hand through his hair and added with difficulty, "I think...I have to know."

"In that case," said Mike quietly, "maybe what you should do is ask her."

"Chris—phone for you," Roxie called, beckoning from the receptionist's window. "Line one. It's the hospital—Pediatrics. Sounds urgent. Why don't you take it right here?"

Pediatrics? The only patient she had in pediatrics at the moment was Kevin, and she'd left him barely two hours ago.

She leaned across the counter to take the receiver. "Hi, this is Chris." She listened for only a second or two, then gasped, "Be right there!" and thrust it back at Roxie. "I have to go. Where's Wood? Has anybody seen him? Oh, God..."

"I saw him come in a little while ago," Roxie told her, looking anxious. "But I don't know where he is now. Maybe he's using the rest room. Chris, what's wrong? Did something—"

"Find him. I can't wait—have to go." She could hardly marshal enough breath for words. Her heart felt as if it was jumping right out of her chest. "Tell him I couldn't wait for him, okay?" She was dancing sideways, already halfway to the double doors. "Tell him I've gone to the hospital. Tell him to meet me there. Tell him..." She shoved the door open with her hip and backed through it, almost hopping up and down in her excitement. "Oh God... tell him *Kevin moved his toes!*"

And then she was outside, sprinting for the signal at the corner. She was still yards away when she saw the Don't Walk sign blink on. "Oh, no..." she moaned. It was such an interminable light, what with left turns and pedestrian crossings. How would she ever manage to live through the wait?

Of course, the tunnel entrance was there, only a few feet away on her right. Oh, but she hated the tunnel. She never used it unless someone was with her. But just this once...what harm could possibly be waiting for her down there, anyway? The police were on the lookout for Alan, and besides, why would he be waiting for her in a place she'd never, ever go? She was just being childish, afraid of the ghost in the closet. The fact was, she'd probably be safer in that tunnel than she would be anywhere else. Alan would never look for her there.

She ran down the steps on legs that shook from excitement more than fear, fingers skimming the handrail, her feet ringing on the concrete, sending eerie echoes down the brightly lit cavern. There was no one else in the tunnel at that hour. Up ahead she could see the darker half circle that was the entrance from the hospital's basement parking garage. She focused on it and quickened her steps, almost running now.

Closer and closer that dark opening came, and closer still. Her heart was pounding; she knew her legs were moving, but still that tunnel entrance seemed just out of reach. Her side ached.

It's my dream, she thought suddenly. The nightmare she knew so well. It was all here. The sense of lurking evil, unreasoning fear, the endless, slow-motion flight on legs that felt like lead. *But that was only a dream... only a dream.*

And then suddenly, unaccountably, the tunnel entrance darkened. Someone was there. Someone who had stepped from the shadows at the side of the opening to block her escape.

The light was on his face; there was no mistaking him. Nor the long, gleaming blade of the knife he held in his hand.

"What do you mean, she's gone?" Wood said in a voice brittle with irritation. "Gone where—to the hospital? Who went with her?"

Roxie lifted her shoulders, looking unhappy. "Nobody. She went alone. She said to tell you—"

"Dammit!" He brought his palm down hard on the reception counter. "She's not supposed to go anywhere without someone with her. Why didn't somebody stop her? Why didn't you call me?" He shoved himself toward the double doors, swearing vehemently.

"She left just a minute ago," Roxie offered eagerly. "Maybe you can still catch her. She said to tell you—"

But Wood had crashed through the doors and was plowing across the waiting room, leaving several people staring after him over the tops of their *People* magazines.

Outside, he paused briefly to survey the parking lot and street. Damn. He couldn't see her anywhere. Roxie'd said she'd just left. Okay, so where in the hell was she?

He could see that the signal light at the corner was red. Had Chris made it across before it changed? Or had she taken the tunnel? In any case, for him the tunnel would be faster than waiting for the damned light to turn green. Provided he didn't have to wait for the damned elevator.

It had to be at the bottom, of course. He stabbed at the call button, then waited in nail-biting frustration, pounding on the arms of his chair and bitterly cursing elevators, cursing steps. Cursing himself. Premonition curled chillingly around his spine.

If anything happens to her...

He was unshaven; his teeth shone white against the dark stubble in a travesty of a smile. Softly, he crooned, "Hello, Chrissy, remember me?"

He seemed heavier than Chris remembered, but otherwise, except for the growth of beard, very much the same. He hadn't lost his winning, tractor-salesman's smile, or that strange little light in his eyes that he always got just before he hit her. He hadn't lost the ability to make her feel powerless and afraid.

"That's right, Chrissy." His voice was so smooth, almost silky.

For some reason it made her think of Wood's scratchy drawl, and her heart contracted painfully. *Oh, Wood, I'm sorry.*

"Yeah...it's me, your loving husband, Alan. Remember me? Seems to me like you've been forgetting you even have a husband lately, haven't you, Chrissy?"

She licked her lips and took a step backward as she pleaded with him, knowing in her heart it was futile. "Alan, you're not my husband anymore. We're divorced, remember? Why are you doing this to me? This is crazy...."

His stance, which had been relaxed and confident, suddenly stiffened. "How do you dare say such a thing to me? I'm your husband—you took a vow in front of God. No paper's gonna change that. You're my wife." He shook his head, like a bull preparing to charge. "You've been unfaithful to me, Chrissy. I have to punish you for that."

She took another backward step, threw a quick, desperate glance over her shoulder, gauging the distance to the far end of the tunnel. She could run...could probably even outrun him. But her legs wouldn't obey her. They felt leaden and stiff, as if they'd been fastened to the floor.

He'd advanced as she retreated, step by step. He was so near she could feel him, smell the fetid heat of his body. One sudden move and he'd have her. And then the knife...

She shook her head and whispered, "No, Alan, I—"

"Don't lie to me!" His voice cracked like a rifle shot. "I know you've been with that cripple. I'm going to have to kill him for that—I was going to kill you, too, but I don't know now if I can do that." His voice had turned high and plaintive, as if he was on the verge of weeping. "I love you, Chrissy. You're mine. So what I'm going to have to do is make it so nobody else'll ever want you, see? That's what this knife is for. I'm going to cut you, Chrissy. I'm going to cut your face... maybe your body, too. I haven't decided. And after that..."

Oh, please, God...somebody... Wood, please come....

As if in answer to her silent prayer, the far end of the tunnel, the elevator door clanged open.

"Chris!" Wood's shout filled the tunnel, echoing like cannon fire. *"Run,* dammit!"

And suddenly her legs would move again, obey her commands. Wood was here! With a sobbing gasp she lurched toward him. Something hot grazed her arm, but she hardly felt it. Wood was here! She wasn't alone anymore. She was safe.

Then a terrible thought hit her. Alan had vowed to kill Wood. He had a knife. And Wood was trapped in a wheelchair.

She whirled like a cornered vixen. But Alan had vanished.

"Stay there," Wood thundered as his chair whizzed past her, his powerful arms pumping the wheels like pistons. "Don't move!"

She was right on his heels as they burst from the tunnel into the hospital's basement garage, but Alan was nowhere in sight. Above their own labored panting Chris could hear running footsteps, echoing, fading away in the distance.

There was an emergency telephone on the wall near the elevator. Wood made straight for it and yanked the receiver from the wall. His face was frightening, black with fury.

"I'm in the basement," he bellowed into the phone. "This *is* an emergency, dammit. There's been an assault. Give me 911 and send security down here, pronto."

Then he dropped the receiver onto the pavement, reached for Chris and pulled her to him. She felt his body vibrating with deep-seated tremors as she cradled his head against her breasts.

"It's okay...I'm okay," she murmured brokenly. "He didn't hurt me."

"My God, Chris—why did you do that? I told you not to go anywhere alone. Why couldn't you have waited? If I'd been a few seconds later..."

"I know...I know. I'm sorry." She began to laugh, crying a little, too. "I got a call— Oh, Wood—Kevin moved his toes."

He lifted his head. "Kevin moved—oh, man, that's great news. Fantastic news." Then he gave her a shake that was poignant in its restraint. "But dammit, Chris, it could have waited. Just a few seconds...minutes—hours, even. Kevin's toes are still going to be there. Don't you know you could have been killed? If I hadn't—geez, you *are* hurt. The bastard cut you. Look at your arm—you're bleeding!"

Chris stared in surprise at the runnels of blood that striped her forearm, the drops that stained Wood's sweatshirt. Then she shook her head rapidly, reassuringly. "It's nothing—I didn't even feel it. Wood, he was going to cut me—my face, he said—so nobody else would want me."

"God . . ."

"But he wasn't planning to kill me," she whispered, staring bleakly over his head, her mind following the path of her assailant's escape. "It's you he means to kill."

First thing Wood did was take Chris upstairs to Emergency to have the cut on her arm tended to. After that they went together to see Kevin.

Flanked by his tearfully happy parents, he was looking pale and a little dazed. Like someone who'd just been hit by a miracle.

"Hey," he said when he saw Wood; evidently the Southern style had rubbed off on him, too.

"Hey," said Wood, bumping knuckles with him. "How ya' doin'?"

"Pretty good. Guess you heard, huh?"

"Yeah, we heard."

A smile hit his thin face like a floodlight, wavered and then vanished. The look of solemn determination that took its place made Wood's throat ache. "I'm gonna do it. I'm gonna walk again. Just like that buddy of yours you told me about."

Wood glanced up at Chris. She had her back to the kid's bed, and he could see that her eyes were shimmering. "Never doubted it for a minute," he said gruffly as her eyes met his . . . and spilled over.

She reached blindly for his hand. He caught it and gave it a squeeze. Go ahead, cry, the squeeze said to her. Crying's good.

He leaned over, plucked a tissue from the box on the bedside table and casually handed it to her. "Here—have one. On Kevin."

She uttered a sound, halfway between a laugh and a sob.

Even after all that, and again over Wood's strenuous objections, Chris insisted on going back to work. He kept wondering when it was really going to hit her, the fact that she'd just been assaulted by a maniac with a knife. He knew she had to be upset, but except for the tears she'd shed over Kevin, she'd seemed almost frighteningly controlled. As though, he thought grimly, she'd crawled back into her shell of ice.

When they got back to the clinic, Roxie was on the phone, jotting down a message.

"Oops, here she is now," she said when she saw them. "Police," she hissed, and thrust the receiver at Chris.

Wood intercepted it. He listened, asked a question or two, said, "Thanks a lot," and handed it back to Roxie. He sat for a moment, then let his breath out in a rush. "Well, they got him," he said quietly. "Picked him up just a couple of blocks from here. They have him in custody now."

"Have *who* in custody?" said Roxie, her head snapping back and forth between them.

Wood glanced at Chris. Her face was set and pale. "Chris's ex-husband," he explained, without taking his eyes away from her. "He attacked her in the tunnel this morning."

"That's what I don't understand," Chris said, her voice low and only for him, barely audible over Roxie's shocked gasp. "How could he have been there? How could he have known? I never use that tunnel alone—never."

"He didn't know," Wood said grimly. "He was across the street, watching for you—had both the hospital and the clinic staked out. When he saw you come out of the clinic and go into the tunnel, he scooted around and into the parking garage. Just in time to intercept you at that end."

"Well," said Chris on a soft exhalation, "I wondered. Roxie, is my one o'clock here yet?"

Wood's stomach clenched. It was that cool, remote voice he hated so, her face pristine and untroubled, her perfect smile in place. There was no mistaking it—she'd retreated, back inside her shell. And in the depths of his guts he was afraid. Afraid he might never find a way to bring her out of it again.

There was nothing for him to do but stay close, keep an eye on her and wait. Be patient, Grady would have told him, and he tried his best. He kept telling himself that she'd suffered an ordeal, that people reacted to these things differently. She'd asked him to stand back and give her room. And that's what he tried to do. And to be there when she needed him. That's all he could do.

That evening after work they made another try at cleaning up the mess in Chris's apartment. They worked until almost midnight, filling plastic bags with trash and piling broken lamps and furniture in a corner to be taken down to the bins. Anything salvageable they moved across the hall to Wood's apartment. And from the way Chris moved through the rooms that had been her home, detached as a browser at a garage sale, he had a feeling she wouldn't be moving back there, no matter what Mr. Spickler did to restore the place.

There was no love play that night. Wood held Chris while she slept curled on her side, facing away from him, but snugly nestled in the protective curve of his arm and body.

Alan's arraignment was scheduled for Thursday, his bail hearing for the following Monday. Chris planned to testify at the hearing. She meant to do everything she could to insure that bail would not be granted, and that Alan stayed in jail for as long as possible.

On Friday afternoon Wood was scheduled for X rays. Though she hated to admit it, it was almost a relief for Chris to have an hour or two to herself. Ever since the attack—no, ever since he'd found out about Alan, Wood had been hovering over her like a mother hen, anxiously watching every move she made. On the one hand she understood and even enjoyed the unaccustomed cherished feeling it gave her; on the other hand, it made it very difficult to do something she needed to do, something she'd been thinking about for weeks.

She arranged to take a late lunch hour. And as soon as Wood had wheeled himself off to X ray, she went in search of Sal Ramos.

She tracked him to the hospital cafeteria, where he was having lunch with several other orderlies before going off shift. She picked up a salad and a bottle of vegetable juice for herself, carried her tray over to Sal's table and, steadfastly ignoring the interested stares of the other orderlies, said, "Sal, can I talk to you for a minute, please?"

Sal colored noticeably, but picked up his tray without hesitation. "Sure, Chris, what's up?"

She led him to an empty table some distance from any that were occupied. When they were both seated, she pushed her salad aside, leaned forward and said in a low voice, "Sal, I want to ask you a question . . ."

"Sure—shoot."

"And a favor."

"Hey," said Sal. "Anything. Just ask."

"Do you know where I can buy a gun? I mean right away, without the waiting period."

"Geez, Chris." He sat back in his chair as if she'd just pulled one out and aimed it at him. "Yeah, I think I do. But—"

"Okay." She let her breath out and sat back, but left her hands tightly clasped in front of her on the table. "That's the question. The favor is, I want you to take me there."

Wood was waiting for her in the radiology department's waiting room. She thought he must have been there awhile, too, since he was thumbing impatiently through a copy of *National Geographic Magazine* and glaring at the door instead of at the pages.

"Where you been?" he asked mildly, but with an air of tension.

"Having lunch." She waved the juice bottle at him. "What's up? Have you seen the doctor yet? What did he say?"

Wood let out a breath and leaned back in his chair, unable to contain his triumphant grin any longer. "Casts come off on Monday."

"Oh, Wood! Oh, that's wonderful. That's...oh." She pressed her fingers to her mouth in consternation. *"Monday?"*

Wood's grin had faded, too. He was nodding somberly. "Monday morning. Same time as the bail hearing."

"But can't you—"

"I already asked. The doctor's got surgery scheduled every day this week. It's either Monday or wait another week. Darlin', I'm sorry. I know how much you wanted to be here."

"But I *have* to be here. Wood, this is important."

"So is that bail hearing. You want to make sure that maniac stays in jail, don't you? Look, you have to be there to testify— that's all there is to it. Hey, we can celebrate afterwards."

"You don't understand—you're not going to feel like celebrating. This is a huge, huge step. It's frightening, painful, standing up for the first time. It's just the beginning of the hard stuff. You'll probably faint again. You can't just—"

"Chris." His voice was soft, his eyes intent, black as onyx. "I'm a big boy. I can handle this. Remember what you said to me about keeping your hands off? This is maybe one of those times. You are going to go to the hearing. No arguments."

She studied him for a few moments in silence. When did this happen? she wondered. When did he become an indispensable part of me? More than a lover, more than family, much more than a partner and a friend. *A part of me.*

"We'll talk to the district attorney," she said calmly. "See what she says. Then we'll decide."

"Come on, you can do it," Chris said briskly. "I know it's scary the first time, but I'm right here. Hold on to me."

Wood glared down at his legs. They were pitiful, useless as wet noodles. He was convinced that the minute he put his weight on them, they'd snap like twigs.

"Why does it have to be a walker?" he croaked. Walkers were for old people. *Doddering* old people, hobbling around in nursing homes. "What's wrong with crutches, anyway?"

"You're not ready for crutches," Chris explained patiently, as if to an intractable child. "The walker gives you stability. Right now you'd probably keel right over on crutches. You have to regain your equilibrium first. One step at a time. And the first one begins with putting some weight on those legs. You have to get the feel of standing again. So come on, quit stalling. Up, up, up!"

"*Okay,* Coach. All right, I'm doing it...." He gripped the arms of his chair, gritted his teeth and pushed down with all his might. The bottoms of his feet pressed down on the floor and sent shock waves through his legs. Sweat began to pour off of him. Cold sweat. His legs quivered. His muscles cramped.

"That's it, Wood. Come on, you can do it."

Of course he could do it. He was a United States Marine, dammit.

He summoned all his courage, closed his eyes and let go of the chair with one hand. Groped for Chris, found her shoulder and held on for dear life. Waves of nausea and dizziness swept over him. He paused, breathing deeply until they'd passed, sort of, then slowly, slowly peeled the fingers of his other hand off the arm of his chair.

I'm a U.S. Marine, dammit!

"Wood, that's great! You're doing it—you're standing up. How does it feel?"

"Tall," said Wood faintly. "Very... tall."

"Okay, now here's the walker. Got a good grip? Both hands...that's it."

He opened his eyes and saw Chris smiling at him. "Hey, Coach, look at me," he said in a voice that echoed. "I'm standin'...."

The next thing he knew he was lying on the floor with his head in Chris's lap.

"I told you you'd faint again," she said tenderly as her cool hands smoothed the hair back from his forehead. "It's a good thing I didn't go to that hearing."

"Yeah, well..." His voice was thick and slurred. He frowned and thought about it. "All I can say is, that D.A. better be right."

"Shh...lie still for a few minutes. It'll be okay. Look, you heard her. She assured me that with all the evidence they have, there's no way Alan will be granted bail. She said they didn't even need my testimony."

He thought about it some more, for quite a long time, it seemed. Then he sighed and said, "Well, I'm glad you're here." He reached up and found her hand, pulled it down to his mouth and kissed it.

He knew with absolute certainty then that he wanted her there for the rest of his life. No matter what her problems were.

Chapter 17

I feel like I'm going to burst, Chris thought. Love and pride...what was it about those two emotions that was so impossible to contain? So many emotions she'd learned to hide well over the years—anger, fear, shame. But love had a way of seeping through her strongest barricades; shining in her eyes as she watched him through the long afternoon, facing that walker as though it were an adversary, psyching himself up for yet another try; curving her lips into a tender smile when he triumphed.

Each time he made it to his feet, Wood would look over at her, catch her watching him and smile, and she would feel warmed as if by the touch of the sun. It's a miracle, she thought, his loving me.

But then the truth would come sneaking in like storm clouds to blot out her joy, and she would turn away, feeling shaky and cold inside. *But he doesn't know me. He doesn't know who I really am. He wouldn't love me if he knew.*

Tell him, Mike Lanagan had said. Give him a chance.

She knew she had to tell him, and soon, before things went any further between them. But...oh, dear God, she was afraid.

"I don't know what's wrong," Wood said that evening, pounding the wheels of his chair in frustration. "I can stand up okay, but I can't seem to take a step. It's not like being paralyzed, either. It's not like my legs can't move, it's more like they *won't*. Like they just don't want to, you know?"

"It's perfectly normal," Chris assured him. "It's a matter of shifting weight and balance. You actually have to learn how to walk all over again. It's not as bad as it sounds—it gets easier with practice. You won't have any strength in your legs for a while yet, though, not until we get those quads and hamstrings built up again. You have to be patient—you can't rush this."

A pained look flashed across his face. "Patience..." he muttered with gravel in his throat. "I guess I was hoping for some kind of miracle—get rid of the casts, rise up and *walk*, brother! Ah, hell..." He reached for her, pulled her to him and pressed his face against her soft, flat belly. "Ah, Chris...you have no idea how much I want to be able to make love to you— *really* make love to you. With two good legs."

She felt the floor drop out from under her. Longing overwhelmed her; she felt as if she were drowning. *I don't care about your legs,* she wanted to cry, as she held him close, stroking his hair, his neck, his shoulders. *Don't you know, I'd love you if you had no legs at all?*

"You know, you can take a shower now," she whispered, quivering inside with butterflies. "If you want to."

She could feel his body shaking with laughter. "It's a damn poor substitute," he growled. "But yeah, I'd like that. Is it okay? I mean—"

"Of course," Chris murmured thoughtfully, "there is a chance you might faint again. So I couldn't possibly let you go in there alone."

Wood pulled back to look at her with burning eyes. "That's right," he said slowly. "I suppose you couldn't."

Later he wondered why he didn't faint—from sheer pleasure, sensory overload. First the deliciousness of warm water sluicing over his head, his face, cascading down over his shoulders and arms, drumming like rain on his chest. God, what a simple joy, another one so easily taken for granted. How he'd missed this.

But then Chris slipped through the curtain, and he felt her wet, slippery hands and body caressing his, and he didn't even feel the water anymore.

She soaped him all over first, sliding around him in that confined space, agile as an eel. He grew hot and tight under the tender stroking; his hands gripped the bars of his walker like a lifeline; his arms, bearing most of his weight, began to quiver with the strain. He groaned aloud.

As the water rinsed the soap from his body, her mouth followed, sipping from his skin, tasting him all over, drinking him in while the water rained down on her head, ran in silvery rivers over her face and beaded like tiny diamonds in her lashes.

"Chris," he sputtered desperately. His hands flexed spasmodically on the chrome bars of the walker, cramping with the intensity of his need to touch her. "That's . . . enough, dammit. I've got to . . ."

She rose instantly then, slithering upward along his body, molding herself to him, fitting her slender belly against his buttocks as she reached around him to shut off the water.

He was never quite sure how they got themselves to bed. He remembered tumbling gratefully onto the sheets with Chris on top of him, both of them still damp from the shower, too heated with inner fires to be concerned about the chill of cooling moisture.

And that was when he discovered for the second time that, if something was meant to happen, the mechanics—or the position—simply didn't matter.

He forgot he even had legs. Remembered a condom barely in the nick of time. After that he was conscious only of her, of her lithe and slender body wrapped closely in his arms, the weight of her breasts on his chest, the round, firm shape of her buttocks in his hands. The tender resistance of her body's feminine defenses . . . the minute breaking as they gave way before the pressure of his masculinity. The feel of himself inside her, with her softness closing around him, sheathing him in honeyed warmth.

He heard her faintest sighs and whimpers, felt her heart beating, the pulses and clenchings deep inside her. He felt her as if she were a part of him, as if they shared the same heart and nervous system, the same mind, the same soul. His body moved to rhythms not of his making or even of hers, but rather a common impulse, as if they'd truly become one body. It was a union so complete and profound it overwhelmed him, his release so much more than physical, a cataclysm he knew even then would leave him forever changed. He knew that from this night on and forever he would be incomplete without the woman he now held trembling and sobbing in his arms.

The words came from him so easily, so naturally he was hardly aware of having spoken them aloud; they seemed only an extension of his thoughts and deepest desires. "Chris... marry me."

She went so utterly, so completely still that he felt for a moment as if she'd gone away... somehow *left* him, left her body behind lying full length on his in an emptiness like death.

Then she carefully separated herself from him, eased herself away and sat on the edge of the bed, groping blindly for a towel, a sheet, anything with which to cover herself. What she found was the tunic she'd tossed across the foot of the bed when she'd undressed so hurriedly for the shower. She pulled it on, moving stiffly, like an old woman, and buttoned it with fingers even he could see were shaking.

"Chris, what's wrong?" he asked as she walked away from him. She paused by the window, but didn't turn around, just went on hugging herself as if she were cold. "I know it's sudden, but it can't be a surprise. You know how I feel about you." His voice was rusty, betraying a fear so profound he couldn't even name it. "I thought you loved me, too. At least... you told me you did."

Love you? Oh God, if you only knew how much. Earl Brown, if I loved you one iota less I'd never find the strength to do this. But I must. I must....

"Wood, I have to tell you something." Her voice was thick, her throat clogged with pain. "Something you don't know... about me."

"My God, Chris..." He sat up and eased his legs over the side of the bed. He looked around until he located his sweats on the other side of the tumbled bed, snatched them up and began to struggle into them. "Don't you know... there's nothing in this world you could possibly tell me... that would change the way I feel about you?"

His chair was there, parked beside the bed. He yanked it around almost angrily and eased himself into it, not even aware, she was sure, that he moved his legs in the process. Realizing that he meant to come to her, she put out a hand in desperation.

"No—don't say that," she cried, gulping back a sob. "You don't *know*. Oh, please, Wood, stay there. If you touch me I'll never be able to say this."

"All right." His voice was deathly quiet, his eyes so intent they burned her. "Tell me, Chris. For God's sake, just . . . tell me."

She nodded; her chest was so tight she couldn't seem to get a breath deep enough to sustain her. Oh, how she longed to look away, to shield herself from those terrible eyes. But she had to see his face when she told him. She had to know.

"You know, I guess . . . that I married Alan when I was very young. Just seventeen. But . . . he, um . . ." She drew breath at last, and it was like a shaft of flame. "He wasn't the first man I'd . . . ever been with."

"For God's sake, Chris! Whose husband is, nowadays? If that's all—"

"It's not all. Don't you understand? It was my father. *My father.* He . . . raped me when I was ten. After that . . . until . . . I thought the only way I could escape him was to run away with Alan. For all those years, he—he . . . Oh, God." She clamped her hand across her mouth.

Wood's face had been drained of all color. "My God . . . my God . . ." he whispered. "So that's it. . . ."

Watching him was agony beyond anything she'd ever known. It was everything she'd feared, but even she wasn't prepared for the intensity of the pain. His face darkened, contorted until she didn't recognize the man she'd come to love more than life itself. And then he dropped his head back until the cords in his neck stood out like blades, uttered her name in a harsh and anguished cry and suddenly spun his chair around.

Her eyes were closed, squeezed tightly shut, so she only heard him leave.

With the closing of the apartment door came the sobs—terrible, almost silent sobs that doubled her over and threatened to tear her apart. They didn't last long—they were too violent and too painful. In their stead came a kind of peace, an almost fatalistic acceptance. So she'd told him.... And he'd reacted just as she'd always known he would. At least it was done. The worst that could possibly happen to her had happened. Now there was nothing left to fear.

She finished dressing slowly and methodically, moving like an invalid. Of course, she couldn't possibly stay here now. She'd gather a few things, go back to her own apartment. Tomorrow...oh, God, tomorrow. It seemed to her like a sentence of life in exile.

She was searching for her purse when the telephone rang. Jangled and shaking, she went to pick it up. Clearing her throat, she managed to say evenly, "Hello? Yes...this is she."

"Ms. Thurmond, I don't know how to tell you this. I don't know how he pulled it off. These things happen sometimes, I guess. Ours isn't a perfect system. But I was just so sure..."

Chris listened and felt her body grow still and cold. "When?" she said in a voice that splintered. "How long has he been out on bail?...I see. Thank you for telling me.... Yes, I'll do that. Good night."

She let the receiver drop from her stiff and icy fingers. She'd been wrong...dead wrong. She'd thought the worst that could happen to her had already happened. Now she knew that the worst—the very worst—was still an imminent possibility. Somehow Alan Bendix had managed to pull it off. He'd managed to charm a judge into granting him bail. The man who'd vowed to cut her up and kill Wood had been walking around a free man since eleven o'clock this morning. And Wood was out there somewhere right now, alone and unsuspecting. Trapped in a wheelchair. Defenseless.

Oh God—Wood! Adrenaline surged through her body, melting the icy dread that had temporarily immobilized her. Her heart racing, she snatched up her purse, tore it open and dumped the contents onto the sofa. The gun Sal had delivered to her just that morning lay in the jumble, gleaming a dull, ugly black.

She picked it up, hefted its weight and felt its shape mold to her palm. It was loaded; Sal had done that for her, and had showed her how to cock it before firing. She made sure it wasn't cocked before she slipped the gun into the pocket of her tunic.

The elevator ride was interminable; she counted the seconds in multiple heartbeats. She stepped warily into the lighted vestibule, knowing she was as visible to anyone outside as someone in a store display window, while she herself could see nothing at all beyond the plate-glass walls, only her own image reflected back by the darkness outside.

She opened the door cautiously, sniffing the air like a wild animal. It was balmy; the air smelled of grass and flower blossoms. It's spring, she thought irrelevantly. At last . . .

She started down the walkway, searching the shadowy landscaping, the lighted parking areas, the empty spaces between cars. All her senses were on overload, every nerve alert.

And it still wasn't enough.

He came out of nowhere. One moment there was no one there, and the next she felt herself being jerked backward, and his arm was like a bar across her chest. Brutal fingers clamped over her mouth and forced her head back; she felt the prick of something sharp and unyielding just under her chin.

"That's right, Chrissy . . . it's me again." His panting breath gusted hot in her ear and reeked of alcohol. "Thought you had me, didn't you? I told you, you should know better. Okay . . . okay, now—this is a knife here, see? You make a sound and I'll cut you. Understand? Now, we're gonna go back inside and wait for your boyfriend. I want to make sure he's there to watch what I'm gonna do to you. Then I'm gonna kill him. And you're gonna watch me do it. Okay, now, easy does it. . . ."

"Let her go, Bendix!"

Wood's bellow must have startled Alan, because Chris felt his hold on her ease—just for an instant, but long enough. With all her strength she drove her elbow backward into his soft belly, heard his grunt of surprise and pain with a surge of primitive triumph. Then all at once she was free, and the gun was in her hands.

She felt very calm. Alan was standing only a few feet away, his head lowered, swaying slightly, like a bear at bay. Chris held the gun in both hands, the way she'd seen people do on television, held it straight out and pointed it carefully, right at Alan. Her thumbs pulled back the hammer. She took a deep, steadying breath. . . .

"Chris—no! For God's sake, *don't shoot.*"

She heard the whirr of wheels. In the last instant before her finger tightened on the trigger, Wood's chair came between her and her target. Her arm trembled, turned to ice water and fell limply to her side.

Things happened so quickly. One moment she was looking beyond Wood and seeing Alan's face, his teeth bared in a grin or a snarl, the knife ready in his hand. A moment after that, the knife was skittering, spinning along the concrete walkway, and Alan was on his knees on the ground, struggling futilely to free his arms from the painful restraining hold Wood had placed them in.

"Go inside," Wood growled at her. "Call the cops. He's not going anywhere. Go on . . . *go.*"

Chris didn't move. Well, she was in shock, he supposed. So he was glad to hear a couple of car doors slam, followed by the slap of running footsteps.

"He's all yours," he said to the first cop to reach him, and backed up his chair to give them enough room to lay their captive out properly in classic police style—belly down in the dirt. Which, as far as he was concerned, was exactly where a snake like Alan Bendix belonged.

"Nice job. Where'd you learn those moves?"

Looking up, Wood recognized the take-charge cop from Chris's apartment. "Marine Corps," he grunted, reaching across his body to offer his hand. "Twelve and a half years."

The cop shook his hand and grinned. "Thought it looked familiar. *Semper fi.*"

"Yeah? No kidding—you, too?"

"Marine Corps Reserves."

"*Semper fi,*" said Wood. He and the cop bumped knuckles and gave each other the ol' thumbs-up, and then he went rolling over to where Chris still stood motionless in the shadows.

"Hey, darlin'," he said softly. He was careful to keep his chair between her and the cops while he took the gun from her slack fingers, eased the hammer into place and tucked it down beside his leg. As far as he was concerned, the fewer questions asked about that gun, the better for Chris. She didn't need any more hassle right now.

"I was going to shoot him," she said through the clattering of her teeth. "I wanted to. I wanted to kill him. I would have."

"Easy, darlin'," he said, taking her cold hand in his. "You didn't, that's what matters."

"But I wanted to."

"Big difference between wanting to kill somebody and actually doing it. Believe me, I know. Come on—the police have everything under control here. I don't think that bastard'll be getting out on bail this time. Let's go back inside."

But her hand remained rigid in his, cold as an ice sculpture. "I thought...you'd gone. I thought...you didn't want..." She sounded dazed, confused as a child waking up from a bad dream.

"You thought I didn't want what?" he prompted carefully.

"Me." It was a whisper, so faint he barely heard it.

"God..." He let his breath out in a rush, hoping it would ease the ache and swelling in his chest. It didn't, much. He drew her out of the shrubbery, guided her around and settled her onto his lap. It was beginning to feel familiar to him, having her there.

He sighed as he wrapped his arms around her and nudged her head into the nest below his chin. "You have a lot to learn about me, lady," he said softly. "I was upset, sure. I was angry, hurting—for *you,* you idiot. I needed to get out of there for a few minutes—get some air. I was about to lose it, and I didn't want you to see me. Okay, so maybe I have a lot to learn about some things, too. But...not *want* you? Don't you know yet how much I love you?" He tipped her chin up and kissed her, kissed her for a long, tender, throat-aching time.

"I guess we have a lot to talk about," he said somberly when he finally lifted his head, gazing down into the miraculous, silvery glow of her eyes. "But first, there's a question I asked you awhile ago that you haven't answered yet...."

Wood stood on the back steps of the crossroads church, sweating in his rented tux under a July Iowa sun and fidgeting while Lucy fussed needlessly over his tie. "Leave it—it's fine," he said irritably. "Maybe you should go and get yourself dressed instead of fussing over me." He nodded at the faded cotton duster she was wearing.

"Not until I absolutely have to," his sister said darkly. "Where's Rhett? Why isn't he here yet?"

Wood chuckled. "Because he's Rhett, that's why."

"You'd think he'd at least be on time for his only brother's wedding.... There—that's better." Lucy stood back, scowling at him like a little hawk all set to pounce. "You look...nice. I'm glad you shaved off the beard."

"Well, I didn't think I ought to look like a pirate on my wedding day."

"Oh, Earl..." Her face was suddenly fragile and transparent. "I wish Mom and Dad could be here to see you. They'd be so proud of you."

"You think so?" Wood's throat felt raw.

"I know so. You going back to school, becoming a teacher..."

"I have Chris to thank for that. She seems to think I have a way with kids." He smiled crookedly and couldn't quite prevent a wistful glance at Lucy's burgeoning stomach. "I don't know if she's right. I just hope someday she gives me a chance to find out."

"Give her time," said Lucy, giving his chest an awkward pat. "She has a lot of healing to do first. She'll come around. I know it's hard for you, but you just have to be patient."

"Not as hard as it used to be," Wood said ruefully. "She's taught me a lot about patience, believe me. But she's worth it."

"Oh, look, here comes your best man now. Will wonders never cease."

"Good ol' Rhett. Don't be too hard on him, Luce." He smiled down at her and caught her in a one-armed hug. "Hey, who knows? Maybe he'll find his way back home, too, some day. I did."

The minister stuck his head out the door, pointed at his watch and said, "It's time. Best man here yet? Great...let's take our places, shall we?"

A few minutes later Wood was standing on the chancel steps in almost the exact same spot where a lifetime ago he'd stood with his mother and Rhett, singing the old-time hymns. Sunlight was streaming through the stained-glass windows behind him, gleaming on the polished wood that edged the chancel and pews. He could almost see his mom and dad there beside Gwen in the front row, smiling, with eyes brimming with happy tears.

The double doors at the far end of the aisle opened, and there was Lucy, all decked out in pink lace, for Pete's sake. Wood grinned at her as she made her way slowly toward him, vowing that he was never going to let her live down that dress.

Next came Rosie Ellen with her tongue planted firmly in her cheek, trying her best to look solemn as she dribbled rose petals down the aisle, looking at her mother to see if she was doing it right.

The organist finished playing "Church In The Wildwood" and struck the opening chords of the "Wedding March." Wood's heart began to pound so hard he could feel it rocking him, and he had to lean hard for a second or two on his cane in order to maintain his equilibrium. Then he drew a deep breath and pulled himself up until he was standing straight and tall, squarely on his own two feet.

And then she was there in the doorway, her hand tucked in the crook of Mike's elbow. Chris . . . the woman he loved. She looked straight at him and smiled, and he felt as if the sun was rising.

* * * * *

COMING NEXT MONTH

#643 ANOTHER MAN'S WIFE—Dallas Schulze
Heartbreakers/A Family Circle
Gage Walker knew the value of friendship—enough to have taken responsibility for his best buddy's widow and young son. But his sense of duty had *never* included marriage—or fatherhood. Then he learned that Kelsey had a baby on the way—*his!*

#644 IAIN ROSS'S WOMAN—Emilie Richards
The Men of Midnight
Iain Ross had no idea that the woman he'd saved from drowning was the embodiment of his own destruction. Feisty Billie Harper seemed harmless—and charming—enough, but an age-old curse had rendered her his sworn enemy. But Iain was powerless to resist her—and their destiny....

#645 THE WEDDING VENTURE—Nikki Benjamin
Laura Burke would never give up her son. Timmy was hers, and no mob kingpin would take him away—even if he was the child's grandfather. Desperate, she turned to Devlin Gray, a man shrouded in mystery. Then she learned that Devlin's idea of protection involved trading danger for wedding vows.

#646 THE ONLY WAY OUT—Susan Mallery
Andie Cochran was on the run, struggling to bring herself and her young son to safety. Yet Jeff Markum was the only man she could trust—and the one man who had every reason to hate her.

#647 NOT WITHOUT RISK—Suzanne Brockmann
Emily Marshall had never dreamed of seeing police detective Jim Keegan ever again. He'd dumped her years earlier without warning—or explanation—and now he was masquerading as her "brother" to catch a drug smuggler. But the feelings that stirred between them were anything but familial.

#648 FOR MERCY'S SAKE—Nancy Gideon
Sheriff Spencer Halloway knew a person in hiding when he saw one, and Mercy Pomeroy was one woman who didn't want to be found. He couldn't figure out what a classy lady and her cute daughter could possibly fear, but he would move the heavens to find out....

Take 4 bestselling love stories FREE

Plus get a FREE surprise gift!

Special Limited-time Offer

Mail to Silhouette Reader Service™

3010 Walden Avenue
P.O. Box 1867
Buffalo, N.Y. 14269-1867

YES! Please send me 4 free Silhouette Intimate Moments® novels and my free surprise gift. Then send me 6 brand-new novels every month, which I will receive months before they appear in bookstores. Bill me at the low price of $2.89 each plus 25¢ delivery and applicable sales tax, if any.* That's the complete price and a savings of over 10% off the cover prices—quite a bargain! I understand that accepting the books and gift places me under no obligation ever to buy any books. I can always return a shipment and cancel at any time. Even if I never buy another book from Silhouette, the 4 free books and the surprise gift are mine to keep forever.

245 BPA ANRR

Name	(PLEASE PRINT)	
Address	Apt. No.	
City	State	Zip

This offer is limited to one order per household and not valid to present Silhouette Intimate Moments® subscribers. *Terms and prices are subject to change without notice. Sales tax applicable in N.Y.

He's an everyman, but only one woman's lover. And we dare you not to lose yourself—and your heart—to these featured

In May: NIGHT OF THE JAGUAR, by Merline Lovelace. Jake MacKenzie was a seasoned operative used to calling the shots. But when feisty Sarah Chandler and her three young charges became his newest mission, he knew he'd lost all control—along with his heart.

In June: ANOTHER MAN'S WIFE, by Dallas Schulze. Gage Walker had only intended to get his best friend's widow back on her feet. His idea of help had *never* included marriage—or fatherhood. Then he learned that Kelsey had a baby on the way—*his!*

In July: WHO'S THE BOSS? by Linda Turner. Riley Whitaker *never* lost a good fight. So when single mom Becca Prescott threw down the gauntlet in the race for sheriff, Riley accepted her challenge—and offered a seductive one of his own....

Heartbreakers: The heroes you crave, from the authors you love. You can find them each month, only in— INTIMATE MOMENTS® Silhouette®

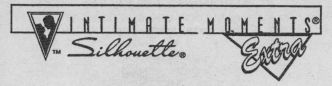

CODE NAME: DANGER

Because love is a risky business...

Merline Lovelace's "Code Name: Danger" miniseries gets an explosive start in May 1995 with

NIGHT OF THE JAGUAR, IM #637

Omega agent Jake MacKenzie had flirted with danger his entire career. But when unbelievably sexy Sarah Chandler became enmeshed in his latest mission, Jake knew that his days of courting trouble had taken a provocative twist....

Your mission: To read more about the Omega agency.

Your next target: THE COWBOY AND THE COSSACK, August 1995

Your only choice for nonstop excitement—

Kathleen Creighton's

RITA Award-winning author Kathleen Creighton brings Midwest charm to the Intimate Moments lineup in her ongoing miniseries, "Into the Heartland." A WANTED MAN, IM #547, introduced Lucy Brown to readers in February 1994. Now meet Lucy's brother, Wood Brown, in ONE GOOD MAN, IM #639, coming your way in May 1995.

Wood Brown had been to hell and back. And no one knew his pain better than physical therapist Christine Thurmond. But as she healed his battered body and soul, she yearned for some loving all her own. And only one good man would do....

The Browns—one sister, two brothers. Tragedy changed their family forever, but never their spirit—or their love for the heartland. Look for Rhett Brown's story in 1996 and venture once again "Into the Heartland"—*because sometimes there's no place like home*—only in

Announcing
the New Pages & Privileges™ Program
from Harlequin® and Silhouette®

Get All This FREE
With Just One Proof-of-Purchase!

- **FREE Travel Service** with the guaranteed lowest available airfares plus 5% cash back on every ticket

- **FREE Hotel Discounts** of up to 60% off at leading hotels in the U.S., Canada and Europe

- **FREE Petite Parfumerie** collection (a $50 Retail value)

- **FREE $25 Travel Voucher** to use on any ticket on any airline booked through our Travel Service

- **FREE Insider Tips Letter** full of fascinating information and hot sneak previews of upcoming books

- **FREE Mystery Gift** (if you enroll before May 31/95)

And there are more great gifts and benefits to come!
Enroll today and become Privileged!

(see insert for details)